Marked by Scorn

An Anthology Featuring Non-Traditional Relationships

Edited by Dominica Malcolm

[handwritten signatures and inscriptions]

I feel silly writing. But...
To Ahadeen
To Aladeen, you're great.
Teddy

SOLARWYRM PRESS
2016

Thank you for supporting Solarwyrm Press.

Published and produced by Solarwyrm Press
http://www.solarwyrm.com

Marked by Scorn: An Anthology Featuring Non-Traditional Relationships

Cover design and illustrations by Grace Jensen
http://gracejensendesign.com/

Production by Dominica Malcolm

ISBN: 978-0-9805084-5-1

Contents

INTRODUCTION

Dominica Malcolm

Since before I finalised my previous anthology, *Amok: An Anthology of Asia-Pacific Speculative Fiction*, I had been ruminating on a theme for this one. In its early stages, I'd planned to put together a collection featuring polyamorous and other non-monogamous relationships. Being the only person to have written a story that featured a polyamorous relationship in *Amok*, I wanted to see more focus on such relationships.

Additional inspiration for this anthology came from someone I was very close to; a man who became involved with a polyamorous woman of another race. Early on in their relationship, race had not been an issue for them. He was concerned about how his friends and family would view them together, given the married and polyamorous labels she carried, but their racial differences never factored into that. Unfortunately, toward the end of their relationship, he became paranoid about how those closer to his race and nationality would see them together, as an interracial couple. Knowing how she felt about his concern with strangers judging them, to the point he would no longer hold her hand in public, led to the expansion of the theme for *Marked by Scorn* from a polyamory focus, to other non-traditional relationships, too. Additionally, as I self-identify as bisexual, bringing in the QUILT-BAG spectrum was another important aspect for me to include in this anthology.

For my second anthology, I am very proud to include another diverse collection of pieces. I love that I can share with you how the highlights and challenges of non-traditional relationships can be experienced in various parts of the world, including Cambodia, the Philippines, Malaysia and Indonesia, India, Singapore, Senegal, South Africa, Haiti, Denmark, Australia, the United Kingdom, and the United States.

Mirror Sunsets

Kelly Burke

"I just spent the last hour being chased by an ostrich."

Thomas glanced up from the spaghetti circuitry vomiting from the back of the microwave. Although the disheveled state of Anbu's clothes was an evident indicator of some struggle or another, Thomas was disappointed by the lack of feathers which he expected to have been knotted in his hair.

"Should I be jealous?" he asked, ducking back into the clumps of wiring.

"No, I told her how it is. She didn't take it very well though."

Anbu slumped into the apartment, setting his camera on the kitchen table with a heavy clunk across from Thomas's impromptu workstation. He gave it a quick survey from around his tools, looking between its scarred lens and Anbu's coiled shoulders disappearing into the next room.

"Anything I can fix?"

"I've got to replace the lens and I think the shutter's jammed," Anbu called back.

"She really did a number on you, huh?"

"You can't see it, but I hope you feel how hard I'm flipping you off right now."

Thomas rolled his eyes and resumed working, hastening his progress now that he had another patient awaiting his diagnosis. Anbu returned to the tiny kitchenette in a change of clothes and with a need for beer. His feet took him straight to the fridge and to their dwindling stock of Sam Adams.

"I'm starting to regret signing up for this," he groaned, flopping into the croaky chair across from Thomas. "I think Mother Nature has it out for me."

"That's the beauty of being in engineering; Mother Nature can't touch you if you don't go outside."

As if to prove him wrong, one of the tinkered microwave wires sparked against Thomas's smugness. He scowled at the offending chord and Anbu laughed.

"Well, I'm glad *you're* at least having fun," Anbu teased.

"Define 'fun' for me, please?"

Thomas leaned away from his mess of tech, clutching the nearest sweat-stained dish towel to his forehead. Scarce strands of black hair escaped from a sloppy ponytail, matting with the sweat. Signing on for the African exchange program had seemed like such a good idea at the time. It was a chance to get away from the states, an exotic locale to explore, and a welcome retreat from the two-faced hypocrisy of his peers.

After a month spent in Botswana, getting acclimated to the changes of their lifestyle, Thomas thought that the country was a vast improvement over the US just by the tone of its people alone. Even though he was only just integrating with their language, words were hardly necessary to interpret when smiles were open on every face. His complaints laid with the climate, and the only thing he missed about New York were the fair summer temperatures in comparison to the blistering heat huffing in through the window.

"Drink?" Anbu offered, leaning the neck of his bottle towards him.

"As soon as I'm victorious, I'll have one to celebrate."

Anbu adjusted his glasses—which, by some miracle, survived an ostrich chase when they could hardly avoid volleyballs back in gym class.

"Do you at least know why it's acting up?"

"Yeah, I know how to fix it. It just takes time and the patience of Gandhi to finish."

"Can't be as easy as just cutting the red wire, right?"

"Well, A, it's not a bomb and B, this isn't 'Mission Impossible.'"

"And yet here I am, sitting across from Tom Cruise," Anbu said, grinning around his bottle.

"Smooth," Thomas chuckled, tossing the dish towel at his face.

Anbu scrambled to dodge and the offending rag landed with an unsavoury slap on the floor behind him. Thomas averted himself from Anbu's scalding glare by burrowing back into his microwave intestines. Anbu set his beer to the side and pulled his injured camera closer, examining the damages while he waited for Thomas to finish. He cradled the machine between his palms and stared at the chips in the lens. He wore the most woeful expression Thomas hadn't seen since they'd watched Les Misérables.

"It's an easy fix, Bu," Thomas tried to reassure him, carefully replacing a stray wire.

"That's what you said about the microwave."

"So, tell me more about your day!"

Thomas quickly veered the topic of discussion away from his present predicament and the threat of an "I told you so." He was finishing it *today*, probability be damned. Anbu rolled his eyes, but conceded to his request anyway. Besides, Thomas suspected that if he didn't put it into words, Anbu would hardly be able to believe the story himself.

"Alright, so there's one other photography major with me on this safari tour, along with our guide and a group of tourists—three or four, don't remember. We're going along, the tour guide's doing her thing, and I wish you could have come, Tom. It's incredible out there. The Discovery Channel's got nothin' over actually being out there yourself."

"Next time," Thomas promised, lip curled beneath his teeth as he concentrated on the circuit in front of him. "Barring any more faulty appliances. How did you meet your new girlfriend, the ostrich?"

"Okay so, ya'know the whole 'keep your hands and feet inside the vehicle at all times' rule? Yeah well, it's impossible to get a decent shot over all those big, floppy hats and if I don't get a few good ones, I'm flunking this project. We take a rest stop at a little oasis—I know, an actual oasis; they're not just a mirage like in the movies—and across the water we spot this flock—me and the other photography major. And we're both in the same boat, desperate for some close-ups, and we figure it's not like it's a lion or anything. It's not going to get us killed to get a little closer while the tourists reapply their suntan lotion, right?

"So, we sneak over—and that was really like 'Mission Impossible,' let me tell ya—and we get a good haul of shots in before they notice us. And, I swear, they would have never known we were there if the other guy didn't have a pocket of granola in his pants."

Thomas set down what he was doing and sent Anbu a long, heavy stare from across the table. Anbu shifted in his chair, dark curls of hair falling forward as he tipped his head down in guilt.

"Okay... If *I* didn't have a packet of granola in my pants. Ostriches are like bloodhounds, man. I didn't think they could smell from so far away."

Thomas's brow cut up his forehead as a very skeptical scythe. The effect of the precision stare was instantaneous. Anbu folded over his half empty beer bottle, cringing with squeezed shut eyes and hissing teeth.

"Okay... I *may* have gotten closer than might be considered an 'appropriate distance.'"

"You antagonised an ostrich for a grade."

"I did not 'antagonise' it..."

"Anbu! You know you can't mess with wildlife. It's dangerous!"

"Says the guy with his hands tangled up in a high voltage death trap."

"Machines you can control. You always know what they're going to do, even if you make a mistake. You can't control nature."

"I got some great action shots out of it though," Anbu mumbled, lips quirking at the corners in pride.

Thomas was determined to stay outraged. He was determined to glare some sense of self-preservation into the man for the next time he decided insignificant worth out-weighed considerable risk. He was determined, but Anbu was stubborn and committed to his chosen career path. Thomas remained quiet, observing the man across from him. Dark, maple-wood skin the colour of his father's old fishing boat after a fresh polish; bright green eyes like the summer leaves of the tree he used to climb in his backyard; faded checkered shirt like his grandmother's picnic blanket. All things that reminded Thomas of a home he could never go back to, but had started following him again anyway after a late night of retreated studying in the high school library. Anbu had taken a picture.

"What are you doing?" Thomas had asked, eyes bruised with stress and a broken heart.

"It's a reminder," Anbu had told him, quiet in the empty library. "One day, you're going to be happy. No one will be able to hurt you like you're hurting right now. On that day, you should look back at this. Not as a reminder of why you shouldn't be happy, but as a way of showing yourself that things are always going to get better. You can never go back to being as low as you are in this moment. And when you realise that, you take the photo and you burn it to smithereens."

"Did I hear that right?" Thomas had laughed—a bitter sound in his aching throat. "A photographer just told me to burn one of his photos?"

"I photograph nature, not people. I take pictures of the things that have no voice to say that they're beautiful. You'll be able to say that about yourself. I'll print this for you and when you can see yourself as beautiful as I see sunsets, promise me you'll burn it."

The only love Thomas had ever known before then was of family. That night, he'd learned love as being a farce. People only loved the idea of what they wanted you to be, not who you really were. In the instant he'd come out to his parents, the polished boat in his memory sunk to the depths of the lake. The summer leaves in his back yard were set on fire. His grandmother tore the picnic blanket in two.

When Anbu reached across the bookshelf to press the photo into his hands, those lost loves of his past slowly started to resurface and he learned how much more there was to love than expectations. He stepped back from the edge of the building and kept going until it was a thread of a line, so far away on the horizon of his pain. He grew his hair out, he moved to Africa, and he went where Anbu went. He rescued their broken machines because Anbu had salvaged the pieces of his heart before they threw themselves to the concrete.

"Be more careful?" he ended up sighing into the tropical heat, because he could say nothing else that summed up just how afraid he was of losing him.

"Definitely," Anbu laughed. "If I don't have to run another day in my whole life, I'll be happy. My thighs are going to be *so* sore in the morning."

He groaned into the rough wooden table, pressing his forehead against it. The aftermath of the ordeal was more harrowing than the event itself. Thomas didn't know how he did it. If he was standing face to face with a giant bird that wanted to nibble on his pockets, he wouldn't have the foggiest idea about how to react. He'd probably be too frozen where he stood to even comprehend running.

Photographers were crazy. He'd told Anbu such the night he'd met him. His immediate response had been, "Yeah, but we're never boring."

"Aren't you ever worried about getting yourself killed out there?" he'd countered.

"That's the last thing on my mind. There's so much the world wants to show us that we'll never see if we let fear keep us at home. As a photographer, I have this obligation to share the world's secrets with those who can't see it for themselves. And I have a responsibility to present those secrets—those beautiful moments—in the best way I know how. Through this."

He'd indicated his camera. It had been brand new then, filled with a reel of random still life and vague conceptual stuff that Thomas didn't understand. Anbu had held it like an ancient treasure, like it was the key to a deity's Heaven, and Thomas remembered thinking that the true treasure was standing behind the lens. It wasn't the lens itself. He'd loved him before he knew that he could.

Thomas put some microwave components back into their appropriate notches and prepared to test the functionality of his repairs. The issue had been the machine releasing a power output which blew the fuses of their shack of an apartment every time they tried to use it. If those past two years of college were truly paying off, then the lights would stay on once he hit the power button.

"Fingers crossed," he warned Anbu, who sat at attention and braced himself to duck for cover in the event of an explosion.

Thomas made certain everything in the machine was safely secured and that nothing was out of place. Judging that everything was as it should be, he rocked back on the legs of his chair and dragged the plug into the nearest outlet behind him. No sparks there so, that was a good sign. He leaned forward again and reached around to the front of the microwave. Pressing the button was like ripping off a Band-Aid: do it quick and all at once instead of dragging it out. They both tensed at the familiar 'beep' before breathing out in unison when the turn table started moving. The apartment lights didn't so much as flicker in response.

"You earned this," Anbu declared, sliding the bottle of beer over to Thomas.

"Damn right I did," he agreed, slumping back into his chair and basking in the glow of accomplishment. "I'm a fucking genius."

"Okay, Steven Hawking."

Thomas finished the beer with two rewarding gulps and took a moment to admire his handiwork before switching it off.

"We should go out to celebrate," Anbu suggested, eyes lighting up at the idea. "We haven't gone on a single date since we got here."

"Kind of hard to have a sit down dinner when you're always looking over your shoulder for another ostrich assault."

"You're never going to let me live this down?"

"How did you know it was a girl ostrich, by the way?"

Thomas set the microwave back at home between the toaster and the coffee maker. The lonely countertop was finally complete again. Heaving a contented sigh into the balmy air, Thomas loosed the band from his hair and ruffled the long, loose waves back into their chaotic cascade. Anbu declined to specify an answer to his question and Thomas instead found him analysing the thin split down the centre of his camera lens when he glanced up.

"So, if you can save the most hopeless appliance in here, a broken camera should be no biggie, right?"

"Right," Thomas confirmed, returning to his surgeon's chair and plucking the patient from Anbu's fretful grip. "Besides, nothing is going to stop me from seeing the photographic evidence of your little adventure."

"Your concern for my wellbeing is overwhelming, thanks," Anbu snorted, leaning his cheek against his knuckles and watching Thomas go to work with renewed fascination.

Thomas smirked in amusement, a small curl of the lips that he knew drove Anbu crazy enough to shut up a second for him to concentrate. While it succeeded with its desired intent, it didn't last quite as long as Thomas would have preferred.

"How are you going to fix it?" Anbu asked, bouncing up to his feet.

"With my mad skills, what else? We've established I'm a fucking genius, remember?"

Thomas turned the camera in his hands, looking for any more external abnormalities before addressing Anbu's main concern with the stuck shutter. Anbu—precious, devil-may-care Anbu—paced behind Thomas's chair, peering over his shoulder every time he passed. The man could be just as infuriating as he was endearing, Thomas thought. Using Anbu's steps to set his own pace, Thomas clicked this, opened that, fiddled with more, and after a few quick tweaks, faced the camera to himself and snapped a selfie when Anbu passed behind him.

"There."

"What?"

"Done."

"No way!"

Thomas held out the camera for Anbu to snatch up and stare at in mouth-agape disbelief. He snapped a quick picture of the kitchen counter and made a noise not unlike that of a delighted puppy rolling through the snow on Christmas morning. He scrolled through the digital images and laughed in relief, finding all of his day's work still intact and the rest of the camera fully functional for him to continue said work.

As Thomas was about to stand, he was forced back into his chair by the weight of Anbu's arms flung around his neck. He growled out some disgruntled protest about being strangled, but Anbu just crushed him closer, streaming a volley of "thank you" in his ear.

"Thank me by being more careful," Thomas said, voice muffled behind the smothering of his rolled up sleeves.

"That's all? That's the only way you'll let me thank you?"

Anbu unwound himself from Thomas enough for him to tilt his head back against the chair. Even upside-down, Anbu's pout was just as adorable as it was right-side-up.

"I *may* accept a down payment now if it's followed by that extended investment."

Anbu smiled bright enough to give his glasses a glare. Soft hands that were never burnt by hot wires or scarred by jagged plastic combed through his tangled hair. Anbu's face lowered to meet his lips—small kisses for small favours—and that was all the reward Thomas really needed.

He'd burned that photo—a sallow-faced shadow of himself in a dim library—only a month ago. It felt much longer than that. He hadn't told Anbu when he'd done it, but he knew either way. Sometimes Thomas thought Anbu saw more when he wasn't looking through his lens. The first time he knew that happiness had found him in all its completeness had been when Anbu turned to him as he stepped off the plane. His eyes were wild with wanderlust, camera slung around his neck and cleared to fit only new pictures. None of the old remained. The sun had been setting when they landed, the untamed savannah black against the deep orange light descending beneath it.

"Like looking into a mirror, isn't it?" Anbu had said to him.

"*...you can see yourself as beautiful as I see sunsets...*"

And he had.

"I'm hungry," Anbu stated when he pulled away, slipping his hand down to thread through Thomas's.

"You're never going to believe this, but we have a microwave now. It makes food edible and everything!"

"That's great, but frozen meals don't exactly scream 'celebration.' Want to go out?"

"Fine, but if you go chasing the tail feathers of another pretty bird, I'm breaking up with you."

Anbu laughed and made a promise, and Thomas fondly squeezed his fingers between his own, watching the contrast of skin against the other. Tanned suede beside winter sky; nails like glass above blackened callouses. Art and science—right brain, left brain—were two halves of one whole. One designed the tools for the other; the other discovered what one needed to create. The wild terrified Thomas, but not nearly as much as it terrified him to think of Anbu not doing what he so desperately loved. He showed people the beauty of the world when it was still and silent. The profundity of that stillness quieted the tumult of a person's soul. It parted the curtain from over the mirror and showed him a sunset for a reflection.

So, he kept saving his camera so he could save people like he'd saved him. His photographer was crazy—crazy enough to let ostriches chase him if it meant showing someone what freedom felt like. He was crazy enough to kiss him like Thomas was every picture he'd ever taken. It was Anbu who was the architect of the person capable of loving him in return. He was a better mechanic than he gave himself credit for. Sometimes Thomas thought he didn't deserve this. He didn't deserve to be loved by someone so selfless, who could take all of his scars and make them into a work of art. Maybe engineers were a little crazy too, because he was crazy enough to know that he deserved this. To know that he was right where he needed to be. To be for one person that could never discriminate beauty, whether it was in a picture or outside of it.

"I'm in the mood for chicken," he announced. "Maybe turkey. Some kind of poultry?"

"You're the worst, Tom," he laughed.

Sometimes, but I'm my best because of you.

ABOUT KELLY BURKE

Born and raised in a small town in Northern New Jersey, Kelly has been a lover of words for all of her life. Books and stories are her passion, and it's a passion that has been kindled by dedicated and loving parents, one crazy comedian of a brother, and two unique cats.

WAKING DREAM

Jeremiah Murphy

The mornings were always the hardest. Everyday he had to ask himself why he should bother to continue living. He was never sure what the correct answer was, so he promised himself he'd figure it out later. Everyday, then, he'd roll onto the floor, put on some pants, generate some coffee, ignite a cigarette, consume the coffee, and determine the class to which he would devote most of his attention. Gradually he'd forget the question until the next morning.

Some days didn't fit into this otherwise ironclad routine. This was one of them. Slowly he drifted into partial consciousness, and as soon as he realised that the pillow pressing against his skull wasn't his own, he woke the rest of the way up.

Oh. Right.

So instead of clothing, coffee, cigarette, and class, he was reduced to deciding whether he should roust the woman beside him on the full-sized bed.

Lying on her stomach with her blonde—but not naturally so, as he'd found out recently—and slightly matted hair splashed across her shoulders and her makeup smeared, she still looked like a gorgeous sex kitten.

A heavy snore rattled out of her nose.

A matching snore from the living room shook the apartment.

That one came from her boyfriend.

Last night was... weird.

He'd been sitting on a stool, admiring the bottles lined up behind the bar. Not a day went by that he didn't think about his old friend, scotch. They went way back, and it was really too bad things had to go the way they did.

If he could, he'd walk backward, past one hundred and ten weeks of sobriety, and then twenty-something weeks further, until he reached a time when he still enjoyed drinking. While there, he'd order a double and toast this night, which happened to be the worst Valentine's Day of his life.

"Last call," said Craig the bartender. "Not that it matters to you."

Sean grunted.

Craig slid a glass over to him. "Here's your ginger ale, big spender."

Sean pointed across the room to another of the bar's occupants, the blonde with a thousand-yard stare. "What's her beverage of choice?"

"Gold-label tequila," he replied. "Top-shelf. The sipping kind."

"I'd always assumed she'd be daiquiri girl; maybe a margarita if she desired fire in her water."

Craig shrugged. "She's usually a gin and tonic. Must be a special occasion."

Sean threw a ridiculously large bill onto the counter. "I'd like one more of those."

"Gin and tonic?"

Sean picked up the bill and laid down a different one. "The denomination will decrease every time you ask a stupid question."

"Seriously?"

Sean switched the bill again.

Without another word, Craig poured a glass of gold-label tequila. Sean replaced the bill on the bar with the one he'd originally left, smirked at the bartender, took the drinks, and strolled over to the blonde. "Shannon," he said as he sat next to her, "you seem contemplative."

She blinked, but didn't look up. "Valentine's Day."

A seismic guffaw rumbled from behind him. Wincing, he turned to the pool table, over which was bent the mountainous torso of her live-in boyfriend, the aptly named Rocky. An epiphany struck. "Oh," he said. "I assume you're disappointed in a certain lack of Valentine-related activities."

She shrugged.

Rocky was the extrovert to Sean's introvert; the party animal to his sobriety; the muscles to his skeletal frame; the masculinity to his ambiguity; the optimist to his resignation. Despite all of this incompatibility, Sean really liked the guy, so he too was disappointed. "If there's any comfort to be had..." He glanced at the bar clock. "...we're nearly two hours into February fifteen."

She scrunched up her face. "That makes it worse."

"You know he really loves you," he assured her.

She giggled and slapped his arm. "Of course he loves me, you goof."

"Then perhaps you should say something."

"Maybe I should." She furrowed her brow. "How should I phrase it?" She bit the inside of her cheek in deep concentration for a moment before lunging forward and kissing Sean ravenously.

It had been far too long since lips had even brushed his, much less attacked so furiously. Her fingernails reached through his hair to dig into his scalp while her other hand steadied his cheek with an equal and opposite amount of tenderness. His body tensed and melted. When she pulled away, Sean took a moment to blindly fan himself with a beer coaster.

His eyes opened to find hers focused on something over his shoulder. His mind sharpened enough to remember that the pool tables and its players were behind him. His head turned to find out if her boyfriend the behemoth had witnessed this unexpected turn of events. His vision focused on the words "ROKK ON," which were stretched out on a black t-shirt, only inches from his face.

"I suppose you might have some questions," Sean said to Rocky's enormous pectorals.

Rocky guffawed again. Through the ringing in his ears, he heard the giant respond, "Hell yeah, I do."

Sean's mouth had gone dry from her kiss, and somehow it now became even drier. "I'm certain we can—"

"What the hell am I going to do with the rest of my night?" Rocky continued.

"After you dispose of me?"

Rocky punched his arm so hard he almost fell off of the stool and onto the floor. "Buddy, you crack me up! You know that?"

"There's a lot I don't know," he replied.

Rocky punched Sean's other arm, stabilising him. "You guys have fun, okay?" Rocky said, "Unless you want me to..."

"To what?" he squeaked.

Shannon took Sean's hand. "I think I need to handle this alone, Rocky." She turned to Sean. "Do you trust me?"

He nodded, because she was one of the few people he did trust. He couldn't say exactly why, but he did.

She kissed him again. "Then let's get out of here."

He had a lot of questions, but no idea how to phrase them. He had no idea how to walk any more either, but Shannon assisted by guiding out of the bar and down the two blocks to her apartment.

She skipped the pretence of coffee or small talk and led him directly to the bedroom. She shrugged off her February coat and scarf and reached under the hem of her skirt, and slipped her panties down to her knees and onto the floor.

"One second…" She opened the door long enough to loop them over the knob. "Unless you want him to join us."

The matching bruises on his biceps flared up. "Pardon me?"

"Usually he just watches," she told him and nodded to an easy chair in the corner.

"Pardon me?"

"Well, okay," she admitted, "it only happened once, and it made the boy I brought home all twitchy and no fun, but Rocky liked it, though, so we keep hoping…"

"Pardon me?"

She closed the door and pressed a finger to his lips. "You want me to stop babbling like a brook that talks a lot, don't you?"

He nodded.

She backed away and giggled, "Then lose the sweater, or you're sleeping on the couch."

Sean didn't want to sleep on the couch, so he tossed his omni-present, stretched-out cardigan to the floor. Based on the way her eyes caressed his arms, it occurred to him that she'd never actually seen him without it before. He felt kind of naked now, and he still had a lot of baggy layers to go.

Blushing, she asked, "Is this really crazy, or is it just me?"

It wasn't just her. "Perhaps you'd feel more comfortable if we simply retired to our corners for the night."

Shannon bit her lip in thought before crossing her arms in front of her and whipping her t-shirt over her head. "It's Valentine's Day," she replied, "and if I don't romp with someone tonight, I will not be happy." She began to pace deliberately, like a cat about to rub up against him. "And you like it when I'm happy, right?"

Most men who knew Shannon were endlessly fascinated by her cleavage. She accommodated them by making it highly visible, regardless of the weather. A part of Sean wondered how wearing a push-up bra at least three-hundred-and-sixty-five days a year could possibly be comfortable, but the other part was just grateful. And, given the snug fit of her blouses, the shape of her body was no secret. His imagination had always enjoyed speculating how her bare skin might curve and glow and tease, and it turned out his imagination had speculated pretty accurately. It even got the goosebumps right. But he hadn't counted on her bra, which wasn't lacy or see-through or even all that interesting.

Because of that detail, he finally accepted that this was really happening.

"Yes," he replied.

With a grin, she told him, "Okay, now *you* go."

Fumbling with his t-shirts, he asked, "I can't comprehend why you don't just fuck Rocky."

"I thought you didn't want to babble about my boyfriend."

"This is true," he replied, "but—"

"You are such a goof, you know that?" Balancing herself carefully, she kicked off her fashionable boots. "I can think of four hundred and thirteen guys off the top of my head who would trade places with you so fast your shoes would fall off." She stepped forward, penetrating his comfort zone. "You don't think *I'm* a goof, do you?"

Flailing and backing away, he attempted to reply, "I..." He lost his balance and fell onto the bed. "I don't often find myself in this situation."

"Really?" This revelation seemed to utterly baffle her, so she put all of her thought into sorting it out—unzipping, dropping, and stepping out of her skirt didn't seem to require any concentration at all. That was when he discovered that the actual colour of her hair was a dull, medium brown—as remarkable as her bra.

Again, the detail only solidified the reality of the situation, making him shudder.

"Because you're totally rompable," she continued.

"That's something I don't hear a lot," he told her as she crawled onto the mattress next to him.

"Are you *sure*?"

"I have... problems..." His sentence stalled when he realised that she was unbuttoning his pants. He tried again. "I have problems being intimate."

She stopped mid-zip and frowned. "Who said anything about being intimate?" She turned her attention to untying and yanking off his shoes. "You don't need to be intimate to have sex! My boyfriend and I are totally intimate, but he's probably at some really late party, looking for lonely girls to comfort."

"Ah."

After peeling off his socks, she added, "And he's not being intimate with them."

"Your relationship confounds me," he told her.

"Well, *I'm* not confounded." She freed his pants completely from his legs with a sharp tug, but sacrificed her balance in the process. He leaned over the edge of her bed to find her on the floor, laughing uncontrollably. "Please don't tell anybody about this," she begged.

With a smirk, he hauled her back onto the bed and kissed her with the same ferocity she'd unleashed on him in the bar.

Her back arched, her hips rose, and her throat moaned. As soon as she could speak again, she sighed, "So I have to be a total goof to make you brave?"

"You just had to remind me why you're one of my favourite people in the world," he replied.

"Because I'm clumsy like a clumsy lizard?"

He shook his head. "That you're not even remotely the person you look like." This close to her face, and with this much light, he could make out crow's feet around her eyes, which was odd, considering that she was two years younger than he, and he was only twenty-three. "So who are you?"

"I'm Shannon, you goof."

"Seriously, who the hell *are* you?"

"Shannon Veronica Heidebrect?"

"I mean..." he began.

"No," she told him. "I am not going to tell you my whole poopy story so you can fall in love with how deep you think I really am."

"I don't fall in love that easily."

"I'm not that deep."

"I don't believe you."

"You want to talk about the scars on your arms?" she asked. "The ones that don't look like an accident?"

"No," he admitted.

"Well, I don't want to talk about my poop." Her fingers crept under the elastic of his boxers. "So how about you take these off, and I'll get a condom, and we can romp."

He couldn't argue any more. "Okay."

She rolled over to her nightstand. "A *lot*."

Hours later, in the morning, he had no idea what to expect from tomorrow, or the day after, but today, he had an answer to his daily question.

His finger tickled the small of her back, and she squirmed.

"Good morning," he whispered.

She reached for his waist and pulled him closer. "Good morning," she replied.

"Good morning!" shouted Rocky from the living room.

ABOUT JEREMIAH MURPHY

From New Mexico to Nebraska to New York to Indiana to Qatar to Washington D.C., Jeremiah Murphy has lived everywhere. And he writes a lot. His work can be found in anthologies such as *Fae Fatales*, *The Dark Lane Anthology, From the Corner of Your Eye, Pagan*, and others, as well as at www.jrmhmurphy.com.

ACCEPTANCE

DJ Tyrer

When you knew me before
I was very different
Yet to your charm
I wasn't indifferent
Not that I would've
Dared admit aloud
My feelings for you
Felt they weren't allowed
Suppressed them
Hid them away
Scared of being labelled
Branded as gay
Uncertain quite what
It was that I felt
Uncertain at the hand
I had been dealt
But over the years
You helped me to see
Just who it was
I was meant to be
Admitting the truth
Of my confusion
That the life I'd lived
Was just an illusion
Until I admitted

I was a girl not a guy
And embracing that fact
Decided to give it a try
And after some practice
Getting used to the role
I finally felt
I was finally whole
And as an act
Of coming out
We agreed to meet up
For a day out
So we each boarded trains
And met up halfway
I was elated, yet frightened
Of what you might say
This truly was me
No longer a lie
But did I look awful
Despite my best try?
But I needn't have worried
You said to me
"You look great—
I like what I see"
We walked through the streets
And you put me at ease
Slipped your hand into mine
And gave it a squeeze
Unselfconsciously we
Walked hand-in-hand
And finally I felt
Life could be grand
We shared a meal
And, yes, some stopped and stared
But with you with me
I didn't feel scared
And when finally we parted
You told me this
"I love you"
Sealed with a kiss

ABOUT DJ TYRER

DJ Tyrer is the person behind Atlantean Publishing and has been widely published in anthologies and magazines in the UK, USA and elsewhere, including *Between The Cracks* (Sirens Call Publishing), *History and Mystery, Oh My!* (Mystery and Horror LLC), *State of Horror: Illinois* (Charon Coin Press), *Steampunk Cthulhu* (Chaosium), *Irrational Fears* (FTB Press), and *Sorcery & Sanctity: A Homage to Arthur Machen* (Hieroglyphics Press), and in addition, has a novella available in paperback and on the Kindle, *The Yellow House* (Dunhams Manor). DJ Tyrer's website is at http://djtyrer.blogspot.co.uk.

EMERGENCY ENCOUNTER

Cindy Stauffer

Normality has become foreign. It could be the sandals on my feet, the crashing sound of the waves, the 30°C or the dirty scenes from the polluted streets I just witnessed, but it just doesn't feel like New Year's Eve. I'm still distressed by the scene I witnessed on our way to Lambi Beach Hotel.

Our two Toyota Land Cruisers were pulling out of the alley in front of our Cholera Treatment Center (CTC) and about to turn right onto the main road. The car's headlamps shed light on the two overflowing rubbish bins by the alley's rusted entrance gate. Suddenly, I noticed two people standing face to face between the open gate and yard wall. My eyes widened, but I was unable to speak, so I simply nudged the expatriate next to me and pointed towards the scene. She nodded. I wondered if she also saw what I saw. Finally, I managed to say, "They are having sex". Nobody said a thing.

Standing alone on the side of the dance floor, I wonder if I am wrong to be so shocked. These were people, not just two street dogs mating amidst the rats and rubbish. This is Port-au-Prince, a city victim of an earthquake and cholera. Unfortunate souls live cramped in crumbling buildings and under make-shift tents. Are these two people not just two people trying to meet their basic needs? The scene becomes a reflection of survival amongst misery. My troubled thoughts are interrupted by the anaesthetist from our team.

"Nice evening," says Dr Jon.

I'm not sure if this is a question or a statement so I simply nod.

Dr Jon and I have been living and working under the same roof for the past three weeks but I actually know very little about him. We start talking about our previous work experiences and about why we decided to do humanitarian work.

"What are your wishes for the new year?" he asks.

"Hmm... no huge dreams or aspirations... no special resolutions... just to have a nice year and spend a lot of time on the beach here in Haiti then in Costa Rica and then in Turkey," I say casually. "I'd also like to do some writing."

As I expose to him my plans for being a vagabonding hippie, for living in Kabak Valley in a tent, there seems to be a sparkle in his blue eyes. I imagine he finds these plans appealing and must be fond of such freedom, but then he says, "I am getting married after this mission".

"Oh, wow, that sounds exciting..." I say, still a bit surprised.

As we go on chatting about life and relationships, in my mind, I move his name to the "taken" section of males on the mission. I do so without any special thought or feeling. I don't find Dr Jon particularly cute or sexy, just a friendly type.

After another half hour passes, I suspect he may stroll off and talk to any of the other dozen members of our team; instead he asks me to dance. When we discover we are both horrible dancers, we revert to drinking ice cold beers and chatting. We do so until our 2am curfew, time at which all eleven expats pile back into the two Land Cruisers and return to the expatriate house.

In the car we are still holding hands. I don't even remember when, how or why we started holding hands, all I know is that now we can't seem to let go.

Four in the morning and perhaps fourteen (small) beers later we are alone on the balcony—still holding hands. The last drunk expat just went to sleep. We sit in silence.

Confusion rolls around my brain, *What is this? What is going on? This is madness, he is getting married! I don't know what this is but I don't want it to stop. So, what next? Oh, my God! He wants to kiss me! Should I kiss him?*

I reason that since it is New Year's and we had a few drinks a kiss can be forgiven. Besides, I love kissing and am not the one getting married. As our lips meet all the harshness of the city around us disappears. The dilapidated buildings, garbage-lined streets, exhaust fumes, tents, chlorine smells, and cholera are erased from my mind. There is only desire and tenderness now. Alarm bells start ringing in my mind when our lips part. Such a sweet drug could become addictive.

"Would you like to come sleep in my room?" he asks timidly. "I mean just to cuddle... I mean just as friends. I promise nothing will happen..."

I smile and kiss him once again.

"Ask me this question in three days," I reply and then go down to my room.

✐

The next evening, Jon and I are left home alone. On the balcony, I sip a beer and contemplate the wonderful day I had at Petit-Goave Beach. A forty-mile drive had taken two colleagues and I from Haiti's gloomy face to its sunny one. We had observed the dreary brown and grey tones transform into vibrant blues and greens. For a few hours we had no longer been on a humanitarian mission but in a tropical paradise. Surrounded by lush green hills, we had lay on the beach and observed local fishermen pull out lobster from the Caribbean Sea. Stephane, my best friend from Switzerland, and I had savoured beef brochettes at the French-owned beachside café. Only Jon had been missing in this perfect picture. Now, as the other expatriates are out for dinner, Jon is probably in his room. Perhaps he is talking to his fiancée.

Then I hear the footsteps in the kitchen. Finally, Jon appears on the balcony. He sits across from me on a wooden chair. We discuss and reflect on past experiences, globalisation, consumerism, and movies such as *Hotel Rwanda* and *Darwin's Nightmare*. It is a harsh world and a hard chair. Before another ten hour day at the CTC tomorrow, we need some comforting. He joins me on the faded, dirty taupe couch.

I stretch out my legs over his lap to get comfy. Our eyes meet but we do not speak. We must both be thinking about last night. Perhaps I should remove my legs. No, this is supposed to be relaxing. I just want to lay in silence and feel his breath mix with mine, to see his chest go up and down as air goes in and out and to think of nothing.

"It was nice on Friday night... really nice..." he says in an unsteady voice.

I can't tell if he will apologise for kissing me and tell me it was a mistake or he will do it again. I interrupt.

"Yes, yes... I respect your personal situation and apologise if—" I say but stop when in his eyes I see that we are already too far off track.

"It was not because I had so much to drink... as you said. I really think you are beautiful..." he continues.

My mind finds itself indulging in the sweetness of the moment and blocking out all the other messages and dark realities.

He then adds, "I don't usually do this... I never did this before..."

Regret, confusion and desire intertwine on his lips as he speaks. He leans forward and we indulge ourselves in hugging and kissing.

✦

Being on his first humanitarian mission abroad Jon may not know of the "Emergency Sex Phenomenon." He needs to be reassured that it is normal for him to act and feel different than he may have back home. He has been working at least sixty hours a week for the past two months. He is not betraying his fiancée, but simply meeting his own immediate mental health need for a bit of love and caring. Since this needn't involve sex, and in respect of his relationship, I suggest we define sex as a no-go area. We shall find sufficient comfort in touching, hugging and kissing. Thus we consciously abandon ourselves to a moment of intimacy confined in space and time. That night, the images of dying children, collapsing ceilings and creeping snakes that I so often see at night are kept away by the warmth of Jon's body and soul. At 6am I sneak back to the reality of my room.

✦

A year before my first humanitarian mission I read a book called *Emergency Sex and Other Desperate Measures: a True Story from Hell on Earth.* In this book, the authors, three humanitarian workers, describe the romantic and sexual relationships they enjoyed throughout their missions in hot spots such as Cambodia, Somalia, and Haiti. At the time, I was rather shocked by some of the stories. For instance, I did not comprehend and approve of Heidi's relationship with a local Somali soldier. It seemed that social and moral norms as well as security rules would dictate otherwise. Yet later I would discover that the stories of the authors are hardly extraordinary. They are part of what I have come to call the "Emergency Sex Phenomenon."

Emergency Sex is a rampant phenomenon. When I finally went on mission, I observed numerous relationships including expatriates dating other expatriates and expatriates dating locals. A year later, I read that a 1991 survey of 1,018 Peace Corps Volunteers in 28 countries indicated that 39% reported having sex with locals in their country of assignment. If other relationships with other foreign volunteers had been included it is highly likely that this number would vastly surpass 50%. So what really is this Emergency Sex phenomenon which is experienced by the majority of humanitarian workers?

Emergency Sex has more to do with fulfilling an emotional need rather than a physical need. The word "sex" can be misleading, as the aim of the relationship goes beyond having sex. Actually, intimate encounters and relationships may not even involve sex at all. The aim is comfort. It is about finding sunshine amongst the misery. The brain wants to switch off and the body wants to relax. Only love and affection can have the power to erase the surrounding hopelessness and daily frustrations. Sunshine may be found in a kiss, in a message, or simply in a smile. Looking forward to that piece of sunshine can be enough to give much needed positive energy and get a person through the rough times in the day.

When I arrived on the Cholera Treatment Project, my second mission, I immediately recognised the Emergency Sex phenomenon operating strongly. The Canadian nurse in her fifties kisses the German nurse in his thirties on his mouth to say goodnight, and holds the hand of the British nurse in the car on the way to work, as a child clinging to its mother. A German doctor in his sixties awaits eagerly in the staff lounge for a shoulder massage by the Canadian Water and Sanitation Manager, in her early thirties. I catch the house cook and Project Coordinator hugging in the kitchen.

"*Bonsoir ma Cherie... Ta robe est trop belle.*" (Goodnight my darling... your dress is too nice).

Another night yet, I catch a glimpse of the Canadian doctor and German Logistician sharing a kiss. We all need love and affection. Considering that our lives are strictly confined between the Cholera Treatment Center and the expatriate house, except for an occasional trip to the city centre or to the beach on Sundays, it is normal that we find this love in the people around us. At times our *real* loved ones are too far away to understand and give us the comfort we need, so we engage in relations we may not in different circumstances. For instance, under "normal" conditions the brain would say, "You know he is married?" or "She is your staff, not your mother."

Social scientists call the space where the "normal" rules of constraints of society are suspended the Liminal Zone. This usually happens when an individual enters an alternate reality and is on the "threshold" of or between two different existential planes, therefore experiencing a temporary loss of identity. It is common for travellers to experience this, as travel in itself creates an alternate reality. For the humanitarian worker the alternate reality is even more pronounced. One is no longer in his/her familiar "home" environment and not fully part of the new environment. Interaction with local people in the mission country is often limited to the workplace. The expatriate or volunteer lives a disparate social life which is essentially composed of other foreigners from diverse countries and cultures. In a sense, the humanitarian worker becomes a new person for the duration of his or her mission as he or she has a new home, new colleagues, a new job, new housemates and a new confrontation with misery. When everything is new so are the rules; normality becomes foreign.

❦

When I look up from the computer, I see Jon standing beside my desk. A lump forms in my heart. I was not expecting to see him. He has been hiding behind a wall of silence since we woke up together three days earlier. We sat in the same car and meeting room in the morning. In the evening, our paths crossed on the house terrace, but mostly he spent his free time in his room. From across the hall, in my room I could hear him speaking on Skype, probably to his fiancée. I wondered if she had seen the blue love bites on his neck and if he was angry at me for this. He begins to speak but stops and starts again when he realises he forgot to greet me, "Oh… sorry… hi… how are you?"

"I am well, thanks, and you?"

"Good."

I am tempted to request a justification for his silence, but remind myself that I am in my office and not at the house. Private matters should be kept for later. He asks me for the contract start date of his translator.

Cold and numb fingers struggle to type the last name of the employee in my Human Resource database. A cramp could handicap my arm at any moment. Anger enters the lump in my heart. I should not be affected so much by Jon. Finally, I manage to find the information and he is gone again.

I return to typing the memo announcing the one year commemoration ceremony that will take place in a week. January 12, 2011 will be considered a public holiday and all essential staff working will gather in the courtyard at 4h53 for a minute of silence in honour of those that perished in the earthquake a year earlier. I can't believe that it's almost been one year since a magnitude 7.0 earthquake rattled Port-au-Prince and the surrounding regions, taking the lives of over 230,000 people and leaving more than 1.5 million homeless. Driving down the street nowadays, I see little improvement compared to back in April. Some 800,000 people remain living in temporary camps. Sorrow joins the anger in my heart.

When I step onto the balcony to breathe this out and let it all go with the cigarette smoke, I am confronted with cholera. Our offices and stores are in a two-storied school building converted into an orthopaedic hospital following the earthquake and into a CTC following the confirmation of the cholera outbreak on 22 October 2010. By the end of December 2010, cholera had already claimed more than 3,000 lives in Haiti. Down below in the courtyard, the tents are still filled with patients.

Where children once used to play, they are now lying in cholera beds—plastic sheeting with a hole in the middle and a bucket beneath. Some of the younger children shriek as IV lines of Oral Rehydration Solution (ORS) are jammed into their bony arms. Those that I can catch a glimpse of appear between four and eight years old. I exhale another cloud of white smoke and mumble an encouragement to myself, "They will go home soon and then back to school, back to playing in this courtyard."

Indeed, with proper care most patients hospitalised recover within three days. According to a report of the Ministry of Health on 29 December 2010, of the 87,639 cases hospitalised, 85,331 returned home recovered, that is 97.3%. These figures provide space for optimism.

I turn my gaze from the children to a man that represents hope. Clad in green scrubs, black rubber boots and a stethoscope around his neck, Jon, accompanied by his translator moves from one tent to another. A smile crosses my lips as affection and admiration transpire through me. Jon is saving lives and while doing so does not neglect the small attentions toward his patients—a soft pat on the hand or shoulder, a reassuring smile, a friendly word.

Twenty minutes before the supervisors meeting, instead of going through the points I shall cover at the meeting—new working hours, overtime policy and contract renewals—I am performing a session of personal counselling.

"Yes, you are good. You are strong, you are professional and you are beautiful. Don't let someone else's weakness become your weakness and your problem. Yes, he is indeed weak. See how he fumbled. He is the one avoiding you. I have done nothing and been strong by not reacting. I shall not make a fool out of myself because that Red Lobster Face is," I say as I pace back and forth in the staff lounge.

⬦

Another day is almost over. There are only twenty minutes left before darkness and along with it our curfew. I decide to read the e-mails containing the latest press coverage on Haiti. In a 9 January 2011 Reuters article, "A year on, hubris and debris clog Haiti quake recovery," International aid organisations express their frustration with slow progress in reconstruction efforts. Another mail contains blogger Tim Large's piece "One Day in Port-au-Prince - THE SEX WORKER: 'God didn't give me a body to sell'." Large tells the story of Evelyne Pierre, a 23-year-old beautician who had to turn to prostitution after she lost her mother, her baby's father and her house in the earthquake. Unable to contain my tears any longer, I shut-down my computer, light another cigarette and sit in silent numbness; drops fall onto the dusty cement floor.

Evelyne is still in my mind when I arrive at the expatriate house half an hour later. I attempt to wash her away with a cold Prestige beer. Jon is also sitting on the street-side balcony. Now, I don't care about his fiancée or about the wall of silence he has built between us.

"Would you like to go have a beer on the back balcony?" I ask.

He accepts. The generator noise in the back is more constant, thereby less nerve-racking than the traffic noise in the front. I drag a mattress out. We sit, we talk, we touch, we talk, we drink, we touch, and we listen.

Our fingertips encounter each other. Cities all over the world are full of misery. Masses of people from the rural areas arrive filled with the belief that better opportunities will be available there—a better life. They are then confronted with overpopulation, scarcity of jobs and housing, prostitution, and lack of support mechanisms. Money is king, but there are few kings and many hyenas around. These refugees abandon green pastures for the devil's den. Our fingers intertwine. The crescent moon is slowly disappearing behind the building in front of us.

"If IKEA was here, it would not have been the guy down the street who would have made our wooden chairs," I comment.

His fingertips caress my inner wrist and crawl up the length of my arm and back down. The touch is ever so soft and faint, like a light breeze over my skin. Copper strands of hair seep through my fingers. I draw contours around his freckles. Then we are back at the fingertips. We are like two blind people discovering the sense of touch for the first time in our lives. I never knew such a soft touch could be felt so strongly. Everything else disappears—the moon, the rest of the expatriate team on the front balcony, the sound of the generator, Haiti, and the cholera. It is like a yoga of fingers.

Jon brings more beers and some music.

"Today I found a way to remove four daily worker working days from the schedule by optimising on contract staff hours. I was doing my job, avoiding us unnecessary expenses and sticking to budget, but part of my heart hurt. I felt as if I had robbed someone of much needed income," I confide.

Moby starts to play. The song goes, "Why does my heart feel so bad, why does my soul feel so bad." The grip of our fingers tightens as if to transmit necessary encouragement. When a more uplifting melody begins, "These open doors. These open doors. These open doors," fingers still intertwined, our arms open to the side, gently rise up and curve as in ballet's fifth position or *bras en couronne*. It is as if we feel a need to open up—to let our soul breathe, the butterfly fly. Fingers let go, inner wrists touch, turn, now the encounter is between our complete forearms, before our fingers touch each other's upper arms. Our fingers and arms are engaged in a mystical dance. The mood saddens again in the last seconds of the song. Arms close, fingers clasp; we are like a closing waterlily.

I lay my head on his chest. Two pairs of blue eyes gaze at each other. Focused on sight now, fortunately the words "So this is goodbye" of the next song go unheard. Jon's end of mission is in three days, the day after the earthquake commemoration. For the next six weeks, I will have only memories to escape to. Our lips call at each other but are left waiting until we move to the privacy of his room.

Jon reaches out through the mosquito net and gets hold of my ringing cell phone. The ringing stops. There is no caller ID. I replace the phone on the white tiles beside our mattress. After pondering for a moment on who could call me at 4h30am, I decide to switch off my brain for a last hour. The "bloody" rooster is already or still screaming outside. Other phones start to ring in the house.

During this election period, the situation is volatile. Anything could happen anytime. Do I dare consider the possibility of this not being my last morning with Jon? The Port-au-Prince airport had already been shut-down due to unrest for a few days this past December.

An hour later, I leave Jon to pack his luggage and go up to the terrace.

"No movements," the Project Coordinator (PC) announces.

Manifestations have taken place on the road between Carrefour and the city centre during the evening and early morning he tells me. Although the airport is open, our organisation has suspended all movements of our vehicles until further notice. The PC makes a series of phone calls to the security advisor, the flight coordinator, and some national staff.

I have really been looking forward to spending these four days of "Rest and Relaxation" on Playa Esmeralda. It can't fall through now!

We get the green-light shortly before 8am. On a "normal" day when traffic is so heavy and clogged, it would be almost impossible to go from Carrefour to the airport in less than an hour. At times, that road can take up to three hours. This morning, the day after the earthquake commemoration, the roads are almost vacant, except for a few motorbikes, tap-taps, and about a dozen police vehicles.

Jon and I hold hands and are silent as we pass through this sad and now familiar city—the crumbling buildings, the plastic bottles floating on the side of the road, the white Styrofoam boxes shining among the rubbish overflowing in dried riverbeds, the monstrous grey boars delighting in the filth, the collapsed presidential palace and the faded blue and white plastic sheeting tents. Today, the streets and walls are black and remnants of burnt tyres can be seen near Martissant.

In twenty-four hours Jon will fly away from this and from me permanently. All will be just a memory, but one, that I believe remains engraved in one's heart forever. Another life, another world awaits him in Berlin. The car pulls up to the departure terminal.

I scramble out of the car with my backpack already on and glance at Jon one last time. He realises we haven't exchanged e-mail addresses. We could have a million times in the past month, but I knew this relationship had an expiration date I had to respect. This is now.

We had agreed that we would not say goodbye, so we just say, "Thank you."

❧

Six months later, as I sit under an olive tree back in Europe, I realise that Emergency Sex is simply a sub-phenomenon of what is called "Romance" or "Sex Tourism." Both the tourist and the expatriate or volunteer find themselves in a new reality, dazed and seduced, as they navigate through what was mentioned earlier as the Liminal Zone.

Jeannette Belliveau, author of *Romance on the Road*, on women who travel for sex and companionship describes the women more likely to have travel romance as having the following profile: from a nation in the West or Japan, in her thirties or forties, having an adventurous and risk-taking attitude, history of broken relationships, smoking cigarettes, and using more alcohol than others.

Most female humanitarian aid workers are likely to fit this profile, with the exception that they may also be in their late twenties. For instance, of the six women in our cholera project, two were from Canada, one from Germany, one from Switzerland, one from France and one from Japan; four were in their thirties or forties; only one was in a steady relationship; only one did not drink alcohol or smoke regularly. We are all ambitious professionals, seeking to help the world but also probably trying to fill a gap in our hearts.

Women certainly don't go on a humanitarian mission for romance, but that is nonetheless often part of the package. Movies such as *Beyond Borders*, focusing on humanitarian aid workers, also portray the romance or Emergency Sex element. While on a holiday, fling sex may be commodified into another pleasurable thing one could enjoy in, such as an ice-cream. On mission, it acts as a band-aid for the heart.

My encounter with Jon turned out to be far more memorable than any other romantic or sexual encounter I have experienced on mission. Even when he was gone, his pink Converse shoes—they were originally blue but the chlorine bleached them—remained at the entrance of the house and greeted me every morning and every evening, until my end of mission about a month later. I was tempted to ask colleagues for his e-mail address and to tell him how much I missed him. But then I remembered that he was now already in a different dimension and that one definition of the Liminal Zone is that it is doomed to end. Instead,

I attempted to seek comfort in the presence of a tall, dark-haired, married Italian working in our coordination office. It didn't work. His touch did not manage to warm my heart and fill it with tenderness; his kiss did not stop my brain. Until the end of my mission, I remained in the same dimension: one where I missed Jon.

Months later, finding a scientific explanation to what had happened to my heart in the form of liminality helped me remain practical about the encounter and prevented me from delving into too much romanticism. Now that the story is told, the magic of that moment captured and analysed to the best of my ability, my encounter with Jon just remains a sweet memory that occasionally brushes my thoughts.

ABOUT CINDY STAUFFER

Cindy Stauffer was born in Switzerland but raised in Turkey by her Swiss parents. Since obtaining her degree in HR Management in 2009, she has been working as a humanitarian aid worker and done missions in places including Swaziland, Haiti, Myanmar and Turkey. She has attended several courses in creative and travel writing and enjoys writing poetry and creative non-fiction for which she largely draws on her work and travel experiences. When not on mission, she lives on the Mediterranean coast of Turkey, indulges in writing, painting, reading, and teaching English.

BREAKING POINT

Tara Calaby

The ute's left headlight pointed in the wrong direction. The two weak beams of yellow met somewhere right of centre, the cross-eyed effect leaving the left edge of the road shadowy and unlit. At dusk, it didn't make a lot of difference. The last rays of sunlight ricocheted off the side mirror and into my eyes whenever the ute broke free of trees and sheltering hills, blinding me and burning a crimson glow through the pinpricks of my irises and right into my brain.

Ruth was silent, her knuckles white against the black of the steering wheel. When I dared to look across at her, I could see the twitch of her jaw as she clenched and unclenched her teeth. Her face was pale, save for a small circle of pink in the centre of her cheek, almost imperceptible but ringed by a faded aura. I got the impression that if I had touched her she would have turned and killed me with her gaze. I wasn't that stupid, though. I had plans for a long and fruitful life. Preferably one without her in it.

The paddocks seemed ominous in the half-light: long stretches of cows and nothing, divided into neat oblongs by hedges and fences. My eyes grasped at the occasional light that seeped from farmhouses and milking sheds, but it felt almost as though the metal shell of the ute had become the boundary of my universe. I checked to make sure that my door was unlocked. Just in case.

The silence stretched through one village and into the outskirts of the next. When she finally spoke, her voice was so quiet that I could barely pull her words from the rush of wind against the windscreen and the whirr of heated air escaping through the dashboard vents.

"I fucked up, didn't I?"

I understood that denial was the preferred response. The curve of her lips was too casual for the question to be rhetorical and I struggled with the conflict between charity and honesty in an attempt to forge my reply, discarding inflammatory words in a desperate attempt to find a non-offensive synonym for 'psychopath.'

"It just wasn't working," I said finally and cringed at the cliché of my own words.

That's what break-ups were, though, when you stripped away the emotions and sifted through the remains. Someone had to be the bad guy, full of bleak 'it wasn't you's and engineered 'I tried's. Ruth didn't believe in following the rules. She wanted conflict and accusations so that she could cry on her friends' shoulders and curse rivers about the horrible girlfriend I'd turned out to be. The required words were deep inside me, but I was loath to let them out. Not here, at least, belted into the passenger's side of the bench seat as she sped ever faster through the growing night.

"I'm a horrible person, you mean."

Yes, I thought, but I shook my head and bit my tongue. "We're not right for each other."

"In other words, I'm not good enough for you."

"I didn't say that."

"You didn't have to."

Ruth's mouth tightened and she leaned forward over the steering wheel, peering through the windscreen at the road ahead. Once, I might have attempted to comfort her, but I was sick of her endless bullshit. We weren't together any more; her emotional stability was no longer my responsibility. I had my own wellbeing to think about and, trapped beside her in the ute, it was continuously at the forefront of my mind.

It had been a while since we'd last passed through the street-lit shadows of a town. Even the farmhouses seemed to be coming at greater intervals as the hills marched on towards the horizon, swelling and bloating and congregating in a blue haze of distant mountains. Behind us, the sky was a swirl of peach-tipped clouds. Soon, the darkness would be complete and the glass in front of us would become smeared and spattered with insects. I wondered whether the left headlight would still appear crooked on high beam.

The stars out here were different, almost threatening as they glowed ever brighter against the blackening sky. I felt surrounded, cornered.

I pictured the world spinning faster and faster, the stars becoming a dizzying whirl of blinking light as my feet found it ever harder to remain steady on the ground. It was a nauseating image and I found myself instinctively clutching at the front of the seat to either side of my legs. The cracked leather was slightly greasy beneath my fingers. I fought the urge to wipe my hands.

"Do you have any idea where you're going?" I asked when the silence started to feel painful and claustrophobic.

"I'll know when we're there."

My stomach twisted. "You can't drive forever. We'll run out of petrol, if nothing else."

"There's still half a tank." Ruth glanced across at me, her eyes challenging. "I'm not an idiot, Melanie."

Frustrated, I jabbed a hand towards the surrounding countryside. "Why can't we just stop here? It's not going to make any difference."

"It has to be the mountains. Don't you read the papers?"

"Not if I can help it."

I slumped back against the bench seat, my neck curling over the top as I gazed up at the torn fabric that stretched across the roof, blemished by cigarette pockmarks and smoky streaks of ash. The owner of the ute was obviously a dedicated smoker. Even the dashboard was stained. It was too easy to imagine him behind the steering wheel, smoke curling around his fingers as he tapped out the drum patterns to the static-distorted music blasting from the ute's primitive AM radio. The Loony Tunes air freshener hanging from the rear-vision mirror was faded. Someone had drawn blue biro glasses around Sylvester's eyes.

"Do you still love me?"

Ruth's question was more predictable than she would have liked to believe. As precarious as my situation was, I was reluctant to lie about something so immense.

"No," I said, looking straight ahead in an attempt to evade her gaze.

"See, that?" She hit the curve of the steering wheel with the flat of her palm. The sound reverberated throughout the ute, harsh against the steady throb of the engine. "That I find impossible to believe." Turning, she looked at me, her face grey as it wavered in my peripheral vision. "Unless, of course, you've been lying to me all along."

"I don't lie about things like that."

"What, then?"

I hated romantic confrontations. I chewed my thumbnail as I constructed responses inside my mind, eyes fixed upon the asphalted road ahead. "You're not the person I fell in love with," I said finally, crossing and uncrossing my legs.

"What the hell is that supposed to mean? I just turned into a whole other person overnight? You're full of shit, Melanie. It's about him, isn't it?"

"I—"

"We broke up months ago," she said. "I know you're possessive, but this is ridiculous. I'm not about to get back together with him now, am I?"

"I'm not being possessive, Ruth."

She laughed bitterly. "What is it, then? Biphobia? For God's sake."

"Biphobia?" I bit my lip. "No, not biphobia."

"I know what you lesbians are like. So I don't have my Gold Star. I've dated men. That doesn't mean I'll dump you for one of them!"

The remains of a fox came into a view as the ute reached the peak of the slight hill we had been climbing. Its body lay towards the right side of the road, looking whole and perfect in the fading light. My throat felt swollen.

Ruth yanked at the steering wheel, guiding the ute over to the wrong side of the road. "Bloody foxes," she said, knuckles whitening. The sickening bump was almost lost amongst the potholes in the road. "Well?" she demanded, steering the ute back towards the left verge.

"I've, um, learned a few new things about you today," I began. "I need time to reconcile them before we can move on."

"Whatever." She shook her head and took a sharp left onto an unsurfaced road.

The ute looked old, but the suspension was remarkably good. If it hadn't been for the company, it would have been quite a pleasant ride, even once we began to climb and the road became narrower and more ridged. We were making our way into the mountains now and at times the only view from the passenger window was a shadowy rock-face, formed when the road had been cut through the hillside. On Ruth's side the ground fell away in a mass of gums and tree ferns, muted greens and browns becoming indiscernible metres away from the ute's path.

"How much further?" I asked when we had reached the top of one mountain and were on our way to scaling the next.

"It's like having a child in the car." Her eyes remained on the tightly winding road. "Soon, okay? I have to find somewhere it'll be safe to park. Otherwise we might find ourselves walking back to civilisation."

I nodded and started scanning the roadside for areas wide enough to accommodate the ute, the task becoming ever more difficult as the last light faded from the sky and Ruth switched the headlights to high beam. Finally, I spotted a possibility, a grassed area that sloped gently downhill for a few metres before quickly being swallowed by the usual trees and scrub.

"There!" I said, pointing towards it.

Ruth reacted, breaking sharply and guiding the car onto the grass. Once she'd killed the engine, she turned off the headlights as well, stretching as she unbuckled her seat belt and slid from the ute.

"Won't you need the light?" I called after her, reluctant to leave my own seat.

"Too risky. The moon will have to do."

"We haven't seen anyone for miles," I protested. "Who else, apart from us, is going to drive up here at this time of night?"

"You never know." Ruth slammed the door before walking over to my side of the car and knocking on the window. "Come on. I can't do this myself."

I retrieved my sweater from the floor at my feet, pulling it over my head as I opened the door and jumped to the ground. "Shit," I said, as the full force of the mountain air surrounded me. "It's goddamn freezing."

Even with the extra warmth of my sweater, I felt like I had been dunked into a tank of icy water. My breath seemed to freeze as soon as it hit my throat and for a few seconds I gasped compulsively, hoping that it wasn't so cold that my heart would forget to beat. I jiggled up and down for a moment, hugging myself, and tried to ignore the bite of the wind against my cheeks.

"Wimp." Ruth shook her head as she moved to the back of the ute, lifting the tarp and retrieving a spade from the tray. "Catch," she said, throwing it in my direction and laughing as I fumbled for a moment before gaining a firm hold.

"I don't see why I have to be a part of this," I said, as she took a second spade for herself and made her way into the bush several metres to the rear of the ute.

"If you don't shut up, I'll be digging two holes."

I bit my lip and followed her through the undergrowth, silently starting to dig once she paused and indicated her chosen spot. To be fair, she did her share of the work, brushing her dark hair back from her face when it became annoying and leaving muddy finger-streaks across her forehead. Ruth was stronger than she looked; I'd discovered that months ago. She didn't pause until the hole was close to a metre deep, finally tossing her spade to one side and wiping her hands on a nearby tree trunk.

"Come on," she ordered, leading the way back to the ute and unlacing the tarp on two sides, pushing it back into a loose roll.

I cringed as she climbed in, using the tow-bar as a narrow step and easily scaling the back of the tray. For a moment, she stood there, her hands dark against her hips and her face eerily white beneath the moonlight. If she had been seeking resolve, she found it quickly, soon bending and lifting her cargo to waist height. With more effort than she would probably admit to, she managed to drag the dead weight forward so that it was hanging half over the back of the tray.

"Well?" She jumped to the ground and glared accusatively at me. "Are you going to give a girl a hand?"

I paused to breathe for a moment before lifting one heavy arm over my shoulder, mirroring her own movement. My neck twitched as it was surrounded by cold flesh and bile rose within my throat. "What was his name?"

Ruth sneered as we slowly made our way into the trees. "Does it matter now?"

"It matters to me."

"His name was Michael. Still is, I guess, if you want to be philosophical."

I looked down at his face, smudged and distorted at the bottom of the shallow hole. His nose looked broken, and his lips were bruised. "He looks like a Michael."

"He looks like a corpse," Ruth said, and kicked a clod of earth into the hole.

I watched as she covered him, patting the dirt firm and collecting bark and decaying leaves from the surrounding area to camouflage where he lay. When she finished, the area was discernible only by the too-even arrangement of the curling strips of bark. Even in daylight, it would go unnoticed from the road.

She picked up her shovel and slung it over one shoulder, calling back to me as she headed towards the road. "He didn't love me either."

Frowning, I bent to arrange two pieces of bark into a crude cross. Ruth revved the engine. I wiped my hands and went to join her. It was going to be a long ride home.

ABOUT TARA CALABY

Tara Calaby is a a British-Australian writer, currently living in the eastern suburbs of Melbourne. Her work has appeared in such publications as *Grimdark Magazine*, *Daily Science Fiction* and *Aurealis*. When not writing or editing, she can be found researching her family tree or attempting to learn Welsh.

Find her online at http://www.taracalaby.com.

A Love on the Other Side
of the World

Men Pechet

After many days of silence—no meetings, no calls, no text messages—my phone suddenly alerted with a text message in my inbox while I was sitting in my classroom. I did not anticipate that anyone would be sending me a message at that moment. I did not have many friends and most of those I did have were with me in the classroom. When I took my phone out of my pocket, it turned out to be your name in the inbox. I was very happy to see your text message. You asked me how I had enjoyed my lunch. You may not realise how very happy I was to read your message. I felt as if I were flying. I smiled to myself and my classmate asked me if I was okay! I told him, "I'm fine." I lowered my head back to my phone, and smiled again. I wanted very much to reply to your text message and tell you how much I missed you. However, my phone had no credit remaining to either reply to your message or make a call. Having no means to respond to you, I remained silent.

An hour passed, and you texted me again. This time your message was not as sweet, but instead was heartbreaking. You asked me if I wanted to meet you, "for the last time?" My nerves were on edge and my heart raced. My body was trembling and my world was crumbling. I could no longer concentrate on my class. Thousands of thoughts, thousands of them, suddenly flooded my mind. I repeatedly asked myself why you had suddenly changed your tone?! When you texted me, I thought you understood my feelings after our last disagreement. But the matter became more serious. I still responded only with silence, and that was how our love ended. No matter how tightly we had once held each other's hands, when our Karma ended, we eventually had to separate from one another.

This is our love story. You were my first love, first kiss, first hug, and first person with whom I made love. Our love was a secret one, I believe, among the thousands of other loves in our society—Cambodia. Our love was different, unusual in the eyes of others. No one in our society could accept us as we were, though our hearts were as pure as those of other lovers. People in our society, including our parents, could not acknowledge us as lovers, so we lived in the dark side of our society. We met in public as mere friends. You would tell your friends or relatives that I was your friend, and I would say the same about you. We lied to everyone we knew. We could not hold hands or kiss in public; if we found ourselves about to hold hands or kiss, thousands of curious eyes would turn in our direction and gossip would ensue. Those inquiring eyes were very cruel, sending us a message of hatred and discrimination. They seemed to scold us for being different. I wanted to kiss you and hold your hand as loving couples do, but instead I had to internalise my feelings. I knew I was forbidden from showing affection for you in public. Sadly we were forced to admit that we could not live together happily for the rest of our lives if our society could not accept our love. We had to break up. Because we were boyfriend and boyfriend.

After your last text message, we fell silent and became what we used to be—strangers. Our relationship lasted exactly twelve months from autumn 2007 to autumn 2008. Then, you stopped calling and texting me. I did not call you or text you either. You walked your way and I walked mine without acknowledging each other's whereabouts. However, one thing was very clear to me—my heart had been shattered into small pieces. I lost you and was drowning in pain because I missed you so much. It felt like my world was falling apart. I believed you missed me too, and your heart was also broken. We both needed time to heal our wounds, wounds which would take a long time to heal since we could not share our pain with others, not even our relatives or friends. We had to rely on ourselves, and this aggravated our suffering.

We hated our own society for not accepting us. We used to talk to one another about other countries where our kind of love is accepted, where we would be permitted to get married, and where we could express our affection publicly. We were not weird animals, but merely human beings with hearts full of love. As such, we needed comfort and warmth from our relatives and friends. Most of all, we needed their acknowledgement and encouragement. We used to make promises to one another that one day we would leave this society to settle in one of those countries, yet that promise was never fulfilled. And now, I have no idea when the biased mindset of our people will change. If it takes thirty or fifty years for attitudes to change, of course, we would never have a chance to be together, nor would any other couples like us. They would end up with a similar fate—breaking up and living their lives separately. Some people like us choose to marry someone they have no sexual desire for in order to hide their sexual orientation and to be accepted by society. However, if they marry someone for whom they do not have feelings, they are hurting both their spouse and themselves. They destroy both families—their own family and their spouse's family. In our society, people live their lives for others, not for themselves. They do many things to satisfy others rather than to satisfy their own heartfelt desires. And we did likewise; we chose to break up in order to please our parents.

I knew you had become very tired—tired of lying to everyone we knew, tired of hiding our kind of love, tired of making excuses when we wanted to be together, simply tired of everything. Ultimately, we became very exhausted holding hands while walking through the endless obstacles we encountered. We always lived in fear, just like a thief always fears being caught. We had come so far, but still we could not move on. Sooner or later, we had to let each other go—not because we were not strong, but because we simply did not want to burden each other. We did not want to damage the harmony and reputation of each other's family. We did not want to be despised and discriminated against. We wanted to be seen as normal people again. That's why, when you distanced yourself from me and kept silent, I knew very clearly that our love had reached a dead end. Though we no longer talked or met each other, one treasure remained in my heart—you were my first lover and our love was very honest. We loved each other heart to heart. More than that, our love harmed no one. There was nothing wrong about our love, nothing wrong about being born as the persons we are. Even today, I still miss you and still regard you as my lover, and you will always exist in my lonely heart. I cannot forget you.

THE FIRST DAY WE MET EACH OTHER

After we broke up, I went on living with all the energy I could muster. Every day, I got up, brushed my teeth, ate breakfast, changed my clothes, left my room, and arrived at school. I returned to my usual life. I was a third-year student at the state university in the capital of Phnom Penh, where I was born and raised. I met my friends and talked to them as usual. It seemed as if nothing had happened in my life for the past year. No one would ever have considered that something significant *had* happened to me, neither my parents nor my friends.

One day in autumn 2008, I missed you terribly. The autumn wind was blowing a cool breeze. I missed the first day we met under the moonlight the previous autumn. On the first day we met, you touched my face and I felt the warmth of your hands. That was soothing, and from that moment onward I fell deeply in love with you. I did not know why I decided so quickly—to love you—but I felt that you were right for me.

We were strangers at first, but we progressed from strangers to friends, and from friends to lovebirds. I remember precisely that you and I began talking with one another after I first signed up a for a Hi5 account under the name of Joo. Hi5 is an online social network to which many young people in our country are addicted. You asked me to be one of your friends on Hi5, and I was happy to accept your friend request. Perhaps, you saw my profile photo. After that, we exchanged phone numbers and started to get to know one another. Gradually, we made less contact through Hi5. Instead, we often shared information by sending text messages. In honesty, I told you that the photo posted on my profile was not mine. I was hesitant to disclose that information, for I was afraid of losing you after revealing the truth. However, my decision to be truthful about the photo occurred just before our first date.

Our first date took place soon after we became acquainted. I was young and it was my first experience in meeting someone considered a stranger to me. I had no idea if you were right for me. We discussed where we should meet. Again, I had no idea, since you were my first date. However, I didn't feel secure meeting you somewhere quiet and unfamiliar. Finally, we agreed to meet around 6:00pm at a bus stop in front of my school.

I was nervous before meeting you. I supposed you felt the same way. I was nervous because on one hand, I was afraid that you may not like me after seeing the real me; on the other hand, I was afraid that you might not be compatible with me. These feelings were normal, since generally everyone has an image in mind of the kind of person they like and admire.

I was waiting there, in front of my school, at the agreed-upon time. It was Sunday evening. There were many people and thus it was difficult to identify you. Some people were sitting on benches, while others were sitting on the grass. I was sitting on my motorbike looking around. Suddenly, my mobile phone rang, and it was you on the line. You said you were there driving around looking for me, and I asked where you were. You then directed me to a spot nearby where there were very many people. You asked me to meet you at the bus stop at the north end of my school gate, along Monivong Boulevard.

The public bus in Phnom Penh had never functioned and eventually closed down. Few people in Phnom Penh prefer public transportation, though it is inexpensive. Most people own a car or at least a motorbike.

I drove my old Chaly brand motorbike over there and looked for you. I made a call to your phone, and you raised your hand as a sign to show me that you had spotted me. You sat on your motorbike, and I sat on mine, close to one another. We were silent for a minute, just smiling at one another.

"How are you?" was the first question to begin our conversation. The sky was a little darker than usual for autumn. I could not see your face clearly under the low light of the street lamp, but I felt affection for you immediately. You were tall, but your skin was not light, which didn't matter at all. What a love at first sight it was! I was totally blinded. I loved your smile, which caught my full attention. Unconsciously, I slowly moved my legs and walked over to sit beside you on the seat of your bike. I could not control myself. I could not restrain my feelings toward you. We were engaged in happy conversation, and from that moment onward, I felt there was no one nearby. Only you and I existed; we were the only people in this world. How nice it was!

Intentionally, you raised your hand up and softly touched my face. I was so shy that I blushed. Again, that was a new experience for me. Soon the sky became darker and darker and I had to rush back home. Time had flown during those happy moments. Two hours had passed in a single wink. I could not stay out late at night; my parents would not allow me to do so even though I was male. My parents were strict with my brothers and me because they were concerned for our security.

They did not want us to hang out at night in Phnom Penh.

I told you that I had to leave, explaining my family situation. You asked me if you could accompany me home. I said I could drive home alone, but you insisted and I agreed. In this way, you impressed me even more. After arriving home, I could not help thinking of you every single minute. I wanted to know if you had reached home safely.

After you arrived home, we continued talking on the phone and revealing our feelings toward each other. Every single word of yours touched my heart very deeply. You once told me that you wanted to kiss me, but it wasn't possible because we were sitting in a public place—everybody was driving back and forth along the street and could see us every single moment. You respected me in this way by not kissing me. How sweet that was! Every word from your sweet lips was like honey, and I never tired of hearing them. I could hardly close my eyes and sleep well that night because I was thinking about you the entire time.

It was easy to fall in love. You gave me a novel feeling and for the first time I learned the word "LOVE." That first day, I began to experience the sweetness of love. I had already fallen for you. You were my first love and I etched your name in my heart. My sky was pink.

*

THE SECOND DAY WE MET YOU BROKE UP WITH YOUR GIRLFRIEND
After our first meeting, we talked more frequently on the phone and got to know one another. You told me that you had a problem to solve. You finally admitted that you had a "girlfriend," with whom you were not really in love. She had given you her mother's ring as a token of her love for you, and you accepted her ring. So what could I say about that? I was disappointed to hear this news. You seemed sad about the situation and troubled about making a decision. I told you that I did not want to be the third person in a relationship. I did not want to compete with anyone, but I did not want to say "goodbye" to you either. I asked you to choose between her and me—to choose the person you loved the most.

You told me the story of your relationship with her. You both grew up in the same village and had been classmates since high school. You had known each other for years and shared a lot of mutual memories. And me? You had known me for only one day. I could not compare with her. No matter whom you chose, I would respect your decision.

53

I did not want to force you to break up with her, because that would make me feel unhappy. After I gave you time to think it over, I felt very nervous waiting for your decision—a decision which was sure to disappoint either her or me.

Having awaited your answer for a few days, finally you rang me and asked me out for a chat. I was so nervous that I could not do anything, for I could not imagine you telling me that we could not be together. The thought of having this talk made my heart beat so fast, it felt as if it would leap out of my chest. This was a talk that I had longed for and dreaded at the same time. My mind was in complete confusion. I was not sure what I was going to do.

You drove to my school after class and we sat on the green grass in front of the school. I told you to meet me there because I had no energy to drive anywhere before I learned your decision. I prepared myself for disappointing news if it was going to happen, because I realised that I could not compare to your girlfriend. What card could I hold to compete with her? You could discern my sadness just by looking at my face at the time.

After we sat down on the grass, you went straight to the point. Just before you opened your mouth to speak, my heart was beating so fast that I could hardly breathe. I almost fainted. Yet, I kept telling myself to maintain my composure. Sooner or later, I had to face your decision. You revealed your feelings by telling me that you felt as if you had known me a very long time—an unusual feeling that was difficult for you to explain—and that you could not stop yourself from seeing me. Therefore, you had decided to break up with your former girlfriend.

You told me that you had already returned your ex-girlfriend's ring. Having heard your words, I was in a confused state. I was not sure if your love for me was real when you told me that you had broken up with your girlfriend. You changed your sexual desire so quickly that I could not believe it. How could a man with a girlfriend choose to love another man within a few days of contact? Had I changed you? I was not sure if you were born this way and were afraid to admit that to yourself. However, after hearing your decision, my body seemed to be full of energy. My smile began unconsciously. At the same time, I felt sorry for your ex-girlfriend. The experience was heavenly and I wanted to say "thank you" for choosing me. You saved my heart. Our relationship then developed further.

We enjoyed a nice dinner together at a vegetarian restaurant behind the Royal Palace and then drove along the riverside. Afterward, you dropped me off at my house before driving yourself home. As usual, we chatted briefly on the phone before going to bed.

Lying on my bed with my eyes closed, I again contemplated the words you had spoken that evening. I told myself that "you're the one I need." I turned on my iPod, placed the headphones to my ears, and switched to Michael Learns to Rock's "You Took My Heart Away."

"Goodnight my dear, goodnight world."

*

PINK BUBBLE TEA SHOP

I can recall an occasion one weekend when we accidentally came upon a tea shop called "Pink Bubble Tea" on our way to the park in front of the Royal Palace. The shop was located between Sorya Shopping Centre and Lux Cinema. After parking your motorbike, we walked into the shop with curiosity to discover what it was like.

Inside it was so dark that we could hardly see each other's faces. I saw no customers, but there were a lot of motorbikes parked outside. I did not see any tables either. "What kind of tea shop is this?" I thought to myself.

Then a waiter came carrying a flashlight in one hand and a menu in the other hand. He walked toward us and asked, "How many people?"

You promptly responded, "Two."

After that, we were guided into a so-called "closet" set with a small table and long chairs for two people, as requested. After we were seated, the waiter closed the "door" softly to avoid making any noise. He handed us the menu and left our table, waiting for our order.

There were many kinds of bubble teas listed on the menu. Food was also served at the shop; however, the price for every dish was a bit expensive for us compared to other places. Despite the high prices, we each ordered a bubble tea. We then realised what kind of place the tea shop was—their target customers were couples or lovers. The setting was like a VIP room. Silence and privacy were the hallmarks of the place. We might find it uncomfortable outside, in a public place, to kiss or hold hands with our partner. Traditionally, we were not supposed to do those kinds of things in public because such behaviour was not culturally-accepted.

We spent hours there comfortably doing what couples do, but not in excess. I can recall that we kissed each other; we sipped water from each other's mouths; we shared the same chewing gum; we also hugged each other.

After that first occasion, we frequented the tea shop more often so that we could share sweet time together. It seems disgusting to other people when two men kiss each other; but as long as we were in love, that's all that mattered to us. Because we were in love, we had no idea how misguided we were. I came to learn that love is blind.

✿

A VISIT TO YOUR ROOM

You and two of your cousins shared a room near Tuol Kork in the capital of Phnom Penh. Depending on the traffic, it took about ten or fifteen minutes from my house to your room by motorbike. You came from a small village in Kampong Thom Province, Cambodia's second largest province which is about 162km north of Phnom Penh, in order to pursue your undergraduate degree. Your room was not private, and we could only enjoy privacy while your cousins were attending their English class.

One evening, a month after our first date, you showed me your room. You skipped your class that evening because you wanted to be with me. We were alone at last. You told me that your cousins were at school and would not return home until 8:30 in the evening. You then closed the door behind us, and we sat down on the bare floor next to one another. We exchanged some conversation and discussed what each of us had done during the day, whom we had met—you name it. We rarely had free time to see each other and only met during the weekend when no classes were held.

A few minutes later, I reached my hand over your lap, with my nose to your face. Then we embraced one another tightly. I whispered in your left ear that I missed you very much. We stood still for a while with our bodies pressed together. I could hear your heart beating and feel the warmth of your body. It was the first time I smelled your body and I tried to hold onto the memory. Because I loved you, I appreciated everything about you.

Though your room was relatively small, it was just large enough for the two of us to be together in privacy. We stopped thinking about the world around us for a while and focused only on our world. We wished the room had been our own shelter, our own place to express our love and longing.

Time passed by quickly and your cousins were already knocking on the front door. We shared our last kiss before you opened the door and introduced me to your cousins so that I could get acquainted with them and vice versa. I visited your room often, particularly when your cousins were not there.

MY FAVOURITE SONGS

I was not really sure how much you loved me. I was uncertain whether you changed from heterosexual to homosexual just to experiment with something new. That was still an unanswered question for me. However, our relationship was moving on. I did not ask you and you did not reveal anything about that; time would tell me everything.

You knew that I liked listening to music in times of both happiness and sadness. While listening to the lyrics of a song, my mind would fly through the wind up into the sky. I felt elated when listening to my favourite songs. You were a romantic person too, and every time I visited your room, you would play my favourite songs on your computer. You had noticed the kind of music I liked and did not like. Sometimes, you sang along with the music you played, and I laid my head down on your lap, listening to your sweet voice. I looked at your face and could not help touching it. You were everything to me. I felt satisfied just to spend time alone with you. I demanded nothing more than the two of us together.

One day, you showed me my favourite song—Baby Girl sung by Inner Voices—on your phone. You said you had downloaded it from the Internet and set it as the ring tone on your phone. I then made a call to you to test it, and of course, I heard the song.

You were a smart person. You knew how to make me smile with just the simplest of things, and I was moved by you. You did many incidental things to make our love memorable and brilliant: you put our photos together in Adobe Photoshop; you made video clips using our photos and my favourite songs; you waited for me to leave my office for lunch; you took me home from school, to name just a few. Though your actions were simple, to me, they were wonderful. They pleased me and I could not erase those gestures from my memory.

THE NIGHT BEFORE CHINESE NEW YEAR

You and your cousins planned to visit home during the Chinese New Year when you had three days off from school. Actually, Chinese New Year, which falls in January or February every year, is not a public holiday in Cambodia. However, since most Phnom Penh residents are half-Chinese, it is commonplace for students to celebrate the New Year with their families. Taking advantage of this opportunity, you and I made plans to spend a night together before the Chinese New Year celebration.

I asked permission from my mother to stay over at your house, lying that no one would be there, and promised her I would return the next morning to help her prepare the New Year feast. My mother agreed with my request. I told you the good news and our plan proceeded.

At 5:30 in the evening, you picked me up at home. I said goodbye to my parents and got on your motorbike. I was excited about the upcoming evening. As we travelled, we discussed our plans. We selected a restaurant for our dinner. We had saved up some pocket money because we wanted to have a Western-style dinner along the riverside. We each ordered a glass of red wine, proposed a toast and took a sip of our wine.

After dinner, we drove to a guesthouse across Chroy Changva Bridge, along National Road N°6 in the direction of Kampong Thom Province, your home province. We did not go to your room, since your cousins were home. The guesthouse room was fine and affordable. As soon as the door closed, we kissed one another, which was what we both desperately wanted to do. We held each other tightly. You helped me unbutton my shirt, and I helped you with yours. Our mouths were still together. I unzipped your pants and you unzipped mine. My hand touched your erection and yours touched mine. Our naked bodies pressed together, feeling hotter and hotter. I felt like I was in heaven, and that night we made love.

On the New Year morning, you drove me back home. I helped my mother with her New Year banquet as if nothing had happened the previous night, but I smiled to myself and my head was filled with the memory of the previous evening.

Happy Chinese New Year to you! Thank you so much for everything you've given me. Have a safe trip home, I texted you when you left my house.

YOU GOT SICK

During the rainy season, you caught a cold after driving home from school for several days in the rain. You sent me a text message one morning, saying that you were home alone and feeling sick. You had chills and a headache, yet you could not stop thinking about me. You said you felt lonely and you wanted me to be near you. I was at my office, working. At that time, I had taken a part-time job as a salesperson at a private company.

Having read your text, I asked my boss if I could leave early because I was not feeling well and wanted to go home and relax. Without hesitation, my boss gave me permission. I thanked him and drove to your room as fast as I could, arriving there in no time. I knocked on the door and realised that it was not locked. I opened the door and there you were, lying under your blanket, shaking.

When I touched your forehead to check your temperature, you were really hot. You opened your tired eyes to have a look, and then closed your eyes again when you saw me. I gave you a smile and a kiss on your forehead. I told you to continue sleeping so as to save your energy. I then placed a cold towel on your forehead to help reduce your temperature. I asked you if you needed anything. You said "no," but asked me to hug you. I lay down next to you and held you. I shared your body temperature and hoped you would get better soon. After a while, you fell soundly asleep. I held you until your cousins returned home from school.

I did not want to leave you, but I had no choice and you understood. We could not let your cousins see us holding one another, otherwise they would be shocked to death. We were not supposed to be doing that.

YOU RAN AWAY FROM HOME

As a very private person, you rarely expressed any personal hardship to me or anyone else. This quality helped to make you unique, and it was what I both liked and disliked about you. What I liked about your uniqueness was that you would not complain if something bad happened to you or your family. What I did not like about this unique quality was that you were not very open with your feelings and it was difficult to get to know you better. The space you opened to me was quite narrow. What I knew about you was very superficial; you didn't reveal your inner self. This tendency led to frequent arguments between us and eventually to your disappearance from home.

One early morning during the summer of 2008, my phone rang. When I first picked up the phone, I heard the sobbing voice of your cousin on the line. I recognised her voice because I had met her on several occasions. I asked her why she was crying. However, it took her a few minutes to compose herself before she began to tell me the whole story.

You had left home that morning as usual, carrying a bag and wearing your school uniform of white shirt and black trousers. However, you did not take your motorbike, which you left locked in front of your room. You told your cousin that it was broken. You left no reason for suspicion with anyone. Not long after you left, you texted your cousin, telling her to check for something you had left behind underneath your motorbike. What your cousin found was a goodbye letter you had written to your parents. You told them that you could no longer bear their frequent arguments, but instead wanted to have peace of mind. You no longer wanted to hear your mother sobbing on the phone whenever they had an argument. You no longer wanted to hear their promises not to argue with one another again and again, because they never held that promise. You wanted a peaceful family, and you felt it was beyond your reach. Your feelings were exploding inside and you chose to leave for a location which you did not cite in your letter. You told your family not to look for you, and you promised to keep yourself safe. After your letter was found, you turned off your phone.

I left my office that morning and went to your room, where your cousin showed me your letter, as she continued shedding tears. I did not know how to comfort her, but nevertheless told her that you would be fine. She called me because she thought I was your best friend, since I had always visited you in your room. That morning, she revealed everything about you to me. She told me that you had found another girl and broken up with your ex-girlfriend, whom she regarded as her sister-in-law. She said that "that bitch" had broken her sister-in-law's heart, and that you had changed after meeting her. I knew pretty clearly that "that bitch" was me, sitting there in front of her. She was talking about me and blaming me for stealing you from her in-law. I did not know how to respond. Instead, I told her that I knew very little about "that bitch" or about your family. She then put me on the phone with your father, who had learned the news from your cousin. He talked to me and asked me to help locate you. I told him that although I was your "best friend," I did not know your whereabouts. However, I assured him that I would try to find you. I turned off the phone, left your cousin and returned home.

Once I arrived home, I kept dialling your number but was unable to reach you. Your phone was turned off the entire time. I then sent you a text message, saying that I missed you and wanted you to contact me once you saw my message. I believed my message would reach you when you turned on your phone. After that I tried to calm myself down and started to think of possible places where you might have gone. I remembered that you once told me that you loved the beach, and that you would really love to go there with me. Unfortunately, we had never had that chance. There was nothing I could do. I had to wait for your response.

Your dad called me again to find out if I had made any contact with you. I said "no." He said that if I was able to contact you, he wanted me to tell you that he was sorry, and if you needed any money please let him know so that he could send some to you. The words of your father and your cousin hurt me very deeply. I felt guilty about everything, especially about not being able to tell your cousin and your father that I was "that bitch." I wanted to let you go, but I couldn't. I did not want to abandon you in that situation.

Later that evening, my phone rang and it was you. You told me where you were—standing on the beach and breathing in the fresh air of the sea. I could hear the sound of the wind blowing through your line. I was right in guessing where you had gone. I was happy to hear from you and told you everything about what had happened in your family after you'd left. I begged you to come back because your family members were worried about you and I begged you not to leave me alone, for I missed you very much. You told me that you were going to turn off your phone again and would return in a few days when you felt better. I felt a bit relieved after talking with you and learning that you were fine. I reported to your father immediately so that he wouldn't worry about you.

A few days passed and you returned safe and sound. I hugged you when I first saw you. You held me tightly and the world seemed to stop moving. I really loved it when we were together. I did not want that moment to end. Your family was happy and so was I.

◢

I'M SORRY
We did not talk for more than a week after you returned from the Khmer New Year celebration in your hometown. I was angry with you, so I decided not to call or text you. We were both very stubborn. You said that I ruined your New Year celebration with your family. Khmer New Year was the only occasion on which you could visit with your family. Maybe I was the one who was wrong, because I was very demanding and selfish, wanting you to spend time only with me. I wanted you to come back to the city to celebrate my birthday, which fell on the day of Khmer New Year. However, you didn't come and I got angry. I told you not to come back again, even after the New Year, and that I did not want to see you. You did not know how much I missed you and wanted to celebrate my birthday with you.

You returned after the Khmer New Year. Still, we did not talk. Since I missed you so much, I picked up my phone and texted you, *I am sorry to have upset you while you were having fun with your family during the New Year celebration. But I really missed you and wanted you to be with me. I hope you understand how much I was missing you.*

Soon after that, we started to talk to each other again, but I could sense that our relationship was not the same as before—not close and sweet. You said we could not be so close. We should keep some distance so that we could understand each other better. You told me that I was too young and childish and every time I had a problem, I always overreacted. You told me not to behave like that. You asked me to call or text you less frequently. I tried to digest what you said and comply with your wishes, for I did not want to lose you.

◢

A MYSTERIOUS HEART-SHAPED CHOCOLATE
I remembered that on Valentine's Day in 2008, you gave me a gift which you had personally wrapped. It was small like a ring box, which I supposed it was. It was wrapped with palm leaves and on the top you made a bow which was painted colourfully. When I received it, I shook it, and it produced a sound like something inside was bouncing against the box. I was very happy and extremely curious to see the inside. However,

you asked me not to open it and warned me that if I secretly looked inside, then our relationship would be broken.

I did not believe in such a thing. Out of curiosity, I tore it open and had a look inside as soon as I arrived home. It was a heart-shaped chocolate costing 100 riel—nothing expensive. I was upset because the content of the box did not meet my expectations. It was true that love should not be measured by wealth, but you did not even consider what your lover preferred. How could I be happy? We had arguments every other day. I had no idea how long we could stay together. Every time I wanted to get to know you better, you hid your feelings and never shared your inner thoughts with me. Sometimes, I felt that you did not love me. I felt that you just wanted to taste something different or abnormal. I expected you to buy me a ring—the only gift I desired—but that never came true throughout our relationship. I did not want to tell you if I liked something. I wanted you to willingly buy it for me from your own heart, not from my suggestion. You treated me well only after we had an argument. Later, you behaved the same as always. I was upset to see your gift. Maybe I was being greedy or materialistic. After having a look at it, I put it back and rewrapped it.

Our relationship was not strong enough to endure the heavy rains and storms ahead—family, friends, society, culture, and our own selves—which were blocking our path. After twelve months, we broke up without a conversation, only a heartbreaking message you sent to me. I cried again. This time I cried because I lost someone I loved very much, but you would never know I was crying. My heart was burning with anger and pain. I went back to your Valentine's Day gift. I angrily tore it out and wanted to swallow that small chocolate to end everything. I wanted to erase all the memories we had together. I wanted to get rid of everything from the past so I could be reborn in the future.

However, something strange occurred—the strangest thing I had ever experienced in my life. When I tore open your gift box, I noticed that the box was empty. I was very sure when I first had a look inside that it contained a chocolate, and it had also made a sound when I shook it. But what had happened? It was empty and no longer made any sound. I was confused. What had happened to the chocolate? I did not believe in mysteries. How could this be? That question still remains unanswered in my mind. However, the chocolate really was gone and so were you.

It was unbearably sad and painful to no longer see you, whom I loved with all my heart. What could I do now? Was I supposed to live my days without a soul? Inside I was so cold, I was almost frozen. I seldom spoke and had no desire to talk with my friends. They asked me if I was okay. I told them "I'm fine, but just a bit tired these days." I didn't know how long I could bear that broken-hearted feeling. Unfortunately, I had to keep my feelings to myself, for the sake of both of us and our families.

Only a cruel world does not allow us to love someone we love, or to meet with someone with whom we want to meet. No amount of tears could bring you back. I had to admit that. There was nothing I could do but adapt myself to my new circumstances—to live my life without you and to plan my days without your company. The healing gradually took place, yet I did not know how long it would take for me to get over you and start a new life again. I had to go on living my life, but please don't worry. I will remember you as my first lover. I will remember that you once loved me. You were once my boyfriend.

ABOUT MEN PECHET

As the third child in a small family, Pechet was born in Phnom Penh, Cambodia. Pechet received a BBA in Tourism from the National University of Management, Phnom Penh and a MA in International Development Studies from Chulalongkorn University, Bangkok, Thailand. Pechet is also the author of Part of Human Story Blog (www.partofhumanstory.blogspot.com).

THE WAY LOVE GOES

Dana L Stringer

our hearts broke easier than the vows

we made

we were just not good at taking

shots of love

chasing it with fear

it burned like hard liquor

trickling down the back of the throat

but at least we got drunk

for a moment

lost our keys and couldn't leave

laughed at ourselves

trapped inside a bubble

of temporary bliss

somewhere in neverland

we were there until the well ran dry

and our highs wore off

then we both said never never never

again and it was true

love goes in threes

ABOUT DANA L STRINGER

Dana L Stringer is a writer, playwright, poet, screenwriter, and instructor. She holds a Masters of Fine Arts in Creative Writing from Antioch University Los Angeles and a Bachelors of Arts from Morehead State University. Her debut collection of poems, *In Between Faith*, was published in 2014. She has been a featured poet in venues throughout Los Angeles, Atlanta, and Louisville, Kentucky. Some of her other work appears in anthologies, literary magazines, and online. Dana's produced plays include: *Colored in Winter*, *The Costume Waver*, *ID*, and *Kinsman Redeemer*. She currently resides in Atlanta, Georgia where she works as a writing instructor, freelance writer, tutor, and book coach. For more information visit www.danastringer.com. Follow Dana on Twitter @DanaLStringer.

ALONE TIME

Viny

At some point during the four months I lived with my husband and son in Denmark, I saw a collection of photographs documenting the final resting places of people so profoundly disconnected from their fellow human beings that no one noticed when they died. When their bodies were finally discovered, weeks or months later, in various stages of putrefaction, authorities were unable to find even one friend or relative to notify.

One of these images made a particularly strong impression on me, possibly because, according to the note card pinned below it, the man who died in that lonely room had been quite young. My same age, in fact. In the very centre of the photograph, there was an inflatable mattress. At one end of this makeshift bed, a pair of stout work boots. At the other end, an almost obscenely neat array of cans and canisters: spray paint, oven cleaner, and I don't know what-all, since the labels were in Danish, but nothing you'd normally find in someone's living room. A television, the only piece of solid furniture, its cord snaking along the shabby carpet to an unseen outlet. And, lined up against each of the two visible walls, orderly rows of empty liquor bottles, as if the man who once lived in that place had been a castaway, marking the passage of his meaningless time with bits of beach glass, one for each dark night of exile. How long until rescue?

Not me, not me, not me, not me.

🖋

I have never lived alone. At the age of eighteen, I went from living with my parents and siblings to sharing a dormitory apartment with five roommates. At nineteen, I got married. At twenty-two, I gave birth to my first child. At twenty-four, I took my first lover. A few years after that, my husband began an extra-marital relationship of his own, and our network of intimates has just expanded from there. Now, at the age of forty, I live surrounded by friends and neighbours in an eco-village in Portland, Oregon, sharing approximately 600 square feet of private space with my husband, our eighteen-year-old son, and our seven-year-old daughter. In the past twenty years, I might have spent a grand total of twenty nights by myself. Maybe not even that many.

These numbers add up to one singular fact about me: I have lived virtually my entire life in the company of other people. Lots and lots of other people.

Sometimes I fantasise about what it would be like to live on my own, far away from everyone – in a cabin in the redwoods, say, or a palm-frond hut at the edge of a blue lagoon. In this fantasy, time would freeze for everyone else: I could go missing without anyone missing me. I might, if I liked, inhabit my very own time slot for months, or even years, and no one would know that I was keeping that meanwhile all to myself. Who would I be, without someone else to corroborate my existence?

⟋

It was my husband who first brought up the idea of a semester abroad. One day, he came home from school looking glum. He told me he'd found out about this great architecture program in Copenhagen, but alas: it was set up for your typical unattached undergraduate. This was always happening to us. We were twenty-nine years old. We wanted to do the kinds of things other people in their twenties did, and so many of them were incompatible with having a ten-year-old marriage and a seven-year-old kid.

"Why can't we all go to Denmark?" I wanted to know.

Tyler listed off all the reasons why not, I countered them, and, because I'm usually the practical one, the one whose job it is to rain on his frequent fantasy parades, that's all it took to make the semester abroad a *fait accompli*: we would be going in August and returning home some time before the new year.

Yes, I willingly signed up for four months in a chilly Scandinavian country, during a time of year when the light would fail a little more with each passing day. I knew that Tyler would be completely preoccupied the whole time we were abroad. I knew that all the domestic chores and child care would fall to me. I knew that none of my friends would be there. But I was desperate for a change, any change, from my life in California.

The way I saw it, going to Denmark would be like entering the magic box my sixth-grade math teacher used to draw on the chalkboard, the one with a slot for 'input' at the top, and a slot for 'output' at the bottom, a dusty green rectangle in which some mysterious mathematical function changed x into y. Back in sixth grade, the object had been for us to guess the function based on the pattern we noticed: if, for example, the teacher put in 5, and 8 came out, and then she put in 11, and 14 came out, we were supposed to deduce that there must be a '+3' in the box. The equations were never that simple, though. This was a class for gifted children, and I was the least mathematically gifted of the entire bunch. I never saw the pattern until every other child had marched to the front of the class, grabbed the chalk, and squeaked out the correct 'output' number on the board, and sometimes not even then. For me, what happened in the box seemed like wishful thinking, a kind of voodoo.

My life was x. I wanted it to be y. Not that there was anything so terrible about x, mind you: I had family, friends, meaningful work, a house and a garden, and enough money that I could even splurge, occasionally, on nice clothes or dinners at schmancy restaurants where obsequious waitstaff would come by with a little silver crumb comb between the duck *demi-glace* and the grapefruit granita. Given my thus-far-unremitting good fortune, I figured, I was probably just a greedy bitch for also wanting a few other things. Namely, although not necessarily in this order: a finished dissertation, a second child, and permission from my boyfriend to have sex with a Certain Someone Else, permission he had grudgingly granted, kinda-sorta, once, and then later had definitively revoked.

So, I would go to Denmark, where there would be subtractions (teaching duties, parties, overnighters with my boyfriend, etc.), additions (sea air, meatballs and smoked herring, peculiar vowels, hats with cute little ear-flaps, etc.), and a shuffling of variables (did I mention that the Certain Someone Else happened to be living in Italy, practically next door?). Yes, I would go to Denmark, and somehow, *somehow*, by the time I returned to California, all my problems would be solved. I would have x plus a three-month pregnancy, a complete draft of my dissertation, and memories of a super-sexy Italian interlude with CSE, with the promise of more to come. Oh, and flawless skin. I would also have flawless skin. Or at least a moderately clear complexion. Was that too much to ask for?

✒

My acne had resurfaced in my mid-twenties, after all but disappearing in my late teens. My mother-in-law, no doubt intending to be kind, gave me a gift certificate for a deluxe facial for my twenty-fifth birthday, and the aesthetician spent what seemed like hours squeezing crud out of my pores. She toiled at her task in silence, her immaculately plucked eyebrows knit together in what I took to be disgust, disapproval, or some oily/dry combination thereof. Then, abruptly: "Do you smoke?"

No, I told her, I did not. She expressed surprise: usually people with skin this bad were smokers. She said I should definitely buy a big bottle of their most heavy-duty cleanser, the one with salicylic acid in it. I thanked her for her advice, privately vowing that this would be my last facial. But I did buy the cleanser.

My face bloomed red for weeks on end, until I finally consulted a doctor, who, as soon as he learned that I was a graduate student, put down his pen and laughed. "Your face will clear up as soon as you get your degree," he assured me. "It's just stress."

Stress, huh. That doctor didn't know the half of it. That year, the year I turned twenty-five, I was teaching two undergraduate composition classes as sole instructor, taking three graduate seminars, and studying for my Master's exams. My son was only two years old, and I was his primary caregiver. Also, I had begun an affair, or something kind of like one, with Scott, a fellow graduate student who was engaged to a woman who didn't know he was cheating on her, which meant that I had to keep a very big secret. Not from my husband—Tyler knew the whole story, and was nominally okay with my gallivanting, just so long as I put out at home, every single night, sometimes more than once— but from everyone else: my family, Tyler's family, Scott's family, Scott's fiancée, and Scott's fiancée's family, not to mention all of my colleagues and students at the university. As if that weren't enough, Tyler and I were also in the process of selling our house. I had to keep the place sparkling all the time, just in case the realtor wanted to pop by with some potential buyers. No wonder I broke out. I was probably swimming in cortisol.

There is a photograph of me taken in Ithaca, New York, right around that time. It would have been late May or early June, because we were at Cornell for my little sister's graduation ceremony. I'm standing between two wooden posts, with my right hand on the chain connecting them. Behind me is a stand of young trees, and behind those trees, a stream cascades down a series of steeply slanted rock terraces into the gorge below. I'm wearing a lilac-coloured tank top and a silver necklace, the one Scott had recently given me for my birthday. A long curtain of hair falls over my left shoulder and covers my left breast, reaching almost to my waist. In the dappled, diffuse sunlight, my arms and face glow gold. I'm smiling widely, two rows of white teeth, as though I am aware that, at this moment, in this light, the way the camera sees me, I am as perfect as I'll ever be. Not a single blemish visible.

Something else not visible in that photograph: what I had been thinking about just minutes before Tyler snapped the picture, as I stood on the high bridge that spanned the gorge and watched the stream winding through the jagged boulders far below me. I was on top of the world, at the pinnacle of my power. *Down* was the only direction left for me to go. So: quick drop, or slow decline? It would be so easy to throw one leg over the railing, and then the other. To simply let go. I would be over in an instant.

✐

Our attic apartment in Copenhagen was tiny, and only half of the floor space was even usable, since the ceilings sloped so dramatically that you had to hunch over if you walked too close to the walls. Day after day, I spent the hours of 10am to 1pm sitting on the black IKEA sofa in the living room, staring at the blank screen of my laptop. It amused me, in a dark sort of way, that I had come from America to the land of the Vikings for some breathing room, a little bit of alone time, in which I hoped to write the first draft of a dissertation. How many academic papers of mine had made reference to American literature's preoccupation with its own newness, its blank slate? All those early American writers: dazzled by the expanse of possibility, like a snowfield as yet unmarred by a single footprint.

Unfortunately, I couldn't escape my crowded past. And as for my future—well, that was completely inaccessible to me. Unimaginable. I was stuck in the here-and-now, pinned by a force that felt damn near material. A stone on my chest. This feeling wasn't just about the dissertation, either. It was also about Scott, who had recently asked me, "Do you know that you make me feel incredibly self-destructive?"

He and I had been making our strange situation work for five years by then, but there was no way we were going to be able to keep ourselves together, and we knew that already, and also we didn't know it yet, and as I sat there, in that lonely room, that psychic place-that-was-not-a-place, Schroedinger's mangy Siamese twins clawed each other's eyes out in the dark.

On the way to Mendocino, Scott starts feeling carsick, so he stops to smoke some dank. When he offers me some I say, "No thanks, I'm good," and he says, "Whatever, you're so judgemental."

We stand on the cliff looking at cold turquoise water sluice between black crags. Swell and fall, spume and spray. Two seals swim into the crevice during an ebb, pink and green ribbons of sea grass exposed and dripping down the craggy rocks far below us. The waves rush in from either side of the channel and crash together, water rising into rolling foam, flecks of spray thrown so high into the air I can feel them on my face, even standing way up here. I worry about the seals because I never see them swim back out.

In the hotel room, Scott paces the small strip of carpet at the foot of the bed, telling me I'm selfish, telling me that since I'm married to another man, I have no right to make things difficult, I have no right to feel even the tiniest bit bad about this new girlfriend, because when he was forced to choose between me and his wife, he chose me, his marriage actually ended because of me, and what this means is he's got every right to date whomever he wants now, he deserves to be happy and if I can't just shut up and be happy for him while he tries to find a life partner then I am a horrible person, a person who doesn't deserve the love he's been wasting on me all these years. I sit on the bed, staring at the green and gold pattern of diamonds and pineapples on the wallpaper while he yells at me and I cry and cry and cry.

On the way to Big Sur, I am driving and Scott is yelling at me again and the Coldplay CD is making both of us cry while the road curves and curls along the sea cliff and sunshine streams through the windshield into our eyes. He says he can't do it, can't stand the thought of me sleeping with another man, it's going to kill him. I remind him that I had to choke it down when he started dating again after his divorce, I did the hard work of wading through the muck of my jealousy, and now I'm on the other side of it simply asking him, begging him really, to make the same effort for me. Please. He says it's not the same thing at all, he's still looking for a new life partner whereas I already have a husband and a boyfriend, and what the fuck's wrong with me if I can't be satisfied with the two men I already have?

At the Copenhagen airport, Scott kisses my cheek with a big wet sound. I grit my teeth. It's been two months since we last saw each other. The whole time I've been in Denmark, I've missed him terribly. But now that he's here to visit me, I can't wait for him to leave.

In the hotel room in Amsterdam, Scott gets on top of me in the neat white bed and I lie there under him thinking *I have to get out of this, I have to get out of this somehow,* and by *this* I mean *him,* so the next night when he wants to have sex I tell him no, which I have never done before, ever, or anyway not like that, and he says he's got to get out of here who cares if it's the middle of the night in a foreign country he's not going to stick around if that's how I feel. I am afraid he is going to do something stupid so I start to cry, and he says fine then, he'll stay, but first he's going to go take care of himself in the bathroom down the hall.

Back in Copenhagen again, in the tiny garret apartment I share with my little family, I tell Scott I think I am going to sleep with Tyler tonight, and Scott says if that's the case he will go out, maybe to a nightclub so it's not like last time, when he had to lie awake listening to us make love all night, and I say, "Oh you mean like last time when you were imagining things?"

He goes out. At three o'clock in the morning I hear him let himself back into the apartment and I get out of bed and pad softly into the living room where he is hiding in a corner as though he thinks I'm not going to notice him there, six-two and reeking of alcohol and cigarettes, repeating over and over "the Danes hate the English, the Danes hate the English," and I don't want him to wake my husband or my son with his drunken muttering so I make myself keep it sweet.

I soothe him and shush him and tuck him into his temporary bed on the floor, and I just keep smoothing his smoky-smelling curls back from his sweating forehead until he stops trembling and falls asleep.

In Davis, California, Scott sits with me on the bed I normally share with Tyler while I explain that I will be leaving again in a few months, for good this time, and Scott is crying and I am not crying and suddenly two somethings hit the bedroom window, one after another. Both of us run outside to see. Downed hummingbirds. One still alive, one already dead.

🖋

The death of my relationship with Scott happened in so many places. It happened time and time again. And what kept happening was simply this: stuck in a given 'here' and 'now,' I would realise that what I wanted to be, more than anything, was *elsewhere*. In the future. Looking back. Only from that vantage point, in retrospect, would I be able to see how I got there.

It feels like I lose everything, like I've lost what's best about everything, I wrote in my journal on December 17, 2003, a week or so before I left Denmark to return home with my family. *Somehow I have turned into THIS, and what is THIS? Not much, it seems.*

I had failed to finish a draft of my dissertation—had never properly started it, even. I had also failed to get pregnant with a second child. And I had utterly failed to get permission from Scott to act on my sexual attraction to a Certain Someone Else. Nothing had changed: I still had no idea who I was or what I was going to do with the rest of my life. I was just killing time.

🖋

In the middle of that semester abroad, I did manage to arrange for an Italian interlude of sorts. In late October, my husband and son and I stayed with CSE in Rome for several days, and then the four of us took a car trip through Umbria, overnighting in Orvieto. Not a single one of the dozens of photographs we took on that vacation survives. We discovered, too late, that the memory chip in our new digital camera was defective, and all the image files were blank.

So, I remember. I remember an old man in rubber boots trudging slowly up the steep hill to his tiny village with a load of sticks strapped to his back. I remember an old woman, seemingly the only other inhabitant of that same forlorn town, standing by a crumbling wall.

"Is that your child?" she asked me, in Italian, gesturing at one of the three figures walking toward us. "Ah, what a beautiful bambino! And which is your man? The shorter one with darker hair, or the taller one with lighter hair?"

For one crazy moment, I wanted to claim both men as mine, in defiance of my other man, the jealous one with the curly red hair. I didn't have time to answer, though, because the old woman launched immediately into a long tale of woe: her husband had died many years ago, and then her only daughter moved to the city, leaving her all alone in the world. She told me I was very lucky. *Fortunata.* The word took a bite out of my heart. I wanted to share some of my good fortune with her. I wanted to tell her she ought to ask the old man with the sticks to join her in the deserted piazza for a glass of grappa some evening. But I didn't know the right words. I smiled at her, fumbled out something about the weather, and fled.

That night, CSE and I went for a walk alone together, through the crooked streets of Orvieto. At one point, we reached a dead end.

"All these dark corners," he remarked, reaching out for me.

I stepped into his arms and pressed my ear against his chest. His heart was beating very fast. Then we moved apart again. Retracing our steps, we made our way to the ancient city wall. A light mist was falling.

We talked for a long time, standing by that wall, looking out over the burnished blacks and greys of the night-swathed countryside. I don't remember everything we said to each other, but I have never forgotten the story CSE told me about a friend of his—a journalist, I think, who'd been active in the Serbian resistance. This man was kidnapped in the middle of the night by Milosevic's henchmen, taken to a field far from town, and forced to kneel in the frozen dirt. Someone pressed a gun to the back of his head. *Click.* Intending only to issue a warning, his captors had fired a blank—but to a man expecting death, it was a skull-shattering sound. He lost consciousness. Hours later, he woke, alone, with the rest of his life in front of him.

The next morning, I had an epiphany, although I promptly forgot it afterward, and it wasn't until many years later that I would finally understand what I'd seen. Before leaving Orvieto, all four of us descended the ancient stone steps of the Pozzo di San Patrizio, which was constructed in the 16th century to provide the city's inhabitants with access to water in case of a siege. At the bottom of this well, deep in the heart of the hill, there is a small bridge that connects the spiral staircase down to the spiral staircase up. I remember pausing for a moment on that bridge and gazing down at our own reflections gazing up at us, framed in a perfect circle of silvery sky.

◢

For my thirty-eighth birthday, my husband gave me one of the best gifts I have ever received: three days alone at Breitenbush hot springs. Their busy summer season had not yet begun, and I was there in the middle of the week, so I had a little cabin all to myself. No cell reception. No Internet. Plenty of opportunity for reflection. For some reason, I found myself flooded with fond memories of that semester abroad back in 2003: how my son would reach for my hand as we walked to the bus stop at Feldparken or the skating rink at Trianglen; how he loved to stop at the ISO bakery on the way home from school for a crème snaigle or a loaf of fresh ciabatta; how he marvelled at the seaweed roofs of the old fishermen's cottages we toured together at Fridlandsmuseet. There wasn't a single second I spent with him that I would go back and change. Even as miserable as I was at that point in my life, I instinctively knew how important it was to treasure the time I spent with people I loved. But I had not yet learned how to value the time I spent by myself.

Alone in my little cabin in the woods, feeling not the slightest bit lonely, I thought again about that art exhibit in Denmark, and the photograph I saw there, which had etched itself so indelibly into my brain all those years ago. And I realised that the true horror of that image was simply this: the man who died in that room might as well have been me.

How I wished I could reclaim all the hours I had squandered during that semester abroad, thinking I had to figure it all out and not knowing how, punishing myself for not doing anything important by not allowing myself to do anything at all, feeling trapped in the interminable present, just waiting for the future to rescue me. How I wished I could travel back in time, and give that sorry self some good advice!

Sweetie, I wanted to tell her, *It's all going to work out. You're going to decide you don't need that PhD after all. You and Scott will figure out how to salvage a friendship from the wreckage of your romance. Four years from now, on a crisp Christmas day, you'll give birth to a beautiful daughter—and trust me, she'll be worth the wait. Listen, there are some amazing people in your future. Luckily, by the time you meet them, you'll be able to love them better, without all this unnecessary drama. Stop killing your precious time! Read books, write poetry, explore the city, paint your nails five different shades of pink, whatever—it doesn't really matter what you do, because there is no waste of time, only waste of self.*

This is what I would have told that younger me if only I could have communicated with her—but of course, I couldn't. Such is the nature of regret.

On the last morning of my stay at Breitenbush, after a solitary soak in one of the hot pools, I opened the door to my cabin and accidentally caught a glimpse of myself in the full-length mirror on the wall. I had been so deep in thought that I didn't immediately recognise myself. For a split second, I believed I was greeting someone else. Whoever she was, I instinctively liked her, and I smiled. It was the most natural thing in the world: time doubled back on itself, and there I was, at the bottom of an ancient well in Umbria, looking up into the beloved face of the woman I had once been, as she gazed down at her own reflection and saw, for one fleeting moment, the face of a woman who had finally begun to enjoy her own company.

ABOUT VINY

Having located her true calling in life, which is somewhere near the 3-way intersection between stories, sex, and relationships, Viny enjoys writing letters and essays, teaching workshops, participating in live storytelling events, and spending time with people she loves. Her advice column for people in alternative relationships can be found at dearviny.blogspot.com.

IF IT AIN'T BROKE

Sara Dobie Bauer

There was no physical reason for Professor Nate Evans to have a crush on Henry Oliver. The boy was twenty-one, a university senior, graduating early, who cared for nothing but books. He was tall and too thin with appendages that looked like octopus arms. There was widespread suspicion that his mess of curly, blond hair refused the use of a comb. His blue eyes were too small and set too far apart. One only noticed the enormous size of his nose when Henry stood in profile. His expressions were overwrought by wrinkles as if his body was covered in too much skin. Worst of all, his clothes never fit: either too tight or too big, like he couldn't be bothered to look at labels when he shopped because there were too many words tumbling around that rather large head of his.

Girls sort of liked him, Nate suspected because Henry smelled good and carried the mysterious allure of a troubled loner. Girls tried talking to him but were often ignored. His fellow male students only talked to him if they needed help on a final paper. Most of his professors hated him because he interrupted class and told them they were quite simply wrong. They were happy to see him go.

Yet, Professor Nate Evans woke every Monday morning of that fall semester and couldn't wait for 10am—for the part of his Henry week to begin—and, if he had really considered the situation, Nate might have realised he saw Henry Oliver as a puzzle in need of solve-ation.

❧

Camden University was situated in the cold, draughty corridor of Southern Ohio, nuzzled between rolling green hills that turned a depressing shade of grey every winter. Camden was the oldest school in the Buckeye state, so its buildings were no higher than three storeys and built of beautiful, red brick—the very same brick that paved the main streets through a quaint downtown filled with artsy shops, bookstores, and bars in abundance. Students climbed nearly vertical hills to get to class, and in winter, those hills were like sideways skating rinks, impossible to traverse without the help of thick winter boots—and even then, dangerous. Classes were occasionally cancelled due to winter weather, and when that happened, students stole lunch trays from the student union and used them as sleds.

It was mid-December. The holidays crept up like ice over a pond, and finals were a week away. Then, for six weeks, the students of Camden would run home, including, Nate assumed, Henry Oliver, although he had no idea where the boy came from. In fact, it was Henry's final semester at Camden. He would graduate a semester early due to his overabundance of intellect. Then, Nate supposed, he would be gone for good.

Monday morning, students walked into Nate's Book Censorship class wrapped in wool coats, scarves, and gloves. Their wind-chafed noses shined red like Rudolph, and he watched them shiver as their bodies slowly adhered to the new rule of electric heat. Several students didn't bother to remove their coats. The building was old, after all, so up on the third floor, the heater did little more than belch the occasional wave of tepid warmth.

Nate thought to take a hurried bathroom break before class commenced, but as he rushed through the exit into the corridor, he smacked into a tangle of long limbs, wrapped in nothing but a large, green sweater, torn jeans, and a holey scarf, obviously secondhand. Nate held onto Henry's upper arms to keep them both from tumbling across cold linoleum.

The young man's face was completely red. His lips were pursed into a thin, pink line. Even his blue eyes looked frozen wide.

"Henry, don't you have a coat?"

He looked down. "Must have left it in the library."

Nate sighed. "You know, if your body freezes, your brain won't work." He ran his hands quickly up and down the outsides of the skinny man's arms. "Good weekend?"

He grumbled. "Too much Dickens."

"For a class?"

Henry sniffed. "No." He sneezed.

"Go back to the library and get your coat. You can be late to get your coat; otherwise you'll catch a cold and miss class. Class is boring without you."

"Most professors prefer when I have a sick day."

"I'm not most professors."

Henry's face did something like a smile: a quirk at the side of his lip that made Nate's chest tingle. Then, his soon-to-graduate student plodded off toward the steps, almost tripping over his own very large feet.

Class began without Henry. It ended without him, too. They were in the midst of discussing two books: *The Electric Michelangelo* and *The Book Thief*, both banned or challenged by American public schools. The class had to decide what quantified each book for censorship, and Nate was pleased by the cross-section of right- and left-wingers, Christian and angry atheist. Made for wonderful discussion. But the discussion would have been better with Henry who, if Nate knew the boy at all, had probably found his coat and then stumbled into a stack of Tolstoy, not to be interrupted until he had devoured every word.

✦

At the end of the school day, Nate met Ella for drinks at a tiny, dank bar on the corner of Main Street across from Camden's wide college green. A sprinkling of white covered the pavement as he slid his way across the uneven brick road and into the warm, beer-scented embrace of Tony's Tavern. She waved at him from a side booth, book in hand.

Ella was always reading. As a fellow English professor, her love for literature was almost a tick. An ex-smoker, books were now her nicotine.

Nate ordered the darkest beer on tap—some heavy stout made in Michigan—and slid in across from his comrade. She looked up over the brim of *Fifty Shades of Grey*.

He and Ella were both around the same age: upper thirties. Ella fit in better with the student body, though, as she was covered in tattoos and had face piercings that set off metal detectors at airports. Nate was handsome, tall, and conservative. He wore suit jackets over nice, pressed shirts and dark jeans to work. He kept his brown hair clipped short. He shaved every morning. Ella's hair was tinted purple.

Nate took a sip of beer and rolled the flavour of coffee, vanilla, and yeast across his tongue. He swallowed. "You are not reading that."

She put the book down, wide open, bent at the binding: an obvious sign of disrespect. "I'm thinking of pitching a new class for twenty-fifteen: The Art of Bad Writing. Show kids what not to do, you know?"

"Oh. That's actually a good idea." He took another sip and felt warmer already. "Did you see Henry today?"

She shook her head. Large, silver earrings danced across her neck. "No."

Nate tried unsuccessfully to stifle a yawn. "He showed up to my class today then bailed."

Ella shrugged. "What can you do? He's a weird kid."

Nate knew Ella had been privy to Henry's odd behaviour for two semesters: once in her Introduction to Creative Writing course, which was like forcing Einstein to sit through ten weeks of arithmetic. Secondly, Henry attended Ella's Gay and Lesbian Literature course, where, she claimed, he mostly behaved himself but continually begged the question: "Why do we have to label everything? Why can't this just be literature?" Ella's response: "Because the university needed something diverse in the course catalogue, Henry."

Ella used a thin, red straw to stir what Nate knew to be coffee spiked with Frangelico. "What are you doing for Christmas break?" she asked.

"Staying here."

She gawked at him. "Again? It's a ghost town at Christmas. There's supposed to be some deadly ice storm coming. Plus, only rejects stick around."

"Hey, my parents are dead, and I can't stand my sister and her homophobic husband." He shrugged out of his wool winter coat.

"Why don't you go somewhere warm? Get away for a while."

"Even better idea: I should go on one of those gay cruises."

She chortled. "Yeah, right. They'd boot you first day. You're the grumpiest gay dude I've ever met."

"I'm not grumpy."

"Okay, well, you're, like, anti-flaming." One of her lip piercings twinkled in the light when she smiled.

"True." He glanced toward the bar where Monday Night Football played.

"This thing for Henry Oliver... You've got it under control, right?"

"Of course. I'd never do anything about it."

"You are kind of touchy-feely with the kid."

Nate slowly turned his mug on the sticky, wooden table. "God, am I?"

Ella shrugged one shoulder. "A little. I think it's cute, but other people might not."

"I just worry about him. Have you ever seen him eat?"

"No, but I've never seen any of my students eat. It's not like I chill out in the student union."

"He forgot his coat in the library today," he said over the sudden sound of a jukebox, playing Journey. "He looked like an iceberg when I saw him before class."

"I think it's a miracle the kid remembers to put on pants in the morning." She slurped at her steaming brew. "He's like an idiot savant or something. Although he does have a lush little ass. And Henry Oliver would make an excellent transvestite."

Nate chuckled. "Yeah."

"You want to fix him."

Nate cleared his throat.

"You're always trying to fix people."

"Obvious diversionary technique: how are you holding up with Christmas two weeks away?"

She rolled her eyes. "Well, Monica is the crazy one. I'm the one working overtime to get ready for finals. Then, I'll be grading papers. I haven't even gotten her a Christmas present yet."

"After ten years together, can't you just say, 'Our love is enough'?"

"Tell her that. If our track record is any indication, she's probably expecting jewellery." Ella itched at her nose ring.

"Tough being the man in the relationship."

"No shit. Know what she got me last year? A tool set, like I should start fixing things around the house." She held up her copy of *Fifty Shades*. "Hello! I know books, not wrenches."

"I assume you're going home for Christmas."

"Monica's family. It's their year. Upstate New York, because Ohio isn't cold enough." She sucked her cheeks in and puckered her lips like a fish. Nate recognised this as her 'I'm slowly going mad' face, which often made appearances during finals week and English department staff meetings. Her cell phone beeped in her canvas bag on the table. "Speak of the devil…"

Nate watched her fiddle with her phone until her face was lit blue in the bar darkness.

"Dinner time. I gotta go." She finished the dregs of her alcohol-spiked coffee and slid from the booth into her heavy, down coat the colour of a shiny York wrapper. "You should start dating again."

"Right before Christmas? No."

"Oh, yeah, and then you've got—"

"Valentine's Day."

"Right. Best wait 'til spring."

He lifted his beer in a non-reciprocated toast.

Ella yawned. "Alright, I'm out. See ya." She gave him a high five as she left. Nate ordered another beer and watched a quarter of football before tracing his own snowy path to his apartment above a bar further down Main Street, where a glass of scotch patiently waited beside a stack of ungraded research papers.

Finals week flew by in a blur, and then grading commenced. Although some would posit paper-grading to be subjective, Nate had a rubric system that was hard to argue. With most of the student body gone, he spent his afternoons in the university library reading papers. Final grades were due; then, Christmas.

Nate hadn't properly celebrated the holiday since his father died, his mother first. The parental units were the only things that brought his family together, as he truly did dislike his elder sister, and her husband was disgusted by Nate's sexual preference, which he'd never tried to hide. The last Christmas they spent together, Nate had mentioned his "boyfriend," and his brother-in-law feigned vomiting into the sink. The relationship was strained ever since, and with Mom and Dad gone, there was no reason to force things. Christmas was dead, and Nate was resigned to winter loneliness.

He was almost finished grading Henry's brilliant final essay on why censorship actually was a good thing in some cases—a tall order for a student who obviously saw censorship as some form of American Nazism. Henry Oliver had made it abundantly clear through the semester that the only thing worse than censorship was chemical castration. Still, Nate admired that Henry had challenged himself to understand the other side. The paper was an obvious A: the last Nate would give one of his favourite students.

For a moment, Nate closed his eyes. The Camden University library was blissfully silent. There was the occasional squeak of a wet boot as the Ohio snow had begun in earnest that afternoon. The smell of old paper. The occasional fart scent of stale heat. Nate found peace in the familiarity.

Then, some idiot knocked what sounded like a dozen books from a nearby shelf, and Nate opened his eyes to glare.

"Henry," he said.

The man's shaggy blond head shot up from where he crouched between bookshelves. "Sorry."

Nate stood up and knelt beside his student to collect the mess of hardcover books that scattered around their feet. "What are you doing here?"

"I'm always at the library," he said as his long, bony fingers shoved books back on the shelf. Nate noticed at least he'd found his coat: a rather large black wool jacket that looked to have once belonged to someone twice Henry's weight.

Nate chuckled. "I know that, Henry. I mean, why aren't you home for Christmas?"

Henry paused. "Why would I go home for Christmas?"

Nate paused. "I have no idea."

They continued rearranging books on the shelf, which gave Nate the perfect excuse to be close to Henry. Nate had always noticed Henry smelled comfortable. There was no other way to describe it. Henry smelled like toothpaste and baked goods and lightly scented bar soap—comfortable or perhaps comforting.

High on the scent, Nate said, "I'm glad I ran into you. I thought I might not get to say goodbye before you left Camden. I assume you'll graduate Summa Cum Laude?"

Henry nodded. "I guess they do those things."

So close to his student, Nate had the sudden realisation: Henry wasn't actually his student any more. Without proper consideration, he blurted, "What are you doing next week for Christmas?"

The young man shrugged, his light blue eyes drawn to one particular book in the pile, which he brushed at with the palm of his hand. Nate recognised the book: *A Christmas Carol*, Charles Dickens.

"More Dickens?"

Henry shrugged again.

"Would you like to join me for dinner on Christmas Eve?"

Henry's eyes appeared to shrink a little in his head as he appraised his professor. He tucked the book into his coat as if he meant to steal it and toed at an aged edition of *A Tale of Two Cities*, still on the floor. "Do you *want me* to join you for dinner?"

Nate tilted his head. "I wouldn't have asked otherwise."

"Okay."

"No one should be alone on Christmas, right? I can give you my address."

"I know where you live. I walked Ella there once."

That came as a surprise. "Are you close with Ella?"

"She's nice to me. She thinks I'm funny."

Funny was not a word Nate would use to describe Henry. "Okay, well, seven o'clock?"

Henry nodded. He wandered away, leaving books in his wake that Nate eventually knelt down to reorganise. Henry was indeed an odd duck. Few people looked sadder following a Christmas dinner invitation, and yet, as he turned around, Nate couldn't help but feel he'd just done something to disappoint his favourite student.

🍃

Nate wandered the aisles of the tiny grocery store within walking distance of his apartment the day before Christmas Eve when his phone rang.

"Hello, Ella," he said with a bunch of fresh kale in one hand.

"You're not going to fuck him, are you?"

"What?"

"Henry."

He threw the kale in his basket. "Why would you think that?"

"He said you invited him over for dinner." In the background, the sound of Christmas bells echoed down what sounded like a very large hallway.

"Well, I didn't think he should be… Wait, how often do you talk to Henry?"

She did her annoyed grunt. "More often than I've let on. I really care about Henry, and, well, we've got something in common. All of us do."

Nate paused and considered tomato sauce before the cogs slid into place. "Henry's gay?"

"Yes," she hissed, "and he's kind of a slut, and I don't want you fucking him. And he's still sort of one of your students until final grades are in..."

"Final grades are in, but I'm not going to have sex with Henry. I might have a crush on him, but I'm not an idiot. I just thought he shouldn't be alone on Christmas, and I didn't really want to be alone either."

"Fine." He heard her blow air out through her nose. "He's different, Nate. Why do you think he lives in books?"

"Why do any of us live in books, Ella?"

The sound of shouting muted her voice, followed by a barrage of Christmas carols at full volume: the Frank Sinatra album.

"Sweet baby Jesus, they're making me trim the tree."

"Ho-ho-ho."

"I hate you," she said. "I'd much rather get drunk with you and Henry."

"You know so much about the guy. What does he drink?"

"Who, Henry? Anything. He's like an alcohol garbage disposal." The phone clunked like it'd been dropped, but then, Monica's voice was on the line.

"Nate! I need my wife!"

With that, the line went dead, and Nate tossed a can of basil tomato sauce into his basket with a sigh.

Henry Oliver was gay. It came as a surprise since he seemed asexual, like a man made of paper and words, not of flesh and especially not flesh that wanted to be touched. Nate's crush on the young man had always been innocent. Alone in the shower, Nate never pictured Henry's brilliant mouth. He had never once mentally undressed his most gifted now ex-student. Henry was alluring like a torn page in a first edition.

Ella was right; Nate saw him as something to be fixed. If he started seeing Henry as someone good for bedding, well, Christmas Eve could be disastrous. He spent the rest of his grocery store time choosing a mid-priced Cabernet and never once thought of Henry's long fingers. Not once.

❧

When the weatherman said they'd have an "icy Christmas," he was not joking. Nate stood by his front window and watched the constant precipitation outside: a mixture of white and wet. His mistake? Not getting Henry Oliver's phone number. He'd tried calling Ella to no avail, and despite creeping disappointment, Nate knew it was dangerous to be walking around out there. He needed to cancel with Henry to keep the young man safe. Maybe he just wouldn't show, which would be the intelligent thing to do, considering there was a stage three weather emergency.

But then, the doorbell rang at seven-fifteen, and Nate opened the door to someone he didn't quite recognise. The tussled blond hair was there, dotted with as yet unmelted snowflakes, as were those wide-set blue eyes and pale skin. Henry didn't wear the awkward-fitting coat, though; no, he wore something Nate himself might have donned: a black wool suit jacket over a perfectly fitted white button-down with dark jeans and shiny leather shoes. He looked older and almost handsome.

He walked inside without an invitation and kept his hands in his pockets.

"I can't believe you made it here in this weather. I was going to tell you to stay home and stay warm," Nate said as he shut the door.

"What weather?" Henry asked.

Nate walked toward the stereo against the side wall of his small apartment to hide the amused roll of his eyes. Through the front windows, he saw the snow continue to fall on Main Street. He had a single candle lit, pine-scented, although it battled with the smell of garlic and pasta sauce in the kitchen. Nate wasn't one for decorating, but he did have Nat King Cole prepped and ready to sing about the Christ child and Christmas trees. He started the music and turned around to find Henry in his face and the young man's lips on his mouth.

"Henry," Nate murmured and gently pushed Henry back with a hand on his shoulder.

For the first time in their relationship as teacher-student, Henry Oliver looked confused. "Did you want me to take off my clothes first?"

"What? No." Nate shook his head.

Still confused: "Didn't you invite me here for sex?"

"No, Henry, I invited you here for dinner."

"Oh." He cleared his throat and stared at the floor. Seemingly unsure of what to do with his hands, he put them back in his pockets.

"Have other professors..."

Henry shrugged. "We usually just have sex, and I go home. Older men have always liked me, and since I'm not your student any more, I figured..."

Nate ran his hand through his brown hair and clenched his fist at his side. He felt an unwelcome pressure in his chest: rage.

"Do you want me to go?"

"No." Nate took a deep breath. "Can I get you some wine?"

Henry stared at him and then smiled: a massive, unfamiliar grin that made his eyes crinkle. "Yeah."

Nate took heavy steps toward the kitchen, trying to calm himself and erase the picture of other men like him—his coworkers, for Christ's sake—using Henry as a pretty little fuck toy. His hands shook as he poured two glasses of red, but when he returned to the living room, he found it empty.

"Henry?"

"Mm?" The sound came from Nate's office.

He walked in to find Henry in his stocking feet, standing on an ottoman, inspecting the top shelves of Nate's private bookcase. "What are you doing?"

"Nothing more telling than a man's bookshelf."

Nate handed a wine glass to his student and watched Henry study each book. Occasionally, he plucked one from the shelf, only to put it back a moment later.

"You're a romantic," Henry said.

"How do you know that?"

"Byron. Shelley. A practically destroyed copy of *Fahrenheit 451*."

Nate sipped his wine and took a slow, calm breath. "There's nothing romantic about *Fahrenheit 451*."

Henry stepped down from the ottoman and sat. "Of course there is. How much would you give up for the love of books?" He drank the wine like beer and emptied his glass.

"Why aren't you with your family at Christmas?"

"Why aren't you?"

Nate smiled and sat down in his reading chair: a faded recliner that no longer reclined. The piece of furniture was close to breaking apart, but it fit Nate's body perfectly. Most nights, he fell asleep in that chair reading.

"I like Christmas," Henry whispered. "But I don't need all the trappings. I like the quiet and the cold. It's so loud most of the time. Makes it hard to read." He sipped from his empty cup, which made Nate stand up and return with the bottle, happy he'd decided to buy two.

"What do you plan to do now that you've graduated?"

Henry took another gulp of wine and smiled.

"What's so funny?"

"No one's asked me that except you and Ella."

"You two are close?"

He shrugged with one shoulder. "She doesn't judge. Or use me."

"Do you feel like I'm using you?"

"Maybe a little." He paused. "Ella says you like to fix people."

"I'm not trying to fix you, Henry."

The young man bit his bottom lip. "She says you like puzzles and projects. You like to save people."

"I just like to make sure people are alright."

"What does that mean? To be alright?"

Nate considered the question and thought back over all the troubled men he'd loved in the past, the work he'd done to make things alright when they never were.

Henry must have construed his silence as an end to the conversation. "Did you know they're playing *The Christmas Story* on repeat for twenty-four hours?"

Instead of eating at the carefully set dinner table in Nate's small kitchen, they loaded their plates with spaghetti and meatballs and kale salad, sprinkled with oil and vinegar, and headed for the living room. Henry sought the film and soon found it, mid-way through. They sat down to the stuck tongue scene, and Henry laughed quietly as Ralphie and his friends escaped punishment from poor Flick. Nate had never heard Henry laugh before.

Henry only finished half his plate before setting the remainder on the coffee table between the couch and TV. He sipped from his wine glass. Once Nate was done eating, his plate joined Henry's. He was surprised when Henry slouched down on the couch and rested the side of his head against Nate's shoulder. He wound his long fingers around Nate's hand, and they watched the rest of the movie that way, over the sound of ice *tink-tinking* against the front window.

When the credits rolled before a backdrop of Ohio snowflakes outside, Henry said, "I'd better go home."

Yes, you'd better, Nate thought. He liked the feel of Henry's hand too much, and he would not be one of those professors. No, he would not.

Nate remained on the couch as Henry carried both their plates to the kitchen and reached for the suit coat he'd thrown on a table by the front door earlier.

"You're going to freeze out there."

"I told you; I like the cold."

Nate smiled. "Well. Merry Christmas."

Henry leaned forward and pressed a single kiss to Nate's cheek before leaving the professor, cozy and warm in his foyer. Nate stood and listened to Henry's feet descending the steps. Then, he fell back onto his couch and sighed... only to be interrupted a moment later by a knock at his front door.

Henry stood there, a bemused tilt to his lower lip.

"Henry?"

"I... Your front door is frozen shut."

In his slippers, Nate descended the wooden steps that led to his apartment and pushed against the door that led to Main Street. He pushed—hard.

"It's the ice," Henry said from the top of the steps. "Can I sleep here?"

Nate stared up the dimly lit staircase at his former student.

They were crossing a line, but he thought Henry could take his bed; Nate could sleep on the couch. He enjoyed the young man's company. It would be nice to wake up Christmas morning and make coffee for them both, so he acquiesced and ushered Henry back inside.

"You can take my bed," Nate said. "I'll sleep on the couch."

"But I don't want you on the couch."

"Henry..."

"I won't try anything." He looked up at his professor, a soft, friendly expression on a face that was usually distracted and numb. He took steps toward Nate's bedroom. "I get cold when I sleep alone."

Nate used hygiene as an excuse to lock himself in the bathroom. He stared at his own chiseled face in the mirror and spoke: "You're a creepy old man." The sensible side of him knew Henry couldn't go home, and the fix-it side danced a joyful jig. But Nate told himself nothing would happen. They would sleep. Nothing would happen.

Nate brushed his teeth and splashed ice-cold water on his face. He returned to his bedroom to find Henry already under the covers, bare-chested, reading a copy of *The Great Gatsby* from Nate's shelf. Nate noticed the younger man had a perfectly hairless chest. He grabbed his flannel pyjamas and changed in the living room before sliding in next to his student, careful to keep to the absolute opposite edge of the bed.

"Have you ever loved anyone the way Gatsby loved Daisy?"

"Yeah," Nate said.

"Do you think about him often?"

"No." He closed his eyes.

"I've never been in love."

"You're young," Nate said.

"I don't think I have the heart for it." He turned off the bedside lamp.

"I think you do."

Nate felt Henry roll around on the bed for a moment before rolling right next to him. He put his face in the nook between Nate's neck and shoulder and wrapped his long arm across Nate's chest. Nate was surrounded by the homey smell of Henry Oliver. He put his arm around his student's back to try to keep him warm.

Henry sighed, and Nate said, "Cuddlers always have good hearts."

*

There was no Christmas morning coffee as Henry was mysteriously vacant. Nate must have been in a deep sleep to miss the boy's disappearance, but when he rolled a little right, he caught the scent of soap and cinnamon on his pillow; so Henry had been there after all, not just a comforting Christmas dream.

The world outside his front windows was coated in a thick, satiny layer of white that shimmered in the early morning sun. Ice crept up the outside of the glass like spider webs, but apparently, his front door had thawed enough for Henry's departure.

Nate made himself a single cup of coffee and watched the snow blow. He opened his one gift, from Ella: a signed copy of Neil Gaiman's *Neverwhere*. No one called, not even her, surely too busy feigning enthusiasm over a new sweater she would never wear. He didn't expect to hear from his sister; he still didn't have Henry's phone number, and Henry didn't have his.

He should have felt guilty, having woken from a teacher-student slumber party. Instead, Nate felt warm and, frankly, filled with Christmas cheer, sort of like Scrooge with a second chance at life. He spent the day putzing around the house, reading segments from his favourite books, never once considering a shower or change of clothes. He remembered Christmases of his childhood when pyjamas were a requirement and when his mom used to make broccoli soup for dinner, followed by Christmas cookies, a glass of milk, and a kiss before bed.

By nightfall, though, Nate began to think about Henry, worry about Henry. Where was he? Why had he left without saying goodbye? Where was his family? Furthermore, who were the professors who had used him for sex, and how could Nate quietly get them fired?

He thought about bothering Ella again. She would have Henry's phone number. Maybe she could call the young man to make sure he was alright. Maybe Nate could even take to the streets. The town was shut down by the ice storm. It wouldn't be hard to find a tall, toe-headed skeleton wandering the streets, probably without a coat, probably reading a book and sliding into walls.

Then, the doorbell rang.

Henry stood in the hallway with a paper bag in his hand. His hair was damp. His nose was red. His eyes watered at the exterior cold, which made Nate drag him inside and immediately attack his head with a dry towel.

"Where's your coat? You need a coat," he muttered.

Henry chuckled under the fabric onslaught.

"Are you okay?" He removed the towel, and Henry's usually wild yellow hair stood in valleys and hills across his head.

Henry held up the damp paper bag in his hand. "It took me awhile. Merry Christmas."

"This is for me?"

"Take it."

Nate reached inside the crumbled bag and pulled out a Rubik's cube.

"Solve it," Henry said.

"I've solved Rubik's cubes before."

"Not this one. It's unsolvable."

Nate sat down on the couch and started twisting away at red, green, white... "That's not possible."

Henry sat down next to him. "I switched two squares."

Nate paused. "You what?"

"I switched two squares, which makes it impossible to solve." He smiled the smile Nate had only seen once before, the night before, when Henry realised he'd actually been invited to a man's house for a meal.

92

Nate shook his head and smiled. "Trying to tell me something?"

"May I take you out to dinner?"

Nate almost dropped the cube. "What?"

Henry slid closer. "I'm not your student any more. We're not breaking any rules."

"But now that you've finished school, won't you be moving back home to your family?"

"I grew up here. My family lives five minutes away. I just don't like them."

Nate laughed. He laughed hard until little white dots lined the edge of his vision. He realised it was snowing hard again outside.

"Will you, then, Nate? Come to dinner with me?"

Nate Evans had a crush on Henry Oliver. He had it since he first heard the young man talk about the ingenious way Chuck Palahniuk could make written words sound arrogant. He'd never once considered what the bright-eyed boy's mouth might taste like, although he now knew, thanks to a hurried Christmas Eve kiss. He'd never wondered what that boney body would feel like pressed against his, but he knew that, too. He knew what Henry's hand felt like, the weight of his head against his shoulder. And he finally knew why Henry smelled so good: he smelled like Christmas.

ABOUT SARA DOBIE BAUER

Sara Dobie Bauer is a writer, model, and singer with an honour's degree in creative writing from Ohio University. She is a book nerd and sexpert at SheKnows.com and author of *Life Without Harry* and *Forever Dead*. Her fiction has appeared in *Stoneslide Corrective*, *The Molotov Cocktail*, and *Chicken Soup for the Soul*. Her short story, "Don't Ball the Boss," was nominated for the 2015 Pushcart Prize. Read more about Sara at http://saradobie.wordpress.com or find her on Twitter @SaraDobie. She lives in Chardon, Ohio.

KEEPING MUM ABOUT DAD

Vanessa Ng

> *What's in a name? that which we call a rose*
>
> *By any other name would smell as sweet;*
>
> *– Act II Scene II, Romeo and Juliet*

My father is the greatest person in the world—I assert that without any tinge of doubt.

He is not what most would term to be a conventional or expressive Dad. Never once have I heard him utter any "I love you"s, or given me verbal encouragement for examinations. He never initiates any family outings and never suggests celebrating, be it festive holidays like Christmas or personal occasions like his own birthday or Father's Day. Being passive, he would spend his free time relaxing by watching Mediacorp shows and playing classic games on his phone and laptop. Many would label my father as boring or uncaring due to his overt nonchalance.

But this is because they do not know my father.

My father does not say "I love you" for it is taken to be always true. There is no need for explicit mentions of something he practices ever so often. Just as how one does not always proclaim that he is breathing, my father finds it unnecessary to tell me or my mother that he loves us. Instead, he affirms his emotions with tangible actions. He does not see the need to celebrate Christmas or Father's Day for he believes that everyday is a celebration in itself and should be treasured. My father's love is constant and consistent—he does not deviate and always gives his best. In such stability and reliability, I find reassurance. He never initiates outings as he prefers to stay indoors with the family to save on travelling time. Despite him not presenting emotions in the most expressive of ways, I never fail to see the hidden stashes of adoration that he has for me.

Every Monday, he would leave three bottles of herbal tea on my table to ensure that I do not fall sick due to my heatiness, or as my *Ah Ma* would say, *pu dwah*. Regardless of how much I tell him not to, my father would always insist on carrying my everything, be it shopping bags or school bags, and leave me empty-handed. Whenever I had cramps, he would always give me a hot water bottle and every pillow in the house such that I can build a fort of softness around me. All these silent yet undeniably thoughtful and sweet gestures warm my heart.

Unlike my mother who would tuck me into bed and ask about my day, my father would just watch TV until he dozed off due to fatigue from work. Nearly everyday, drafts of logo designs would flood his table messily while his marketing power point slides fill his blinding screen. Despite the tiring work, weekends were always set aside for the family. My father has a passion towards kite-flying, and not just towards any regular kite, but kites that stretch up to 8.5m in width. These kites conquered the skies and my father would fly them from evening until night. Even in the darkest times, the kites brightened the night sky with shimmering LED lights, resembling diskettes of UFOs.

At exactly 5pm, just before the ice cream vendor leaves, my father would buy my mother and I one-dollar ice-creams wedged between two pieces of crispy biscuits. All these and hearty laughs complete the family's weekly ritual.

✎

Before my father leaves the house, he would always wrap himself tightly in a chest binder. If he was not in a rush, he would use a long, beige cloth and wrap a few rounds more, flattening his breasts downwards and outwards to conceal. After checking in the mirror from various angles, he would change into a loose tee or a structured, collared shirt and put on matching pants. Rubbing some hair wax on his palms, he would turn on the hair dryer and style a slick backcomb which is aptly reflective of his forty year old self.

At the end of the day, he would remove the bandage and the chest binder so that he can breathe normally again. Taking a big gulp of air and exhaling slowly, my father would proceed to take a shower. The binders would always leave burning red marks around his chest and it pained me to see that. I once asked if it hurt, but he would simply smile and ruffle my hair.

Over the years, I have learned that this ritual instilled walls of confidence in him as the public constantly tries to break it down.

*

Unlike what others think, I lead a wholly normal, if not privileged life. My parents taught me to pursue and secure my dreams in writing by going through university. We are not rich, but my parents worked hard to provide me with what is *enough*. I never had to worry about money and I had sufficient to splurge on myself every once in a while.

Like every other Singaporean girl, I had plenty of tuition for both my academics and musical endeavours. Guitar lessons were on Saturdays whereas Mathematics and Science were on Sundays. My parents think it is important for me to learn how to defend and protect myself so I go for Aikido classes too. The key thing is that my parents do not believe in forcing me to go for such lessons. Essentially, I wanted them for the betterment of myself and my parents worked hard, as a Designer and an Accountant, to enable me to receive the education and self-enrichment that I opted for.

Funnily, a lot of my friends ask if I am straight, and my response to them would always be a confused, raised eyebrow. My parents neither dictated nor forced me to love in a certain way. They guided me, as all parents would, to love whoever I want so long as I believe the relationship will better both our lives and no regrets will linger when I am old. They taught me to commit only if I believe that the relationship is worthwhile, enriching, and meaningful.

Beyond that, I learned how to love by observing how my parents cared and sacrificed for each other. The consistent mutual adoration, sacrifices and respect kept my parents together—it was the effort that made them last.

*

Unlike them, I am straight—I am straight purely because the man I love is male. Never once have they questioned or tried to convert me. Never once have I felt obliged to be a homosexual. I never felt that I was adopted for they loved and cared for me as though I was their own.

Love was not bound to the narrow social circle of relationships. Love was extended to those who needed it. We gave to others when we could afford to. Our money to the tissue-paper aunties and our time to all sorts of charities. It was not a lot, but it was sufficient to remind ourselves of how fortunate we are and how we should never be selfish.

*

As the only child, I have always been doted upon. As much as I love my family, I used to feel afraid. People would stare when we go out and that disturbed me quite a lot when I was younger. Friends who came over often commented that I have a "weird uncle" and it did not help that my father was quiet. I have to admit that I am often too lazy, or rather, a tad ashamed to explain the circumstances. I used to just call my father "*jiu jiu*" in the presence of others just so I can avoid the topic. I am overwhelmed with guilt and I think nobody deserves to be treated this way, and especially not my father after all the love he selflessly gave me.

That was in the past for the old me was young, ignorant and afraid of steering away from the norm. I was not aware that in trying to hide what should not be deemed as wrong, I was mindlessly feeding the colossal monster of homophobia. In essence, I was guilty of perpetuating this irrational fear of something natural and beautiful. During that phase, I was overly concerned with getting our *kay poh* neighbours to stop gossiping. I wanted to hide when nothing wrong was done. I should never have been ashamed of my father and I should have never let my insecurities blind me.

Over time, I allowed myself to search for an inner courage. With my father's unparalleled love, my courage soon grew into pride as I became open about who I am and who my parents were—

I finally decided to not keep mum about Dad.

*

I told my friends that I was adopted by a loving lesbian couple when they asked me about my "strange uncle." Some did not know what to comment and merely tried to shift the topic in the most awkward of manners. Others would be overtly casual, yet stutter at certain instances to reveal the recovery of shock. Some tried to process what I said and proceeded to have an in-depth questioning about what it is like to have homosexual parents. Some judged me and we talked lesser afterwards.

Of course, some of the most hurtful comments were made by the closest people. My paternal grandparents, particularly my *Ah Gong*, utters the most cruel of words, often in Hokkien. Some of my relatives go the extra mile to pretend that my family is not there during reunion dinners. Still, we remained strong and did our part, together. I was forced to greet those relatives despite not wanting to. My parents never once got angry despite the treatment and taught me to be respectful of other people's choices and actions.

"Family comes first," my parents would always remind me.

"No matter what."

Besides the unconditional love that can get very discouraging, my family also faced the problem of extra attention when we head outside. Precisely due to my parents' sexual orientation, coupled with their duty as parents to bring me up, the public tends to judge. And precisely due to the judgement passed, my parents often cannot express their love for each other as how any other regular, normal couple would.

I remember a fateful incident in which my mother gave my father a casual peck on his cheeks in the mall. It was nothing close to an unacceptable public display of affection, but a mere, quick peck on my father's cheeks. I remember an angry middle-aged woman with permed, short hair staring in shock at my parents as though they did the most repulsive thing ever. The woman shook her head in disbelief and annoyance before telling her friend, in an unnecessarily loud volume, that, "This kind of people should just stay at home."

I ignored her offensive remark at first. But from the corner of my eye, I could see my mother turn away from me. The thing is she only does that when she is tearing. I felt so terribly angry.

"What do you mean by stay at home?" I walked up to the woman, fuming madly inside.

I was in secondary two then and all of me just wanted to hit her in the face for making my mother cry. *For making my mother cry.*

Upon confrontation, she just tried to appear calm and walked away, saying that she would not "argue with the poor kid" and that I "don't know anything." I started tearing out of anger as I felt so helpless and undignified. Her words lingered and echoed in my head as the scene of my mother crying behind me started replaying:

"This kind of people should just stay at home."

I felt that it was so unfair to be judged without justification or reason. It was just plain wrong and insanely upsetting.

❧

Thankfully, such experiences made me treasure my family all the more. It made me appreciate my understanding *Po Po* whom we visit on a weekly basis. We would even roll Peanut *Tang Yuan* together randomly just because my father likes it. It made me appreciate that one, nice aunt who is the only person that says hi to my family during new year reunion dinners. It made me glad to assert with truth and relief that my parents rarely quarrel. They have fought so many treacherous obstacles and came so unimaginably far to be together, to adopt me, to start a family. Nothing else mattered and nothing can bring them down.

I am happy and proud of my family.

❧

Rorschach, a Swiss psychologist, once asserted that three aspects need to be fulfilled for a healthy growth in one's character. They are genuineness, acceptance and empathy. In that vein, I know that I have been showered with infinite love and affection from my parents whom I am eternally grateful for.

❧

What's in a name? that which we call a rose

By any other name would smell as sweet;

A rose by any other name would smell as sweet. A father by any other gender would love as much. We have been through a unique set of challenges that I foresee will become less of an obstacle as society progresses forward into acceptance. It is a special kind of love—a love that conquers all odds to emerge triumphant and ever-lasting.

It is a contemporary love that strengthened through hard times and it should be respected, if not embraced.

"Pu dwah" is Hokkien for "heaty food" which is a category of food that most doctors practising traditional Chinese medicine (such as acupuncture, etc.) would say. Essentially, heaty food are food that will cause you to have a fever, cough, or an ulcer if eaten in excess. For instance, chocolate, durian, and fried food are heaty in nature. There is also "liang" food, which literally translates to cooling food. For instance, certain types of herbal tea and mangosteen are considered cooling. We are supposed to combat heaty food with liang *food. So if we consume too much fried chicken we have to drink some herbal tea to even out such that we don't fall sick.*

About Vanessa Ng

Vanessa Ng got first runner up in NUS's Creative Writing Competition 2014. Her short story was adapted into an animation and ticketed for the Singapore Writer's Festival in August 2015. She was published in *From The Belly Of The Cat* (Math Paper Press, 2013), *A Cup Of Coffee And A Suicide* (Budding Writers League, 2012) and the *Ayam Curtain* microfiction anthology (Math Paper Press, 2012). She studies in Nanyang Business School and is a recipient of the Singapore-Industry Scholarship.

THE ALLEYS OF THE MIND

Cathy Bryant

Down the alleys of the mind
they chase me, yelling abuse,
as they did when I was young.
I learned to run, to hide, then.

Do they still race down alleys
to hurt, to kill the different?
Are they still defined by that
narrowest road of hatred
and fear of those not like themselves?

So long ago. I chase, now,
most intoxicating love,
the giddy starship freedom
and the warm highway of bi-sex.
I climbed out of those alleys
into a wide boulevard,
friend-filled—a village, no less,
on a planet of courtesy
and acceptance of all love.

Resentment still swells towards
the thugs who chased me for fun
but now I feel pity, too,
for those ugly pounding minds
self-trapped in narrow places.

ABOUT CATHY BRYANT

Cathy Bryant worked as a life model, civil servant, and childminder before becoming a professional writer. She has won 19 literary awards and her work has appeared in over 200 publications. Cathy's published books are: *Contains Strong Language and Scenes of a Sexual Nature*, *Look at All the Women*, and *How to Win Writing Competitions (and make money)*. Cathy is bisexual, and mentally and physically disabled/exceptional. See Cathy's monthly listings for cash-strapped writers at www.compsandcalls.com.

DEER HUNTING WITH THE PREY

Tom Trumpinski

Teddy walked into their computer room and stood behind John, who was manipulating ship construction in the *Star Shield* game on his screen. He wiggled his partner's earphones until he looked up and then leaned down and whispered, "The guys at the store want me to go out hunting with them this weekend. I want you to come with—it's opening day for deer."

John grunted. "And I would do that... why?"

"Come on, man. It's hard enough for me to work outside the community—I've got to watch what I do and say every second. If you do this, it'll make it a lot easier for me. Please?"

John pushed back his chair and stood up all the way, running his hands through his long, blond hair—once his pride, now thinning as he approached middle age. "I don't see why I should hang around with a truckload of straight normal. Worst of all, they're a bunch of fucking rednecks."

Teddy looked him in the eye. "Rednecks like me, you mean. Look, I didn't get to go to a fancy college like you did. I can't work from home doing game design. Every day, I get up and go off to Wal-Mart to stock shelves in sporting goods. All day, I try to ignore the smells of shoppers who only bathe occasionally and I have to fight from salivating when a baby is left unattended in a cart while its mother runs back to exchange a nursing bra."

"You could go to a community college."

"Right, go with kids ten years younger than me. This comes up again and again and that's always your answer—improve myself. God-damn it, I like the way I am now. Studying never appealed to me, I'd go crazy cooped up in a classroom every night. I'm a farm boy—I want to hunt; I want to fish; I want to fuck under the moonlight while the cows run away from us in terror. Say you'll come with me."

"It'll make work better for you?"

"Damn right it will. Can you butch it up for a day?"

John growled and swiped at him, playfully. Teddy laughed. "Yeah, that'll do," he said. "Now, I'll have to get my old man's gun out and clean it up. You ever used a shotgun with slugs?"

"Never used a shotgun—never a gun at all, really. I hate them—unnatural things."

Teddy sighed. "City boys—so easily scared. Just gotta make sure you don't shoot yourself instead of the deer. I'll get you a vest and a hunting license. Give me your driver's license for tomorrow—I'll need it. I can get groceries on the way home."

Thursday morning. Time to set out the new displays on the end caps—the shelves at the end of the rows of merchandise. Teddy had a cart full of orange hunting caps—at least the tags told him they were orange—he couldn't tell colours any better than any other canine.

He had always survived menial jobs like this by letting his mind wander. The scent of a sheepskin vest wafted over from the next aisle. Wool. He smiled as he thought of rolling hills and the herds of sheep his parents had kept for food. *What time was it?* Break wasn't for another forty-five minutes and he was ravenous. The suburbs just didn't have any wild uncooked food running around, unless you counted rabbits and squirrels. Not that much meat and they really, really got old after a while.

"Hey." Randy Withers had come up behind him without Teddy no-ticing. If it had been the old days, such inattention might have gotten a werewolf killed. Teddy, surprised, whirled around so fast that his su-pervisor saw only a blur—fortunately, humans discounted what they didn't understand.

"What? Man, don't do that." Teddy tried to keep from scowling and didn't succeed. "You scared the living shit out of me."

"Sorry, man. When you get this done, Ralph needs some help setting up the license and tagging booth. You still on for this weekend?"

"Abso-fucking-lutely. I wanted to ask—this buddy of mine, John, he wants to come, too. Can we bring him along?" Teddy had put off asking for as long as he could. He figured that they boys would never let a stranger come with them.

"Well, sure. The more the merrier, right?"

"Uh, one thing, though..."

"Uh, oh. I hate when people say things like that. What? He drinks on hunts? He makes too much noise? What, Teddy?"

"He's from Chicago. The city itself. He don't know nothin' at all about guns or huntin'."

Randy looked at him like he had grown another head. "Then what the living hell does he want to go out with us for? We're not some kind of deer-hunting school. This is the only chance some of us have to get our buck. Some city guy fucking it up is not on the agenda."

"Look, I'll take responsibility for him. I've been trying to convince him that this sort of thing is fun. He's not a bad guy, really." Teddy knew Randy was a game junkie. "You know *Car Theft Five* for the X-Box Three-Sixty? He designed part of it."

"No shit? Still not completely convinced, but I think I might be able to find a place for him. You've got to get him dressed proper, though. I don't want us getting noticed by a game warden because he doesn't have the legal hunting vest on. Can he be quiet?"

"I'll gag him if I have to."

"Perfect. Talk to you later."

John hit the alarm snooze button so hard he almost smashed the clock flat. "Crap, crap, damn, it's four-thirty in the freakin' morning. Who set this thing? It's Saturday! Almost full moon tonight, need to rest."

Teddy poked him to keep him from falling back to sleep. "Deer... hunting," he sang, altogether too happily in his partner's opinion. "We have to get up and get ready. We're supposed to be at the timber by a half-hour before dawn."

"Goddamn it, I forgot. I was up working until two hours ago. You go ahead."

"No, John. You promised. We never go out—not anywhere. Remember when I first came to town and we went dancing every night?

Nothing any more—you sit in front of the computer and work. Do it for me... please?"

John threw the covers to the foot of the bed. He sat up and rubbed his eyes until he could finally keep them open. "Alright." He put his head in his hands. "Get some coffee on and I'll go."

All Teddy had to do was throw the switch—he'd set that up the night before. By the time he got out of the shower, the apartment was filled with the rich scent of Jamaican Blue Mountain. John was already dressed and lifting his cup to his mouth when Teddy returned to the kitchen.

"Man, you have to shower. The deer will smell us two miles away if the wind is from the wrong quarter."

John snarled at him, but pulled his shirt off and hung it over the kitchen chair. Teddy took cheese and minced ham from their refrigerator and put together sandwiches for the trip, which he then loaded into their insulated carrier, along with jerky and Oreos for lunch—can't beat chocolate and lard for dessert. He opened their thermos, which he had pulled out of the storage unit and rinsed the day before. As the coffee he was pouring into it passed halfway, its insides shattered into shards of glass. All of the coffee in it was wasted.

"Oh, shit." He looked over at John's first cup. They were going to have to stop at the fast food joint by the expressway and get some of their undrinkable mud to take along. He absolutely hated the stuff they had there.

He loaded the car, double-checking his list. John was not going to get a gun of his own—that much was certain. Teddy figured he'd let him go up onto the stand for a while with his shotgun once he had given the city mouse enough instructions in safety. This hunting trip was important—there was way too much tension around the house.

❧

John didn't notice the lack of a refill until they were already in the car and headed for the interstate. "Where's the coffee?"

"Thermos broke. We're going to have to buy some on the way."

"We need to stop at Starbucks."

"That's in the other direction—clear on the far side of town. We're supposed to be in the farmer's yard by six-thirty. If we're late, they'll go off by themselves and we'll never find where they have the stands set up."

106

John grumbled for a while longer, but after going through the drive-through, the car was quiet while they sipped from their Styrofoam cups. They were playing catch-up and the earliest threads of dawn were erasing the stars in the east by the time they hit the interstate. Once they were beyond the suburbs, they passed rigs parked on the on-ramps—long-haul truck drivers catching some sleep. Teddy took the Emery exit and headed north, away from the river. Cows called for their morning milking; frost made the barnyards and empty fields white in the half-light.

The farmstead was three miles from the state highway on a section road. An F-10 pickup and a souped-up 4x4 sat in the driveway and the Wal-Mart crew—Randy, Ralph, and Ernest—were out in force, unloading the truck beds and spitting on the ground from time to time. Randy unhooked his ladder from the side of the pickup and motioned to the two of them. The werewolf couple pulled their hunting vests over their jackets and walked to him.

"Randy, this is my buddy, John," Teddy said. "John, this is my boss, Randy." Teddy looked his partner right in the eye. *Man, don't screw this up for me,* he thought.

"Pleased ta meetcha," John said, holding his hand out. Teddy exhaled.

"I heard you were a game designer—worked on *Car Theft.*" Randy looked up. John was a foot taller than he was.

"Yep. Worked on the last two expansions—did the colour-blind levels and all of the boss fights for five."

Teddy grabbed one end of the ladder and followed the four of them into the woods behind the farmhouse. The going was easier than he expected—the dairy cows were allowed to graze there in the summer so the wild rosebushes, which had taken over so many of the other hunting areas, were trampled down. The hunters tromped a mile toward a tributary of the large river to the south. At a fence line, they stopped adjacent to a line of tall trees with deer stands built into their branches. On the other side of the fence, brambles and other undergrowth provided cover penetrable only by wild animals who knew where the trails were located.

"Alright—here's our spot." Ernest knew the farmer and had used these stands before. "This tree-line goes a quarter-mile along the fence. There are stands every fifty yards. We'll go up one at a time and one of us will need to stay at the foot of the last tree, quiet, in case something happens or we need supplies.

"Listen, this is important—the guy on the ground needs to stay put. Those of us up in the deer stands won't fire at anything inside of our row of trees. We wait 'til the deer are well away from us before we fire. We do this to make sure there are no accidents. Any questions?"

"I can take first shift on the ground," John said. "Ted showed me how to use the shotgun, but I've never done this before. I'm nervous about missing and scaring the deer away."

"Hey, that's okay, man," Ralph said. "We all had our first hunt some-time. It's just that most of us were, like, twelve, when we did it." All four of the country boys laughed at the same time. John looked down and kicked a root.

"Help me set the ladder up, John," Teddy said, trying to distract him. The two of them went to the first tree and set the ladder up while Ralph climbed to the stand and then they carried the ladder down the tree-line until they reached the next position. "Thanks for coming out," Teddy continued, "I think they like you—they've never met a real game designer before. At least I've got someone who does something cool for a living. I'd hate to be here with a fucking florist—that wouldn't be good at all."

They reached the last stand, which was located in the area with heavier underbrush. "What do I do now?" John asked.

"Sit at the bottom of the tree. Don't move or make too much noise. The idea is to not scare the deer away. If they come, they'll come from upwind." Teddy went up the ladder with his gun.

⟋

The sun rose, burning the frost from the pine needles and fallen leaves of the forest floor. John sat, his back to the tree, trying not to nod off—he figured if he did, his snoring would warn every deer for ten miles. His sense of smell was acute enough that by nine, he knew every path any animal had taken upwind during the last forty-eight hours. He had no idea what kind of animals they were, however. *How could a place make someone nervous at the same time it bored them to death?*

Ten o'clock, boredom. Eleven o'clock—John had debugged three design concepts in his head. Eleven twenty-one—a shot echoed from the treetops. His cell phone buzzed—it was Randy. John was delighted something had finally happened.

"Ernest got one," the hunter said. "Tell Ted we're going to take it to the truck, eat lunch, and then go back up and try an' get a couple more. After he comes down from his stand, bring the ladder down the line."

◢

The deer lay on its side, its eyes open. Blood poured from a chest wound—the shotgun slug had gone clear through it, puncturing a lung. Teddy and John did their best to stay upwind from the deer, but they were distracted enough by the presence of raw meat that the wind blowing the scent away didn't count for much. Teddy, especially, was flexing his biceps and opening and closing his hands. *It's a good thing the three humans are too intent on dragging the deer back to the truck to notice.*

"See," Teddy said, once they were out of sight, "nothing to it. We just stick around for the rest of the afternoon, maybe we see another deer and shoot it, and then we go home and laugh about it."

"Well, this is fun for you, but I'm ready to go nuts. There's absolutely nothing to do—my iPhone's only got one bar and is getting low on battery. If I have to spend another five hours out here squatting by that fucking tree, I'm going to go batshit crazy."

"You want to try it up on the stand?"

"What?"

"You want to try hunting?" Teddy picked up his gun from where it was leaning against the tree. "Here, this is how the safety works—you just move the little lever like this... red means they're dead. Don't take the safety off until you actually see a deer. Put the stock of the gun against your shoulder like this when you aim—there'll be a big kick when it goes off. It's not pellets like in the movies, it fires a big-ass lead slug."

When they finished the lesson, John looked up into the tree and shook his head, no. Teddy put his hand gently on his shoulder. "Go on up the ladder and wait there—at least, you'll be busy scanning the brush for a buck. Maybe that'll be good enough to keep you occupied."

"Really, I want to go home... but if I have to stay, I may as well be up in the Goddamn tree. Sure."

◢

Now John was not only bored, but bored twenty feet in the air. He couldn't tell where the brush stopped and targets began. It wasn't, he imagined, like being human—*those monkeys can see colours—they can see the tan of a deer standing behind a bush.* He would have to rely on motion—keeping in mind that he would have to wait to determine that it wasn't another hunter. *Damn, those vests are supposed to keep us safe from accidents, but they sure as hell do nothing to help us tell the difference. In grandpa's day, we could have eaten the whole lot of them and then moved on.* Living in the city had its advantages, but sometimes his blood sang to him, especially around the full moon. *Maybe this is what Teddy means by the thrill of the hunt.*

John's head nodded against his chest. He fought his way back to wakefulness several times before leaning back against the branches behind him, still standing. He dreamed in shadows and smells, of blood flying everywhere as his talons found the soft spot in the belly of his prey. His mouth lowered to the streaming entrails and he drooled in anticipation of a feast.

BANG!

John, startled, jumped two feet forward, the front two-thirds of his feet landing over the edge of the deer stand. He was in trouble, overbalanced—the safety strap hadn't been made to resist an impact caused by his inhuman muscles. Teetering over the forest, his arms windmilled once, twice, a third time before the strap broke and he fell forward, plunging head first toward the ground.

John's reflexes took over and he watched his descent slow to a crawl as the adrenaline filled his body. He looked his situation over—*the bushes below will break my fall. The question is, should I land feet first or flat? The branches are sharp. If I land on too small of an area, they could impale my foot or hamstring me.* Choosing to land flat, his body twisted in the air, too fast for anyone but another wolf to see. He pulled his head back and put one arm over his eyes to protect them. Slamming into the bush as time returned to its normal rate, he screamed in agony—the fucking thing was a blackberry bramble. His impact scattered berries all over the surrounding area. Thorns penetrated him from every direction.

"Teddy," he moaned, "get me off this thing. Please help me, Teddy."

His partner was there before he could say another word. The two of them worked to unhook John's jacket and vest from the branches of the bramble. Blood seeped into John's shirt from the punctures he had sustained.

"Man, that was a bad fall; you're lucky nothing's broken. You scared the shit out of me." Teddy kissed him, since the rest of the hunters were out of sight. "They shot another one. If you can sit here for a few minutes, I can take the ladder and get them down, we can haul you to the car, and then they can come back for their deer."

"What time is it?"

"Three-thirty; why?"

"It'll be better for me to just wait here. Help them load up the truck. Moonrise is a half-hour from now—an hour before sundown. After they're gone, I can recover fast."

Once down, everyone came over to check out John's injuries. "Damn lucky that bush broke your fall—might have busted your neck," Randy said. "Shame you got stuck. How'd you manage to tear out of your safety harness?"

John shrugged. "I was a dumbass—didn't attach it right or something. When your shot went off, I was startled and fell off the edge. I'm scratched up plenty, but nothing's broken, as far as I can tell." He tried to move a little and winced. "Ted's going to come back and help get me back up to our car."

∅

By the time Teddy returned from the barnyard, the sun had neared the horizon. On the other side of the sky, the moon, one day before full, was already visible as he headed down the last slope to where John was sitting. He crouched next to him and reached behind his partner's head to comfort him.

"It's getting close. You'll feel better real soon, now."

John groaned, struggling to sit upright. "Help me get this shirt off—it's sticking to me now."

Teddy peeled it from him and then stopped to remove his own hunting vest, jacket, and shirt. Their breath steamed in the frosty air as the sun slipped away completely. John worked his belt buckle loose and lifted himself far enough to get his pants off. Within another five minutes, they were both completely naked. For the first time, Teddy could really see the damage the landing had done to John.

"Looks bad—you've lost some blood," Teddy said. "They wanted to call a doctor—to get an ambulance to come out to the farm. I convinced them that I'd drive you to the ER myself. It took forever to get rid of them, but we're alone, finally."

John's back arched into a bow as the first spasms of metamorphosis hit him. He groaned as his ribs swivelled to let his lungs expand. It hurt every time, but the endorphins pumping into his system moderated the pain. Soon, it would feel good, ecstatic, to breathe this deeply. The pigment of his skin darkened, mottling to camouflage him against the sign of forest animals. The guard hairs of his fur extruded from his arms, chest, and face. His accelerated healing closed and repaired the puncture and slash wounds from his fall—this wasn't magic; this was evolution.

The fading light of the woods grew brighter to his perception and he glanced over at Teddy, who was changing, too. John could see his lean form alternating between a crouching and standing position as he tried to stay comfortable. Claws slid out from the tips of the farmboy's fingers—sharp enough to gut an enemy or kill an animal for food.

"Are you alright? Does it still hurt?" Teddy's voice was guttural, now, a low growl shaped into language.

"Never felt better." John looked around, his senses now amplified a hundred-fold from those he had in human form. "This is amazing—everything in this forest is alive. You lived this way?"

"Every day. I've been trying to tell you for years."

"I never knew. I never dreamed all this was here. What do we do now?"

Teddy let fly with a howl. "We hunt, you silly son-of-a-bitch." He cleared the barbed wire fence by two feet and danced on the other side. His voice was alive, anxious with joy. "Come on, John. The deer are waiting for us."

❧

The two of them ran, side by side, down a game trail illuminated only by moonlight scattered by the trees' bare branches. John sniffed the wind, blowing from the north. Their fur and high body temperatures kept them from suffering from a wind chill that he figured was well below freezing.

"We need to come from the south," Teddy said, taking a loop of the trail that would face them that way. "Then, all we need to do is wait until we smell deer."

"What do they smell like?"

"They smell like food."

They crept on all fours, trying to keep as quiet as they could. John smelled something new. "Is that them?" he tried to whisper, not successfully.

"Shh," Teddy replied, "yeah, that's deer. There's a herd of them fifty yards or less straight ahead on this trail. I expect a clearin' to be there. Watch out for the big bucks with the long racks of antlers—they can puncture a lung and even we can't take that. My uncle was laid up for a month from a botched hunt."

They crept closer, Teddy a half-wolf length ahead. As he had expected, the trail widened into a meadow. The moonlight almost blinded them after the half-darkness of the brush that had concealed them. Teddy counted two dozen deer altogether, with the largest buck standing guard. Off to the side, an older deer grazed, oblivious to the yellow eyes, glinting as they watched.

Teddy poked John in the side with his paw and pointed at the prey. He motioned for a charge. John looked at his, raising his eyebrows. "Yes," Teddy said, "you go. I'll protect you from the guard."

John was travelling thirty miles per hour when he hit the side of the old deer. It let out a bellow and jumped away. Like a warrior sentinel, the larger buck charged at John, only to be headed off by Teddy's onslaught of teeth and claws. The rest of the herd scattered in every direction, making too many targets to possibly follow.

John leapt at his victim, catching the isolated deer's shoulder with a bite like a vice made of knives. The shed blood gushed into his mouth—*man, this is better than the best steak I've ever had.* He kicked himself for stopping to think—the deer leapt ten feet away in that fraction of a second. *This will never do. If I don't get him now, I'll never live it down.* He ran beneath the deer's neck and jumped straight up, opening his jaws as he did, hoping to bite through the jugular vein.

Meanwhile, Teddy was weaving and bobbing like a winning prizefighter. *This eight-point buck has fought us before.* The deer lowered his head and charged. *Ha.* Teddy jumped to the side and the attack missed him as he showed the buck his impotence against him. Despite his speed, he was no danger to the buck, either—even if he wanted to, the deer was too fast for him to get a mortal wound and those antlers would throw him fifteen feet if they ever connected. *Now, where the hell is John?*

John felt the soft throat of his deer between his teeth and bit as hard as he could. He could feel them sink in and then he shook his head from side to side, rending and tearing the flesh of its neck. Blood sprayed over his skin, drenching him. The deer stumbled three feet, crashing over onto a pile of rocks.

Teddy smelled the fresh blood, as did the buck. The wolf sidled, one eye on his foe, toward where his partner was standing—panting over the body of the kill. The leader of the deer herd approached close enough to determine that his charge was dead and decided that two hungry wolves were too much of a danger to confront. Teddy padded to John and kissed him, lolling his wet tongue all over his face.

"You did it—I can't believe it. You killed it by yourself."

"Hey," John said, "the damn thing jumped into my mouth. All I had to do was bite down really hard." His laughter was like a pack of dogs yipping.

"Here," Teddy said, "let me show you the best part." He ripped into the stomach of the dead deer and his head disappeared for a moment. He emerged in a shower of gore and entrails, wet flesh hanging from his mouth. He let John take it from him and chow down. "Goddamn it, I've missed raw liver. It's been years."

The two of them took their time, sharing the best parts of the deer. Teddy was in heaven—they hadn't done anything that he had enjoyed so much in years, maybe since they first met. When they were full, they took turns licking each other's fur, taking an extra-long time with the sexy bits.

By the end of the night, they were curled around each other on a hill, watching the moon descend toward the farmhouse below.

"You want to do this again, sometime?" Teddy asked.

"Absolutely," John replied, opening his mouth in a yawn as large as his partner's head. "Let's just leave the rest of them at home, eh? This is just for us."

ABOUT TOM TRUMPINSKI

Tom hails from the American Midwest, where the land is flat, the forests are green, and the rednecks are often the most fun of all the people in town. "Deer Hunting With the Prey" is a side-story from his Iona urban-fantasy universe, which has been featured in short stories in *Fae Fatales: A Fantasy Noir Anthology* and *Latchkey Tales: Elementals, Fire and Ice*.

He lives with his four partners and their teenage daughter, who writes anime fan-fiction.

HOLIDAY MINI-SERIES

Adan Ramie

Sam stared at the flickering screens in front of her, bored and restless, waiting for something to happen. Normally during this time of the year, she could nap through most of her workday, waking up to the sound of her cell phone timer, entering a time-stamped entry into the log her boss insisted she keep.

"Keeps you honest," he said, nudging her in the ribs with his fat elbow. "You can't just lock up and leave if I make you keep tabs on yourself."

Shows what he knows, Sam had thought, setting an alarm to go off every hour on the hour.

During scheduled holidays, the most excitement she got was buzzing in a delivery or maintenance worker once in the span of three days, and it suited her just fine. Sam never cared for small talk, making friends of co-workers, or basic human interactions. They felt phoney to her, as if scripted by unseen hands; she preferred her drama on a television screen, and she watched a show or two on most of her shifts, flipping her eyes back to the security camera footage now and again to be sure no one was waving a high powered rifle over his or her head. People in cubicles were known to be volatile, and she didn't want to be immersed in an historical drama when the shit hit the fan.

This Christmas, however, the office was closed for four days, which should have afforded her plenty of time to catch up on her regularly scheduled programming. Instead, one of the cubicle monkeys and one of the junior executives were at their desks, busily typing and clicking. To Sam, it looked as if they were frenzied, doing all the work for the holiday in a few hours, and it amused her to watch them for a few minutes before she turned her attention back to the rest of the show. Afterwards, she had little to do besides watch them, in case they were engaged in something off the books; her boss would lose his grip if she let corporate espionage or theft go on under her nose without flagging suspicious activity.

So, for an hour, she just watched them work at opposite ends of the building, seemingly lost in their work. She kept dozing off, so she turned her attention to making a pot of coffee in the little security office kitchenette. When she got back to her post, everything had changed. The two employees had vanished, and she wondered if she would soon get the call to buzz them back out of the building. She waited for ten minutes, and was just about to call her boss to report the inconsistency, when first the cubicle girl, then the executive girl, filed out of the bathroom, both still adjusting their clothes as if they had redressed in a hurry.

As Sam watched, the cubicle girl—who she thought was called Calista—covered her mouth as if to cover a sneeze or a sob, and walked out of one frame and into another, covering ground away from the junior executive. The junior executive—whose name was something ordinary, like Danielle or Ashley—jogged after her, a look of remorse or horror on her face, her mouth open and her hand raised toward Calista. As they entered the last frame, near the entrance to the elevators, Calista stopped, pushed the elevator button, and swiped at her face angrily with the sleeve of her cardigan. Danielle, as Sam had decided to call her, caught up, and started talking to Calista, her face contorted with sadness, her hand dropping onto Calista's shoulder.

Calista pulled away but turned toward Danielle, her face a mask of rage as she yelled. She pointed a finger in accusation as she spoke, jabbing it into Danielle's collarbone as she made each point. Danielle's shoulders sagged, but she made no effort to stop the assault on her chest. Calista stopped talking and jerked around to enter the elevator. Danielle moved to stop her, grabbing Calista's elbow, but Calista pulled out of Danielle's grasp and got on. Danielle followed, and Sam lost sight of the two for a tense minute.

Intrigued, she slid away from her controls only long enough to fill her mug with coffee, then wheeled her chair back to see what would happen when they emerged. The elevator doors opened, but neither woman left the space, and the door closed again. Sam sat up, her eyes scanning frantically through the elevator doors of all the floors in the building, waiting for the women to emerge. When they finally did, it was onto the same floor they had left only minutes before.

The yelling and finger pointing had stopped; in fact, they didn't speak at all as they made their way back to their respective desks. The two worked in solitude for another few minutes before the executive picked up her cell phone and typed out a message. She put it down onto her desk a few seconds before the other girl picked hers up. Cubicle Calista turned her head in the direction of Junior Executive Danielle's office, worrying her fingernail with her teeth, then looked back at her phone, and shot a text back. She dropped her phone to her desk, Danielle picked up hers, then shot out of her desk and office, practically sprinting towards Calista's cubicle.

Sam tore open the wrapper of an energy bar and took a bite, washing it down with hot coffee, her eyes focused totally on the drama unfolding on the silent, black and white screens. The two women met at Calista's desk, and Danielle pulled Calista up by one hand and wrapped her arms around her, burying her face in Calista's dark hair. Calista clung to the back of Danielle's business casual blouse, occasionally nodding or shaking her head, presumably to something Danielle was whispering into her ear.

Is it worth it? Is it worth the screaming and the pain, the breakups and the makeups? Or is it better—am I better—without her?

As Danielle wrapped her fingers in Calista's, and the two made their way to the break room, Sam picked up her phone and stared at it. She still had Kiley's number, though she had named the contact 'Don't Do It,' and swore she would never call it again. The picture was an old one, from the beginning of their courtship, when they had taken a "business trip" together to a city a few hundred miles from their hometown. Kiley grinned up at her, tank top showing off golden brown skin, one hand up to hold her mane of poker-straight black hair out of her eyes. It had been windy, hot, and beautiful the whole long weekend. It was the best time of their whole relationship.

After months together, Sam found she couldn't handle the seemingly endless cycle of fight, break up, apologise, make up. With Kiley's living arrangement—deep within her self-imposed closet—Sam felt like a shameful secret. When she told Kiley so, the girl lost it, shrieking and breaking everything in sight, sobbing out words like "betrayal" and "broken" and "mistake."

Sam glanced up from her phone in time to see the secret lovers kiss, then part ways, as each practically skipped to their own desks, their steps lightened by their joy. She wondered if, in calling Kiley, she could salvage something like what Calista and Danielle had. It was more than just sex, she knew, because that was exactly what she tried to tell Kiley. She insisted Kiley's family and friends would eventually get over it; it was love, not sex, so they had to see the light after they saw how happy they were together.

She wondered if Kiley had changed, if she had burst from the closet after their breakup, or if the loss had driven her further underground, hushing her hidden desires in favour of the cookie cutter world in which she had been born. On the screen, Danielle sent a text with a smile, and Calista received it with a laugh that threw her head back and her hand over her belly. In the dark security room, Sam dialled, then lifted the phone to her head, holding her breath as it rang.

ABOUT ADAN RAMIE
Adan Ramie is the author of *Maladaptation* (Deviant Behaviors, #1), three anthologies, and too many short stories to count. She lives in a small town in Texas not unlike Andy Griffith's *Mayberry*, and in her spare time can be found gorging on true crime TV, reading anything she can get her hands on, drowning in gallons of coffee, or spending time with her amazingly supportive wife and rambunctious children. Find her online at AdanRamie.com.

FRAGMENTED

DJ Tyrer

"Who are you?" he asked as I entered the room.

As much as I loved him, I hated visiting him. The smell of the home and its clinical lack of personality were hardly inviting, but his fragmenting, vanishing memory was worse. I loved him, but every visit broke my heart.

"I'm your granddaughter, Sarah."

He looked up at me from his chair with rheumy eyes and said, "I don't have a granddaughter. I have a grandson." He screwed his eyes up, trying to remember. "John. His name is John. Where is he?"

I bit my lip, steeling myself to tell him what I told him every time I visited. "He... is dead." What else could I say? It was difficult enough to explain when he could follow my words. Now...

"Dead?" He looked at me uncomprehendingly.

"Yes," I said, nodding. "Dead. He died a long time ago."

I could see his heart breaking all over again as he processed my words.

"Who are you?" he asked, eventually.

I chewed on my lip. Every time I visited him, it was a battle between persisting with explanation and an easy life. These days, I find myself opting for convenience more and more.

"My name is Sarah and I've come to visit you."

"Oh." He gave me a vague smile. "That's nice: nobody visits me."

I sighed. He never remembered, yet I went there twice a week, minimum. He breaks my heart every time, just as I break his.

I sat with him for a while, telling him all my news, as inane as so much of it was. Every little story I told of life's inconveniences and oddities seemed to enthral him, although I wondered just how much he took in. Sometimes, I thought it was just the sound of my voice that captivated him so; I could probably be speaking a foreign language and he would hang on my every word with a smile on his face. How I wished I could have the grandfather back that I once knew! Not that I was the grandchild he vaguely recalled.

"I have to go now," I told him when I finally found I couldn't keep talking or stand the home any longer. I bent and kissed his cheek. "Bye, granddad."

"Who are you?" he asked and I felt tears prick my eyes.

"Sarah. Sorry, I have to go now. Bye."

"Goodbye." He closed his eyes and began to snore.

With a sigh, I turned and walked away, only to halt before I reached the door of his room. There was a leather-bound folder lying on the sideboard. Something about it caught my eye. It was old and battered, as if it had seen some adventures. I couldn't help but pick it up. I was curious.

Before I could flick it open, a voice from the doorway said, "Hello."

I looked up and saw one of the other residents of the home. I could never remember the man's name, but had seen him around. He was one of the more mobile and articulate.

"It's good to see Steve getting a visitor," he said. "Poor guy's always going on about his grandson and how proud of him he is, but he never comes. I guess he's too busy. Ah, he talks about you, too, of course," he added. I knew it was a lie without his expression giving him away.

He spotted the object in my hands. "Oh, I see you've found his folder." He chuckled. "I don't know what he's got in there, but it's sure important to him. He got it out for John, he said."

"Uh, yeah. He told me. I'm taking it over to him. John, I mean."

The old man nodded, believing me. I was a better liar than him.

"Well, I've got to be going. Bye."

"Cheerio," he said, smiling, waving me off. I wished my grandfather had his good humour.

I took the folder with me. If what the man had said was true, my grandfather wanted me to have it, so it wasn't stealing if I took it. Besides, I wasn't necessarily going to keep it. I couldn't wait to get home and look inside it.

*

Arriving at my one-bedroom flat, I immediately went into the lounge and opened the folder. It was filled with loose sheets alternating between tracing paper and lined paper. The former were scribbled with crayon that revealed rubbings of some engraved surface. The latter were covered in Greek letters taken from the rubbings and, below them, what I took to be the English translation. I flicked through the sheets and tried to make sense of them, but whatever my grandfather had rubbed—I presumed it was him who did the rubbings—it was fragmented and such a cursory glance yielded me nothing.

It was going to take a little more work to decipher them than that.

I went into the kitchenette and put the kettle on and popped a ready meal into the microwave. A couple of minutes later, I settled down to eat a gloopy mess that was nowhere near as appetising as that shown on the box it came in and drink a cup of instant coffee, the only virtue of which was its strength. Still, they were quick and would keep me going.

When I was finished, I made myself another cup of coffee and settled down to examine the fragments in greater detail.

It seemed that no single fragment extended to over twenty or thirty words; and none were contiguous that I could find. As far as I could ascertain from comparing the rubbings and their content, they seemed to be the remains of a plaque or plaques or maybe a set of clay tablets from a temple. Unfortunately, not only did the fragments not form a continuous whole, but many were broken at an angle, cutting words in half and sundering sentences. My grandfather had attempted to fill in the blanks, but the results were still vague and unhelpful.

The fragments spoke of a Dark Mother, which sounded like a late version of the Canaanite Astarte. References to the 'Fecund Black Ewe' who is mounted by the 'Mighty Ram' were clear enough, but many of the passages remained obscure to me and, not for the first time, I wished I'd studied classical languages so that such things weren't opaque to me.

My phone bleeped, startling me from my reverie. A text: that was something of an unexpected occurrence; the coverage here was abysmal. I picked the phone up and read the text. It was from David. That brightened my mood immediately; I always tended to feel down after visiting my grandfather and puzzling over the fragments had done nothing to improve my mood.

David had been my best friend in college and had supported me through the toughest decision of my life. We'd stayed good friends, even when work and an urge to travel had led him away from me. But, he'd recently taken a job near me and we'd started meeting up. I had hopes we could be more than just friends.

Can u do diner tomoro. 7pm? the message read.

I texted back in the affirmative and suggested we meet at an Italian place not far from my flat. I knew he liked Italian food, having spent a year in the country.

A couple of minutes later, he replied, *Its a date.* I felt a pleasant glow as I read that.

I considered putting aside the folder for the night, maybe picking out an outfit to wear, but the temptation to continue was too strong. I just had to make sense of the fragmented words. I needed to understand why my grandfather wanted me to have them. After all, he'd gone to the trouble of copying and translating them. I knew he'd been something of an adventurer in his youth, but he was no archaeologist and I couldn't imagine him making the rubbings out of idle curiosity. And, as much as I might have wished it so, I didn't think it was because of anything as obvious as treasure.

I worked my way through them. I read of eunuchs and hierodules, of sacred mirrors and Tamash trees, of meaningless words such as Kharkhaso and Khasteer and Melekh, and of stranger things besides, things lacking in the necessary context to make sense of them. Had my grandfather actually understood what he had here? It was as if he'd been searching for something, whether an object or meaning, I had no idea, and never found it. I wondered if I could ask him to explain it, but his memories were as fragmented now as the contents of the folder before me: he might remember all or nothing of it.

Eventually, after one last coffee, I set the folder aside and decided to go to bed. I felt as if, perhaps, I'd been concentrating too hard on it. If I had a break, was refreshed, it might be clearer to me. Besides, I wanted to think of David.

❧

The Black Ewe invaded my dreams. I was there in her woodland home on the slopes of the mountains of Canaan. Through the dark, encroaching woods, I followed her as she sought her mate. I felt the same burning desire inside me that I knew inflamed that dark goddess.

Finally, after what felt like an eternity, we reached the mighty Tamash tree, a soaring phallic trunk, beside which loomed the powerful bulk of the Mighty Ram. No sooner were we there than he mounted her and the mountains shook.

Then, I was standing beside a misty, reed-clogged lake. Up from the waters rose great blocks of stone and, somehow, I knew that this was the place where the inscriptions originated. Somehow, I knew that this place was the Kharkhaso of which the fragments spoke. It was a holy place—a profane place—of which the fragments were a latter day record.

A Bedouin in ragged robes approached me along the lakeshore. His face was like a waxy mask and, as he reached me, he reached up a hand to remove it as if sloughing off skin, to reveal David's face below. He dropped the mask to the ground and reached out for me, pulled me to him and embraced me, kissed me.

Bowing his head to my ear, he whispered, "It is a fearful thing," and I awoke with a scream.

✿

Eventually, I fell asleep again. I say eventually, because I was woken in the morning by the insistent whine of my alarm clock, but had no clear memory of falling asleep, merely tossing and turning, jarring images from my dream battling with a feverish desire to recall if those words came from one of the fragments.

I had work, so couldn't spend any real time looking in the folder, but a quick flick through found a piece inscribed 'It is fearful/terrible' before breaking off. I wondered if that was what had inspired the words in my dream. Yet, it felt as if it had deeper meaning than that bald line carrier. Then, there was Kharkhaso. Why had that word, a seemingly meaningless collection of syllables, so firmly anchored itself upon the image of a ruined city? Then there was the image itself, an oddity having no apparent derivation from what I'd read in the folder. I could see no reason why that one word had become attached to it out of all the other untranslated terms.

I fruitlessly pondered those questions on the bus, but had to put them aside when I arrived at the office. It was a minimum-wage data-entry role, mind numbing yet demanding of my full attention. There was no space left in my mind to think about things until I was on the bus heading home; and, by then, I was busy thinking about seeing

David. Our future was a dream I was more keen to consider than some silly nightmare.

Arriving home, I ignored the folder and went into my bedroom where I picked out a suitable dress and leggings. The weather was still warm, so I didn't need to worry about a coat. I looked in the full-length mirror I kept in the lounge—a last testament to my childhood dreams of becoming a ballerina, before reality and my father had battered my hopes into nothing—and decided I looked okay. Even after five years, I still wasn't entirely comfortable with my appearance; too many neuroses were niggling away at my confidence. But, then, who was body confident, these days? Setting aside the worries that always rose up in an attempt to sabotage my self-esteem, I was fairly confident I was presentable. Besides, I told myself, David had never had any problems with my appearance.

"Deep breath," I told myself, before taking one. "No need to panic." Not that I quite believed myself. But, still, I was calm enough.

✐

"Sorry—Sorry—Sorry!"

David was standing outside the restaurant, glancing at his watch; he was the only person I knew who still wore one. He looked up at my exclamations and smiled.

"Sorry I'm late."

"No problem," he said, stepping forward to hug me. I felt an electric sensation at his touch. I'd loved him for so long, but had never told him.

"Shall we go inside?" he asked after a moment.

I nodded and allowed David to guide me inside.

It was strange: we'd eaten out many times before and I'd never felt nervous like this. I think I was finally in a position where I could imagine us as something more than just friends, and that scared me.

The meal itself was nothing out of the ordinary, just spaghetti Bolognese and the sort of small talk that two friends make, discussing work and life in general. I considered mentioning the folder, but wasn't certain what to say, and the opportunity never quite arose. Instead, I told him some inane story about an irritating work colleague and how I wished I could find a better job.

Dessert followed—ice-cream—but what I was eating held no interest for me. It was what David did that held my attention: he slipped his hand into mine and looked into my eyes. I felt that electric shock again, only more intense; a connection.

Neither of us spoke, savouring the sensation.

Finally, when we laid down our spoons, David took my other hand and said, "Sarah, you know I've always cared for you, right?"

"Uh-huh."

"I mean, *really* cared."

"Yes. You were there for me."

"I'll always be there for you." He squeezed my hands in emphasis. "I want to always be there for you." He coughed and shifted in his seat. "What I'm trying to ask is if you'd like to, ah, go steady with me? Now that I'm nearby, it makes perfect sense."

"Yes, I would."

I smiled at him and he smiled back at me, then we leaned towards each other across the table and kissed.

"Would you like to come back to mine?" I asked.

He smiled and nodded. "I'd love to."

✍

It felt amazing to fall asleep in David's arms, to feel protected, to feel loved. To feel accepted. Everything seemed right. Perfect.

I dreamed of the drowned city again.

I stood on the misty shore of that reed-clogged lake, gazing at the stone blocks that were all that was left of the mighty city of Kharkhaso.

I was crying.

It was odd. I'd felt a real sense of bliss as I'd drifted off to sleep and something of that had echoed into my dream. But, with it, and eclipsing it, I felt a sense of sorrow and loss. A longing for some certainty I no longer possessed.

I could recall the city as it had stood at its peak, a great metropolis in which the sacred acts were enacted, acts that I half-perceived as in a vision and which left me recoiling in revulsion. The city of Kharkhaso had been a city of sin. Yet, the fact of its loss saddened me.

The Bedouin in ragged yellow robes stood beside me wearing a face that looked like David's. He turned and reached up his hand to pull it away as if it were just a mask to reveal a featureless white curve of bone.

"It is a fearful thing," I whispered as I stared up at that face that was no face and I awoke with a scream.

"Sarah? Sarah? Are you okay?"

I started awake to find David shaking me, staring down at me, concern etched upon his features.

I looked up at his face and screamed in terror, as I seemed to see him peeling his flesh away.

"Darling? What's wrong?"

It took me a moment to remember the restaurant and the blissful evening I'd spent in his arms and that the horrors I'd experienced were a dream.

My gasping breaths slowed and I calmed down. David tenderly held me and stroked my hair.

When the effects of the terror finally subsided, I told David all about my dream and the fragmented notes that had inspired it.

He gave me a rueful chuckle. "It must've been one heck of a nightmare; you seemed quite terrified! You know, I'm really curious to see this folder of yours."

I persuaded him to wait until morning. I felt as if I needed to steel myself before I looked at it again. But, I couldn't put him off any longer than that and had to hand him the folder to look at over breakfast.

"Okay," he said, at last, "there's some pretty odd stuff in there, but nothing nightmarish—and not much of what was actually in your dream."

I felt a little embarrassed at his observation. "Yeah, that's exactly what I thought." I ran my fingers through my hair. "I think that's why it freaks me out so much. It makes no sense."

"Well, it's all out of your subconscious," he said; "dreams, I mean. Your hopes and fears."

I blushed at that. I hadn't mentioned that the Bedouin had his face. The meaning of that seemed pretty clear.

"What I don't understand," I said, redirecting the conversation, "is why my grandfather wanted me to have the folder. It obviously has some meaning, but what it is..." I shrugged.

"He's senile," David said. "Sorry, I don't mean to be blunt."

"No, don't worry."

"He's senile," he started again, "so whatever his reasons might've been, they might not make much sense. He's thinking of you as you were and, who knows, he might be muddling you up with someone

126

from his youth or something like that. The logic is probably quite confused."

I bit my lip and nodded. I hated to think of my grandfather like that, but it was true. Who knew how his fragmented memories bumped together?

"Maybe," David finished, "he was just proud of his discovery and wanted to share it with you. Or, perhaps he wanted you to pass it onto a museum or something."

"Perhaps." That made sense, yet didn't seem quite right.

"You know..." David pushed the breakfast things aside and began to spread the sheets out on the table. "If you put them in this order..." He picked out some of the sheets. "Yes! These bits form some sort of, what's the word? Litany."

He was right. There were a dozen fragments that, together, clearly formed a complete, or near-complete, tablet with a continuous engraving of words on it.

David began to read the translation.

"Don't! Please," I interrupted.

He looked at me and laughed. "Oh, come on; you don't believe I'm going to summon the Devil or something, do you?"

I shrugged, awkwardly, feeling stupid. "I don't like it."

"It's just the memory of your nightmare," he told me, his tone confident. "Hey, now, you remember you said you dreamed the phrase 'It's a fearful thing'?"

I nodded.

"Well, here it is in full: 'It is a fearful thing to fall into the hands of the Living God.' Hmm... For some reason, that sounds Biblical to me."

"Whatever." I really didn't care. I just didn't want to be reminded of my dream any more.

"I think this Khasteer that is mentioned here is the Living God. I'm not sure if he's supposed to be the Mighty Ram mentioned elsewhere; I think that's Melekh. Hey!" he laughed, "maybe this Khasteer is the Bedouin who's in your dream?"

I shuddered, although I wasn't sure why.

"A god in yellow rags?" I asked him.

"Why not? Jesus wore rags and a crown of thorns."

"Please, don't." David wasn't religious and his irreverence could sometimes touch a nerve with me. I'd struggled with issues of faith and I didn't like him to treat my beliefs as a joke.

"Sorry. I didn't mean to be flippant. I was just trying to point out that not everyone thinks of gods as glorious superheroes on golden thrones. Anyway, let's change the subject. How are you feeling now?"

"Still a bit off-colour," I admitted, "but better. I guess last night was a pretty big deal for me and I need to get used to it."

I was pleased when David reached over to hug me and said, "You'd better get used to it, because you're stuck with me."

I guess it was a corny line, but it made me laugh and I felt a good deal better.

"I'm going to take a shower," I told him. "Make yourself at home."

"Will do," he said as I headed for the bathroom.

For the first time I could recall, I didn't feel the need to look in the mirror. The days of revulsion were long gone and I felt—I hoped—the days of insecurity had been banished to the same bin. It wasn't, I realised, that David had validated me, but that, through having the courage to embrace what he offered, to seize what I'd wanted for so long yet been too scared to seek, I'd finally validated myself.

I took a leisurely shower, savouring the sensation of being fully at peace with myself. As I stepped out of the bathroom, I could hear David reading aloud the text that he'd assembled. I winced. It disturbed me to hear it, even if I couldn't say why.

I was just about to step into the lounge when he gave out a horrible gurgling shriek of inarticulate terror.

Crying his name, I ran into the room only to be brought up short with a shriek of my own. David had fallen from his chair and now cowered on the floor behind the small table, staring in horror at a figure that stood in the corner of the room before my full-length mirror. It was the figure from my dreams: the ragged yellow-robed Bedouin who wore David's face like a waxy, pallid mask. It wasn't reflected in the mirror behind it, it was as if it were a reflection that had stepped out from within the frame.

It stepped forward, saying, "It is a fearful thing to fall into the hands of the Living God," as it reached out towards David.

"Keep away from him!" I screamed. I'm not sure which of them I was shouting at. All I knew was that I had to save David.

I seized a chair and threw it across the room. It didn't hit the figure—I don't know if I missed it or if the chair just passed through it—but the chair struck the mirror, which toppled and fell.

"In Khasteer's Name, leave us in peace!" I shouted as the mirror struck the floor and shattered. I don't know if it was the breaking of the mirror or my words or both together, but the figure halted in mid-step, then seemed to shatter like broken glass before vanishing in a silvery swirl of shards.

I had no idea where the words had risen from, I didn't recall them from the folder, but somehow I was certain I was right to say them. Memories, of a city I was sure could never have existed and I certainly could never have seen, buoyed in the back of my mind, but I suppressed them, scared of just what I might learn.

I helped David to his feet and hugged him. It was like hugging a frightened child.

"It's okay. You're safe. It's gone now. It's all okay."

I led him through to the bedroom and seated him on the bed, then returned to the lounge. Looking down at the fragmented remains of the mirror, I decided the shards could wait. Instead, I gathered up the folder and its contents and dropped them into the sink. Finding a box of matches, I set fire to them and let them burn. Then, before the smoke alarm could sound, I turned the tap and doused the flames, washing away the blackened fragments that remained.

It was over. I was hopeful of that.

*

"Who are you?" my grandfather asked when I entered his room that afternoon.

"My name's Sarah. I'm... a friend of John's. He sent me to, ah, collect the folder you left for him and to ask what you wanted him to do with the papers inside."

After everything, I was still curious to know.

My grandfather smiled, "Ah, John; he's a great kid. Very good to his ol' granddad, you know."

"Yes, I know," I whispered, tears in my eyes.

"A good boy."

"The papers," I prompted. "In the folder..."

"The folder? Oh, yes, the folder. That's for John."

"Yes, but what must he do with the papers?"

"Burn them," he said with unexpected force. "We found the fragments near the ruins of Kharkhaso, but they hold a curse." He sighed.

"I began to reconstruct the words, but realised the danger. I was a fool to keep them! He must burn them!"

I almost laughed as I listened to him. Instead, I said, "They've been burned. It's all okay."

He smiled and nodded in his usual detached manner. Then, he looked at me with surprising clarity and said, "You're a good girl, Sarah."

Then, his features grew slack and his eyes glazed and he looked at me in confusion and asked, "Who are you?"

"Someone who loves you very much," I told him, hugging him tight. Tears were running down my cheeks, but they were as much tears of happiness as tears of sadness. I'd overcome something I didn't understand and my own reticence, and, somehow, had received an absolution of a sort. My life would never be perfect, no-one's was, but it would be good enough. It was no longer fragmented.

ABOUT DJ TYRER

DJ Tyrer is the person behind Atlantean Publishing and has been widely published in anthologies and magazines in the UK, USA and elsewhere, including *Between The Cracks* (Sirens Call Publishing), *History and Mystery, Oh My!* (Mystery and Horror LLC), *State of Horror: Illinois* (Charon Coin Press), *Steampunk Cthulhu* (Chaosium), *Irrational Fears* (FTB Press), and *Sorcery & Sanctity: A Homage to Arthur Machen* (Hieroglyphics Press), and in addition, has a novella available in paperback and on the Kindle, *The Yellow House* (Dunhams Manor). DJ Tyrer's website is at http://djtyrer.blogspot.co.uk.

LESSONS ON LOVING AN ABLE-BODIED MAN

Taylor Lyn Carmen

1. Accept pride as part of the equation
it shouldn't be but is
know that you will have to do things in front of him
be things in front of him
any other woman wouldn't
know some days it will be harder
on you for him to see you weak and fragile
than it is to be naked in front of him
understand it will be hard for him too
for this reason make pride as small as you can
take huge bites out of it and swallow as much as you can
some days this is harder medicine to take than others

2. Some days you will feel like a burden on him
like the weight of the metal in and around your body
is too much to ask him to bare
he's a good man
so he'll tell you it isn't
that the crosses you bare for him
even the scale
sometimes this will be enough to let you sleep
others you'll be awake nights
trying to find more you can offer

just to measure up to his other options
other days you'll convince yourself
he is blessed to have to get past all of the metal and challenges
after all only great gems are kept under such lock and key
have as many of these days as you can
because if he loves you he'll agree

3. Learn your version of beauty
know your curves
your peaks and valleys
show whatever womanly features you have
so he knows your body is unbroken
give him just enough to emphasise
you are a being capable of passion
once you can map your own body
be willing to teach him
he may not always know the best ways to follow your maps
try not to hold that against him

4. When his hands land on the parts
you try not to draw on the map
do not pull away
do not move his hand
let his fingers press into the scars
try your best not to show concern
when his face turns to shock
hope it is not a reaction of disgust
and is simply an explanation of unfamiliar landscapes
convincing yourself of this will be harder than it should be

5. Understand he could choose an able-bodied woman
try not to focus on reasons he doesn't
only he really knows what they are
and no matter what
you'll always find more reasons why he should

6. Appreciate his gentleness with you
not as something fragile
but as something remarkable worth treasuring

don't be afraid to remind him you are not easily broken
take pleasure in showing him when to be rough

7. In the beginning
he'll need you to guide him
you know you love him
when you trust him enough to stop

8. Even if you cannot bare the physical weight
remind him you are someone he can fall into
at times he will forget this
these are the most important moments
to prove just how strong you are

9. Fight the urge to imagine
what you look like to him
on your good days you'll convince yourself
he hasn't noticed your differences
on your bad days you'll convince yourself
he has noticed nothing but that

10. Know that the rarest things
are the most valuable
make sure he knows this too
remind him often
that in a world full of hard edges
you have learned the softness of kindness
even when the world hasn't always known it for you

ABOUT TAYLOR LYN CARMEN
Taylor Lyn Carmen is a poet, activist and wife-to-be. She focuses her work on issues of disability, sexuality, and self-love.

THE KEBAYA KING

Rumaizah Abu Bakar

Raden is at his two-level workstation, with a pencil in hand. I approach him from behind to take a peek; it's a new design.

"Cream *kebaya* for the flower girls, for Puan Sri's daughter's wedding," he explains.

"Oh, I see. That's pretty."

I sit on the wooden stool next to him.

He tosses me today's copy of the *New Straits Times*, "Page three."

I turn to the Lifestyle section, spreading the sheets on the round table and holding it down with my elbows to prevent the pages from being blown away. Raden has turned on the portable fan at full blast.

"Aahh!" I gasp.

It's a full-length photo of me in a blue shirt.

I read the headline out loud, "'Being single in your thirties'... oh my God! I didn't think the picture would be this big. Everyone's going to see this."

Raden laughs. "Well, that should bring in single women and divorcees in droves," he teases me.

I punch his shoulder. "Yeah, right! Thank God it doesn't say I can't sew a button," I laugh.

"What? You told her that?" He raises his brows in disbelief.

"Yes, she also asked me when I was last in a relationship. I told her I couldn't remember."

"You don't know when to stop, do you?"

I continue reading the article quietly, wondering when he would bring up that dreaded matter again.

My eyes feel heavy. I get up and push the stool back, cringing as it scratches the parquet floor. I put the folded newspaper on the floor.

"I'm going to make some coffee, you want some?" I ask as I walk to the kitchen.

"I'm fasting. It's Asyura Day, remember?"

"Oh!"

Raden had mentioned it yesterday. He had practically pulled me out of bed before the dawn for *sahur* this morning. I had stubbornly crept back under my warm blanket.

"You should have joined me. All your sins over the last year and next year would have been pardoned."

I say nothing, and sip my hot black *kopi luwak*, my favourite brew; Raden had brought the beans from his hometown in Indonesia.

I carry my cup to the display window and caress the soft lacy dress on the mannequin. I bask in its floral scent. It's a real work of art; the amber material has been carefully selected and beautifully cut; the intricate gold embroidery and beads have been sewn with passion and care.

Puteri Sisir Emas is a masterpiece, a proof of Raden's genius. Tunku Sasha's engagement will be aired live on national television. The entire country will see the Princess in that *kebaya*.

I return to the table and switch on the laptop to check my inbox.

"New fabrics arriving next week," I tell Raden.

"Good, perfect for the flower girls," he is happy.

"The accounts figures are good. It's the best year for Qiera yet."

Raden stops sketching and looks up.

"A month left in our fiscal year, and we have already exceeded our highest annual sales," I say. "We should take our staff out for a vacation."

"Why not just the two of us?"

I remain quiet and avoid his gaze. A lump forms in my throat. My mind flies to the gala dinner last week.

*

We had been invited to the grand opening of The Opulence, a new luxury hotel in the city.

Glamorous, excessively made-up women had flirted with Raden all evening, some pretending to seek his advice on their wardrobe while others were bolder.

135

"I love your designs, but I don't have the body for a *kebaya*," many women said to him.

He'd smile and say, "The *kebaya* was created for all body types and sizes. A well-cut one should fit a woman like a second skin. The 'polar' is a secret formula that has been passed down for generations in my family…"

And with that, they'd agree to visit the boutique and have their measurements taken.

During the drive back home that night, his phone had beeped continually with text messages. He had simply ignored them. I had laughed, although I noticed he looked a bit worried, and was not his usual easy going self. It was strange. Just a minute ago he had been friendly and charming, and now, he had turned mysterious. I wondered if Raden was aware of the effect he had on women.

It was three o'clock in the morning when we reached home and settled down on the Berber carpet to watch *Forrest Gump* on HBO. He leaned so close to me that I could smell the faint remains of his after-shave; his shoulder felt warm against my bare arm.

"We should be together, you and me. I've had feelings for you for years, you know," his voice was soft, but clear.

I was not sure what had shocked me more; what he said, or the fact that he said it so effortlessly, as if it was the most natural thing in the world.

"At least, think about it," he pleaded, looking at me.

Speechless, I got up and shut the bedroom door behind me.

*

I walked along the busy alleys of Yogyakarta, past rows of boutiques and textile outlets, holding my umbrella, enjoying the sights and gentle taps of raindrops.

Then, I saw it.

The stunning sheer blue-black *kebaya* on a mannequin at the entrance of the shop beckoned to me. It was tastefully paired with a hand-painted batik sarong. I was mesmerised. I stood there staring at it for a full fifteen minutes. I knew I was in love.

Unlike at other shops, nobody stood at the door to call out to passing shoppers. The place had a certain air about it, as if it was of a different class. Entering the shop, I felt as if I was walking through a sea of colours; rolls of fabrics were lined upright on the cemented floor, all the way to the back. A man was holding the finest lacy material I had ever seen in a light shade of blue. He looked up and smiled widely when he saw me.

"*Selamat siang, Pak.* Welcome to Qiera. May I help you?" he greeted me warmly.

I smiled. "I was looking at that blue-black *kebaya* at the window."

"Oh, that's *Puteri di Bulan*, my latest creation."

"It's beautiful. So, you are the designer?"

"Yes, I'm Raden."

I learned that he was born into the business. His father, grand-father and great-grandfather had all been renowned *kebaya* designers. He and his brothers took over ten years ago. They became the *kebaya* master's apprentices after finishing high school. None of them had college education.

He gestured towards a rattan chair in the corner and offered me a cup of brewed Javanese coffee. I was delighted with his company; we talked for hours. He told me about the origin of the *kebaya*, and showed me his many designs. I was astounded. He could transform a plain spider-net fabric into a work of art with his meticulously hand-sewn embroidery and beads.

After that, I visited his boutique every day during my vacation to watch him work.

"Raden... have you ever thought of opening a store in Malaysia?"

He looked surprised. "Malaysia?"

"Well, why not? I'm looking for a new business opportunity. *Kebaya*s would be great," I smiled.

❧

Unfortunately, people around me were sceptical.

"What? Do you know anything about women's clothes? You're not even a fashion junkie." This would be followed by hysterical laughter.

"You're not cut out for business; you're too soft. You'll be dead in no time," said one with genuine concern.

"You're an auditor. You're doing well where you are now."

"You have no people skills."

"You've got to be kidding. Have you become gay?"

I ignored their remarks. I was stubborn. Having my own business was a dream I had had for a long time. It was the right time, and a man didn't have to be gay to sell women's clothes. On the contrary, I felt I'd fail miserably if I tried to sell men's clothes.

Raden had agreed, after a long discussion with his family. Young and adventurous, he was up to the challenge. I had returned to Malaysia in a joyous mood, as if my life had new meaning. I felt like a man with a purpose.

I resigned from my job as the head of internal audit at a multinational company a month later. My boss was stunned; I had been at that job for eleven years. He made me many counter offers, including a substantial raise. However, my mind was made. I dreamed of running a *kebaya* boutique with my new Indonesian friend. After several weeks of looking, I found a two-storey house with a compound in Damansara. Raden arrived just before they put up the signboard.

One of our first few customers was a celebrated actress who walked into the boutique barely a week after we opened. She saw Qiera's gilded plaque on the gate when she was walking along the street. Being a *kebaya* fan, she was impressed with Raden's intricate handiwork and agreed to let us sponsor her attire for the most prestigious artistes' award presentation ceremony. When people saw her on live telecast, they started asking about us.

✍

I am about to stretch out on the plush sofa after an exhausting workout at the gym, when Raden calls out to me, "*Solat maghrib, ay*o!"

He has already changed into his *baju Melayu* and *kain pelikat*. I hear the call to prayers on the radio. I grumble and reluctantly go to the bathroom to perform my ablutions before maghrib prayers. The cold water from the tap is refreshing. I quickly pull on a clean t-shirt but my body still feels sweaty and sticky.

Raden has spread out two *sejadah*, velvety prayer mats, on the living room carpet. After we complete the three-*rakaat* congregational prayer, Raden grabs two copies of Surah Yassin from the coffee table and gives me one. I remember it's Friday night. After reciting the verses, I plop on the couch and lean back while he folds the prayer mats.

Then, he sits next to me. A few minutes pass before he touches my arm. "Have you given the matter some thought?"

I jerk my hand away, unsure how to respond.

"Adi, at least say something, man." He sounds hurt.

"You know it's forbidden by religion," I blurt. "What about dosa, Raden?"

He says nothing; there is a sad look in his eyes.

"I don't want to burn in hellfire," I continue.

"How could something that feels so right be wrong?" Raden's voice is a whisper. "God knows how I feel, He made me..."

I sigh.

"But... it's wrong. Didn't they teach you that at your *pesantren*?"

"Adi?" Raden is looking at me.

I jump and grab my car keys from the coffee table.

"I'm going to Mahbub. You want mutton *briyani*?"

I had gone with Raden to his village a few years ago. He had wanted to visit his old religious boarding school to catch up with his teacher. Class was in session. We entered the quaint wooden building quietly through the back door and took a seat on the hard wooden chairs in the last row.

There were about twenty boys in white *baju Melayu* and *songkok*, listening and taking notes. I smiled. I didn't recall being so attentive during my school days. The *pak kiyai*'s class was about sacrificing the things we love in this world for something better in the permanent hereafter. His beard matched his white robe and the *ketayap* on his head.

A *santri* raised his hand and asked a question, "What if one has homosexual desires, should the person give that up too?" I heard loud gasps and murmurs from his classmates in every corner of the room.

The teacher seemed concerned. He paused for a moment and explained gently, "If the person can control his desire, In Sha Allah, he and his friend will be rewarded with a better life in the hereafter."

"Will the couple be together in Jannah?" the *santri* continued.

"Allah knows best. Always have faith in Him," the old man smiled.

I whispered to Raden, "Is he saying homosexuals are allowed into Heaven?"

"Shush," he hissed at me, and I felt a sharp nudge of his elbow.

I rubbed my midriff where he hit me, and chuckled at the notion of a group of gay men flapping their feathery wings in the clouds.

"We want to tell our customers that all women can look beautiful in a *kebaya*," I explain to the creative director during our meeting at Starbucks, The Curve. We are planning our new brochure and introducing a new line. "Our tagline is 'Qiera's Indonesian *kebaya* for every figure.'"

Zain nods. He has produced marketing material for us before, and we have been happy with his work, and his costs.

"What does the new line represent?" he asks.

I cringe at his foul breath, noting the pack of Malboro on the table, next to his wallet.

"Like my partner says, it's the corset within that enhances the curves..." I stop when I see a familiar figure at the counter.

It is Raden, laughing and talking to a man in a dark pin-stripe suit. The place is packed and the crowd is loud; I strain to hear their conversation. They pick up their drinks and adjourn to a sofa set on the other side, partially hidden by palm leaves. I wonder who he is. They seem to know each other well.

After Zain leaves, I stay on and watch them for another hour. They hug before parting. I am unable to explain the uneasy feeling I have.

I do not mention the incident to Raden, but two weeks later I see them again at the same outlet. I am meeting a supplier who prints our clothing labels and have not told Raden I'd be there. I feel an unfamiliar knot in my heart. It is unlike Raden to not mention his friends to me. I wonder how long this has been going on.

One day, I return from the gym earlier than usual. Our two staff are about to leave on their motorcycles, and they wave when they see me. I see a blue BMW parked outside.

I walk in and stop before the oak-wood dresser. Raden is talking to the man I saw at Starbucks.

He is holding up the sleeves of a lime green dress, "Kimono inspired," he explains, and moves on to the fiery red one, "Spanish touches; note the Flamenco-styled sleeves."

They stroll to the staircase to admire the ivory piece on the mannequin, "Elegant Victorian collar," Raden says, before pointing to the embroidery on the bodice, "Swarovski crystals." The man touches the precious stones, murmuring his appreciation.

They return to the front and are surprised to see me. The man takes his jacket from the chair. "I'd better leave," he says. He gives me a gentle nod before sliding open the glass door.

❧

Next morning, I carry two mugs of steaming hot black coffee to the workstation, take my usual seat, and sip my drink quietly.

Raden seems deep in concentration, his fingers busy arranging tiny colourful beads on a tray. A fine dove grey material lies on the table. It is as if he does not notice my presence.

I sit quietly and listen to the whir of the portable fan. I have almost finished my drink when he finally puts the dress aside and looks at me, both elbows pressed on the table.

"He is my new business partner."

"Who?"

"The man you saw yesterday."

"What?" I nearly spit out my coffee.

"We have been talking for weeks. Either he buys your share at Qi-era… or I sell my shares and start a new *kebaya* business with him."

"What's happening, man?" My head spins.

"I can't do it any more. You need to find a new partner."

I hit the table hard with both hands; his carefully-arranged beads fly off the tray and roll on the floor. *Plop! Plop! Plop!*

He ignores the mess.

"Raden! What is this? What are you saying?"

"I want out, Adi. I really do," he answers calmly and gets up, grabbing his car keys.

"Hey!" I shout after him. "You're not going anywhere."

"Oh, yeah? Says who?"

A car engine rumbles outside. I rush to the glass door just in time to see him backing his Nissan out.

He rolls down the window and shouts, "You want mutton *briyani*?"

🍃

"You're deep in thought," my trainer says, as he adds more weights.

I called him an hour ago to schedule an extended workout. Fortunately, his other client had called and cancelled. My heart is pounding. Raden has not been picking up my calls all day.

I return to the bungalow in the evening and find a row of big boxes at the bottom of the stairs. Raden's name is neatly written with a marker pen on the front flaps.

Loud traditional Javanese music rises from upstairs. I go up and find Raden sitting cross legged on the carpet. I raise my brows.

He smiles. "I'm trying to draw the spirit of my warrior ancestors before they went to a battle," he winks.

I am about to bring up the subject of our earlier conversation, when he grins and cuts me off.

"Hush," he points to the plastic bag on the coffee table. "Have some mutton *briyani*. We talk tomorrow."

He gets up and goes to his room.

◢

I wake up to find Raden at the round table downstairs, looking at two mugs of coffee and a plate of *lempeng pisang*.

"Assalamulaikum," he greets me cheerfully.

"Walaikumsalam," I reply.

I am still yawning and the piping hot beverage is good. I notice the crisp *kain pelikat* he is wearing and his *ketayap* on the table.

"I've been up since four o'clock," he explains. "I haven't performed the *tahajjud* for a while."

"Oh!"

I had slept restlessly the whole night, but I had not heard him get up for his long night prayer. It's something he did every few weeks.

He bites into his banana pancake.

I take a piece too, cringing at the slightly bitter taste.

"Do you remember how it was when we started Qiera?" he says. "We had to scrimp and save every cent. It's hard to imagine now how we had lived on our awful cooking."

I laugh, and nearly choke on my food. "And your *lempeng* is not any better. It still tastes like rubber."

He grins. "You are cooking lunch today, man. I haven't had *kicap* rice with your over-fried *ikan termenung* for a while."

I stick out my tongue at him.

"I went to the *pasar* to buy some fish. You'll find it in the fridge."

We continue eating breakfast in silence. It has been five years since we moved into this house. It was bare then, without a single piece of furniture. We would yell at each other across the hall, and listen to the echoes of our voices. It was like our own piece of heaven, with crickets chirping at night and birds singing at dawn.

We slept on mattresses on the floor. The boutique and showroom downstairs had to be furnished first. We made do with the minimal living quarters upstairs for the first few years.

"Adi..." Raden's voice turns serious.

I stop chewing and look at him.

"I can't go ahead with it."

"What?"

"I can't do it to you... to us... to Qiera..." his voice trails off.

I can almost hear my heart beat.

"I called him, and told him the deal was off."

I take a deep breath. "Does that also mean...?"

He shakes his head. "Honestly, I don't know. I can't answer that..."

I'm not completely sure if I should feel relieved.

Raden yawns. "I'm going back to bed."

"One step at a time..." he sings softly on his way up the stairs, carefully avoiding the stack of boxes.

Asyura - the tenth day of the Islamic month of Muharram when Muslims are encouraged to fast; Muharram is one of the four sacred months in Islam.

ayo - an expression of affirmation, "come on, let's go."

baju Melayu - a traditional Malay two-piece outfit of shirt and trousers for men, usually in plain colour. The long-sleeved top comes with an upright stiff collar and is occasionally worn with a sarong/kain pelikat instead of trousers.

briyani - Indian rice dish

ikan termenung - Indian mackerel

kain pelikat - a men's casual sarong, usually with checkered design

kebaya - Traditional attire from Indonesia, which consist of a close-fitting long or short blouse often embellished with rich embroidery, worn over batik sarong.

ketayap - a white skull cap worn by male Muslims

kicap - soy sauce

kopi luwak - a gourmet coffee from Indonesia that includes partly-digested coffee cherries eaten and defecated by the Asian palm civet.

lempeng pisang - a Malay-style banana pancake

Nyonya kebaya - a variation of the Indonesian Kebaya, worn by Peranakan people of Chinese ancestry in Melaka.

pak - sir

pak kiyai - the leader of a religious school / an Islamic scholar / a person who is knowledgeable on Islam

pasar - market

pesantren - Islamic boarding schools in Indonesia, usually in Java

puan - Ms

Puteri di Bulan - Princess on the moon

Puteri Sisir Emas - Princess with gold hair-combs

rakaat - a set of prescribed movements and words that accompanies a Muslim's prayers; each of the five compulsory daily prayers have between two to four rakaat.

sahur - the early morning meal that Muslims eat in preparation for the fast; the fast starts just before dawn and ends at sunset.

santri - student at a religious school
selamat siang - good day
Solat maghrib - prayer performed just after sunset; it is one of the five compulsory daily prayers performed by Muslims.
songkok - an oval-shaped, brimless and velvety cap worn by Malay Muslim men; it is usually black

tahajjud - a recommended but not compulsory night prayer performed by Muslims.

ABOUT RUMAIZAH ABU BAKAR

A traveller in life, Rumaizah Abu Bakar treats writing as a personal journey, be it fiction or non. Her public relations career and leisure travels open up worlds that not many have contact with. Among the countries that she has fallen in love with is Indonesia, whose culture and Islamic practices appear similar to her own, but only on the surface. Rumaizah is the author of *News From Home, The Female Cell,* and *A Call to Travel: Muslim Odysseys* (Journeys of a Muslim Woman through Turkey, Saudi Arabia and Indonesia), all published by Silverfish Books. She also contributes literary articles and book reviews regularly to a leading English newspaper in Malaysia. Visit her at acalltotravel.blogspot.com and follow her on twitter @rumaizah123.

THE AFFAIR

Rebecca Freeman

It was a chilly, rainy day, so there was only one other customer at the salon when Eleanor Prescott arrived. She pushed the glass door and the bell at the top jingled. So kitsch, she thought. But that was small town for you. Rob had told her it would be like this, when they decided to move here shortly after they had married. And for a while, it wasn't an issue. It had seemed quaint. It was a change from the hectic pace of the city, and she found a kind of gentle routine: shopping on Thursdays, pub meal on Friday evenings, tennis on Sunday mornings.

But the gossip. If The Painted Lady weren't the only hair and nail salon in town, she would not have bothered with it, but she didn't have much choice unless she wanted to go without haircuts.

Working from home, she only had to deal with the locals when she went to the supermarket or when she was out with Rob. But having her hair done once every six weeks was both a way for her to feel good about herself, and a reminder of the life she'd left behind in the city, when she'd worked in the office everyday, and appearances counted for something more.

Of course, appearances still mattered, here. But compared to the high-powered clients she had met with everyday, it felt like a step down. And Eleanor knew the other women could tell. She knew what they thought of her: she was a snooty bitch, she thought she was better than everyone else. It probably didn't help that she dressed like she had done in the city—tailored outfits, expensive shoes. She wasn't even trying to fit in, and they could tell. Most of the time, their opinions didn't bother her, but she did sometimes feel lonely. Not lonely enough to change how she behaved or what she wore, though. If she wanted to fit in, she would need to be someone else, not herself. She wasn't sure if she was willing to let that go, just yet.

"Eleanor!"

The owner, Sherry, stepped across the floor in her high heels and short, short skirt, and smiled briefly at her. She marked Eleanor's name off in the appointment book. Sherry was always very pleasant to Eleanor, but she gossiped so much about the other clients when they weren't there, Eleanor was under no illusions that she did the same once Eleanor had left the salon. "You're right on time. Take a seat, I'm just finishing up Ingrid over here."

She strutted back to a dark-haired lady with foils in her hair, and Eleanor sat and picked up a magazine from the coffee table.

"And I heard Michelle say he'd been out of town for a week," Ingrid was saying as Sherry fussed and patted the foils in place. "Poor Michelle. As if she's not been through enough. This is her second marriage, you know. And her first husband, well, you know what happened to him. Did you know what happened to him, Eleanor?"

Ingrid looked at Eleanor's reflection in the mirror, perfectly shaped eyebrows arched over accusing eyes, as if Eleanor had asked a question.

"Uh, no," Eleanor stammered, rather surprised that she was being included in the conversation.

"He disappeared. Went off to visit his brother in New Caledonia, of all places, and was never seen again."

Ingrid's voice was full of dramatic cliché. Eleanor half-expected someone to chime in, 'Dun-dun-DUN!' and stifled a chuckle by clearing her throat.

"Poor Michelle," she said.

"Yes, and now this. I don't know how the poor woman is going to cope."

"What is happening, exactly?" Eleanor put down the magazine. She had already read it last time, anyway.

"Well!"

Ingrid half turned in her seat, eager to re-tell the story, and Sherry gently but firmly turned her head back to face forward. Ingrid made do with simply fixing on Eleanor's reflection.

"Sonia, you know Sonia, who works at the chemist? She was at the post office and heard Michelle talking to her husband. And she was trying to whisper, but they were obviously fighting. And she was arguing with him about when he was coming back, and how he always said that, whatever 'that' was, Sonia didn't say. But she seemed so flustered when she got off the phone. And then Sonia said she went up to Mr Riley and asked him about mail redirection, and he said, 'Oh, are you thinking of moving?' and she said, 'No, it's not for me.' I mean, why would you ask that kind of thing? If you're not going to do it?"

Eleanor shrugged, not sure what the appropriate response would be.

Ingrid nodded, seriously.

"So we think it's definitely an affair."

Eleanor tried to swallow and choked a little, coughing into her hand for a moment.

"An affair?" she said, when she had recovered.

Sherry and Ingrid agreed.

"Definitely. Axel is having an affair, and Michelle knows about it."

"Axel is..." Eleanor trailed off.

"Michelle's husband!" said Ingrid, barely containing her impatience at Eleanor's lack of commitment to the town's family trees.

"Oh."

"*Exactly*," said Ingrid, with a knowing nod.

Eleanor didn't follow the logic, but she knew better than to question it. Once again, she was aware that coming to the community as an adult, rather than having grown up here, placed her at a disadvantage. These people had been steeped in the histories of everyone and everything local. Eleanor knew that with some strategic enquiry, she could find out more—the ladies liked nothing more than to share their knowledge—and it would certainly help her integrate. But it all seemed so very judgemental. How was anyone to know what happened in someone else's life? Or in their marriage?

"I just don't know why she's stayed with him for so long, frankly," said Sherry, finishing off the last foil and tapping Ingrid on the shoulder.

Ingrid stood and walked, stiff-necked, over to the other chair where Eleanor sat. She held her silver-clad head straight and picked up a magazine, then put it down as Sherry continued her train of thought.

"I mean, let's face it. Axel Johannsen has always been one for the ladies. I was surprised that Michelle ended up with him, to be honest. She was such a shy little thing back in high school."

"I heard that there was a pregnancy scare," said Ingrid.

"Oh, I didn't hear about that!" said Sherry, indicating for Eleanor to come and sit at the washbasin.

"Yes, and even though there was some talk of him going off with her sister... well, I think we all thought that it might have been a trick on her part to keep him. But you know, I don't think any of us really expected she'd have to put up with all these affairs over the years."

"There's been more than one?" Eleanor said, as Sherry ran the water in the basin, checking it for temperature with her fingers.

"Oh, I'm certain of it," said Sherry, firmly.

Eleanor sat back in the chair, leaning uncomfortably backwards. She tried to relax as Sherry massaged the suds through her hair.

"Ah, these men," said Sherry. "I don't know. I'm sworn off 'em, myself. I'll die an old maid, with my cats!"

She gave a cackle and Ingrid joined in.

"What about your Rob, Eleanor?" asked Sherry. "Got him on a tight leash, have you?"

Eleanor laughed. "Oh, well. There's not much you can get away with in a small town, is there?" she said. "I'm sure if there were something going on, someone would be able to tell me about it."

She kept her voice light, and the other women either missed the innuendo, or chose to ignore it. Instead, there seemed to be an unspoken agreement that this was the perfect place to end that conversation. They moved onto discussing the fact that whole chickens were on special at the supermarket at the end of Ember Road (not the one in Redfern Crescent), and that the high school play had been particularly good this year. Eleanor added in the occasional comment, but for the most part, she let her mind wander and began to think about the dinner she was cooking for friends that evening. She would pick up the shopping on the way home, she thought, and hoped that her Rob remembered to get the wine after work.

*

As she pulled into the driveway a few hours later, Eleanor noticed that the cars of both her husband and their friends were parked on the front verge. She sighed. She had worried that they might not come at the last moment, given the problems they'd had during the week. It would be good to relax together over a hot meal and a few glasses of wine.

Eleanor grabbed the shopping bags and walked in through the side door from the garage. She could hear voices in the dining room, so she was surprised to see a figure in the kitchen, filling the kettle. He turned and smiled at her as she bumped the door open with her elbow.

"Mrs Prescott," he said, putting the kettle on the counter and opening his arms open wide.

"Mr Johanssen," she replied, putting the shopping down and walking over to put her arms around him.

"It's been a long time," he said.

He pulled away slightly to look at her.

"Two months!" she said. "Far too long. And you should hear what the ladies at the hair salon have been saying about you."

He chuckled.

"Oh, don't keep me in suspense! Tell me everything."

She put her hand on his neck and kissed him tenderly on the lips.

"Maybe later," she said. "I need to get this meal cooking. You wouldn't be able to give me a hand, would you?"

He held on to her waist for a moment longer, and lent his head against hers.

"Do I have to?" he murmured. "Perhaps we could put the food off for a while and just…"

"Later," said Eleanor, firmly, but with a smile. "Your wife and my husband will be in here in a minute, wondering how the food is coming along."

Axel sighed, and walked over to pick up the shopping bags for her.

"Right, then. What do you need me to do?"

She placed two onions on the chopping board.

"You know where the knives are. Get chopping. We need some garlic as well…"

They fell into an easy rhythm, cutting up vegetables and chatting about work and laughing about their colleagues. Eleanor was recounting a phone call she'd had the week before when her husband came into the kitchen.

"I didn't hear you come in!" he said, walking over to kiss her on the cheek. "How was the salon?"

"Interesting," she laughed. "I'll tell you all about it over dinner. How was work?"

Rob shrugged.

"Same old. I left a little early. I wanted to be here when Axel and Michelle arrived."

Eleanor smiled at him.

"I'm glad you were. Where's Michelle?"

Rob indicated the other room.

"She should be in in just a moment. She had to use the bathroom. She said she wanted to change before dinner..."

He trailed off as Michelle came through the kitchen doorway. She was dressed in black stilettos, sheer black stockings, and elaborate lace underwear.

The three others stopped what they were doing. Nobody spoke.

"Michelle!" Eleanor said finally, breaking the silence. "Are they new shoes?"

Michelle grinned.

"Axel brought them back from Melbourne last week. You like?"

Eleanor and Rob both nodded without speaking, their eyes fixed appreciatively on the other woman. Axel laughed.

"I thought we were going to concentrate on the food?" he said.

"Oh," said Eleanor, turning the gas down on the stove. "I think it can simmer for a little while. I've made up the king-size in the spare room. We could do with working up an appetite, don't you think?"

She grabbed both Rob and Axel's hands and winked at Michelle, and led them all back through the house.

ABOUT REBECCA FREEMAN

Rebecca Freeman lives on the south coast of Western Australia with her Handsome Sidekick and too many children and pets. When not preparing food for everyone, she works as an editor and freelance writer, and drinks a lot of tea. You can read more of her writing at thisclimbingbean.wordpress.com or follow her on Twitter @path_ethic.

SPAR

Baylea Jones

I lost my virginity in Denton Miller's hayloft while the football team did keg stands in the cow pasture. Buzzed from Fireball whisky and the start of the school year, I snuck into Denton's barn just to show off. Jolie teetered up the wood steps behind me—a bottle of Boone's Farm in one hand. Grabbing her by the forearm, I pulled her so that she fell perfectly against my chest, her chin touching my own. We stared into each other's eyes, all serious trying to hold each other's gaze. When I looked away, overwhelmed by the moment, she laughed and rolled over beside me. I lit a cigarette to calm my nerves, clenched it between my teeth, and stared up at the rafters like they were stars. Jolie took it from my lips like she wanted a drag. Instead she smashed it against her boot and flicked it down to the dirt twenty feet below.

"Smoking ain't as cool as it looks, Myka," she said.

"That's debatable." I blew a perfect smoke ring and smiled. Jolie rolled her eyes.

We laid on our backs holding hands like we'd been doing innocently since grade school. Jolie nuzzled into my shoulder; I put my arm around her. She sang whisper songs to the ceiling like she was alone in the shower and not lying next to me. And her complete comfort around me made my stomach twist in a good way. I expected the kiss that came next because we'd been kissing in secret all summer. Jolie said we needed to practice especially since we'd be Sophomores and would finally get to go to the Homecoming Dance. The only problem was it didn't feel like practice to me. I'd kissed boys before, dares in the schoolyard or spin the bottle at a bonfire. That was practice. This was the real deal.

My stomach had been swirling around her for months, but that Fireball fuelled it even more. As our fingers clasped together, I wondered if she felt it too. All I could make sense of was that she smelled like honeysuckle, and it was intoxicating. I'd been at her heels like a hunting dog, and I kept wanting to sneak off with her, anticipating our next 'practice' session. Jolie sat up, took another swig of Boone's farm, and leaned in close.

"Kiss me. I know you want to," she said.

And I did want to kiss her. I thought about it every second. Sounds from the pasture below muffled becoming distant underwater voices, and it was only us. Just like that we were kissing. I could taste the strawberry wine on her tongue, sweet and tart at the same time.

We rolled around—hands tracing each other's bodies—kept switching positions because we didn't know what we were doing. Her hair was the colour of the hay, and I got my tongue tangled in it a few times, thin strands cobwebbing my mouth. Scratchy needles poked into my back, and mosquitoes swarmed our sweaty skin. I tried to mimic the moves I'd seen on grainy cable channels late at night, but her hip bone pierced my torso as I tried to slide my body smoothly against her own.

"Err... you're kind of hurting me," she said, staring off at a horseshoe hanging on the wall, either embarrassed or embarrassed for me.

"Sorry," I mumbled, pulling myself into a pushup position and hoping it would show off my biceps.

Her body, petite and pale, beneath my own. I wasn't big by any means, but compared to her, I looked bulky. I could slide my hand under her lower back and lift her up, do practically anything with her body, yet she was the one guiding my movements, telling me with her blue eyes what to do next. The air was heavy and humid in the loft, sticky in my throat like flypaper.

She pulled at her western shirt until each pearl snap unclicked and showed her tanned stomach beneath. I tried to unhook her bra, but it got caught so Jolie just did it herself. I put my hand in the waistband of her cutoff jeans. She unbuttoned them, pushing my shoulders down to her legs. I couldn't think, couldn't see, could barely even breathe. I kept coming back up, unsure of what her peaking breaths meant.

"Is this okay?" I asked. She nodded, pushing me back down.

I came up again, "Are you sure?"

"Shhh... shhh. Stop talking."

Afterwards I curled up beside her. The only sound I could hear was my own breathing. We laid in our bed of hay at the top of Denton Miller's barn while Kenny Chesney sang about being barefoot below.

"I love you," I said a few minutes later, sobered by what we had just done.

She shifted away from me, arching her back, a bow ready to spring. My words dissipated into the silence until even I was unsure if I had said them aloud.

"I'm sorry," she said, buttoning her shirt.

I didn't know if she was sorry to me or sorry for what we had done. She climbed down the ladder and walked up to her group of friends like she'd only gone to the bathroom. I breathed heavy, stroked the hay like it was her hair, and passed out alone at the top of the barn—feeling better than I've ever felt before and worse at the same time.

The sting of a horsefly on my cheek woke me up the next morning, circling my sweaty face like it was a pile of manure. I swatted it away and climbed down groggily, back damp from the dew, head pounding from the whisky. Only puzzle pieces of the party remained—Solo cups crushed on the ground, piles of chewing tobacco on the grass, an empty keg.

One of Denton's cows stared at me from behind the barbed wire like it was judging me. I stuck my tongue out at it, and I swear its lip curled up in a smirk. I couldn't believe Jolie didn't come back for me, that nobody even checked to see where I was. My Dad's pickup was still in the yard. Pissed off, I kicked the tyre as hard as I could, but it did more damage to me which only made me madder.

I drove home—huffing, puffing, and cussing at cows since there were no other trucks on the back road that early. It was a foggy, dew-heavy morning, dense air in my dry lungs. When I pulled into the Pelican Trailer Park, I braced. I hoped Dad would be passed out on the sofa or out fishing, but when I opened the door he grabbed my collar before I could even blink.

"The fuck's wrong with you, girl? Staying out all night like that and not telling nobody."

"Sorry," I said, jerking away from his grip.

"Drop the attitude. And give me my goddamn keys. You ain't taking my truck any more."

"Fine with me," I said, chucking them on the table.

I knew I was pushing my limits with him, but I didn't care. I waited for a reaction, but he just leaned back against the counter, cupped his elbow in his palm, and smoked a cigarette. I could feel his eyes on my back, judging me like Denton's cow, seeing that I was different in some way.

"You look like shit," he said, squinting his eyes in curiosity. "Take the couch, you sure could use some resting up."

"Thanks," I said, genuinely.

I slept, deep and dreamless, until dusk. When I woke up, Dad was sitting at the kitchen table, a slice of dusty light from the window illuminating his brow. He looked bored, maybe even a little lonely.

"'Bout time, sleeping beauty," he said. "Hungry?"

"Starving," I answered.

He tossed me the keys to the pickup. I started to say something, but he cut me off.

"Zip it, or I'll change my mind."

I didn't argue there. I just climbed in the truck, revved the engine, and drove to BeeBee Q's. Barbecue sauce—thick, sticky, and sweet—dripped down my chin. Dad and I had the all-you-can-eat ribs every Saturday night. We didn't talk much, never about anything personal, just ate and drank a beer at the bar while the bartender looked the other way.

I wanted to ask him about Mom, but I didn't. It was just something we didn't talk about. It was easier to pretend she never even existed than to remember. Hurt less that way. She'd been gone for four years, 18-wheeler accident on Highway 90. Dad and I had our own ways to deal with it, and that was pretty much to not deal with it at all.

❧

The halls buzzed at Votty High the next day. Everybody was talking about Denton's party. I started walking toward Jolie and I swear she saw me, but she stuffed her books in her locker and shuffled away. A few people looked at me, whispering and giggling like it was a child's sleepover. I just shook it off.

In PE I stood behind my locker door and changed into my gym clothes. Katie Breaux covered her chest when she saw me, a look of shock on her face like I had wandered into the wrong dressing room. I turned around and saw other girls doing the same thing—throw their hands up like it would deflect my gaze, keep them from turning to stone.

"What's going on?" I turned to Katie.

"Don't play dumb, Myka. We all heard about Denton's party," she said.

"What about it?"

"Well Jen saw you and Jolie sneak off in the barn together."

"So? We were... smoking a joint, that's it." I started to get uncomfortable, searching the eyes that were staring at me for Jolie's.

"Deny it all you want, but I'm not changing around a lesbo."

"Don't fucking flatter yourself, Katie." I slammed my locker door.

The locker room got quiet. I puffed my chest and stiffened my shoulders, a kind of posturing I learned from my dad. I wanted to hit her. I wanted to hit all of them. Jolie came up beside me and put her hand on my shoulder, but I kind of wanted to hit her too.

"Leave Myka alone," Jolie said.

"Oh, of course you're gonna stand up for her. What, is she your girlfriend now?" Katie said.

A few girls snickered, Jolie's face reddened. I actually wanted to know the answer. Jolie moved her hand from my shoulder and stepped away from me.

"She's not my girlfriend. I'm not gay," Jolie said.

I tried to catch her eyes, search for my own answers, but she wouldn't look at me. I grabbed my clothes, shoving my way past Jolie and Katie, and changed in the bathroom stall so no one would stare at me which seemed pretty damn ironic. I wasn't used to this kind of attention. People left me alone because I boxed, or they felt bad for me because my mom died.

I decided to stay in the bathroom for the whole class period. I couldn't go out into the gym, beneath all those bright lights, and pretend to care about a game of volleyball. I heard someone's feet shuffle on the tile so I folded my knees up on the toilet seat to keep hidden.

"Myka, I know you're in here."

It was Jolie. She leaned against my stall, her voice echoing off the wood. She spoke through the partition like Catholic confession. Hoping I could hear her breathing, I put my ear to the door. Our bodies were pressed against the thin veil between us, close but not close enough.

"I'm sorry, Myka. I just didn't want people to think anything was going on between us."

"But stuff *is* going on between us."

"Yeah, but other people don't have to know that. They won't understand."

"So, we can still be friends?"

"Always."

My shoulders relaxed, and I slid down to the floor, relieved. Everything would be okay. I still had Jolie.

"Shit, someone's coming!" Jolie said. "I'll catch up with you later. We probably shouldn't hang out as much at school any more."

"Okay, I'll call you," I said, coming out of the stall and facing only my own reflection.

Jolie was popular, but I'd seen her beneath the mask of makeup, in baggy sweat pants with morning breath. I'd stroked her hair when she cried about her dad missing her first gymnastics meet last year. I'd watched her go back and forth from the scale to the treadmill at the gym, saw her pick around her plate at dinner. I'd pretended to do homework while she sucked in her stomach in the mirror. I'd helped her straighten her hair before school most mornings. I'd watched her scribble lyrics about love, loneliness, and beauty in her notebook and strum her guitar the way I hit the punching bag: completely unrestrained. I'd checked out animal science books from the library for her and watched her play dumb in Biology class the next day. And in fourth grade when my Dad didn't have the money for the field trip to the state capitol, I saw her crumble up her permission slip and toss it in the trash. She sat next to me, asked what I was doing, and we became best friends over gossip and crossword puzzles.

She made popularity look seamless even though I knew she worked for it everyday. I might not have deserved what people said about me, but Jolie had a helluva lot more to lose. And we both knew it.

Jolie had been distant all week, but I understood her reasoning. She told me we'd go the first football game of the season together to make it up to me. I don't remember much about the actual game, whether the Pirates won or not, but I do remember her dirty blonde hair in a messy ponytail, that she had powdered sugar from a funnel cake on the corner of her mouth, and that every so often she'd look over at me and smile like I was the only person that mattered. Surprising me, she even squeezed my hand on the touchdowns. The school week was rough—rumours, stares, ostracising—but things were starting to die down, and Jolie and I were getting back our old closeness.

"Myka, can you get me a hot chocolate? Please, please, please?" Jolie asked.

"Of course! Anything else?" I said, jumping up.

"Ummm. Maybe a t-shirt. One with a pirate on it."

"Okay, sure." I said, knowing that I only had five dollars in my pocket, money I'd swiped from Dad's jeans while doing laundry.

The band kids were selling shirts to raise money for a competition or something. I bought two hot chocolates, spilling one on their table so I could stash a shirt in my jacket while they cleaned it up. Jolie said I was so sweet when I told her what I did. I convinced myself it was a date. And it was going perfectly until Colt Guidry showed up, squeezed his way into the six-inch space between us, and put his arm around her shoulder. He was wearing an LSU baseball cap, a blue corduroy FFA jacket, and way too much Axe body spray.

"Dyka!" he laughed, slapping me on the back. "Get it?"

"Fuck off, Colt," I said.

"Just a joke, Rousseau. Don't go all period rage on me."

"Cut it out, Colt," Jolie said, moving her shoulder out from under his arm.

"I'm just saying, Myka. I'm totally cool with two chicks if you know what I mean." He winked at both of us, and it turned my stomach.

"I never said I was gay."

"Trust me. You didn't have to."

Right then I wanted to melt into the cracks and hide beneath the bleachers. And it looked like Jolie did too which only made me feel worse. I left the game, kicking rocks in the parking lot at stupid pickup trucks hoping one of them was Colt's. I thought Jolie would follow me, but she just gave me a sad look and let me walk away.

The thing is somebody had seen both of us sneak off to the barn that night, but I felt like I was the only one getting any real shit for it. I thought about the differences between Jolie and me. She was in gymnastics; I liked to box. We wore similar sleeveless shirts, but hers were called spaghetti strap; mine were wife beaters. She wore makeup—layers of powder and gobs of eyeliner; I wore chapstick. She straightened her hair every morning; I tucked my wavy mess behind my ears or under a baseball cap. She was slim, with defined cheek and collarbones; I was broad-shouldered and muscular. I looked the part and everybody knew it. If Jolie kissed me, she was drunk and confused. If I kissed her, it was proof. And it wasn't her fault, but I blamed her for it.

As I walked across the empty town street, I wanted to smash all the storefronts in with a baseball bat. The lights were out in the drugstore and there was a sign that said: Closed for Friday night football. *Jesus Saves* was written on the water tower, and I thought about throwing myself off of it to see if it was true. Instead I went to Dane's Gym because it seemed a little more productive.

Mr D, Jolie's dad, owned the gym—which also doubled as a dance and gymnastics studio, a video rental store, and a fried chicken joint. He didn't go to the football games, which seemed blasphemous, but somehow he got away with it. When I walked in, Mr D tossed me the wrist wraps from the drawer without even looking up. He was reading the Votty Times, a two page newspaper with bake sale announcements and football victories on its front page. He had a Yosemite Sam moustache, a Marine haircut, and blue eyes a shade lighter than Jolie's.

I learned to fight from my dad, but Mr D taught me how. He was the karate coach and tried to push it on Jolie growing up, but she wasn't interested. When I started hanging around, he took to me like I was his own. We'd be in that gym every Saturday morning while Jolie sat bored in a corner thumbing through a Teen Beat or scoping out the newest video rentals. He'd teach me different stances, how to wrap my wrist, blocking, and new techniques every week. I never learned discipline. Mr D said that was my problem. I did learn how to land harder punches and that's the main reason I was interested in the first place.

"You're too hot-headed, Myka," he'd sigh.

Even though I liked the way I fought—careless and rough—I hated letting Mr D down. But I did constantly. Just like Jolie had by choosing barrel racing and beauty pageants. He thought I'd be the karate kid he always wanted, but I just liked to punch things. He stopped giving me lessons, but still treated me the same, and that was all I could really ask for.

I went a few rounds with the bag, fuelled by adrenaline. Wrist numbing as I landed blow after blow, sweat beading down my forehead, muscles tightening in my arm. I didn't know who I was hitting or what, but it felt pretty damn good. Each punch, controlled and calculated. I had all the power in my hands. I lost myself to the rhythm of the *thrawp, thrawp*. Chain jingling against the hook as the bag swayed. I shifted my stance: left, right, jab, jab, duck, up, uppercut.

"Closing shop, Myka," Mr D said, breaking me out of my trance. "You can fight your inner demons tomorrow."

"Inner demons?" I asked, but Mr D just shook his head and laughed.

I walked back to Pelican Park and watched the MMA fights on the couch until somebody knocked on the door. I opened it as Dad stumbled in drunk off his ass. Officer Toby popped his head in behind him.

"They kicked him out of The Bootleg so he threw a brick through the window and tried to climb back in," Toby said. "We're overcrowded tonight, but he'll still have to pay for the damage."

I just nodded and said goodnight. Really I didn't want Toby to leave him here like this. I kept the door open hoping maybe he'd stay in the driveway for a while, but the cruiser just drove away.

Dad looked at the TV. "Turn this shit off. Only pussies fight with gloves."

I handed him the remote, but he looked confused.

"What? No smart aleck remark?"

"I'm not in the mood. You wanna be drunk and belligerent, find somewhere else. I'm going to bed."

"The hell you are." He grabbed my shirt sleeve as I tried to walk past. "Sit your ass down."

"Dad, come on. I just wanna go to bed."

"Not until you tell me what's gotten into you."

He kicked out a chair. I slid into it, propping my cheek in my hand. He waited, watching me intently. Underneath the stench of smoke and beer, he smelled like Old Spice. He had the weathered rawhide skin of a Cajun who spent too much time in the Louisiana sun, calloused hands stained black from the pipeline, and yellowed teeth from the dipping tobacco he kept in his bottom lip. But right then at the corner of our kitchen table, I saw him soften.

"Wait, you ain't pregnant right?" he asked, almost a whisper.

Part of me wished I was. I just felt like that's what I was expected to be telling him. I shook my head. He took a deep breath, like he was relieved and more nervous at the same time. I sat in silence. I couldn't tell him. He was my dad, someone I hated and loved, but someone I could only connect to over ribs and beer.

Besides, saying "gay" or "lesbian" didn't feel right. It was a shirt I didn't fit in yet. The gays lived in California. They damn sure weren't found in Votty. All I knew was that I loved Jolie, and she was a woman and I was a woman too. It was normal to me even though I'd never met another person like it, even though I'd heard the slurs and knew it was something you didn't want to be.

"I just wish your mama was still here," he said. "I don't know how to do any of this, you know?" He slumped against the counter, something like a tear almost forming in his eye.

"I know, Dad. You're doing alright. Just go to bed, and stop getting into trouble."

Dad was a Gemini, two sides of the same coin. When he drank, it was a fifty-fifty flip. Either he'd be angry and yelling, or he'd be depressed and wallowing. More often than not, he'd go through both sides in the same night—starting high and energetic, breaking bar windows with bricks then wind down to a slumped heap on our kitchen floor.

Jolie and I went to the homecoming dance together near the end of October. Secretly, of course. Same-sex dates weren't allowed to go together so I went stag, and Jolie went with Colt Guidry as a cover. I wasn't particularly thrilled that she went with Colt, but she assured me it was just so people wouldn't talk.

She was beautiful in a sparkling blue dress with black heels. Curled hair in an elegant up do, fingernails painted to match her dress, a white shawl, red lips, thick black eyeliner that made her eyes glow. She looked like a woman, not like a sixteen-year-old girl.

I wore my dad's Old Spice, a pair of thrift store slacks, the cleanest button-up shirt I could find—royal blue to go with her dress. I put my wavy hair in a ponytail because I didn't know what else to do with it. Plucking roses from someone's yard, I made a corsage and pinned it to her dress after she finished getting ready in her bedroom.

"It's beautiful, Myka, but I have to wear Colt's at the dance. You understand?"

I didn't, but I nodded anyway. Even smiled. Her and Colt were in the line to buy their tickets a few people ahead of me. She kept looking back and winking, giving me chills. Our principal, Mr Stephen, was sitting at the ticket table. As I tried to hand him a crumpled bill, he refused it.

"What's wrong? It's five dollars, right?"

He hesitated, then sighed, "Myka, I'm going to need to speak to you. Stand off to the side for now until we get everyone else inside."

The other people in line craned their necks curiously. My face grew hot with embarrassment. Whispers started again like the ones I heard in the hallway the week after Denton's party. People made me nervous with their stares. Jolie looked back to see what was going on, but Colt pulled her into the gym.

"Why? What's the problem?" I raised my voice.

"We can't let you into the dance, Miss Rousseau." He looked me up and down uncomfortably. "Unless you change."

"Are you serious?" I said, heat swelling in my gut, fists clenched.

"We have a dress code. Female students must wear dresses to school dances. It's school policy."

The outfit I had been so proud of before began to suffocate me. I couldn't deal with the crowd of people standing around watching, listening. I walked away without another word, grabbed a flask of Fireball from my truck, and downed it in one burning gulp. Angry and buzzed, I walked around the school, found an unlocked door, and snuck inside. I could hear the bass from the gym, but the halls were eerily quiet and calm, empty and dark.

I ended up in a bathroom, hands bracing the sink, dry heaving with no luck. The face in the mirror didn't look like me. It was distorted, disgusting. I punched the glass, shattering my image into fragments, blood trickling down my knuckles, shards embedded in my fingers. I saw what everyone else had seen when they looked at me: a girl in a wrinkled men's shirt, messy hair in a ponytail, dark eyes, dirty nails, broad shoulders. A freak.

Thinking, in a moment of hope, that Jolie had been looking for me, I found another entrance to the gym. But what I saw was Jolie and Colt laughing together, dancing close, her head on his shoulder, his hand on her lower back. He whispered something in her ear, and she smiled at him the way she smiled at me in dark places. It wasn't fair that they could be together in public in a way that we couldn't. They made sense together, and I knew that, but I was too upset to be rational. All I could do was hate him, hate them both. I walked back to my truck—sharp pain in my gut, heavy head, stinging cuts on my hand. Finding a bottle of Jack Daniels Dad kept in the glove box, I took sips as the minutes ticked by.

Finally the parking lot started clearing out. I waited, watching intently each body coming out of the door. Growing impatient, I decided to find them myself. It was dark in the gym, streamers littering the floor, sticky puddles of punch. I saw their shadows in a corner, and then only flashes after that: their lips together sloppily smacking, her nails in the hair behind his ear, his hand under her dress.

The first hit was hard, split my knuckle right open on his tooth. After that, I don't really remember. I just started laying on him like he was the punching bag at Dane's Gym. We tumbled over onto the floor. I missed a few times because he kept grabbing my forearm. Colt looked up at me like I was crazy, and I felt like maybe I was. He turned his face to the side, peach fuzz stubble, beady green eyes. I missed again as somebody grabbed my shoulder, snapping me out of the rage.

"Stop it, Myka! Leave him alone," Jolie pleaded.

And I did stop, just long enough for Colt to squirm away. But I didn't care. I had a new target. I wanted to hit her so bad. I even raised my fist.

"Shut up, you dumb slut!"

Her eyes watered at the brim. She looked afraid, guilty, and heartbroken at the same time. I had to stop looking at her because it pissed me off. In that moment there was no love, only anger. Colt spit blood into my face, yelled some vague threats, and walked away with his arm around Jolie's shoulder like he was protecting her from me. She looked back, but I never met her eyes. I just stared at the waxy gym floor and pretended not to see.

I decided to drive down Highway 90 to clear my head, trying to finish the bottle of Jack on the ride. Had one hand on the wheel, the other on the bottle. My daddy's Chevy swerved through the back road, the only light from the moon. No houses or street lamps, just cow pastures stretched flat for miles. 18-wheelers roared as I sped past them, mud flaps slapping against big tires. Soon Votty was just a match in the dark, a blip on a map.

The rotten egg smell from the petrochemical plants filled the cab. I straddled what was once No Man's Land, the Sabine River a slit from Jean Lafitte's cutlass creating the border between Louisiana and Texas. The road looked empty and endless, probably not much different from the days of pirates and highway robbers, until it wasn't.

I heard the siren first. I'm pretty sure my eyes were closed so I didn't see the lights until they were blinding in my rearview. I knew it'd be Toby. He liked to hide in the brush and catch kids coming home from parties. He was the only Votty police officer to care about drunk driving or speeding. I just don't think he had anything else to do.

He came up to the side of the truck, twirling his little flashlight and whistling off-key like this was the highlight of his night. I rolled down the window, grinned, and held up my bottle.

"Don't worry, officer. It's empty."

"Jesus Christ, Myka?"

"In the flesh."

"Goddamn spitting image of your dad if you ask me. Drunk, cocky, with blood on your knuckles." He sighed. "Go on, get out of the truck. I'm bringing you home. I won't take you in this time."

"Aw damn. And here I was looking forward to it."

"Just get in the car. I really thought you were smarter than this."

"Yeah well sorry to disappoint you. Seems I'm not what a lot of people thought."

Toby would have let me ride up front, but I didn't want to. I felt like I deserved to be in the backseat of the police car. He didn't try to talk to me, just kept sighing and shaking his head dramatically every few minutes. My head was pounding so hard, my heart actually ached, and I'm pretty sure I dozed off a few times on the short ride.

We pulled up to Pelican Park, and it was weird to be on this side of things. I'd watched from the front door my dad being un-cuffed and brought back like a stray dog many times before. Always drunk, usually bloody, shirtless a couple of times, and cussing at anything that moved. And here I was following in his footsteps, becoming the image of my father I swore I'd never be.

"You know, Myka. You were lucky tonight, driving around the same area your mom was killed, and drinking no less. What's gotten into you?"

I didn't answer, but I wanted to. I was angry at him for even bringing her up, trying to dislodge a memory just to get a reaction, teach me a lesson. Yet I was thankful at the same time that someone remembered, that I wasn't crazy after all.

I just walked away, rounded the corner, and saw Dad waiting on the steps, empty beer cans crushed around him. My stomach hit my feet like a lead sinker. I stood in front of him, sank my shoulders, and braced as much as I could in my drunken state.

His hand was hot against the back of my neck as he grabbed me. My eyes were closed as if not seeing would be the same as not feeling. But when I didn't feel anything, I opened one of them. He was staring me down, unblinking black eyes, chin stubble grey at the tips.

"Are you out of your goddamn mind?" he yelled.

I shrugged my shoulders, stared down at my shoes.

"Look at me! Or I swear to god..." He shook me.

But I couldn't do anything. My whole body ached; I just wanted to go to sleep. I slouched back against the trailer and passed out. Dad shook me awake, and I threw up, all over that blue dress shirt—the stench making me gag again. I choked it down, nauseating artificial cinnamon taste burning my throat. I squeezed my eyes shut so he wouldn't see me crying.

I tried to stifle my tears, but they poured out. I was so overwhelmed. Every emotion I had hid in the past few weeks, years, came pouring out. It was loud and it was messy—throaty sobs, tears, spit, snot, and vomit streaking my face. I'd never cried this way in front of anyone, especially Dad. Hell, I don't think I'd ever cried that way in my whole life. Not even at Mom's funeral.

I was hysterical. I couldn't respond. I couldn't stand up. Everything was heavy. I felt weighted to the ground. The more Dad yelled and threatened, the less I could do. He shook me, he tried to pull me up, but nothing. I just sat there, slumped against the wall, head swivelling back and forth, shaking and sweating at the same time. So he left me out there and went inside.

A few hours later, he kicked my shoe to wake me up. The sun was starting to creep over the trees, a pink and yellow swirl. At least I could stand at that point so I did. He waited for me to say something, give him an explanation. I just laughed.

"You think this is funny? Coming home in a cop car, drinking and driving, getting into fist fights. Huh?"

"I learn from the best, right?"

He slammed me back against the wall, my head jerking, hit hard. Re-energised now, the rage was back. I pushed him off, made him stumble. He caught his balance and popped my mouth with the back of his hand. It stung, hot and prickly. Wiping my lip, I saw blood and it was that and not the pain itself that made me charge at him. I had him

164

like I'd had Colt on the ground, towering over his face, a clenched fist. My adrenaline surged—veins sparking, a live wire. I reared back, but I couldn't hit him.

"Do it, you fucking coward." He spat at me.

I just kept punching the gravel right next to him. Over and over. I'd aim for his face, that scruffy chin, that bulge of dip in his bottom lip, but I'd veer at the last minute and hit the ground, a fistful of rocks. I'd get pissed from the pain, making me want to hit him even more and just end up doing the same thing again.

He was my dad, and I hated him in that moment, but he was all I had. I saw myself in him. Not just the parts I hated about us both, but the vulnerable ones too, the soft spots underneath. I think he wanted me to hit him. I think he thought he deserved it, that if I hit him it would make it okay that he hit me.

"You're the coward! You think you're so tough, but you're not. You're just insecure, weak, a scared little..."

I stopped, not knowing who I was talking to. Him, me, Jolie? He shifted his weight, rolled over, pushing me off, and walked inside. I sat there stunned, shaking and heaving, hunched over with my fist still raised and throbbing. A door slammed and he threw my already packed duffel bag to the bottom of the steps.

I put the bag on my shoulder and walked across town to Dane's Gym. The first morning train roared by and I counted the boxcars like I used to do as a kid. After it passed, kicking up a swirl of dirt-dust, its rumble growing fainter the further it went, Votty seemed even calmer and quieter than ever in comparison. There were no fathers and daughters fighting it out on their neatly mowed lawns, just perfect families sleeping soundly in their beds. The streets were empty, birds were chirping, and the only thing they had to worry about was someone like me hobbling down main street, bloody and confused.

The gym wouldn't open for another hour or so, but Mr D never locked the back door. I snuck in, took a nice hot shower, and washed away the dirt, blood, vomit, and tears. After I tossed my old clothes in the dumpster out back, I curled up on the blue gym mat to rest, feeling safe and protected but completely alone.

I thought Mr D would wake me when he opened the gym, see me bundled up in my hoodie, a duffel bag as a pillow. He'd joke with me, make the whole thing light hearted like it was any other day, maybe even bring me a cup of coffee. But the key clicked in the lock and Jolie's silhouette stood in the doorway. I sat up, looking at her looking at me, waiting to see who would speak first. She tossed the keys on the desk, the sound startling in the quiet. She just came over and wrapped her arms around my shoulders. I wanted to resist, say something mean, hate her, but I sunk into her arms, blonde hair tickling my cheek, that sweet smell of honeysuckle on her neck.

"I'm sorry, Myka," she whispered into my shoulder.

She squeezed me tight then let go. Pulling back, she studied my face with sad eyes. She lifted my chin, brushing her thumb on the split in my lip. Her eyes were on my lip, mine were on hers. We kept glancing back and forth between eyes, lips, eyes, lips. I turned away, embarrassed or overwhelmed. Her touch made everything tingle, hairs raise, heart thump. It was too much.

She sat back against the wall mirrors with me, our shoulders barely touching, a million things unsaid floating around us. We were quiet for a while just listening to each other breathe and feeling the heat of each other's bodies so near, but not quite near enough. Finally she spoke, tension fading with each word.

"I haven't been a good friend to you. I know that," she said, voice cracking.

"It's okay."

"It's not. I wanted to love you back, I tried, but I..."

"Look, you can't choose who you love any more than I can," I said, just so I wouldn't have to hear her say it aloud.

"But you're my best friend, Myka. I need you."

I felt sick. I knew this would be the last time we'd talk this way— honest and intimate. I knew this was the end. It had to be. There was no going back to the way it was before that night in the hayloft.

"I can't be just friends with you," I sighed. "And you can't love me like I do you."

"What are you saying, Myka?"

She found the answer in my eyes and hugged me again, pulling me close into her chest. She held tight like she didn't want to ever let go, and I didn't want her to. I let my body fall limp, resisting the urge to hug her back and make it harder for myself. She nuzzled my neck, kissed my cheek, the side of my mouth, my forehead. I felt the warmth of her cheek against my cheek, the softness of her lips on my chin, the tickle of her touch.

166

I cried, a soft whimper that I let her hear. I'd never cried in front of her before even though she cried in front of me many times. I was the strong one, the protector, and here I was letting her hold me and kiss me and make me feel like everything would be fine when we both knew it wouldn't. So she wiped my tears as we sat tangled up in each other's arms on the floor of her father's gym.

❧

That afternoon I walked to BeeBee Q's, duffel bag on my shoulder like an outlaw. I ordered the usual, ribs and beer, and the bartender slid a bottle down to me even though I wasn't with my dad. I sucked the bones dry, lost myself in the primal feeling of it all. A hand rested on my shoulder and turned me around on the swivel stool.

"I went by the gym today, figured I might find you there and apologise," Dad said. "You and that Dane girl looked pretty close so I just left you alone."

I kept eating, licking my fingers like I couldn't hear him. But my heart was pounding. I fidgeted in my seat, anxious and afraid.

"I can't believe you did all of this—the drinking, fighting, acting out—over a damn woman."

"Well, isn't that what you do?" I smiled, looked up at him.

He shook his head and laughed, "Girl, there's a helluva lot more to aspire to be than me."

"Sometimes, you ain't so bad," I said.

He pulled up a stool, ordered a beer, and we ate our ribs in a quiet closeness.

ABOUT BAYLEA JONES
Baylea Jones is a fiction student in the MFA program at UMASS Boston. Though she is originally from Louisiana, she currently lives in Northampton with her wife. She enjoys the New England weather, but misses southern food.

Draupadi Hallucinating

Rochelle Potkar

My dreams are in five—
fractions of a whole vision.

I am quenched by as many men,
some viciously,
some in pure intent
before my thirst uprises again.

One man usually never has it all, Karna.
If valour, then no moral strength.
If dharma, then also infinite boredom.
If vigour, then oblivious foolishness.
If not, then no good looks or focus,
or muscle power equalling a hundred.

But with you, it shall never be enough, *Surya putra*.
Light not heat is what I seek.
But who ever goes close to the sun that illuminates her?

At a distance I see you whole.
You possess focus, dharma, might, purity, beauty.
Also, I imagine, the cunning of my *Sakha*.

But even if I have it all,
must I also possess this yearning for you,
appropriating in each limb equally,
in the wailing, waiting silences of my unstoppable body?
I am a well-fed woman, Karna,
yet it is your armour that worries me.

It won't feel my warmth nor my reproaches.

In the Mahabharata epic, Draupadi had five husbands. This was in answer to a boon granted by Lord Shiva in her previous birth, where she desired for fourteen qualities in a husband. Since it wasn't possible for one man to have all these qualities, she ends up marrying Yudhithira for his wisdom of dharma; Bhima for his strength; Arjuna for his courage; Nakula for his beauty; and Sahadeva for his patience. Yet, there is a notion that she desired Karna, who fought against the Pandavas—Draupadi's husbands—in the famous Kurukshetra war.

ABOUT ROCHELLE POTKAR
Rochelle Potkar's stories and poems have appeared in several Indian and international publications. A few have won awards. She has read her poetry at several festivals and gatherings. Her first book of stories, *The Arithmetic of breasts and other stories* was shortlisted for The Digital Book of the Year Award 2014, by Publishing Next. Her next book, *Dreams of Déjà vu* is a speculative novel. She lives in Mumbai and blogs at: www.rochellepotkar.com. Twitter @rochellepotkar.

DOMINION HOTEL

Mo Reynolds

Remember the Dominion Hotel, Fiona? Place was so run-down it leaned over the sidewalk onto the street, staring into the windows of the hotel opposite like some red brick Peeping Tom. Before we lived there, it was a residential hotel for sailors and old bachelors. Now it's Single Room Occupancy for the homeless, the addicted, and the lost. In other words, it's for people like me.

It's been eight years since we moved in together. We were nineteen years old then—college kids who couldn't return to school. You wore a sleeveless plaid shirt as you carried boxes filled with our lives up the stairs. I think you wore that shirt to look butch but it only emphasised how small you were, how your blonde hair fell in waves down your back. Our new place was tiny with a mattress, fridge, and hotplate in one room, but it was the first thing that was ours together—our own heaven.

I'm still here at the Dominion and Jean is too, like she's always been. She was here before any of us came and she'll be here after we go. However we go. Rail thin and ancient, Jean occupies her room like she was born there. Her couch, shag rug, and bookcase have been there so long, they're covered in some type of organic fuzz. The rug has balls of food and hash and other crap coming up from its base, like plants growing in rayon soil. Hermetically sealed, that's Jean. Sealed in her apartment baggie just like the ones she sells.

I'm writing this on the roof of the Dominion, my back against the crumbling brick chimney. I like to get up here when I can, when it's not raining too hard and Jean doesn't need me, and have a think. That sounds good, doesn't it? 'Have a think.' But it's not true. I don't think much when I'm up in my chimney seat with the strutting pigeons. I watch. I watch the suburban kids lining up for bars promising cheap drinks. I watch my neighbours, emaciated and twitching on the corner as they resume their search for the perfect poison.

Watching how people walk, I can tell those who have love from the ones that don't—the suburban kids swagger down the street like they own it, while the skids sidle along the perimeter, shoulders hunched to protect their soft bellies from the pack. I understand. I'm alone too, but up here it matters less. Here I can pretend I'm a god watching the world from my crumbling brick paradise—alone and aloof—until I look at the Hotel Winter. You know it, the residential hotel across the street. It's also red brick and old, but its bricks are redder, the windows unbroken, and the doorway always free of shopping carts. I've stared at that building for hours over the years, hoping to catch a glimpse of you. And I did once. Just a slim silhouette on the window shade, but I knew it was you—I could feel it. I told myself I'd be going over there as well soon. Once I got my shit together.

Remember the toilet in our closet? Only our suite and the one above had them, courtesy of an aftermarket septic pipe tacked on the outside of the building. At night the wind would whistle through that pipe into our room like a ghost. It was through that toilet that we met Jean. I should say it was Jean's leaky toilet that led to our meeting, but I won't scratch that sentence out because it's closer to how I feel about Jean now than anything else I can think of.

You noticed the water leaking on that first day. It was coming from the ceiling. It was brown.

"So gross!" you said. "I'm going up there!"

That's the Fi I remember—take charge but never any shit.

Jean was drinking a Bud when she opened the door, her lips furrowed around the mouth of the bottle. She offered us one.

"But it's still morning," I said. The people in Jean's apartment laughed.

"Sorry ladies," she said after we described the leak, "it's an old building and the landlady's a slob."

"Yeah, who *is* that?" I asked between sips of beer.

"Me," Jean smiled.

We all laughed and Jean's helper, Ace, said he could fix the toilet no problem.

"See girls?" said Jean, "I'll take care of you."

Remember the Gravitron ride at the fair? One minute you're standing in a barrel with your friends, then the walls start to spin and the floor drops out. There's a thrill of terror as you go down, followed by delicious relief as an unseen force catches your fall. That's how I felt when my father kicked me out of the house. But unlike the Gravitron, there was no law of physics to keep me from dropping—I just stayed in a queasy free-fall. Then I met you and the falling stopped. We were both broken but, like a miracle, the shards fit.

That first night in the Dominion you came to me in a threadbare t-shirt, nipples shaded pink under white cotton, and I'd never seen anything so beautiful. Your warmth was a beacon to me as you crawled under the sheets. And when we breathed together, I felt losing everything was almost worth it. Almost.

"I love you, Jules," you whispered in the dark.

Every time I see a Christian cross, I hear my mother's voice. Why can't you be like other girls? Why do you dress like that? Cut your hair so short? Why don't you go to church any more? Whatever answer I gave, it was never right.

"Oh God," Mom would whisper, fumbling with her rosary.

"Why are you talking to Him? It's *his* fault, not mine."

"Julia! Shame!" she would say, "It's never God's fault. It's *us*!"

My father said something similar when he found out I was gay, but he was speaking of my shame, not mankind's—certainly not his own. He was a jerk and a drunk but my mother just saw it as bad luck—her punishment for some latent sin. She loved him anyhow. Mom died before I came out. I wonder if she would have still loved me.

You worked nights at the drug store processing other people's family photos while I stayed alone in our room, no money, no computer or phone. Every night I'd lay in the dark listening to the wind whining in the septic pipe, longing and lonely. Jean had a lot of parties. The music and laughter coming from above made me sadder and emptier than I'd been since leaving my father's house, when I'd puked from fear and grief in his hedge.

One night the isolation was finally too much. I knew I had to talk to *somebody* or I'd fling myself out the window. I tamed my curly hair and walked upstairs in my pyjama bottoms.

The people in Jean's room smelled of cigarettes and filthy clothes, but they spoke to me when I came in and gave me beer. Blues music was playing and Jean sat on a couch in the middle of everything, an overflowing ashtray in her lap. With the cigarette in her hand and cross about her neck, she reminded me of my mother—surrounded by people, yet somehow alone.

"Hey, Kiddo," she said as I sat down beside her, "I was wondering when you'd turn up."

Being Jean's friend had perks. Our neighbours were nicer to us and Ace delivered my Welfare cheques on Wednesdays. He walked you to our door after your late shifts and the guys in the building stopped suggesting you suck them off in the stairwell. Then there were the free drugs.

Ace had been enjoying that perk for years. His arms and neck were dotted with needle marks and he often reminisced about the good Quaaludes Jean had in the seventies. His full name was Ignatius, like the saint.

"My mom's crazy religious," he said once, "Awhile back her house caught fire but she didn't call nobody for help. Just stood outside praying for a miracle."

His mom lived on the Rez and Ace talked about going back to see her before she died but he fretted about leaving.

"Jean's been a mother to me too," he would say, laughing. "My Drug Mom."

I don't remember why you and I started fighting but I know it was my fault. I was going to all Jean's parties by then and life had become one long foggy day. I was sleeping when you left for work and partying upstairs when you came home—or puking in the toilet.

"Ain't nothing wrong with losing yourself once in awhile," Jean would say to me. "Don't let that girlfriend of yours tell you what to do."

She gives me advice like that a lot, just like a real mom.

I spotted for Jean yesterday, watching for cops on the street while she worked the rooms. I sat on the hotel steps and held a paperback up like I was reading. It was over an hour before I noticed. And then I laughed. All that English I took in college, yet I'd been 'reading' the book upside-down.

"Working the rooms" is Jean's term for checking the tenants for drugs. Government funding for the Dominion is based on a bunch of rules, including no drugs. Jean's changed this rule to read 'no *outside* drugs' but of course it's not written down anywhere.

"Gotta have rules," she says. "It's a matter of safety."

Residents will do the drugs anyhow, she reasons, and the ones she sells are much safer than what they get on the street.

I rested the paperback on my nose and watched the cart-pushers shuffle down the empty street like it was the day after the apocalypse. The Hotel Winter's entrance was silent and clean but its windows were lined with people's lives: pictures, knickknacks, a shirt on a hanger fluttering in the breeze. I detected a warm presence from somewhere inside—your beacon. Then a car passed and our connection was lost. *No matter,* I thought, *I'll join her soon.* When I get my shit together.

It was through the toilet that we heard Ace die. You were in our makeshift bathroom crying after another fight. Hearing you cry tore at my heart, but I said, "You can't control me with tears!"

It was 3am when the screaming started. I ran in to tell you I was wrong, that I'd stop partying and we'd leave this place, but it wasn't you making that noise. The screams were coming from our toilet, from the pipe—horrible, strangled cries. Listening close we recognised the voice but could do nothing to help. One thing we learned at the Dominion— mind your own business or someone will mind it for you.

"Don't worry," I said. "Jean'll stop it."

Ace was her helper, her servant. She never left the building; he was her proxy in the outside world. Jean wouldn't let anything happen to Ace, I reasoned. She needed him.

But the screams continued.

You ran to the door. I pulled you away. Together we looked into the hall but there was no one there. All those tenants awake behind the walls yet there wasn't a sound except Ace's cries echoing through the place, rattling the flimsy doors.

Back in our apartment we couldn't get away from it. We plugged our ears with toilet paper, beat the couch with our fists, then finally we collapsed on the bed, exhausted, and cried. I covered our heads with pillows and slowly, impossibly, his cries became white noise. I didn't realise we'd fallen asleep until the screech of morning gulls woke me.

"They got him in the alley," said Jean. "Not on my territory. I couldn't trust Ace anyhow. He was always talking about going home to his *mom*. Not like you."

I drank the thick percolator coffee and felt ill.

When I got back to our room you said, "Is it over? Please Jules. Let this be it!"

You wanted to move to Hotel Winter where it was safer but I told you I couldn't leave, that Jean needed me. You cried but I didn't feel I had any choice. We all need family—even Jean.

I have to be careful where I sit on this roof, between the bird-shit, the rain, and puddles of old puke. Vomit is something you tend to forget about until it's happening, again, and you remember how strange it is: visceral and dirty, yet cleansing—a purging of poisons. When it happened again today I thought, *Maybe if I puke enough, I'll get rid of whatever's wrong with me.*

And then I thought of all my neighbours in the Dominion purging themselves in the same way at that very moment.

Does that make this place a purgatory?—I thought, remembering my Latin—maybe The Purgatory?

I wonder what my rosary-fondling mother would have thought about that.

This morning started out as usual. I got up at twelve-thirty, had a whisky for my headache then went up to Jean's for coffee. I'd been dreaming of you again and the warmth of your beacon still lingered around me like a blanket. When I told Jean I was going to Hotel Winter to find you she looked like she'd sucked on a lemon.

"I wasn't going to say anything, cause it's just a rumour," she said, "but Fiona's dead."

The air left my lungs. I couldn't breathe, couldn't speak.

"It's just a rumour. Understand? But yeah, I heard that. Sorry, Kiddo."

Jean's a big liar. I've heard her tell some real whoppers to people: tenants, social workers, the cops, her drug suppliers. Her lies kept people happy and the Dominion running smooth.

"Lies and spies," Ace used to say. He would know. It was then I realised how Jean saw me. Not as a friend or surrogate child—I was her puppet—her property—just like everything else in the Dominion. Her Dominion.

I watched Jean drag on her cigarette then slurp some coffee, then suck on her cigarette again. The lines around her mouth are deeper now and as I watched them converge around her smoke her mouth reminded me of a puckered asshole. How much crap had spewed out of there over the years? I'd lied plenty too, sometimes at Jean's command, sometimes just out of habit. I wondered if my mouth looked like hers now and a wave of revulsion rippled through me.

"I gotta use your toilet."

I didn't throw up right away. First, I looked in the mirror. Some people say they never look in a mirror, like they're so humble, but you can bet they'll at least give themselves a passing glance. Especially women—they know what they look like. I can say for sure that, up until that moment, I had not looked at myself for at least a year, maybe longer. Jean's mirror was corroded and broken, but one corner was still useable. In it I saw a stranger's face, drawn and lined around the mouth and eyes, and surrounded by a pale halo. It took me a moment to realise what that halo was and it was then the fear-sickness really hit. My dark curly hair had gone completely grey.

First I puked, and then I cried, the pale face in the mirror crumpling like a piece of paper. Back with Jean, I held my coffee mug with both hands, feeling the warmth through the plastic, but no longer wanting to drink. Jean lit another cigarette and poured us whiskies.

"We give the finger to the Devil every day," she said, winking at me.

I used to love Jean's sayings—found them comforting somehow—but today I got up and walked away mumbling that I had to check on Lucille in 2B. No one had seen her in awhile and people were complaining about a smell in the hall. I felt Jean's eyes follow me to the door and down the hall.

I've been sitting here in my chimney seat for hours now, trying to think. All the time I've watched people from up here, thought about them and their lives, I'd never once tried to think about my own. It's hard enough to remember the past let alone your place in it, not with my foggy brain, so I decided to write you a letter. I laughed, I cried, I puked some more behind the chimney, but mostly I wrote. Every word I write now, I realise that I was wrong. Oh Fi, I'm so sorry!

I used to think mistakes were just something that happened to you. You'd fuck up, feel regret, then you'd walk away telling yourself it wasn't your fault. Not *really*. Now I know, you make enough mistakes they stop being the exception and become your life. I never became a writer like I wanted, but I saw in Jean's mirror that I'd written a story all the same.

I believed my free-fall ended when I met you, that I was safe at the Dominion. With Jean. But I was falling the whole time. I saw that in the mirror too.

I'm going to Hotel Winter now to find you. If you're not there, I'll look all over this city. If Jean's right, if you're dead, then I guess I'll go find you there. Either way, my time in Purgatory is done.

"Doesn't matter," I say as I get up to leave. Everything ends eventually.

I'm rolling up these pages now and stuffing them in a gap between the crumbling chimney bricks. When the time comes to knock this place down, someone will find this letter. And with every word they read, we'll be together again.

ABOUT MO REYNOLDS

Born on the Canadian Prairies, Mo now lives on the Pacific coast of Canada. She attended the Simon Fraser University Writer's Studio where she studied under mentor Steven Galloway (author of *The Cellist of Sarajevo*). Published in the *Emerge Anthology*, Mo has also written for local music zines and is currently working on a novel. She lives in Vancouver, BC with her partner and two adoring cats and likes music, beer, and dark alleyways—not necessarily in that order. You can find her on Twitter at @mo_reynolds1.

Churriye

Khadija Anderson

The bedroom was dim and smoky. Seynaba was dressing and had not yet put on her top. She didn't care that I had walked into the room, and she didn't try to cover herself. This was typical in Senegal. Women were all sisters, no matter that we came from completely different worlds.

Seyneba greeted me and pulled on her top while standing near the incense and fanning it with her long wrap skirt. She bent over and let the sweet smoke fill her loose top and curl into her braids. She was burning the *churriye* for her husband Modou. It was her night with him and the *churriye*, like the ceramic beads clicking softly around her waist under her skirt, were for his pleasure.

Seynaba lived in a two room shack in Medina, Dakar's oldest neighbourhood. It couldn't be more different from Modou's first wife's house which was in an upper class neighbourhood in Dakar near the University. Seynaba had walked by it once with a friend. Modou and his first wife had been married for twenty years and had three children together. Seynaba was eighteen and had met Modou at a wedding where he was the lead Sabar drummer. She had danced in front of him, her skirt flying open as her knees lifted high while she jumped and spun. The sequins on her short betcho caught the light and glittered around her upper thighs and crotch. Later that night Modou stopped by her house and gave her a gift of a gold coloured watch and a month later she agreed to marry him.

Seynaba's sister Kodu walked in and greeted us. The two started speaking Wolof too fast for me to catch more than only a word here and there. They repeated two words several times, *goor* and *xalis*; man and money.

Yassa, Modou's favorite meal of rice and vegetables, was prepared and Seynaba put on filigreed gold earrings and a bracelet. She turned on the propane furno to boil water for tea. Seynaba was already pre-occupied with the idea of Modou returning to his first wife's house in a day or two. She would try to keep him as long as possible.

Betcho - a short skirt worn as underwear
Churriye - homemade incense considered an aphrodisiac
Ferno - a propane burner used for cooking
Goor - man in Wolof
Sabar - traditional Wolof drumming featuring 7 drummers
Senegal - a country in West Africa
Wolof - the main language spoken in Senegal
Xalis - money in Wolof

Yassa - a Senegalese stew made with onions and rice

ABOUT KHADIJA ANDERSON
After 18 years exile in Seattle, Khadija Anderson returned to her hometown of Los Angeles where she runs a monthly social justice themed series "Poets & Allies for Resistance" featuring poets of colour. Khadija is a Pushcart Prize Nominee, and her first book of poetry, *History of Butoh,* was published by Writ Large Press. She can be found at khadijaanderson.com.

FLESH AND STONE

Dominica Malcolm

Marc was lost to them the moment he set foot in the ocean. He and Felicia had stayed on the beach for some time alone while their travelling party returned to the hotel so the children could go to sleep.

Felicia and Marc laid side-by-side on a blanket, looking into each other's moonlit eyes. Their fingers entwined, dark against light. Felicia's ginger hair streamed across her neck, under her chin, while Marc's black hair lined his head in tight cornrows.

Marc's face scrunched up in confusion. "Do you hear that?"

"The crickets?" Felicia asked.

"No. A woman singing."

Felicia strained her ears with no success. It didn't matter which way she looked. She sat up. Then stood. Nothing. She shook her head.

"It can't just be my imagination," Marc said. He looked out at the Andaman Sea. "It sounds like it's coming from out there."

Felicia's gaze matched Marc's, but still she heard nothing.

🍃

Back in the hotel, as Pradeep was tucking in Felicia and Marc's daughter Kayla, he paused, entranced, and walked to the window overlooking the sea. Mei walked into the room and saw him staring out. Her face contorted, one eye partially squinting as she noticed the sheet only half covering Kayla. She finished Pradeep's task before joining him at the window.

"*Sayang*, what..." she started to ask, only to catch her voice in her throat as she saw Marc in the water, Felicia pulling at his arms, trying to get him back to shore. "Stay here with the kids," Mei whispered, then turned and tried to walk calmly back out of the room.

As soon as she closed the door behind her, Mei ran as fast as she could through the hotel and back to the beach. By the time she got there, all she found was Felicia kneeling in the shallows with her head in her hands.

Mei slowly walked over to Felicia and lifted her up from behind with her forearms under Felicia's armpits. When Felicia turned around, Mei leaned up and kissed Felicia's forehead.

When they were finally able to make their way back to the blanket to sit down, Mei held Felicia's hands in her own and asked, "Leese, what happened? I only saw a little from the window upstairs, but Marc wasn't suicidal. What made him go in the water?"

"I... don't... I don't know. One minute he was hearing things, and the next I was trying to get him to stay with me. It was like he couldn't even hear me by that point."

"What did he hear?"

"A woman singing."

Mei's breath caught in her throat.

"What?" Felicia asked, searching for answers in Mei's eyes, suddenly afraid.

"Did he say what she was singing about?"

Felicia shook her head. "He said it was in Thai."

"Shit," Mei said, standing.

Felicia stood with her, looking directly at her. "Mei, you're scaring me. I didn't hear anything. He was just imagining it, wasn't he?" She paused and looked back out at the sea, half-hoping to see Marc's head pop up out of the water, trying to catch his breath. "Shouldn't we call the coastguard or something? Get a search party out there to look for him?"

Mei's mouth widened across her face and her brow furrowed. "I don't think they can help."

"Why not? He might not have drowned. He could still be out there somewhere. Or... at least..." Felicia took a quick intake of air and tried not to choke on her next words. "His... body. They could retrieve him."

Mei shook her head.

Felicia tapped Mei's chest, pushing her a step backwards. "He can't be gone. What aren't you telling me?" Tears began streaming down her face. "Why can't we just call for a search and rescue?"

"Because they won't believe what actually happened. I don't even know if you will. I'm afraid... I cursed us. I didn't mean to, you have to know that. But it sounds like Sasi is back." Mei paused and took a breath. "I haven't seen her since before we met you and Marc. She tried to take Pradeep from me before. Twice. I had no reason to believe she would come for Marc, though. If I did, I'm sure I would have said something. No matter how crazy it would have sounded. At least then you'd have had some warning... some chance to stop her."

Mei's breath was short and heavy now.

"Mei, you're not making any sense. Who is Sasi?"

Unsure how to explain, Mei started folding the blanket. Felicia watched with concern.

"Who's Sasi, Mei?"

After shoving the blanket into a backpack and throwing the backpack over her shoulder, Mei took Felicia's hand in hers. She started leading them back to the hotel.

"Sasi was a woman Pradeep was with a long time ago. Like, a decade. We were in our early twenties then. He cheated on me with her."

"But how the hell does that relate to Marc drowning?"

Mei stopped walking, and brushed some hair out of Felicia's eyes. "Marc didn't drown. Sasi pulled him under, to God knows where. She's... God, I don't even know how to say this without sounding insane. Sasi is a mermaid now. Or a siren. I don't know exactly. Somehow she turned into one when she died. I only know because I've seen her tail. And she almost took Pradeep the same way."

"Okay... let's say I believe you... why would she do that?"

"She blamed me for her death."

She poisoned me. Felicia went stiff as she heard a thick Thai accent in her mind. She cupped her head on either side of it as those words penetrated her brain over and over. *She poisoned me. She poisoned me. She poisoned me.*

"Oh God, don't tell me she's in your head now too," Mei said, grabbing Felicia's wrists. "You have to block her out."

Mei leaned in and kissed Felicia square on the lips as the Thai woman's voice faded from Felicia's mind.

"She thinks you poisoned her?" Felicia finally asked as they parted.

"It was an accident," Mei replied with defeat. "I was trying to come around and accept her being with Pradeep too. I cooked her dinner and everything. I didn't know she was allergic to peanuts. I mean, she's *Thai*. They eat satay just like us Malaysians. I thought peanut allergies was just a white people problem."

Felicia looked back toward the sea. "Are we safe?"

Mei took Felicia's hand again and started leading her back to the hotel. "I'll feel safer once we're back with Pradeep. I don't understand all of this, but I'll explain what I can then."

They found Pradeep staring out the living room window when they returned.

"Can you hear her?" Mei asked.

Pradeep didn't respond. Mei approached him slowly, then stood in front of him. His eyes didn't see her; they were hollow, looking straight past her. Mei leaned up and kissed him softly on his lips, bringing him out of his trance.

"Oh, Mei, I'm so glad you're here. It's Sasi. She's back."

"I know." Mei paused to take a deep breath. "She took Marc."

Pradeep furrowed his brow and stumbled backwards. "This is all my fault." He turned around and found Felicia staring at him. "Filly, I'm so sorry." He embraced Felicia in his strong arms and kissed her forehead. "We never should've brought you and Marc and the kids to Phuket. This is where she was from." Tears started forming in the corners of his eyes. "I thought this was over." He parted from Felicia and took Mei's hand. "*We* thought this was over."

Felicia looked at the two of them with confusion. It was a lot to take in. Feeling herself lose balance, she sat down on the couch behind her.

"What happened last time you encountered her? How did you survive, Pradeep?"

Pradeep and Mei were eating al fresco at one of the restaurants that overlooked the main canal in old Malacca. It should have just been a routine date night after long days at work for each of them. Mei in the hospital, performing surgeries, and Pradeep fixing cars and motorbikes.

Mei was caught mid-bite of *mee goreng* when she noticed Pradeep sitting unnervingly still and staring at the canal. When Mei followed his sightline, she dropped her fork on her plate and spat out her noodles.

"Miss me?" Sasi said with a sickening grin as she stood against the balustrade, naked.

"But... you're dead," Mei replied.

Pradeep remained eerily stationary.

Sasi's smile widened across her face. "I know. No thanks to you, murderer... you changed me, and you will pay."

Using her hands, she lifted herself onto the balustrade and fell backwards into the canal, snapping Pradeep back to life. Mei swore she saw a large fish tail emerge from the canal for a split-second afterwards.

They spent the next six weeks being haunted by Sasi's voice in their heads. Mei heard disconcerting words, threats, and accusations, increasingly terrifying. Pradeep heard her singing in Thai, but rather than the disconcerting feeling Mei got, Sasi's voice was comforting to him. It was like he understood her, and wanted to be with her all over again.

One night when Mei was working late at the hospital, Pradeep followed Sasi's voice to the beach. She was laying naked in the sand, waiting calmly with her stomach and thighs beneath her, feet crossed above her thighs, and chin resting on her entwined fingers, propped up by her elbows in the sand.

When Pradeep inched closer, Sasi stood, revealing her full form. White specks of sand contrasted against the tan skin on her stomach, thighs, and lower half of her breast.

"I'm glad you finally came," she said, walking toward him. "I've missed you." She leaned up half a foot to pull his head toward hers, and kissed him deeply. When she pulled away, she thumbed the thin scrub of hair on Pradeep's chin and added, "I like this new look."

"You can't be here, Sasi," Pradeep said, stroking her hair. "I miss you, too, but you died. This isn't natural."

"And it was natural for your Chinese bitch to murder me?" Sasi replied through gritted teeth, stepping out of Pradeep's reach.

Pradeep furrowed his brow. "Sasi, that was an accident. She didn't mean it."

"I don't understand why you believe her." Sasi took Pradeep's hand and started walking him toward the water. "You should be with me."

Pradeep's phone started buzzing in his back pocket, but when he went to reach for it with his free hand, Sasi took that hand, too.

"Sasi, Mei is my *wife*. I've known her since we were ten. I know what she is and isn't capable of, and I know she couldn't have done that intentionally." Pradeep searched Sasi's eyes for some semblance of understanding but couldn't find any. "Sasi, I—"

Sudden lips on Pradeep's mouth interrupted him. His memories of passion past overcame him, and he allowed himself to be drawn into the moment. Pradeep gently lowered himself backwards into the sand, pulling Sasi with him.

Sasi pulled Pradeep's t-shirt over his head, discarding it beside them, and pressed her bare breast against his chest. She pushed him backwards so he was laying in the sand. Pradeep's eyes rolled backwards as he closed his eyes, treasuring the trail of kisses she began planting on his hairy chest.

"This is just... like... Cherating," he said between breaths as he remembered one of their secret trips on the opposite side of the Malaysian peninsula.

Pradeep's phone vibrated in his pants again, but he was too involved in the moment to notice.

"I remember Cherating," Sasi said, making her way back up his body. "That was a beautiful beach. You were so adventurous."

"You showed me the ropes," Pradeep said, cupping her buttocks in his hands. "It was like I was doing everything for the first time."

Sasi ran her nails over Pradeep's shoulders, causing him to moan a little. "I still remember when we met. When you walked into my fish spa in KL, looking so unsure of yourself. You didn't want to be there. You told me your wife convinced you to come."

"She swore by the therapy. She—"

"Let's not think about her right now. I don't want to think about the woman who killed me. I want to focus on you. I'm going to make you come, here and now, and later, you will join me, we'll do it in the sea." Sasi smiled and reached into the front of Pradeep's pants.

Pradeep gasped and arched his back.

Then, in a matter of seconds, he felt hot goop speckle across his bare chest and face. When he opened his eyes, he saw Sasi's severed head staring blankly at him in the sand, then felt her remaining body drop on top of him, where more of her blood pooled on his chest from her neck. He looked up and saw Mei in her surgical gown holding a blood-stained machete in her hand.

"What did you do?" Pradeep asked with wide-opened eyes.

"I'm getting rid of her for good, apparently," Mei said, pulling a plastic bag from her pocket before inserting Sasi's head into it. "Which is more than I can say for you. I mean, what the actual fuck, Pradeep? You were going to have sex with the ghost of your ex-girlfriend?" She tied the plastic bag's handles into a double knot.

"I don't know. She wasn't exactly a ghost, was she? I mean, she was corporeal. I can still fucking feel her—" he remembered, then scrambled out from beneath her. He stood up and looked at his chest. "This is disgusting, Mei. Couldn't you have at least waited until I was further away?"

"And miss a perfect surprise opportunity to give her a chance to escape? No way."

Pradeep shook his head. "You couldn't even warn me you were planning something? I mean you must have been planning something. Why else would you happen to have that machete?"

"What, like how you warned me you were going to meet her?"

"No need to get sarcastic about it," he said, and walked into the water to clean the blood off. "How did you know where to find me anyway?"

"You weren't answering your phone. I tracked the GPS and when I saw where it was, I just had a bad feeling. I knew I had to come. Spirits are nothing if not vengeful. Who knows what she could've done if I hadn't come?" Mei swung the head-filled bag around in circles before finally tossing it as far as she could into the water.

Pradeep had a difficult time washing the blood off his chest, getting clumps away from the hair. "She loved me, Mei. I don't think she would have hurt me."

"Maybe not you," Mei said, lifting up Sasi's legs to drag her body to the water, "but she had it in for me. Can you give me a hand with this?"

Pradeep looked over at her and groaned. "This is sick, Mei," he said, moving slowly toward her.

"And what's going to happen if we don't dispose of the body? At least you're already wet."

"Can't you at least show some compassion? I cared for Sasi. What you're asking me to do..."

"She. Was. Already. Dead." Mei pulled Sasi's body right up to the tide, then walked around it and started rolling her into the water with her boots. As soon as the tide washed over Sasi's legs, blue scales started to form, until they fully transformed her legs into a tail. "What the fuck?"

Pradeep stared at the tail. "I guess this doesn't make her a ghost... she's a... a... a mermaid?"

"Whatever the fuck she was, she's dead now. Please just get rid of her."

Pradeep shook his head and closed his eyes before taking Sasi's soft hands in his one last time. He swam with her for a while before pulling her deep under the water while Mei watched from the shore.

When Pradeep returned, blood-free, Mei had already covered up any evidence of blood and body dragging on the beach.

"Thank you," Mei whispered. "It's a relief to no longer have her voice inside my head."

*

"So you killed her again?" Felicia asked. "And she somehow survived *having her head cut off*?"

Mei nodded. "I guess so. How was I supposed to know that, though? We haven't heard anything from her in years."

"Well what can we do now? Can we capture her? Find out if she can bring Marc back?" Felicia spilled out her questions rapid fire. "But if he's dead, I want her dead, too. And if beheading didn't work, we'd better find out what will. I wouldn't be able to live with myself knowing we didn't try."

Pradeep looked to Mei. "What if she can't die?"

"I won't accept that," Mei said. "There must be something we can do to find out what works. I'm not going to risk anyone else's life. If she took Marc, then who knows what else she's capable of?"

Felicia took out her iPhone and started Googling for mermaid mythology and lore. If mermaids were real, or mermaid spirits, then maybe something about them on the Internet was actually true.

"Can we just sleep on this? Maybe it's over now, maybe it's not, but it's late, and we can't think clearly like this," Pradeep said.

"And we have better attention to detail when the kids are awake? I know I can't concentrate when they're screaming in my ears. Especially Jacob. You know how he gets. And what if Sasi comes for him next? He's only two." Mei's breath was loud by the time she finished her thought.

"Why would she come for our son?" Pradeep asked.

"Because she wants to take everyone away from me that she can? Because she's jealous you didn't have a kid with her instead? I don't know!"

Pradeep began pacing the room. "Maybe I can reason with her. Maybe I can get her to leave us alone."

"And if that doesn't work?"

"Hey, I think I found something," Felicia said, scanning the words on her phone. "It talks about spirits becoming mermaids. It says they only every appear between sunset and sunrise. Maybe something happens to them during the day? What do you think?"

"Yeah, maybe," Pradeep said, picking up his pyjamas. He started changing into them as he continued, "That fits. We never saw or heard from her during the day. But would that make it easier or harder to find her then?"

"I suppose it depends what happens to her when the sun is up," Felicia answered, "This site only lists theories. It suggests disappearances, invisibility, hibernation, the sun taking away their power..."

"The Internet isn't going to have answers for this," Mei said with her arms folded. She turned from Felicia to Pradeep. "We may have to use you as bait, *sayang*. Capture her at night and keep her out until the sun comes up. Do the research ourselves. Because even if people have killed a mermaid before, it's not going to be online."

"Well she's not calling to me now, so can we just get some sleep and figure it out tomorrow?" Pradeep moved in to wrap his arms around Mei and kissed her forehead.

"Fine," Mei replied, lowering her head.

Pradeep moved into their bedroom and left the women to get ready for bed. Felicia was still scrolling through blog posts on her phone until Mei came up, turned it off, and took it out of her hands. She put the phone on the table next to the couch, then took Felicia's hands to lift her up, and kissed her on the lips.

"Let's get you out of these salt-encrusted clothes," Mei said, pulling Felicia's shirt off with care, as it was stiff from the seawater from when she'd tried to rescue Marc. "I'm so sorry about Marc," she added, changing the subject, "but we will get her for this."

"What if he's not dead, Mei?" Felicia asked, stepping out of her stiff denim shorts. "What if we can get her to bring him back?"

Mei led Felicia to the bathroom and turned the shower on. "I don't think he could have survived being underwater that long, Leese."

"I want answers," Felicia said, raising her voice. She dropped her panties and stepped into the shower. "I want to know why she took him."

Mei replied as she undressed herself. "Then we'll do what we can to capture her alive, and make her tell us. Leese, I love you." She stepped into the shower with Felicia. "I want to do this for you."

She brushed a lock of Felicia's fringe behind her ear, and Felicia leaned in to kiss her.

Upon turning around, Felicia allowed her grief for Marc to fall from her eyes and be washed away with the shower water as Mei held her from behind. Mei rested her head against Felicia's shoulderblade, and kissed her ever so slightly.

"We'll make this right," Mei whispered. "I'm so sorry."

Just before dawn, Pradeep sat upright in bed. Beside him, Mei laid naked, arms wrapped around Felicia's bare stomach, and head nestled into Felicia's neck. Pradeep followed the song in his mind to the bedroom window, overlooking the sea. The moon was close to full in the sky, and there was no sign of the sun, which would be rising from the opposite direction within thirty minutes.

Sasi's voice called to him, and Pradeep found himself moving toward the door to the hotel's corridor at least somewhat against his will. He wanted to call out to Mei, to let her know he was leaving, to find Sasi, but his voice was gone. He was wearing his pyjamas in the hotel lift by the time Mei felt a chill on her back and she realised he was gone. She quickly searched the hotel room and found no sign of what happened.

Mei shook Felicia awake. "Stay here with the kids. Pradeep's missing; I need to go find him. I have a bad feeling that Sasi might get him too, if she hasn't already."

"Yeah, go," Felicia blurted, immediately jumping out of bed.

The kids were still asleep, but Mei threw on the first things she could find to wear—a pair of jeans, foregoing underwear; a tank top; a hoodie; and her sandals.

When Mei got to the lobby, she asked the lady at the reception, "Did you see an Indian man walk through here recently?"

The lady nodded, and in her Thai accent replied, "Yes, it was very odd. He was moving slowly and I tried to ask him if he needed any help, but he would not reply. He just walked right out in his bed clothes."

"Thank you," Mei said, exasperated.

The lady opened her mouth to respond but didn't have a chance before Mei let loose a series of curse words and ran out of the sliding doors herself.

By the time Mei got to the beach, Pradeep was only a couple of feet from stepping into the water. Mei dug her toes deep into the sand with each step she took sprinting toward him. He was knee deep in the water before she managed to kiss him, jerking him out of his daze.

"Mei." Pradeep let out a long sigh. "Oh my God, Mei. I thought she had me."

Mei pressed into Pradeep's shoulders, urging him to walk backwards out of the water. He was slow to move with her, but focusing on Mei's eyes as she talked helped.

"We only have a few more minutes before the sun comes up. You can hold out until then. We can do this. I'm here with you. But once the sun is up, I'm going back out there. I'm hiring some damn SCUBA gear and I'm gonna find that bitch. I'm not waiting until sunset so she has another chance to overpower you again. And since she seems to have a power over you that Leese and I are immune to, you're staying with Jacob and Kayla, and Leese'll come with me."

They were sitting in the sand by that point.

"I can live with that," Pradeep said. "I don't feel safe going under there. It's too risky for me, no matter what state Sasi is in."

Mei nodded, and grasped Pradeep's hand in a tight grip. "Can you still hear her?"

"She's definitely still out there." Pradeep gripped her hand back. "But I feel like she can't get to me when you're here too."

Mei tried to smile, but Pradeep could tell from her eyes that she was terrified inside. He hoped she had what it took to get rid of Sasi for good, but he didn't know how to tell her that. Up until now, a part of him had believed Sasi still loved him and wouldn't do anything to hurt him. Now he knew the only thing on her mind was revenge, and there wasn't anything he could do to stop it himself. All he could do was let her go.

"We need to go back to the room," Pradeep said.

Mei shook her head. "I want you close enough to the water that she stays there when the sun comes up and we can find her. I'm not letting this go on another day."

"She's getting closer," Pradeep said. "I think this is a mistake."

But before he could get Mei to change her mind, Sasi was walking with her hands, pulling herself out of the water. Her tail soon hit the sand, and transformed into legs.

Mei and Pradeep stood up; Mei standing in from of Pradeep to protect him.

"You can't have him," Mei screamed.

Sasi calmly walked toward the pair. "Twice now you've tried to dispose of me," she said. "When will you learn that you cannot destroy me?"

Mei wanted to scream obscenities at her, but then she thought about Felicia's face in the shower the night before.

"Why did you have to take Marc? He doesn't have anything to do with this."

Sasi continued walking toward them. "You're wrong. I want you to know that anything you touch will be mine. I'll take that Australian of yours, too. You know I'll find a way."

"Sasi, you have to stop this," Pradeep yelled, tears streaming down his face.

The sun started hinting at its arrival behind them, with touches of pink entering the sky on either side of them.

"Keep her talking," Pradeep whispered in Mei's ear. "The sun will be here soon. We'll see what happens then."

Sasi's eyes narrowed on Pradeep and her mouth widened. "I can still hear you. I know what you're thinking, and it won't work."

Sasi rushed at them faster than they would have expected, knocking Mei to the ground. She grabbed Pradeep by his hair and started trying to drag him toward the sea. It was a struggle, though. She may have had some super powers, but she lacked super strength. Pradeep fought with her by planting his hands in the sand every few feet when she continually managed to pull him out. When they were inching ever closer to the tide, Mei managed to recover. She ran toward them and jumped on Sasi, tackling her into the water. Sasi's tail appeared and flailed about, knocking Mei back.

"This isn't over," Sasi yelled through gritted teeth. She dived into the water, leaving Mei and Pradeep alone.

The sun broke the horizon.

"You know why she fled, don't you?" Mei asked, watching the sky get brighter. "We're onto something. We need to find her when the sun is up. I can feel it in my bones."

Pradeep nodded. "Let's get back to Felicia. We need time to prepare, and we need to get out of these clothes."

✐

By midday, Felicia was prepped with the details of what had transpired, and she and Mei hired a boat and SCUBA gear. They directed their driver to various segments of the sea, and searched underwater in thirty minute intervals, trying to find some sign of Sasi.

On their fourth return to the boat with nothing to show, their driver asked, "Why you go where nothing is? Why not search sunken ship from hundred years ago?"

Mei looked at Felicia. "I guess it would be a good hiding place for her."

Felicia nodded and turned to the driver. "Okay, take us there."

The driver manoeuvred the boat to the location, and wind blew Mei and Felicia's hair about as he sped over low waves.

"We only have a few hours of daylight left, Mei. What are we going to do if we can't find her?"

"Don't think so negatively. I have a good feeling about this next spot. It makes sense, doesn't it?"

"Sure, but it's still a risk that we won't find her there. The ocean is enormous; she could be anywhere. Maybe it would be easier to catch her on land."

"Let's give this shipwreck a chance. If we can't find her, we'll go back and try your idea."

The driver slowed down, getting closer to the dive site, and the women began preparing their equipment. They checked their tanks and put their masks back on. As soon as they were told where to dive in, Mei and Felicia were in the water.

Felicia followed Mei to the shipwreck. It was an old eighteenth century-style tall-ship, but looked to have some more modern fixings. Felicia had had a fascination with nautical history as a way to procrastinate from studying computer science when she was at university. She wished there was a way she could have combined the two in her career, but instead she was stuck programming bank security systems in Malaysia. If she was honest, she'd prefer to be programming games where pirates battle the Spanish and English in the seventeenth and eighteenth centuries. She wondered if this whole mermaid saga would be the push she needed to make that change. After all, don't pirates and mermaids practically go together?

Mei and Felicia swam into the forecastle and found remnants of canvas hammocks hanging from various posts. Barnacles and seaweed covered the wood planks. But there was no sign of a mermaid.

Felicia led the way aft to the captain's quarters and found strewn furniture and stone statues. A captain's bust and... a wide-eyed mermaid. Felicia waved Mei over because she didn't know what Sasi looked like. She shrugged her shoulders with a questioning expression, and Mei responded by swimming closer to the statue to inspect it. Mei's gloved hands ran over every inch of the stone, touching the scales on the tail, running fingers over the hair, face, and eyes. The mermaid's arms were outstretched over her head as if she was mid-dive when she was made. Or turned to stone.

Mei nodded at Felicia with eyes bigger than Felicia had ever seen them, then grabbed the mermaid's wrists, and began swimming toward the captain's door. Felicia followed, and grabbed the mermaid's tail to assist Mei as they swam back to the boat.

When they breeched the surface, Mei wrapped her legs around the body of the statue so she could hold onto the boat with one hand and remove her mask with the other.

"Pass me some rope," Mei called to the driver, who did as he was instructed.

Mei passed the rope to Felicia under the water, who wrapped it around the mermaid's body before she, too, surfaced and removed her mask.

"You think this is Sasi?" Felicia asked.

"It looks like her."

"So we're going to drag her up onto the boat? Question her when she comes out of this state?"

Mei nodded. Both women climbed back onto the boat, then pulled on the rope to drag Sasi on board with them. As soon as the stone met the air and sun, it turned to ash.

They stared as more and more ash flaked away the more they pulled on the rope, until Felicia stopped Mei and dived back into the water to grab the tail before the rope let it drop deeper. Felicia wrapped her legs around the tail and pulled herself up over the side of the boat, but as she did so, ash began to cover her legs.

Felicia's breathing got heavier as she considered everything she had just seen. "So," she finally said after a couple of minutes. "Here's my theory. She's properly dead now. Mermaid are never seen in daylight, because that's what kills them, like how it kills vampires in some stories about them. Also, their bodies turn to stone during daylight hours as an extra protection for themselves, so they don't accidentally expose themselves to the sun. That's why Sasi left you and Pradeep when she did this morning. And maybe this is how they sleep, like how vampires are supposed to sleep in coffins during the day to hide from the sun."

Mei looked at the driver who had just witnessed all of this, and heard Felicia's theory. Whilst Mei was unsure how much English he was able to understand, he clearly didn't know where he was supposed to look or what to do next.

"Take us back to shore," Mei instructed, and he was all too happy to go ahead with that, likely not wanting to be part of such a confusing conversation to an outsider.

As the boat travelled back, Felicia asked, "Well? You didn't tell me what you thought of my theory."

"I hope you're right," Mei said. "But what if she can piece herself back together from the ashes the way she did when I'd severed her head?"

"When some of it is still covering my legs?"

"I don't know. I guess we'll just have to see if she comes back to-night. Or in several years."

"Now that's a scary thought. Having to wait years, not knowing if we actually got rid of her for good."

Mei nodded. "But until then, I think we just have to try and lead a normal life."

"What if there are more mermaids out there, doing this to people?" Felicia asked.

Mei took a moment to consider the idea. "I suppose there probably are. But it doesn't have anything to do with us."

"Mei, you've dedicated your life to saving people—"

"Medically, yeah—but Leese, this is different. We got lucky. We were able to do this because she came after us. I wouldn't know the first thing about finding another mermaid who didn't want anything to do with us."

Felicia watched the beach as they neared the jetty to dock. "I guess you're right. But what if we catch wind of any mermaid signs?"

"Are you actually suggesting we become mermaid hunters? Leese?"

"Honestly? I don't know. I didn't get to talk to her. To find out what really happened to Marc. I want to understand, and finding another mermaid to talk to is the only way I can. If they have to die, too, so they don't hurt anyone else, then so be it."

"You're in mourning, Leese. Killing more mermaids will not bring Marc back."

Their boat docked, and Mei paid the driver an extra large tip in the hopes he would keep quiet about the incidents that occurred at sea. They had pre-paid for his time and use of SCUBA equipment.

Mei and Felicia removed their wetsuits, wrapped towels around themselves, and put their sandals on to walk back to the hotel.

"I know it won't bring him back," Felicia said. "But if I can help stop this happening to someone else... if I can help another woman avoid the pain of losing someone like this... then I want to do that. It seems so much more valuable than only spending my days working for a bank the rest of my life."

"What about Kayla? What about Pradeep, and me, and Jacob? Can't we just try and have a normal life together?"

"What normal life?" Felicia asked. "We're already far from normal because we were a quad that'd now turned into a triad with children. Kayla's already lost her father, and I've yet to even tell her."

"How are you going to tell her?"

Felicia shook her head. "I don't know."

*

Pradeep was reading a book to Kayla and Jacob on the floor when Mei and Felicia returned to their hotel room. The women sat down on the sofa while they waited for Pradeep to finish, but when Kayla noticed her mother, she interrupted Pradeep.

"Mummy, where's Daddy?"

Felicia sighed, and took hold of the four-year-old's hands. "Sweetie, I'm afraid there's no easy way to tell you this... Daddy's not coming back. Something happened to him last night, and he's gone to live with the angels in heaven now."

Though Felicia didn't consider herself religious, she figured that if mermaids were real, then there was a chance angels were, too. And that's a more comforting thought to give a child than telling her that a creature like her favourite Disney character killed her father.

"Daddy died?" Kayla asked.

Felicia's eyes welled up with tears. She nodded.

"I want to see him!" Kayla screamed. She jumped up and down and the brown curls atop her head bounced as she yelled continuously. "I want Daddy; I want to see him."

Tears streamed down Felicia's face. "You can't, honey. He's been taken away. We can't find him."

"Then how do you know he's dead? Maybe he just ran away."

Felicia shook her head. "No, honey. I saw him drown. That's why we always tell you to be careful in the water. We didn't want that to happen to you."

Kayla's lower lip trembled before she collapsed to her knees.

"But Mummy's still here. I'm not going to let anything happen to you. And Uncle Pradeep and Aunty Mei will look after us. They won't let anything happen to you either."

Kayla turned her head to look at Mei and Pradeep to see if that was true. They nodded at her with sad eyes.

"I miss Daddy," Kayla said. The light brown skin of her face flushed red.

"I know you do, Kayla. I do, too. And we will miss him for the rest of our lives. That won't go away. He loved you very much. I'm sure he'll be watching over you with the angels."

Kayla just looked back at Felicia.

"We can put more pictures of Daddy around the house when we get home," Felicia said. "Maybe that will remind you that he's still going to watch over you."

Kayla still didn't reply. Instead she stood up, picked up a couple of books from the floor, and stormed out of the room.

Mei wrapped an arm around Felicia's shoulder. "I think that went as well as we could have hoped."

"I feel like I failed her."

"No. You avenged his death. You did everything you could have. When she's older, you can explain it better, but now... this is all you could do."

Felicia shook her head. "No. I can do more. I don't want any other child to lose their father this way."

"God, Leese. At least take some time to mourn your husband before you up and decide to hunt the damn things. It might not be so easy next time." Mei looked concerned with her eyes narrowed in on Felicia.

"I'm not going to jump right into it; that's not what I'm saying. I just... I need to do some research. Find out more. See if I can find others who've had these encounters. Something. I don't want to just sit back and do nothing."

Mei nodded. "In the meantime, I think we should go home. Report Marc's death to the police so we can get his death certificate, and then go home."

"Practical, Mei," Felicia said with a sad smile. "Can you take care of that? I don't think I can leave this place now until it's time to go home."

"Whatever you need, Leese. I love you." Mei planted a kiss on Felicia's forehead. "Marc may be gone, but we will get through this together."

"Thank you," Felicia said, squeezing Mei's hand. "I love you, too."

ABOUT DOMINICA MALCOLM

Born in Australia, Dominica spent half of her twenties living in Malaysia before moving to the San Francisco Bay Area, where she now regularly performs improv with Leela's YUM! and the LGBT troupe LiGht BrighT. In her novel, *Adrift*, you can see where she originally developed the mermaid mythology that features in her story in this anthology. She has also been published in numerous other collections. Her first anthology, *Amok: An Anthology of Asia-Pacific Speculative Fiction*, was shortlisted for Best Anthology in the 2014 Aurealis Awards, and showcased her passion for diversity in storytelling. For more information about Dominica, visit her website at dominica.malcolm.id.au.

SPIRALLING HOME

Karen Sylvia Rockwell

I had a feeling
almost right away
of familiarity
when she smiled
a shy smile
but with a
confident edge
welcoming me
to a place I know now
is home

how does it happen
when beings
born across cultures
in different countries
and years apart
find each other
and know each other
and defying convention
find their way through the controversy
to love each other?

do you think we plan it out before we're born?
playing hide-n-seek
posing challenges to our soul mates

to find us again
a gem in a New York City night?
Or do we just
spiral home?

ABOUT KAREN SYLVIA ROCKWELL

Karen Sylvia Rockwell lives in Belle River, Ontario with her partner Sandy, and their dog Kasey Marlowe. She attributes much of her inspiration to her work as a counsellor and to her colourful, many facetted, extended blended family. Since her Ma passed away in 2008, Karen has become fierce about writing, diving into workshops and readings. She is celebrating the recognition her work is receiving, including being awarded 1st Place in Room Magazine's 2013 Poetry Contest. Karen's work appears in *Room*; *The Saving Bannister*; *Deep Water Literary Journal*; *offSIDE*; *The Grief Diaries*; *Napalm and Novocain*; *Vanessa Shields's Poetry On Demand, vol.2*, and is featured in anthologies by Cranberry Tree Press; The Ontario Poetry Society; Polar Expressions Publishing; Ascent Aspiration; Kind of a Hurricane Press and Womanspirit. Find her online at karerock.com.

THE FINAL ACT

Tom Nolan

Gilroy Dexter was eighty-three years old. He had emphysema, prostate cancer, and no doubts that he had overstayed his welcome in this world. That was okay; he would be happy to move on, if only to escape the bouts of choking breathlessness that seemed to double in number, duration and intensity with every day that ground by. There was just one last thing he had to do before he left the stage and he prayed he would be granted the time to do it. Getting to Christmas was probably within his range but he had as much chance of making Easter as he had of playing Hamlet again, which was mildly disappointing as he had always quite fancied reprising the ultimate starring role (Jesus, not the Dane) and dying on a Good Friday.

Every night for two months, Gilroy had left his ground floor front room window open. "You're asking to be burgled, Mr Dexter," the Community Support Officer had told him, unaware just how accurate his words were. Of course, Gilroy hadn't been holding his crossbow at the time.

Non-theatre people tend to assume that actors function best in the spotlight. Those people have never had to find their way, quickly and silently off stage during a blackout, into wings crowded with things to bump into and trip over. In his heyday, Gilroy's eyes could adjust from blinding light to blind darkness at a speed that impressed even his fellow performers (who are rarely as generous as is claimed at awards dinners). His eyes, like the rest of him, were more sluggish now but that didn't matter as he sat motionless in his damask armchair and let the world darken around him.

Now, at the end of his run, Gilroy Dexter's nights were made on dreams of vengeance, darkness, the open window, and his Superlite crossbow. Only a burglar was required to complete the scene. His, or her, role would be brief but significant because the one thing keeping Gilroy alive against his body's will and his doctors' predictions was his determination to kill at least one housebreaker before he took his final bow and exited to meet his (it was to be hoped, grateful) maker in the green room of eternity.

Since becoming ill, Gilroy had adopted a mainly nocturnal lifestyle, dozing on and off through the day and remaining alert during the hours of darkness. Sleep was easily avoided thanks to his aged bladder and enlarged prostate. This he believed was the universe's way of preparing him for what he had to do and he bore the indignity of a nappy and incontinence pants because they were preferable to alerting a potential intruder by having to move to relieve himself. Now the likeliest things to betray him were the coughing fits and the subsequent inability to breathe that afflicted him several times a day. And still the consultant refused to put him on oxygen—in case he became 'dependent.' Of course, the real reason was budgetary, which Gilroy could understand, having once attempted to produce a small-scale tour of his musical, *Squidge*. Even with a pared-down cast, a pianist instead of a band and everybody sleeping in the van, the costs had proved prohibitive. But that was a long time ago and a lot of Leichner sticks had drifted under the bridge of disenchantment since then.

For heaven's sake! Gilroy shook his head so hard his neck twanged. He cursed his aged brain for drifting down the twisted alleys of memory at a time when he needed absolute focus. He slowed his breathing and tried to empty his mind. Lack of movement and absence of emotion usually managed to keep his congested chest under control. His breathing was still uncomfortably shallow and rattly but at least there were no suffocating spasms.

🖉

Would this be the night? God, he hoped so. Iron determination can achieve a certain degree of mind over matter but his body and time were conspiring against him and those two comprise the one bad-guy tag team that always wins.

Why in more than two months of leaving the window open, had nobody tried to break in? By all accounts the neighbourhood was a popular burglar theme park. Perhaps he was making it too obvious? Were crooks suspicious of anything that seemed too easy? If so, such discernment and shunning of the simple solution went against Gilroy's (admittedly limited and admittedly out of date) experience of the criminal classes. In the course of playing numerous malefactors during his years of treading the boards in rep and standing in front of cameras in a handful of widely forgotten television dramas, he had done his research. He wouldn't go so far as to describe himself as a 'method' actor but he did feel it essential to understand the reality of a situation before attempting to create a facsimile of it.

This dedication to his craft had, in his callow youth, cost Gilroy a part in *Coronation Street*, the one potentially lucrative and secure job of his career. He had been cast to play a small-time local gangster, a type he had found in real life to be dull, unimaginative and, frankly, thick. The producer wanted verve but Gilroy held out for verisimilitude and quickly earned himself another spell of 'resting.' In fact, he was worse off than he had previously been because he was now labelled a 'difficult' actor. Naturally, he defended his integrity by telling himself and anyone who would listen that this had always been his intention. Whenever an opportunity for self-justification arose, he would do a five minute monologue on how he shivered at the idea of forsaking his training to play the same undemanding part for years on end—especially in an uninflected, inexpressive Manchester accent! After three tellings, he believed it himself—although his conviction was frequently tested when the heating went off in his succession of tiny North London flats and he found himself in possession of nothing that the gas meter would accept as a coin.

Then on a wet Tuesday in Covent Garden, Gilroy met Marcus. Marcus worked as a 'suit' in advertising. He was slightly younger than Gilroy; he was beautiful; he was caring; he was emotionally stable (thanks to not being a 'creative') and, for much the same reason, he was financially secure. Gilroy Dexter adored him. The adoration was mutual and three weeks later they moved in together and set about playing the game of openly being a couple in artistic circles while remaining respectably legal to everyone else. In those days, gay rights were still a distant dream.

Then it ended. The world ended. Because of a break-in. Marcus didn't die straight away but he might as well have. That would have been kinder to all concerned.

Now during the sleepless nights and fitful days, Gilroy spent his time reflecting upon what a fool he had been. Like everyone, he had been a fool on many occasions in a great variety of ways but, unlike most people, he could acknowledge the fact. And while he was being brutally honest with himself, he had to admit that in all probability, if he could have his time over again, he would make most of the same mistakes with even more relish. One thing he would definitely not do, however, would be to leave Marcus alone, nursing a summer cold whilst he, the Great Actor, toddled dutifully off to show his face and trot out his inane repartee at that tawdry awards do.

At nine thirty-seven, two men had broken into the flat. They took everything of value including Marcus's life force. It seemed they were infuriated at having sullied themselves by entering the home of a homosexual couple. They beat Marcus viciously, breaking seven bones. Then they urinated and defecated on him and one of them masturbated into his facial wounds before bursting one of his testicles with a parting kick.

In time, Marcus's body was repaired but he was never the same person. The official verdict was that he had taken his own life while severely depressed. As far as Gilroy was concerned, the love of his life had been murdered by the burglars—murdered by *all* burglars.

Not one of them cares about the effect they have on their victims. If they cared, they wouldn't do it.

That he had taken until infirm old age to exact retribution was in Gilroy's mind all part of 'delaying the pay-off to heighten the drama,' 'enjoying a dish best served cold,' and any other clichés he could find that approximately fitted the bill. A more complete assessment would have to include the fact that he didn't want to waste his life by spending a large chunk of it in prison. Marcus would have hated that. But now that the never-great Gilroy Dexter was dying, it would be negligent not to send at least one scum-sucking parasite (thank you, American television) on ahead of him. Assuming, of course, that a member of that bottom-feeding species ever decided to fucking well show up.

10:39pm. Was that someone outside the window? Gilroy left the primed and loaded crossbow resting on his knee and flexed his trigger hand. The other nine bolts were within comfortable reach on the arm of the chair. Crossbows are cumbersome to reload at the best of times and his strength and manual dexterity were not what they had been but that didn't matter. Unlike in films, so long as the first bolt solidly strikes the body, the target is not going to be getting up and moving about very much for quite a while. Shock kicks in quickly after the initial pain and gives you all the time you need.

It was definitely a burglar. He, she, or they were easing the window back wide enough to climb through—and the idiots hadn't even taken the precaution of shining a torch inside. Gilroy had been prepared to shoot them through the glass. That would have enhanced the dramatic impact and would send out a message to make other thieves think twice. He had no wish to escape punishment as he was already serving a death sentence and he had prepared a powerful pre-incarceration speech but this was better; this would give him *time* with his enemy. It would lend extra substance and gravitas to his performance.

Here he comes.

As soon as the intruder was standing in the room, Gilroy put a bolt through his left shoulder, aiming to shatter the clavicle and avoid for the moment any major organs or vessels. The man yelped like a small dog and dropped into a sitting position on the floor. The second bolt pinned his right shoulder to the sideboard. It was a disgraceful way to treat an Edwardian antique but sometimes sacrifices have to be made. In any case, whoever got the furniture next would probably fail to appreciate its value and would consign it to a skip.

Now that the burglar was, and would continue to be, no threat, Gilroy switched on the flexible necked desk lamp and directed it into the man's face. The intruder was young, around twenty, and if you looked past the pain and the sneer, quite handsome. He was casually dressed in jeans, t-shirt, and the obligatory Converse plimsoles. Gilroy had owned several pairs of those in the seventies and had worn them with a black suit until his arches dropped. "One in each shoulder!" the burglar said, squinting to see who had taken him down. "You're a good shot."

"Not really. I was aiming for your eye. But I have plenty of bolts left."

"Why do you want to kill me?" The burglar sounded genuinely surprised and surprisingly cultured—unless the bastard was mimicking Gilroy's trained RP.

"Because you broke into my house."

"That carries a death sentence now, does it?"

"Yes."

The burglar waited with a hint of expectancy showing through the pain in his face. "I have to say I expected more justification."

"Can you justify your presence in my home?"

In the fashion of youths the world over, this one attempted to shrug, which caused each of the crossbow bolts to tear agonisingly through an extra inch of flesh. He gasped and then he said, "No I can't explain my presence here in a way that an old guy like you would understand."

"By 'understand,' I presume you mean 'feel sympathy for'?"

"Sorry if you were expecting a more educated burglar."

The youth was starting to appear disconcertingly relaxed. Was this gallows humour from a man who had accepted his fate? Or was it just how people his age *were* now?

"I think I shall save my breath, which comes in rather short supply these days," Gilroy said. "The type of parasite who breaks into other people's homes and thinks he can take whatever he wants with no thought for the consequences is not worth the effort."

"Getting shot with a medieval weapon was certainly a consequence I failed to consider."

Fury flashed through Gilroy Dexter and he had put a bolt in the intruder's thigh before he realised he had any intention of doing so.

"The consequences to *me!*" he roared. "I was referring to the consequences to me and your other innocent victims." Amazingly, this outburst did not bring on a bout of choking coughs. He slowed his breathing and in the quiet bass rumble he had used to such effect as *Lear* in Bournemouth, he said, "I imagine, if you spare any thought at all for your victims, it is to assume that they will claim on their household insurance and then simply carry on with their lives as if nothing has happened."

"Of course they do and I bet they usually add on a few items they never had in the first place," the intruder said, fighting through the pain.

"You stupid, stupid little boy. It isn't just about possessions. There are psychological sequelae, insecurities, lasting fear. One never again feels safe in one's own home after a break-in. In some cases there is a progressively deepening depression from which the victim never recovers. Their lives and those of the people who love them are destroyed. So yes, in answer to your earlier question, I advocate execution for the taking of life."

The burglar frowned and looked sympathetic, an obvious piece of am-dram. No doubt the seriousness of his predicament was finally penetrating his dim brain. "Did you lose someone close to you that way?" he asked.

"Yes." Gilroy held the pause beyond the appropriate dramatic length. When he was certain he could speak without either tears or breathlessness, he continued: "Marcus took his own life, or what was left of it by then. His misery dragged on for two years. I shall be more merciful with you. In a very few minutes you will no longer be alive. There will be some suffering before oblivion but I think that is only appropriate in the circumstances."

Incredibly, the intruder smiled. "Old man, I very much doubt that in one, two, or twenty hours' time, I will be any deader than I am right now at this moment."

"Really? I have six more bolts, not counting the one that's already loaded and you deserve to get one in the balls for that tautology alone. By the way, contrary to what I may have led you to believe, I am an excellent shot."

"Well, there's no point arguing about it." The youth calmly folded his hands in his lap with a nonchalance that his captor could not help but admire. "We'll just have to see how things turn out and which of us is right, won't we? But before you take your next shot, tell me, was this Marcus your boyfriend?"

"He was the love of my life, my perfect person."

"Yeah, I thought you sounded queer. Not in a camp way like those wrist slappers who can't string three words together without one of them being 'fabulous' but more, you know, posh bender, like."

Gilroy sighed and sarcastically remarked that it seemed almost a pity to end the life of such an eloquently gifted social analyst.

"What did Marcus look like?"

"What is that to you?"

"If he's the reason I'm dying... Do you have a photo?"

"Not of Marcus. He didn't believe in photographs. He thought they celebrate deterioration by holding up to you the mirror of what you have irretrievably lost. By the time he passed, the poor boy resembled a papier-mâché ball that has been fought over by two cats. When I met him he looked like someone who, ten years previously, might have looked something like you, I suppose. How old are you, by the way?"

"Nineteen."

"Dear me. That would be tragically young if there were any hope of your being redeemed."

"Like a Groupon voucher? Are you sure you don't know me, Dex?"

"How do you know my name? And it's Gilroy. Gilroy Dexter."

"Not to Marcus it wasn't, Squidgers."

Gilroy stared. "Have you been reading my letters?"

"No, I wrote them, fifty-odd years ago. Very odd years, as it happens."

"Don't be ridiculous. Apart from the obvious age discrepancy, Marcus is dead."

"That has its advantages too." The man got to his feet, the crossbow bolts seeming to melt through his flesh, leaving no obvious mark. "It's less painful, for one thing."

"I've read about this," Gilroy said. "Visual hallucinations are common in cases of chronic obstructive pulmonary disease. Your brain doesn't get enough oxygen and you imagine your long dead loved ones coming to collect you and take you to paradise. How tiresome not to have avoided the cliché. Still, it doesn't matter if I can't see properly now. I don't need to shoot you again. Eventually you will die of blood loss, or septicaemia or, if all else fails, starvation."

The intruder took a step towards the armchair. "It's not an hallucination, Dex. For us to appear to the living after we've passed on requires Olympian skills so we take all the help we can get. Cerebral oxygen deprivation makes it easier. Stand up and look in the mirror."

"Don't be absurd! I haven't been able to hoist myself out of this damned chair unaided for months now."

"Really? Then who gets your meals?"

"Mrs Rosen. She comes in twice a day."

"Has she been here today?"

Gilroy had to think about that. It struck him that he didn't appear to have seen the redoubtable Mrs Rosen for a while. "Possibly not," he said. "You lose your appetite as you grow old and infirm."

The youth who claimed to be Gilroy's long dead lover nodded. "What about the toilet? Or the lights? Who opens that window when Mrs Rosen closes it because she thinks draughts are bad for your chest?"

No answer presented itself to the baffled Gilroy Dexter. How, he wondered, did this child know so much about him and his domestic arrangements?

"Come on, Dex," the *child* said gently. "You know Mrs Rosen doesn't come any more. Otherwise how could you expect me to starve to death? Step over to this mirror above the fireplace and look at your-self."

With a resigned sigh, uttered to cover the indignity of groaning in failure, Gilroy made the effort to stand—and was astonished to find himself succeeding. He began to shuffle towards the mirror.

"You don't have to do that," the other man said. "Step out with con-fidence."

Gilroy did so—with *semi*-confidence. And the level of surprise that he had previously thought of as astonishment assumed a very minor status as he saw a young man's face looking back at him from the glass. It was a face he remembered and could verify against old photographs should he feel the need. He would fall over now were it not for the other man's steadying hand.

"You're twenty-three, Gilly. I peaked at nineteen and you were al-ways four years older than me, so..."

"So how is this possible?" Gilroy cuts in. "How have you made me younger?"

The young man whom he realises he is beginning to accept as Mar-cus, nods towards the recently vacated chair. Gilroy turns expecting to see his old, shrivelled, dead body. But the chair is empty and there is a layer of dust on the seat.

"You've been dead for six weeks, Dex. You had to be allowed to get the resentment and the hatred out of your system. I put in an applic-ation to prevent you doing anything that might have endangered your long-term post-life prospects..."

"Such as killing an intruder?"

"That sort of thing is rather frowned upon. As is interrupting people when they're speaking—frowned on by *me*, at least." Marcus is smiling.

Gilroy chuckles—something he hasn't done in years because it makes him cough. It doesn't have that effect now. "Yes I remember how much you hated that."

Slipping his arm around Gilroy's shoulders, Marcus says, "It's time to come away now, old boy. It wouldn't be fair on the new owners to have you hanging around. I—"

This time Gilroy cuts Marcus's flow not with words but with a kiss, at first tentative then firm. All thoughts of denture-breath are gone as his tongue feels two mouths full of healthy teeth and gums.

"I'm so sorry if I hurt you, with the crossbow," Gilroy says as he pulls his face away.

"Didn't feel a thing. It was acting. I learned from the best."

"Do you mean me, or have you been having lessons from Olivier or Irving or someone since you died?"

Marcus laughs. And they are outside in the street. The front room window is closed.

"So..." Gilroy says, his young brow knotting into a frown, "I wasted all that time feeling angry and planning a revenge that was neither necessary nor possible?"

"No emotion is wasted, Dex. They all change us in some way. They're a step away from the person we were, into the person we are and towards whatever we're going to become."

Marcus disentangles himself from Gilroy's embrace. "Race you to that lamppost."

"Why?"

"Because we can, Dex. Because we can."

Laughing, Gilroy sets off after the love of both his life and his afterlife. He feels the ground shooting back beneath him in a way he had forgotten was possible. Skinny little Gilroy Dexter never expected to be cast as Superman, nor as a gazelle bounding across the veldt, nor as the wind in the trees but he is now all of those things. He is everything he has ever wanted, everything he will ever want to be.

ABOUT TOM NOLAN

Tom Nolan lives in the UK. Most of his writing has been for performance, with regular contributions to television, radio and professional theatre. He placed second in the 8th Story Pros International Screenplay Contest and is currently working on two novels. More of his stories can be found at http://www.readwave.com/tom.nolan/stories/.

LOVE IS IN THE BLOOD

Kawika Guillermo

The twelfth winter of my youth was especially harsh. Back then I was more of a tool than a human being—something to be bandied about, used or unused, to be kept down, to be worried over. I was the chief's estranged son who preferred crafting and weaving to hunting and killing. But only women weaved and cultivated. Men fished, hunted, and raided.

In the growing cold of winter, as the snow sculpted the distant mountain of our island, I could not help myself in picking up the woman's craft of weaving hats from dyed thread. As the fruit died from cold, I too was remade.

✑

In my fifteenth winter I refused to hunt; I was a corpse for the hunt of our rivals, the Pangcah. To be of my people, the Atayal, was to be hungry with vengeance. I hated going on the hunts the way I hated slapping at mosquitos, but to perform the role of a domineering warrior took an attitude carefully designed as dismissive when I wanted to listen, unhelpful when I wanted to assist, and violent as it was possible for a man to be, all wrapped up in a casted persona, unmeasured in its aggressive posturing. There was no greater pain than this.

✑

When the northern breeze of my eighteenth winter came I was still unable to find a wife. A shaman came to our house dressed with dark tattoos of crescents scattered about her naked body. Banging on drums made of pig hide she summoned the spirits, invoking my unseen past. She sang in a voice from my dream.

"You were in love before you were born," the Shaman told me. "Your past life was of sweetness and ice, a life of eternal winter. In that life you promised yourself to another. Your husband. You promised to find each other in the next life. This life."

Then the Shaman and my brothers tied me down, leaving my stomach exposed as she took a stone knife to my ribs. She let pour the blood where my spirit's memories survived long after death. "Love is in the blood," she told me. I felt my body grow numb and felt nothing but the sharp pain of her blade. On the brink of death, I felt my lost love's sweet kiss.

"You must be cleansed again next winter," the shaman told me. "And every winter hereafter."

*

My twentieth winter was of sunshine and surf. One could barely tell the time of year, but I still went through the blood-letting ritual. I was married then, but the thought of sex still made me nauseous. The sight of a woman's body was all visual rot, like decayed pork marinated in urine. None of it turned me on at all. And how could I be disloyal to the husband of my past life?

When finally I could see snow from our house, my wife came to me in disguise. Her face was masked in the dark tattoos of a huntsman; her body was clothed in the fur and feathers of our chief. I wore nothing save a cloth that I had weaved in my youth. At first I did not know who she was, yet something filled my senses; I felt *him* deep in my throat.

"I've seen you somewhere," I told her. "Somewhere far away."

*

It was on an early morning of my twenty-ninth winter when the Pangcah raided my family. I told my wife Oarcea to stay huddled in the house with our five children. I had seen them, the Pangcah, in their ungovernable lust for blood. To take my wife was part of their ritual to manhood; to take their heads was part of mine.

They entered my house, their mouths salivating at the sight of my wife. I stayed crouched in the corner. Like snakes they snipped at her, undressed her, forced her closer to my concealed axe. When I began lopping at their heads, my children joined my battle cry.

◢

By my thirty-ninth winter I had learned to be discreet. In summer I dressed in the clothes of my father, our great chief; in winter my wife dressed in them as we grew intimate beneath fur blankets. What else was there to do in winter, when every cold breeze felt like his voice whispering into my earlobe? I was isolated with my wife then, my children grown and with their own families. The blood-letting ritual was no cure; its numbness only brought back his scent; the feeling of blood pouring down my skin left me in an avalanche of foaming desire.

◢

On a sallow afternoon during my forty-first winter, I watched clouds like fish-scales over the ocean. On the beach I arranged men made of straw as my eldest grandchild practiced his straight blade. His younger sister bent to take a short knife.

"No, no, no," I told her, taking the blade from her.

"Granddad, why?" she asked.

"It is forbidden," I said, and returned to stringing the bow that would be used in my grandson's raid on the Pangcah, where he was expected to bring back his first head.

"Can I help build it, granddad?" My granddaughter asked, pointing to the bow.

"It is forbidden," I said.

◢

Now, in my fiftieth winter, I spend my remaining days crafting head-dresses, using the weaving tools of my long passed wife. The winter has come again and our family is troubled for food, so when the air feels calm enough I will march to the top of the snow-capped mountaintop. Finally, I will pass out of this life.

"Do not forget," the now aged shaman tells me, giving me a sharp blade, "bleed yourself to death, and in the next life, you will remember nothing. Your spirit will be free."

A great cloud covers all that I can see from the mountain. The snow has already numbed my feet. In the numbing cold I begin to remember all my lifetimes, people after people, furious with lust, mad with murder, pillaging each other's towns, celebrating death. I lie on the iced dirt, feeling his arms embrace me. Perhaps, in the next life, his blood will remember me.

ABOUT KAWIKA GUILLERMO

Kawika Guillermo spends his days traversing among Nanjing, Hong Kong, and Seoul. He has a PhD in English Literature from the University of Washington, and does editing work for *Drunken Boat* and *decomP*. Over two dozen of his stories have appeared in journals like *Feminist Studies, Drunken Boat, Hawai'i Pacific Review,* and *LONTAR: Journal of Southeast Asian Speculative Fiction.* His work has been nominated for the Pushcart Prize and his stories have been featured in multiple anthologies. Recently, he has been avidly seeking publication for his novel about queer ethnic travellers.

HOLI COLOUR

Shruti Sareen

Nobody exactly knows how the tradition began, or how long it had been there, but evidently it was a tradition for the hostellers, after the wild and raucous Holi celebrations, to go to the staff flats looking like a lot of rowdy youngsters and ask the teachers for sweets and *mithais*.

Holi in this hostel began two days before Holi in the rest of the world. Whether it was the hostel mess or whether it was Aarohi's room, it did not matter, the buckets of water came pouring down, cold, cold water in the middle of March, until the place was flooded. Just the previous year Madri had come yelling and running down the corridor, dragging Aarohi out of her room and drenching her with cold water for the sixth or seventh time. And Sweksha had conveniently got the clever idea of throwing water from the balcony on all the unsuspecting people such as Aarohi down below.

There was plenty of water and plenty of colour and yes there was some *bhang* too. Little did the teachers know how Aarohi had handled two wicked *bhang*-ed friends all alone, Neha and Noopur, who insisted on gifting her tiny scraps of paper. Who got insulted when she threw away these scraps. Who said they needed water for riding bicycles and who named the two fans as '*kutta*' and '*kamina*,' and told Aarohi to turn both of them off lest the fans fall down on top of them. So, the water and the colours and the *bhang* and the big music system. And food. The only Holi essential missing in this narrative is food.

There was a junior-cum-friend, Poulomi who once begged Aarohi to take her to *any* teacher's house so that she could have *mithai*. Ultimately it was Aarohi, as usual, who had ended up gorging on most of the *kaju barfis*.

During this particular Holi, Aarohi and her friends had all been getting annoyed by the water balloons that the kids of one of the teachers kept pelting them with and finally decided to make their way back. Aarohi had just decided that she was not going to *her* house this Holi. She had already been the previous two years, and she was *not* going to go this time when... just as they turned back from the water balloon pelting kids, they saw her and her husband coming towards them. Kopilee ma'am, and her husband, Sudhir.

Though Aarohi had decided not to go, it began to seem as if she couldn't escape it. There was this whole crowd of girls, and Kopilee Hazarika, or KH as they called her, began putting Holi colour on them in her typical, graceful way. The very way she put colour suggested beauty.

Sudhir, meanwhile, walked just a little ahead and waited for her to emerge from the crowd of girls. Aarohi usually referred to him as Sudhir, having been told by Kopilee ma'am a couple of years ago that that is how some of her ex-students called him.

Aarohi retreated to the edge of the path, looking on. It did not occur to her to walk ahead on the other side. She stood there at the edge, watching the pretty sight. Standing there, she remembered previous Holis.

The first year, Aarohi had insisted on going to KH's house all alone when she realised that the others had already been and had somehow missed her out. That was just a few days after their initial fall-out, when Aarohi had been a first year kid. Aarohi was crazily in love with her that time. Oh well, wasn't she still? So she hadn't been able to restrain herself from going to her house when she realised that all the others had already been.

She thought festival time was a time when you made peace. That was her problem, restrain, refrain. Refrain itself had become her refrain but the problem was that she was not very successful in this mission of refraining and restraining. And as she stood there, her train of thoughts went to last year's Holi—how KH had marched in when they were all at Saroj Mehra ma'am—SM's—house, and proclaimed that in order to know what 'real' *mithais* are, they would have to come to her house.

Then when they went to KH's house, Aarohi had been the first one to pick up a *mithai* with her dirty fingers from the neat box. Aarohi was so used to being in her house after all, she had been here last year more than anybody else. She had sat here in the inner room of this house and had discussed everything from every small little problem and worry to poetry to college to food and school and problems at home to Kopilee ma'am's family to the menstruation rituals in Assam. When she spoke at all, that is.

Aarohi, who had been quiet and shy most of her school life, used to just sit, and sit there in Kopilee ma'am's house without saying anything. Then Kopilee ma'am would start telling her about how she had stayed in a live-in relationship before she got married. Aarohi would remain sitting silently still after having received this piece of information.

Sudhir exclaimed, "Kopilee, you don't know how to talk! What will the poor girl say if you tell her such things?"

Then Kopilee ma'am had turned to Aarohi and had said that she did not know how to make conversation. Well, neither for that matter, it appeared, did Aarohi. "You will keep sitting here silently," said Kopilee Hazarika, "and then later you will send me a text message."

Aarohi, who had just been formulating a text message in her mind that very minute, blushed a hot red. Kopilee ma'am definitely knew her through and through by now. More than she knew herself, she used to think.

But all this had happened before Kopilee ma'am had decided that she had had enough of all this falling in love. Hence the estrangement, which Aarohi could never keep up fully because she had this habit of not being able to restrain herself. She had eaten *aloo paranthas* and popcorn and had been gifted chocolates and chocolate cakes. She had kept silent even when she had made a mistake, and she had been altogether so comfortable here in this house. It just came to her naturally to be the first one to pick up a white *mithai* with her dirty black-blue-green hands, whereas all the other girls hesitated just a little to do so.

Watching all the girls painted red, blue, purple, green, and more, and the way Kopilee ma'am gave attention to each one of them and put colour in that very graceful way, it made a pretty sight. Aarohi watched with an unconscious smile playing on her lips, which betrayed her. She thought KH would move on, Sudhir was waiting for her, after all. Aarohi didn't understand why she was so interested in this crowd of hostellers. But she streaked them all, even the three or four stragglers. Streak being the closest word the English language has to describe this act of putting on holi colour, though it's no equivalent.

As KH streaked the stragglers, Aarohi sighed. She was to be the only person left out. Oh well. She continued to stand there, the smile unconsciously playing around her face, expecting KH to go ahead and join him after she finished streaking the girls. It did not strike her that she could go ahead on the other side and join the others who were going back to the hostel. Transfixed and rooted to the spot as she was, she thought she would wait until she joined Sudhir, before joining the other hostellers.

But Kopilee Hazarika did not go ahead to join him. Instead, she turned towards Aarohi first. Aarohi wondered if she had been conscious of her on-the-edge presence all the while. Like she knew it in class if Aarohi was there or not, where Aarohi would sit, even if Aarohi decided to stop responding to the attendance call.

Aarohi wondered how she could recognise her in this condition, how she could recognise this open haired, red, black, blue, green, yellow, lanky creature in front of her. She wondered why she turned towards her. If she couldn't see her or hear her, if she complained about her, why did she turn towards her now then, as she stood there on the side of the path, transfixed to the spot with that smile on her face which she did not realise? That is why Aarohi called her a stupid woman.

KH came towards Aarohi with a "Yeah" that was brusque and curt but which was very there all the same, and its presence can never be described in any story. As she streaked Aarohi's face in that graceful, very womanly way of hers, an expression of delight and uncontrolled happiness had sprung to Aarohi's face. The expression was uncontrolled because she never expected her to do it. Had she known she was going to, she would have done her best to make it easier for her by moderating her facial expression, like when she used to sit on the side in class so that she need not look at her.

Aarohi did not know what to say or do. Some vague instinct prompted her to return the streak, the way everyone does to everyone on Holi, though hers was oh! so much more awkward and clumsy than Kopilee Hazarika's beautiful touch. As she looked at the delight on Aarohi's face, her expression turned to one of fear. Aarohi could have sworn that she had never seen such a stupid woman before. Eccentric, idiosyncratic woman.

She sees me standing aside and deliberately excluding myself, then she comes to me, and then does she expect me to be sad? thought Aarohi.

As KH's expression changed to one of fear, it hit Aarohi like someone had just boxed her in her stomach. She cursed herself for not having the presence of mind to control the delight which had sprung up to her face. KH scurried ahead to join her husband.

Suddenly, Aarohi found herself lingering there all alone. The others seemed to have already gone back to the hostel in the meantime. She walked back slowly, this tiny incident which had taken hold of her mind, stuck on repeat, playing and replaying and replaying itself over in her head for years to come.

---

aloo paranthas - fried, round, potato-stuffed Indian bread
bhang - cannabis-infused beverage
kaju barfis - a type of mithai, usually diamond-shaped and made with cashews
kamina - low life/selfish
kutta - dog (sometimes used in jest or as an insult)
mithai - South Asian sweet

ABOUT SHRUTI SAREEN

Shruti Sareen studied in Rajghat Besant School KFI, Varanasi and went on to do English literature from Indraprastha College for Women, University of Delhi. With a keen interest in Indian Poetry in English, her MPhil looks at the depiction of urban spaces whereas she is currently pursuing a PhD on twenty first century feminist poetry from the University of Delhi. She also teaches at a college in the university. She has had poetry accepted by *The Little Magazine, Muse India, Reading Hour, North East Review, Allegro, 1 Over The 8th, Six Seasons Review, The Seven Sisters Post, The Chay Magazine, Ultra Violet, Brown Critique, E-Fiction India, Thumb Print Magazine, Coldnoon Diaries*, and so on. She blogs at www.shrutanne-heartstrings.blogspot.com. She is passionate about music, poetry, birds, rivers, trees, and of course, love.

PENELOPE

Eve Kenneally

I played not knowing about nights and girls,
reaching out to clutch our shadowed bed,
thinking of fair eyelashes and spitting
curls, their sighs escaping in your vivid red.

I knew you this way since we were seventeen, twisted
on rooftops in our skirts and crosses.
I settled for being your in-between, prickling
with the count of long-legged losses.

We fought into walls, you swore to stay home;
grew sick of those girls clinging lust-struck. You said I loved harsh
and needing, through bone, 'til I answered that call groggy, tongue stuck.

I chew through those screeching brakes, the ones that left me grieving,
but how could I have known you if you weren't always leaving?

ABOUT EVE KENNEALLY
Eve Kenneally is a second-year MFA student at the University of
Montana, from Boston by way of DC. Her poems have appeared or are
forthcoming in *Cutbank* (All Accounts and Mixture), *Star 82 Review*,
baldhip, *Bluestockings Magazine*, and *Sugared Water*, among other
journals. Follow her thoughts on food and Winona Ryder @eveveve418.

SIMPLICITY

Donnelle Belanger-Taylor

The sunshine splashed scarlet against Jean's eyelids as she gently rocked her chair. Her gnarled hands, paper-skinned and traced with veins of blue, lay limply in her lap. She ignored the staff bustling to and fro, answering the impatient demands of distant bells; she ignored the crochet blanket slipping off her lap; she ignored the wafting scent of cabbage that suggested it was nearly time for what passed as dinner here at The Golden Oaks.

She was too busy for any of that.

Deep in reverie, Jean remembered. Her memories took the form of a house, her childhood house. Jean wandered through it, her gaze sliding over the cluttered knick-knacks and minutiae of ninety-two years of life. She mentally picked up a snow globe and shook it; she smiled as tiny flakes settled over the squat brick building of the Moore School of Electrical Engineering. She'd never admitted it to anyone, but the war years had been the happiest of her life. It had always felt wrong to be happy in war, but the challenges she'd faced, the problems she'd solved, and the complexities she'd mastered while working on ENIAC had fed something deep in her soul.

And the friends she'd made, oh, the friends. A whole group of women who loved maths and spent hours working on solutions to problems they didn't even have words for. It was Evelyn who had taught her the 'memory house' technique, a way to visualise and memorise complex information. Evelyn had taught Jean other things, too, that made her blush even now. Jean put the snow globe back on the mantelpiece, smiling to herself.

'Computers,' they'd been called. Just like the grey plastic boxes her grandson was so obsessed with. She gripped the handle of the drawer labelled 'James' and slid it open, keen to replay her first cuddle, his first steps, his high school graduation.

The drawer was empty.

Jean frowned. It had been happening more and more lately; things weren't where she expected, or just looked strange. Too often, it was only an empty space that told her something was wrong.

It was those gaps that had sent her here, to The Golden Oaks. Things had gone missing from what she called 'her running memory,' a joking reference to the fact that she stored short-term tasks as pictures stuck on her virtual refrigerator. Three burned dinners in a row, three fire engine call-outs, and she'd ended up here, tucked up with blankets and cabbage-smell. Her grandson had brought her here... what was his name? It started with a 'J,' she was sure of it. She looked for the drawer, but it was gone. A blurry discolouration on the wall was the only sign that something of import had once been there.

Things seemed to disappear so fast, these days. It's why she was spending so much time here, in her memory house. Reinforcing, re-membering... defending.

Jean reached for a silvery silk scarf, draped next to the snow globe. She started to bring it to her face, to inhale the scent on it, Evelyn's scent, but a hand on her shoulder and a repeated "Mrs Gabouldi? Jean? Mrs Gabouldi?" brought her back to reality.

One of the staff was crouching next to her, watching her face with professional concern. "Are you alright, Mrs Gabouldi?" She reached for the slipping blanket and pulled it back onto Jean's knee, without waiting for an answer.

"I'm fine," Jean answered, crossly. "Call me Jean. Gabouldi was my husband's name, and I didn't like him much."

The staff member laughed, not quite concealing a patronising tone. "Alright then, Jean. I'll remember that. It's dinner soon, won't that be nice?" She stood up. "Oh, I'm Sue. I'm here most nights." Sue turned and bustled away, summoned by a bell, but Jean still caught the muttered "Not that you'll remember."

Defiantly, Jean returned to her memory house, with an image of Sue gripped in her fist. She looked around. So cluttered, so full, so many memories... yet gaps glared at her, painful and raw, like the bloody hole where a tooth should be.

There was a space on the wall, faintly discoloured. Something tugged at her memory—a snowy-blonde head of hair? A boy at the beach? No, it was gone. She filled the gap with the picture of Sue, taking pleasure in using a ridiculously large nail to fix it in place, before scrawling 'Sue' across it in red ink.

She'd always used red as a warning, for people and things to be careful of. Funny how none of the red things seemed to be missing. They glowered at her, garish and unharmonious, dominating the room. Reds were like that.

She reached for the nearest one. A shoe, in a shade of burgundy that almost looked attractive until you realised how odd it looked on a man's penny loafer. She'd stuck it here in her memory house, as a reminder not to get distracted by theorems while cooking. Vincent had beaten her with it, holding her down like a three-year-old, punctuating each of his words with a painful *thwap*. "All—I—want—is—meatloaf," he'd panted, before making her eat the blackened lump that remained.

Jean contemplated the shoe. A thought occurred; if things were disappearing... could she *make* them disappear? She threw the shoe at the wall. It bounced off and lay stubbornly on the floor. Hmm.

She concentrated for a moment, with a knack made easy by years of practice. A rubbish bin appeared, a replica of the foot-pedal one her daughter, Barbara, had bought her for Christmas one year, after carefully saving her pennies. How Vincent had laughed. She stepped on the pedal, amused as always by the way the lid flopped upwards, and dropped the shoe in. She let the lid close, then opened it again. The shoe was gone.

She felt better already.

What else could she get rid of? She found the strawberry jam jar she'd carefully stored pennies and dimes in, saving for a trip back to Pennsylvania, where Evelyn and several of the other girls had settled. It had disappeared after Vincent came in ranting one night; she'd started to ask him about it, but quickly changed her mind. Into the bin it went.

Jean picked up a carmine-covered book, *What Men Don't Like About Women*. Vincent had thrown it at her one night, making a point about... something. The corner had nicked her forehead, and the sight of blood, as always, had made him apologetic and charming again. Barbara had been conceived that week. Jean laughed bitterly at the reminder that she'd thought things would get better.

As she dropped the book in the bin, a playing card slipped out from between the pages and tumbled to the floor. The two-faced king of diamonds stared up at her, both heads grimacing and grotesque. She'd put it there the day after Vincent's funeral, when a pale, sweating lawyer had revealed that Vincent had left her nothing but gambling debts.

There were more, many more, mostly to do with Vincent and the things that made him angry. She'd spent a lifetime cataloging them. Jean scooped up armfuls and dumped them into the bin. He was gone, and she didn't need them any more.

She reached for the next red that caught her eye, and found herself holding a faded rose. It wasn't red with warning, though perhaps it should have been; it was the rose that Vincent had brought her, the first time she went out with him. She'd been happy then, flattered by his attentions and his smooth words.

The rose went in the bin. The only red remaining was the fresh 'Sue' scrawled over the picture of the rude nurse. Jean snorted and snatched it off the wall. Sue didn't deserve a space here. Into the bin she went. A patch on the wall wavered and firmed, shaping a drawer with a label on it. 'James,' that was his name, of course it was!

The room was much emptier now, spacious, clean, tranquil. Jean was drawn to the silvery silk scarf on the mantelpiece, lying next to the snow globe. She caught it up, held it to her face, breathed in its sweet scent. Evelyn, oh, Evelyn.

A hand brushed down her arm. Jean turned, and smiled.

"Mrs Gabouldi? Mrs Gabouldi? Jean?" Sue shook her shoulder. No response. She reached to check Jean's pulse, but without much urgency. She'd seen that smile before.

ABOUT DONNELLE BELANGER-TAYLOR

Donnelle is a software developer, a tuba player, and a mum to twins plus one. Her house is a mess, her head more so, but there are always new things she wants to add to the mix. Writing is one of them.

ROULEZ

Teddy

GK Hansen

Beau sprawled against the wet pavement, gasping and trying not to gasp, one hip and both hands flat on the stones. They could feel the rainwater seeping into their skirt, but it wasn't really a priority; not the way the pain in their side was. Out of the corner of their eye Beau saw a woman roll the now-unconscious man to the side of the street. With the amount of alcohol he had in his system, waking him up wasn't exactly a concern—and she must have hit him hard, to drop him like that. Whoever she was. Small blessings. And she was in heels, Jesus, and not even panting.

Another wave of pain; Beau closed their eyes briefly, trying to take shallow breaths, and when they looked back up the woman was crouched down beside them. Not touching, Beau noticed, and that was interesting; just waiting.

"*Bonswa,*" she said, almost ironically, in a not-quite-familiar accent. "You okay?"

"*Byen q' non,*" Beau shot back, but tried to smile. "I think he cracked a rib, but I got off easy this time."

"Oh, honey." The sympathy—empathy, even—was clear on her face. "Yeah, you did. Come on, let's get you up."

She offered Beau a hand, and they took it without thinking; broad palm, strong wrist, warm skin. After a moment they were both upright, with the woman steadying Beau in a way that was extremely careful to invade no further into their space than necessary. They were so grateful it hurt, and held on until their breath steadied.

"I think," Beau said, as the woman eased them onto a bench across the street, "he thought I was a trans woman." They glanced down at themselves, the skirt Teesha and Alice had talked them into, and felt a hot flush of something like shame. Beau had liked this skirt. "From what he said, anyway."

There was a short silence; Beau glanced over to see the woman looking at them with her head a little on one side. "You'd think any idiot could tell a binder from a bra," she said, finally, and grinned just the slightest bit. Beau tried to laugh and coughed instead, and she put a hand gently on their shoulder.

"I'm Kath. I work just down the street." She nodded in the direction of a club whose crowd—gay men, a scattering of women—was just starting to spill out onto the sidewalk.

"Beauregard. Beau."

"Creole?"

"Cajun. Probably." Beau glanced across the pavement to the man's unconscious body for the third time in as many moments. "It's complicated."

"What isn't?" Kath followed their gaze, then looked back at Beau and said, casually, "And what pronouns do you use?"

Beau froze. After five seconds of dead quiet between them Kath said something embarrassed-sounding in a language that wasn't either Creole or English, and began talking just a little too fast. When Beau managed to unbend enough to look at her, it was clear—despite her dark skin and the sodium-yellow of the street lamps—that Kath was blushing.

"I—*Dyeu*, I'm sorry, I'm terrible at the boys, I know I am, I'm okay at spotting other trans women, but I'm always asking trans guys for their pronouns and making an ass out of myself, and you've had a shitty enough evening—"

Beau put up a hand, shaking their head, and Kath reined in, though she still looked humiliated.

"I'm not," Beau said, and then stopped, and then started again. "I'm not female to male. I'm not anything, really, I'm just." They shrugged, and pain shot through their ribcage. "Between. Or neither. I'm not sure."

Kath looked at them sharply, seeing the wince before hearing the words, and her hands moved like she wanted to check Beau over, right there on the bench.

"So neutral pronouns then," she said, cheerfully, as she glanced them over in lieu of a physical examination. They were almost of a height, though Kath was broader all over than Beau, who was just short of being too thin, though the bones that showed were strong. Adolescent thin, Beau knew—like they'd grown tall without getting older.

"If you can coin some here and now, yeah," they said, and it was almost bitter. "I just use they, and everyone argues grammar instead of gender, which I guess is better." Beau laughed, which was followed almost instantly by a shallow pained breath. Had to stop doing that; a surreptitious check while Kath was moving the man had revealed nothing out of place, but it was badly bruised at the least.

When Beau looked back to Kath her face was mildly surprised.

"Not ze and hir?" she asked, and for a moment they felt as if they'd been knocked against another wall, dizzy and reeling in the giddy space just before the concept took hold, the pronouns slamming into them the same way the word intersex had five years ago. All they could do was shake their head, helpless, and Kath put her hand back on Beau's shoulder, as if they needed steadying again. Which they did, although their body on the bench was still.

"Don't worry about it," Kath said, and squeezed gently before letting go. "Look, do you want to go to the ER? My shift just got over, I can take you—"

"No." Beau said it too fast and didn't care. "No, I... don't like doctors, I'd rather change my flight home and see one who's known me for a while, it's. Safer." Their hands clenched the edge of the bench, knuckles going pale. "But thank you."

Kath opened her mouth as if to argue, then took a long look at Beau, the way their head was hunched down between their shoulders, and seemed to think better of it. Parallel experiences, concluded the part of Beau's brain that was still calm and collected. Good. Unlikely to argue. Their eyes stayed on the ground as the silence stretched again, while Kath watched the entrance to the club she'd pointed at earlier, gaze distant and thoughtful.

"Do you live around here?" she asked, finally. Beau shook their head.

"Streetcar, then a bus," they said, and shrugged, carefully, stiffly. "It's still early enough that I should be able to get home."

"Is there anyone you want me to call? Did you come into the city with someone?" Kath sounded worried, and Beau, in an abstracted sort of way, was touched.

"No, I—it's fine. My friends are probably halfway home already, it's pointless to call them back, if they're even paying any attention to their phones." Beau doubted it, judging from the look in Teesha's eye the last time they'd glimpsed her, and the position of Alice's hand. "I know the way, and I didn't have much to drink. It's okay."

"Won't they be worried—?"

Beau half-laughed again, a shallow little sound that only hurt right at the end of it. "They'll just think I went home with someone. It's happened before."

Kath cleared her throat, and then said, very delicately, "Would you like to? Go home with me, I mean. Not—I live close by, and you're not in the best shape. And I'd sleep easier if I knew you weren't trying to make it home when you'd already had one bad run-in." She waited a heartbeat, then followed up, hurriedly, "I'd let you have the bed, there's a pull-out couch but you're hurt so I'd take it."

They couldn't do anything but stare at her for a second or two, and Kath ducked her head, hands folded in her lap as if to keep from reaching out like she had before. "Not if you don't want to, but—my coworkers would vouch for me, some of them are still wrapping up, and you could tell your friends where you were, and. It'd be safer than the RTA."

When Beau still didn't say anything Kath shrugged awkwardly, clearly embarrassed. "Sorry, I—sorry, I don't even know your last name and I'm offering to put you in my bed, *Dyeu*, I'm sorry. I'll walk you to the streetcar and then be out of your way."

"St Cyr," Beau said, without thinking, and then blinked and looked up at Kath. "It's Beau St Cyr. Are you... you wouldn't mind?"

Kath touched their shoulder again, tentatively. "I wouldn't have offered otherwise. I've been in a... a similar kind of shitty place myself a few times, Beau, and if I can keep you out of it I will."

Beau thought it over, tracing the seam of their skirt with fingers that were still stiff and tense with adrenaline. They'd gone home with people they'd known less long, and with worse motives, and something about the deferential, too-casual tone of Kath's voice when she said a similar kind of shitty place made Beau think she was unlikely to pose any sort of danger.

"If you really don't mind," Beau said, finally, and Kath looked up from where she'd been examining the cobblestones. She was also so clearly relieved that the last of Beau's fear drained away, leaving them tired and shaking.

"I really don't," Kath repeated, then got to her feet. They stood too, a little more slowly, as the woman curled long, self-conscious fingers around her strong-boned wrist—and Beau realised, suddenly, that Kath couldn't be much older than they were. "I can have my boss vouch for me, if it'd make you more comfortable."

"No. It's alright." Beau glanced across the street to where a leggy black woman, maybe ten years their senior, narrow-hipped, in a short skirt but eminently sensible shoes, was watching the two of them with a protective look like the one Beau's mother wore sometimes. They almost smiled. "She probably thinks it's me that needs vouching for, so."

Kath followed their gaze and her half-smile was the echo of Beau's. "Yeah. No, I wouldn't be surprised. Give me two minutes to reassure her."

Beau stood quietly as Kath loped across the street, one hand on the back of the bench for balance. While the woman leaned across the wall next to her boss, Beau touched the pocket sewn into their binder and nearly crumpled with relief, despite the support of the bench. Bad enough that they were hurt; it would have been the last straw to lose both the fake ID and the real one, not to mention enough cash to pay their tab and Teesha's, and to get the bus home. They ran a shaking hand over their face; by the time they dropped it Kath was most of the way back over the road.

"Madame Papillon's satisfied you won't kill me in my sleep," she said, only half joking. "Can you walk, do you think?"

"If you keep an eye on me," Beau replied, and gingerly stood without a steadying influence. One step, then another; and the third came easily. To keep from thinking too hard, they said, "That can't actually be her real name."

"As much as Kath is mine." The reply was very mild, and Beau glanced over to see her giving them a skeptical kind of look. "Or Beauregard yours, I'm guessing."

Beau snorted, and immediately regretted it. "Touché. Though I came by Beau honestly—family nickname. I just extended it." Speaking wasn't precisely difficult, but doing it at the same time as walking created a kind of stretchy pain in their right side, unpleasant and peculiar. Kath offered an arm, diffident enough for them to refuse easily—Beau took it with a stiff little nod, and Kath took as much of their weight as was feasible.

"Everyone assumes mine's short for Katherine," she said, clearly trying to distract them both as they made their slow way down the street.

"Taking it it's not."

"Nope." Kath paused before crossing the next street, even though no cars were coming; Beau was almost sure it was to let them catch their breath, and was obscurely amused at her gentle chivalry. "Liked the sound, and it was—compact. I was getting tired of long strings of saint-names, even if they were only middle ones."

A number of hints slid into place at that, and Beau finally placed Kath's accent; Haitian, leavened by a more generic Louisiana drawl. They grinned, just a bit—Teesha's maternal grandparents had two first names each, all of them indisputably saintly, and so did her mother. Teesha counted herself lucky to have escaped.

"I see you've run into the affliction before," Kath said, pausing in front of a worn but not derelict building and rummaging in her pocket for her keys.

"One of the women who ditched me tonight—part of her family is from Haiti." Beau steadied themselves on the railing as Kath unlocked the door, and then moved carefully into the entrance hall behind her.

"Five siblings, and they've got fifteen names between them, *Bondye ede m'*. You doing alright? There's a flight of stairs to go, but if you need to rest..."

"I'd rather get somewhere I can sit down." Beau took the deepest breath they could manage and, with Kath's hand on the small of their back to steady them, began to go up the short flight of stairs to the second-floor walkup. They barely had the presence of mind to register that she was less hesitant to touch this time, and the contact itself less delicate; by the time they got to the landing, Beau was just glad for the help.

Kath let go only long enough to open the door, and steered Beau to a chair before returning to close it. They shut their eyes as soon as they were seated, trying to quiet the slight whirl of the room, and didn't look up until Kath said, softly, "Beau, *cher?*"

"I'm alright," they said, automatic; but Kath's brows were drawn together with worry.

"You're not, but there's nothing much I can do about it except point you towards the bed." She gestured towards a folding screen, and Beau realised slowly that it was two rooms, one the kitchen and living room combined, the other big enough for a bed and dresser and not much else. "I'd offer you something to eat, but I doubt you want food."

Beau shook their head and took Kath's offered hand, levering themselves to their feet with more effort than they really liked. She held onto them, fingers curled strong and steady against Beau's wrist; and they wanted to break down and weep.

"Sleep will help," Kath offered, almost wistfully, like she wanted to say or do more but was lost as to where to start. Beau mustered up a smile, and let her lead them fifteen feet to the bed, and sit them down on it. It took everything Beau had not to collapse backwards as Kath dug through her drawers for pyjamas, but they knew from experience that leaving a binder on with a cracked rib was a recipe for disaster.

Beau didn't particularly want to think about trying to get it off.

They waited through Kath shyly handing them a men's shirt and boxers and saying, "I thought you might be—ehn, more comfortable, with these. I haven't worn them for years, and they're clean," and through her pulling down an extra blanket for the couch; it was as Kath was adjusting the screen across the doorway to give them privacy that Beau said, very small, "Kath?"

She stopped, just out of sight, and was still for a moment before she said, "Yeah?"

"I don't dare sleep in the binder, with my ribs." Beau let that hang in the air, and then swallowed hard. "And I can't. *Pardonnez-moi*, I know this is a lot to ask of you, but I can't get it off by myself."

There was another moment where no one moved, and then Kath sidled back into the bedroom. "You don't have to be that formal with me," she said, half-gentle, half-teasing. "Not if I'm going to be taking your clothes off."

Beau made a noise between sob and laugh, and got out, "I had to forget to pack the one with the zipper, didn't I?"

"Shame to make things easy." Kath didn't come any closer until Beau stood up and turned around. The shirt was almost easy to wriggle out of; not comfortable, but loose enough that they could get one arm from its sleeve and push the whole thing off without too much more than a pang through their side. Beau dropped it, and swallowed again, then said, "Alright."

They could hear Kath's bare feet against the carpet as she came up behind them. Beau went tense when Kath made contact, and then tenser as her hands began to work the binder up over their hips, even though she was clearly trying not to touch them more than she had to. After too little time their belly was bare, and Kath began easing up the more heavily-elasticised section that bound Beau's ribs and chest, keeping her hands as close to their back as she could.

When the binder cleared the bottom of Beau's sternum they made a desperate stifled noise, and Kath froze, palms warm against their sides. Beau bowed their head, hands over their face, and struggled for their breath back; the woman took a step away, putting space between them without letting go.

"I'm not going to do anything, " Kath said into the silence, low and clear and firm. "Beau, I am not going to hurt you. I'm not even going to look at you, I'll shut my eyes until the binder's off and you get a shirt on. Okay?"

The noise this time was helpless, and then Beau managed to get themselves together long enough to choke out, "Okay."

They could hear Kath draw a slow breath, and then she continued easing off the binder as if she'd never stopped. After a few seconds Beau shut their eyes too, and managed to get both arms up long enough for Kath to work the fabric up over their shoulders and off.

"There," she said, sounding as tense as Beau felt, and as breathless. "There. You're okay. *Tout se byen.* I'm gonna go into the other room, yeah?"

When Beau didn't say anything, Kath turned and went out, stumbling a little; they could hear her footsteps, hear her drop onto the couch and then go still. After another few heartbeats, Beau opened their eyes, blurry with tears, and reached blindly for the shirt.

⌀

When they woke up, Beau had no idea where they were. They stared blankly at the ceiling for a while, and then rolled over; it was when their elbow hit their ribs with a spasm of pain that Beau remembered whose bed it was, whose white sheets were tangled around their legs.

It was another four or five seconds before they remembered that they'd spent the night alone, and by that time Beau was already upright, scrabbling for their binder. They dropped it, feeling awkward and almost angry at themselves, and sat down on the edge of the bed.

"Beau?" Kath sounded like she was just outside the screen, voice hesitant but cheerful. The apartment smelled like fried bread and syrup, and Beau couldn't quite decide if they were hungry or nauseous. Both, probably; the feeling was slowly becoming identifiable as a hangover as Beau struggled the rest of the way out of sleep. "You awake?"

"More or less." They rubbed at their face. "I'll be out of your way soon. Sooner if I can beg a cup of coffee."

"I'll do you one better; there's breakfast if you want it." Kath shifted her weight.

Beau could just see her outline through the screen as they tried to decide if their skirt was wearable. The blouse was probably fine, but the skirt was still damp, and dirty at the hem. They had to chew on the inside of their lip to keep from cursing out loud, and there was a strained quality to Beau when they said, "I could eat, gimme a minute."

"I have a wrap skirt that might fit you," offered Kath as she went back into the kitchen; the apartment was small enough she barely had to raise her voice. "If your things are still wet. I forgot to find the drying rack last night, and hip size won't matter if it's a wrap-around. It's hanging over the screen."

"I have no idea how I'm going to repay you, Kath," Beau said fervently, and pulled the brightly-patterned piece of fabric down.

While they were wrapping the length of it around their waist Kath chuckled, and set what sounded like a pan down on the stove. By the time Beau came out into the kitchen she was looking contemplative, one elbow on the countertop, spatula dangling from her hand.

"There is something you could do," Kath said, straightening up to reach for a plate.

Beau watched the line of her for a moment, then realised what they were doing and looked away, embarrassed. "Name it," they said, grinning a little, and Kath laughed again, set down two plates.

"You might not like it," she warned, going back to keep an eye on what appeared to be French toast. "I called the clinic I go to, and they said they could have you in for an x-ray this morning." Beau went still, and Kath nearly dropped the piece of egg-soaked bread she was about to put into the pan in her haste to say, "They're used to transgender—to people who don't match up to the binary, it's where I pick up my oestrogen. I mean. Beau. You don't have to, but I'm worried about you getting on a plane without knowing what's wrong."

"You have a point," Beau said finally, only a little stiff.

Kath looked visibly relieved, and they unbent enough to give her a small smile and reach for the coffee pot. She immediately handed them a mug, and grinned in return.

"*Di Bondye mèsi.*" Kath's voice was matter of fact. She must be almost bilingual, to have that be the first thing to her tongue. "I thought you might get offended."

"I thought about it." Beau stirred in sugar, and watched her from the corner of one eye. "But it seems like you might be hard to argue with once you've made up your mind."

Kath made a small, nonspecific motion, then flipped the piece of bread over. "Sometimes. Call it a... a kind of familial obligation, *se wi*, to make sure you're okay?"

"Familial, huh?" drawled Beau without thinking, and felt a rush of surprise and delight to see Kath's cheekbones darken in a blush.

"You know what I mean," she said, tart.

Then she set two pieces of toast on each plate, turned off the stove, and dropped into the chair across from Beau, who finally took a good look at her. In the full light of morning, Kath was more clearly only a year or two older than they were, with dark brown skin and shoulder-length black hair in tiny, careful braids. A mouth that smiled easily, long eyelashes, light brown eyes. Square across the wrists and a little in her shoulders but mostly curved, casually feminine even in running shorts and a tank top—Beau cleared their throat.

"I really can't thank you enough for, well. All of this, really." They waved a hand.

Kath turned her mug a quarter turn and looked embarrassed. "You looked so worn down is all," she said. "Like it hadn't just been a long night? And I know that feeling and figured, why not, I don't work today."

"Thank you," Beau said, and meant it. "You didn't have to do anything."

"Yes, I did." Kath's response left no room for argument, voice calm and very firm; and Beau couldn't help but smile.

❧

Kath's hand settled tentatively on the back of Beau's neck and they let her keep it there, appreciating the steady, steadying warmth of her palm. Deep breath; another one, and a third, so that none of the clinic's neutral, antiseptic scent remained. The sense of a rising tide began to ebb back, wave by wave, until Beau's lungs felt less like they were being squeezed.

"*Sa va?*" Kath said it very softly, so as not to intrude if things weren't yet alright, and Beau wanted to lift their hand and grip her wrist to hold her there, in case she took it into her mind to move.

"Yeah," Beau said after a minute or two; and after another few breaths they managed to sit up straight again.

Kath let them go, reluctantly, and Beau leaned their head back against the brick wall, looking out over the water. They had walked down from the clinic at a fast clip, in silence with Beau leading; and now there in front of them was the river.

"At least it's not broken?" offered Kath, pulling up stems of grass and dropping them back onto a little pile next to her hip.

Beau nodded without opening their eyes, letting their body relax and register the air around it, the smell of road tar and just-opened flowers and the ocean never very far away. Eventually they sighed. Blinked once or twice, and got to their feet, offering a hand to help Kath up. Without either of them saying anything, they started up towards the Canal streetcar line, matching stride easily.

"Thank you again, *cher*," Beau said when they reached it. "I'll give you a call when I get back home. Let you know I made it okay."

"I'd like that." Kath sounded almost wistful.

"Would you?" Beau could hear the same tone in their own voice, and kicked at the ground to try and cover it.

Kath licked her lips, made one false start, and then said, "*Wi.* Yes. Very much. If you don't mind."

Beau went to try and shove their hands in their pockets, but the wrap-around skirt didn't have any so they just ended up smoothing both palms over their thighs. Around the corner, they could just hear the streetcar ding, and Beau said in a rush, "If I were to kiss you—"

"That," Kath said very carefully, "is a thing I would like even better than you calling me."

Bondye ede m' - God help me
Bonswa - good evening
Byen q' non - of course not
Cher - various; most closely 'dear' as in 'my dear'
Di Bondye mèsi - thank god/thank the lord
Dyeu - God
Pardonnez-moi - Excuse me (formal)
Sa va - okay / it's okay
Se wi - yes/yeah
Tout se byen - Everything's fine
Wi - yes

ABOUT GK HANSEN

Currently living in Somerville, Massachusetts, GK Hansen is a multi-genre writer interested in exploring complex relationships and complicated—mostly queer—people. Previously published in *Liminality: A Magazine of Speculative Poetry*, "Roulez" is Hansen's first short story publication. If social media used sparingly is your thing, click follow at gofindout.tumblr.com.

UNDER THE SYCAMORES

Terry Sanville

The rain sounded like a snare drum solo, beating against platter-sized leaves that covered the creek bank, beating against the slickers that Mason, Jerome, and I wore. I shielded my eyes and gazed into the upper branches, searching for Aiden. He'd removed his raincoat, shirt and shoes and had scrambled up the massive tree, moving fast like a monkey. That's the nickname our classmates at Westside Middle School gave him. He hated it.

Mason dug me in the ribs. "Forget about him. Come on."

"Wait just a fuckin' minute. He could fall."

"If he does it's his own damn fault. It's stupid to be climbin' in the rain."

"Yeah, well you and your punk friends have been ragging on him all week... and messing with his head in front of everybody really sucked."

Mason glared at me but said nothing. I'd know him since first grade. He used to like me. But that got lost in Junior High when I became just another nerd cruising the hallways, and he became a cool jock.

Jerome had already unhooked the rope from the exposed root at the base of the tree. The swing had a huge knot tied at its end to support the rider's feet. I stared upward to where it was looped around a limb as thick as my waist. The tree stood atop a bank next to Mission Creek that flowed out of the Santa Ynez Mountains and cut across Santa Barbara on its way to the Pacific. Along this stretch, concrete walls boxed it in. During the summer, it barely trickled. But during a storm, it almost topped the walls, a raging torrent of brown water carrying logs, stones, trash bins, and anything not nailed down.

"Here, gimme the rope," Mason demanded.

Mason grasped the swing with both hands and Jerome and I gave him a push. He swung out over the creek, cutting a wide arc through the rain-thick air, the rope barely clearing the water. On the backswing we gave him another shove and he gained momentum, lengthening the arc. After four passes, we hauled him in.

Mason grinned. "Epic, man." He scraped matted hair away from his green eyes. "Seeing that water thunderin' below... I about pissed my pants."

"Yeah, yeah. Just get outta the way," Jerome snapped. "It's my turn."

A huge log rounded the bend and surged toward us. Jerome swung out over the creek. The log dipped forward, speared the bottom, and shot out of the water, tumbling end-over-end. It narrowly missed him. He shrieked. On the backswing Mason gave him a hard shove, sending him out again.

Jerome yelled, "Stop the swing, stop the swing."

We hauled him in after just two passes.

"Did... did you see that fucker?" he said, gasping. "It nearly knocked me off. I woulda been screwed if..."

We stared at the churning water and I thought about our next moves. I glanced upward into the treetop but still couldn't spot Aiden. He had a way of disappearing when he wanted to, like a brown salamander against a muddy creek bottom.

Aiden had showed up in third grade at Harding Elementary. His family had moved to Santa Barbara from somewhere in Michigan. He sat next to me in Mrs Molina's class. For the first year or so he kept griping about being away from winter and how cool it was to build snow forts and go ice-fishing on frozen lakes. I ignored him, until I discovered that if I had any schoolwork problems, he could help. The dude was a genius, especially in math and science. Later, he became my go-to guy with tech stuff, helped me set up my laptop and load my cell phone with all the cool apps.

But of all of us, Aiden seemed to glom onto my friend Jerome. In seventh grade I caught them in a bathroom stall during lunchtime. I didn't see anything, but it seemed pretty weird. Neither of them looked at me when they came out.

"What were you guys doing? I asked.

"Nothing," Aiden said, his face red and sweating.

"What do ya mean, nothing?"

"Whatever we're doing is none of your business," Jerome said. "Just shut up about it."

"What's there to shut up about?"

"Nothing, I tell ya." Aiden glared at me.

"Alright, alright. But the guys need you to go get their baseball."

A three-storey apartment bordered the schoolyard and the jocks would sometimes hook a high fly over the right field fence and onto its roof. Aiden would shinny up a drainpipe, pull himself over the parapet, and retrieve the lost prize. If any of us had tried it, we'd have ended up as a grease spot on the concrete below.

Aiden frowned. "Yes, I'll get the ball if you promise to keep quiet."

"Okay. Jesus." I gave him a shove.

"Do you know about... about being gay?" Aiden asked.

"Yeah, it's not my thing. I'm just starting to, ya know, like girls."

"Jerome and I have known since fourth grade... and... and it's getting stronger."

"Huh. I've been his friend longer than you. Jerome, you never seemed queer to me." I wanted to end that conversation fast and get the heck out of there.

Jerome still wouldn't look at me. He washed and dried his hands, then ran for the door.

I'd kept their secret. But by the next year, everybody at school had found out and the bullying kicked in big time—loud conversations at the vending machines, cat calls, 'fag' and 'queer' scribbled on their lockers with ink markers, the special sessions with the school counsellor. Right after Thanksgiving, Aiden started missing school—a day, sometimes two a week. And he seemed to get even skinnier and jumpy as hell. I felt sorry for him and Jerome, knew something about being picked on; the jocks called me *lardass* or *douchebag*.

❧

During lunch hour that day, the bullying got really ugly, and Mason was one of the worst. He stood a head taller than any of us, sported bulging arms and a flat stomach. Aiden, Jerome, the jock table, Billy grinned while the rest of them cracked up.

"Real cute. What a bunch of troglodytes," Aiden said, loud enough for them to hear.

"What'd you call us?" Billy rose slowly, a sneer creasing his face.

"Google it, moron," Aiden shot back.

Quick as a cat, Billy crossed the floor to our table with Mason right behind him. Billy grabbed Aiden's shirtfront and hauled him up. "How'd you like me to kick your queer little butt?"

"Oooh, that sounds interesting," Aiden said in the high voice he sometimes used with Jerome.

I looked around the cafeteria for help from the monitors and teachers. But they'd crowded into a far corner, trying to stop a bunch of gang bangers from fighting.

Mason shoved Billy aside and pushed Aiden to the floor, straddled his body, and smeared mashed potatoes onto both of my friend's red cheeks. "Shut up you little monkey before I pound you."

Aiden struggled to get up. "Get off me, creep."

Mason pushed him hard and Aiden's head cracked against the linoleum. Mason reached into his jeans pocket and pulled out a red marker, the kind taggers use that doesn't come off. He grabbed Aiden's head. Aid struggled and Billy stepped in to hold him while Mason painted 'Fag' across his forehead.

It all happened so fast that the monitors couldn't get there in time. When they did, we all marched off to the Vice Principal's Office, sat through interviews, had our statements recorded, pictures of Aiden taken, parents called, and disciplinary paperwork filled out for Billy and Mason. We finished just as the buzzer ended fifth period. Jerome and I took Aiden to the bathroom and tried to scrub the marker off his face, with no luck. Jerome offered him his knit cap to hide the slur. Aiden pulled it on, glowering.

The three of us headed home along Modoc Road, not saying anything. We'd been walking to and from school together for years. Finally, I tried to get Aiden and Jerome to talk about something.

"Hey, you guys wanna go to the creek? I'll bet nobody's using the swing."

"Yeah, I guess," Jerome mumbled.

Aiden kept his head bowed, fists clenched, and wouldn't look at us. We hustled down the sidewalk, whipped by the wind and rain, and turned onto Mission Street. I felt ashamed that I hadn't stood up for Aiden during lunch hour, even if Mason and Billy would've kicked my ass. As we neared the creek, I took him aside.

"Hey man, I'm like, really sorry I didn't help you fight Mason."

"Yeah, so am I. He's been doing that shit for years to Jerome and me. You just don't know about it. I'm not looking forward to high school. I... I can't take much more..."

"Don't worry, man. I'll help." I reached out my fist to bump knuckles. But he just stared at me.

"No you won't. Nobody will." He dashed to the sycamore, stripped off his slicker, shirt, and shoes, and disappeared into the twisted treetop.

I heard a shout and turned to see Mason hauling ass toward us.

"Crap. Now what?" Jerome muttered.

Mason caught up. "I should kick your butts from here to Carpenteria," he said, snorting.

"Why? You guys started it," Jerome said.

"Yeah, well Aiden had it comin'... and that bullshit story he told Mr McMillian really pissed me off. Where is that little shit, anyway?"

I pointed into the treetop.

Mason glanced upward then stared at the chocolate torrent. "Jesus, look at that fuckin' creek. You guys gotta help me swing across."

"Why should we?" Jerome said.

"Because it's fun, stupid." Mason gave him a shove. "You little fairies like fun, don't ya?"

✿

"Quit your daydreaming," Mason snapped. "It's your turn. You gonna swing or what?"

I flipped him off and grabbed the rope. They gave me a hard shove and I sailed out over the creek. The rain pounded me and I ducked my head to keep it out of my eyes. The bottom of the rope skimmed the water. The swing slowed. A chill ran through me. If it stopped over the creek, I'd be stuck and have to climb to that high limb; I'd never make it. On the backswing, I barely cleared the concrete wall before they grabbed the rope and hauled me in.

"The creek must be coming up," Jerome said. "We should quit."

"Whatcha worried about?" Mason said. "You just gotta lean back and bend the rope upward with your feet. Here, I'll show ya."

He grabbed the swing and we gave him a hard shove. He pushed the bottom knot outward with his legs, sailing over the creek in an almost-horizontal position, yelling the whole way. He kept at it, three, four, five passes. On the sixth pass, the swing trembled. As Mason arced over the tossing water, the rope went slack. With a scream, he plunged into the torrent, arms flailing, and disappeared. I stared at Jerome. His lips quivered, eyes huge. My stomach lurched and I bent over and barfed.

"Wh... wh... what happened?" Jerome stuttered.

"I don't know." I leaned my head back and let the rain wash my mouth out. High above, a movement caught my eye. "Look," I said and pointed.

Aiden sat precariously on the limb at the point where the rope had been tied off. Both his legs hung over the edge of the thick branch. The light flashed off something silver in his hand. He held it away from his body and dropped it into the abyss.

Jerome gasped. "What did you do, Aid? What did you do?" He continued to gaze upward.

My heart thundered as the water's roar faded into the background. The light dimmed. I felt like I would glide off that creek bank and sail into the trees, be left grasping at branch ends as they floated past. But the creek's rumbling slowly returned and with it awareness that Mason's death was a fucking big deal, something that would get the cops involved. I glanced at Jerome and knew that we couldn't keep it a secret. With his rain-hood pushed back, he gazed upward, muttering "Shit... shit... shit... shit... shit... shit..."

From his perch high above us, Aiden raised a hand and waved. Jerome waved back. Aiden slipped from the branch and dropped without making a sound. The brown water swallowed him. Jerome howled, and took off running. I caught up with him a hundred yards downstream. He stood sobbing on the creek bank with his hands covering his face. I put an arm across his shoulders but he pulled away.

We stared at the creek for a long time. More debris shot past. The sunlight faded and darkness closed in. I imagined Mason and Aiden rolling and tumbling in the torrent, banging into rocks and bridge supports before reaching the sea and being sucked offshore by the riptides into the wide open channel. Jerome stopped sobbing.

"Come on, we gotta go," I muttered.

"Where?"

"The police."

"Can't we just text 'em or something?" Jerome dug into an inside pocket for his cellphone.

"No. They'll wanna know... everything."

"But... but can't we make it, ya know, sound like an accident?"

I shook my head. "They'll know somebody messed with that rope."

"It's just... Aiden is... *was* my friend."

"Yeah, he was mine too. Look... better let me do the talking."

Jerome nodded. We walked along familiar streets, the four of us having lived within a block of each other. The police substation loomed ahead. Jerome looked ready to flee, ready to cry.

"Hey, dude, pull it together, man." I grabbed his arm.

He yanked it from my grasp and pushed through the station's front door.

ABOUT TERRY SANVILLE

Terry Sanville lives in San Luis Obispo, California with his artist-poet wife (his in-house editor) and one skittery cat (his in-house critic). He writes full time, producing short stories, essays, poems, and novels. Since 2005, his short stories have been accepted by more than 210 literary and commercial journals, magazines, and anthologies including *The Potomac Review, The Bitter Oleander, Shenandoah,* and *Conclave: A Journal of Character.* He was nominated for a Pushcart Prize for his story "The Sweeper." Terry is a retired urban planner and an accomplished jazz and blues guitarist—who once played with a symphony orchestra backing up jazz legend George Shearing.

ON BEING LOVED BY A WHITE BOY

Kiki Nicole

One.
He cradles my face in his hands,
admires the skin I have hated for years and says:
"You are gorgeous."
I wonder if this is true or if he really means: "You are Different
and New to me and I don't know what else to say to you,"
but I've never thought of myself as someone who could be beautiful—
I cling to these compliments like a strange fruit on his poplar tree.

Two.
I let him speak first to sales associates,
so they listen.
I make him cross the street before me,
so cars will actually stop.
I realise I am holding hands with a privileged white male patriarch
and use this to my advantage.
Most days, I feel like Beyoncé in the beginning of the Partition video,
when she drops her napkin on the floor for the white maid to pick up.

Three.
I tell him to choke me during sex and he asks me if I'm sure and my anxiety
hesitates longer
than any other part of my body.
It wonders if this could be some sort of slavery metaphor.
It wonders if he wonders that everything could potentially be some sort of
slavery metaphor.

He asks me if I'm sure.
I tell him, "Of course."

Four.
We only go to parties where people socialise with each other and drink;
I am too afraid to watch him try to dance.

Five.
I am harassed on the street. Another white man praises the boy on my arm
for getting the privilege to hold hands with "a sista" like me
and I squeeze that hand tighter,
hold my breath until we reach the train platform,
and hastily pull down my shorts to make sure none of my Black was escaping
through the bottom.

Six.
I am harassed in the park. We sit up from our blanket as another white man
inches closer to us.
He dissects my body through a neocolonial slur of the lips,
puts me on display like an animal in a cage.
He gets drunk on my hair, lingers too long on the fullness of my lips, the dark-
ness of my hips,
tells me how "beautiful" I am—just look at my nails, my eyelashes, my skin.
We pack up our things.
I leave trembling.
He asks me if I'm okay.

Seven.
Notice his ease and my discomfort.

Eight.
At night, he envelopes me in a sheet of freckles
and I've never seen so many stars this close before.
While he sleeps, I count them,
imagine connecting them in black ink.
I notice how far apart each freckle is from the other,
how he's always been light years away from me.

Nine.
I am "other" and you are white.
I am "ebony whore" and you are white.
I am "nigger bitch" and you are white.
I am Victim and you
are white.

244

I am afraid.
You are white.

Ten.
Notice his ease
and my discomfort.

Inspired by Rachel Wiley's 10 Honest Thoughts On Being Loved By A Skinny Boy

ABOUT KIKI NICOLE

Kiki Nicole is a black femme poet and sometimes artist currently writing in Portland, Oregon. Their work has been featured on websites such as Bitchtopia Magazine, Drunk in a Midnight Choir, and Voicemail Poems. They work in publishing for the indie poetry house Where Are You Press.

They can be found at kikinicolepoetry.weebly.com and on Twitter, @princesspoesia.

PARTNERS

Jude Ortega

DJ sensed right away that Enzo was jealous. When Enzo took the beer from the counter, the bottles clanked aloud.

"What's the matter?" DJ said as they walked away.

"Why don't you ask yourself?" Enzo said.

"What did I do?"

"You were flirting with the bartender."

DJ snorted a chuckle. "I just said thank you to him."

"Did you have to smile and show him how cute your dimples are?"

"Stop that, Enzo. I wasn't doing anything."

"You were checking out his butt while he was—"

"Enzo, stop. People might think we're having a lover's quarrel."

Enzo froze.

"Go make a scene," DJ said. "I have no problem with that, you know. The whole of Cebu knows I'm gay, so they won't be surprised if I have a boyfriend and I'm arguing with him in public. But you..."

Enzo clenched his jaw.

DJ tapped Enzo at the back and said, "C'mon, man. Let's have some fun." They continued walking, and the music became louder as they got closer to their table. "We're two hot-blooded men on a Saturday night-out," Enzo said aloud. "Look at those girls, those boobs."

"Shut up," Enzo said. "Let's just go home."

"We can't leave my friend here," DJ said. They reached the table, and nobody was waiting for them. "Where's Lee?"

Enzo shrugged. He placed the bottles of beer on the table and sat down.

"Oh my god," DJ said, looking at the dance floor.

Lee was dancing with two girls, and he was grinding with one of them.

DJ chuckled and sat down opposite Enzo. "That gay guy Lee is sure confused," DJ said.

"We can go home now," Enzo said. "Looks like your friend is enjoying himself."

"He's not," DJ said. "He's never going to enjoy here in Alcho or any other heterosexual bar. He really wants us to go to Doce so he can hook up with a gay man. But because you don't want to, because—"

"Is it really Lee who wants to go there?" Enzo said. "Or you?"

"Why would I want to go there?" DJ said. "Enzo, I've long stopped going out at night. I've never been to Doce or to any bar since we moved in together."

"Are you trying to make me feel guilty?"

"I'm not. I'm just telling you that I have never given you any reason to think I want to fool around with other men. And as I've told you, I'm just going out tonight because I can't say no to Lee. He's here in Cebu for just a short vacation. He's going back to Mindanao tomorrow. Now stop being a party pooper. I want to enjoy the night with Lee."

"You want to enjoy the night with Lee? Why did you ask me to come with you?"

"Don't hint at something, Enzo. Lee and I are just friends. We're even distant relatives, for crying out loud!"

Enzo didn't say anything and took a swig at his beer.

DJ sighed. "C'mon, Enz, do you really think I would exchange you for anyone? There's nothing going on between Lee and me, and I don't like that bartender. He's skinny, has a thick accent, and doesn't seem to be gay. You know that I'm not into straight men."

Enzo remained quiet.

DJ knew the quarrel was nearly over. All he needed to do was hug Enzo and give him a peck on the cheek. But he couldn't do it now at the bar, so what he did instead was run his foot up Enzo's shin under the table.

Enzo's leg moved away. "Don't," he told DJ. "Lee's coming, and I think I know the girl he's with."

"Hi, guys!" Lee greeted DJ and Enzo. "Jenni here said she knows Enzo."

DJ and Enzo exchanged glances. Both of them knew what was in DJ's mind. *So this is Jenni, your infamous ex.*

"Hey, Enz!" the girl said. Before Enzo could greet her in return, she leaned down and kissed him. It didn't escape DJ's attention that she pressed her lips a hairbreadth away from Enzo's lips.

"Jen," Enzo said. "It's nice to see you."

Jenni sat beside Enzo, and Lee sat beside DJ.

Enzo told Jenni, "It looks like you already know Lee. This is DJ."

DJ and Jenni exchanged hellos.

Enzo asked Jenni, "Did you and Lee know each other before?"

"No," Jenni said, giggling drunkenly. "I just saw him earlier sitting here alone, so I pulled him to the dance floor. I'm with some old college friends. Oh, you know most of them, Enz. Some of them were in the soccer team with you."

"Really?" Enzo said.

DJ noticed Enzo fidget on his seat. DJ knew that Enzo was getting paranoid. Enzo didn't want to be seen in public with DJ because people who knew him might have funny ideas about the two of them.

"Join us at our table," Jenni told Enzo. She turned to DJ and Lee. "I'm sorry, guys. I have to borrow Enzo for a while." Without waiting for anyone's answer, she stood up and pulled Enzo along with her.

DJ sent Enzo off with a murderous stare.

Lee chuckled. "Hey! DJ, don't tell me you're jealous with *a girl.*"

"She's not just any girl, Lee," DJ said. "She's Enzo's ex."

"Really? Gosh, it's a small world."

"For Enzo, it is. He went to college here in Cebu, so he knows a lot of people here."

"No wonder you gave me a hard time persuading you to go out tonight. Your closeted boyfriend has a whole city to hide from."

"You bet," DJ said. "I no longer have a social life because of him. He even had me deactivate my Facebook and Instagram accounts. He's afraid our photos might be seen by his family and friends."

"Gosh, isn't that suffocating?" Lee said. "But well, if I were in your shoes, I also wouldn't mind holing up with Enzo. With such a piece of ass, I can stay in bed the whole day every day. Enzo is so hot, friend. Where on earth did you find him? Does he work for Convergys too?"

"No, he works for JP Morgan. I met him in Alba Uno, a dorm right inside IT Park. We both used to stay there."

"You were roommates?"

"No, we're not. But he's Ilonggo, like you and me. He's from Bacolod. And the Ilonggos in the dorm sort of had this loosely formed organisation. We would go out drinking together every Friday night."

"Drinking buddies to fucking buddies."

"Well yeah," DJ said. "But it didn't happen overnight, of course. When I first met Enzo, he was straight, or acting straight, if you know what I mean. He had a girlfriend and all."

"That was Jenni?"

"No. Someone else. Jenni was his girlfriend when he was still in college. He never really ran out of girlfriends. Anyway, as I was saying, everyone in the dorm was thinking Enzo was straight, but I kind of, you know, smelled him. I knew that if I was patient enough, he'd be mine eventually."

"I bet you could smell him," Lee said. "You'd been in countless same-sex relationships. You already knew all types of gay guys and how to ensnare them."

"Lee, it's not like I manipulated Enzo into this relationship. We... fell in love. And the relationships I had weren't really countless. I just don't want to count them." DJ chuckled but in a moment went back to being morose.

"Alright. Easy. I know you're not like me. You don't like one-night stands. You're into long-term stuff. Now go back to how you and Enzo, well, fell in love."

"So there. He was lonely, he was confused, and I was there to listen. Besides, as he confessed when we were already living together in Talamban, he was taken by my dimples." DJ smiled, showing Lee what he meant.

Lee giggled. "You're such a slut. Now tell me, if Enzo is out only to you, or to a few people, then you must be his first time. Gosh, DJ, I can't believe how lucky you are."

"Actually no," DJ said. "I wasn't his first time."

"What do you mean?"

"He's fucked girls before."

"That's gross!" Lee giggled again.

"He had girlfriends, I told you."

"But you're his first gay experience."

"Well, yeah. I popped his cherry."

"Ohhh." Lee covered his mouth with his fingers and gave DJ an envious look, but his expression changed when he spotted something behind DJ. "So Enzo has reached the point of no return," Lee said. "He has done the gayest of things. Why is it then that he's still pretending to be every inch a man? Why is he doing body shots with Jenni?"

DJ turned to the scene behind him. Enzo and Jenni were several tables away. They were hugging each other tight, and Enzo was licking the salt on Jenni's shoulder. DJ pursed his lips and gripped the bottle of beer tighter.

"Calm down, DJ," Lee said. "Don't make a scene."

"He's such a bitch."

"It's harmless, DJ. He's just putting on an act. You should pity the girl."

"I told you, that girl is his ex, and she's not yet over him. She texts him all the time."

"Shouldn't you be proud? Girls run after your boyfriend. Don't act as if you're a woman, DJ."

"I'm not acting as if I'm a woman."

"You are."

"The thing is, Enzo accused me earlier of flirting with the bartender."

"Were you?"

"I wasn't."

"C'mon, DJ. I know you. Just like me, you have a thing for bartenders."

"Alright. I smiled at the bartender and said thank you to him in my nicest voice. But that was all, Lee. That was all, yet Enzo was pissed. Now if he doesn't want me flirting with anyone, why is he flirting, much more dirty-dancing, with his ex?"

Enzo and Jenni were at the edge of the dance floor, and Jenni was grinding her butt on Enzo's crotch.

"DJ," Lee said, "what you did and what Enzo is doing are two different things. There's a possibility that you'll cheat on Enzo with the bartender—"

"There isn't. The bartender's not gay."

"Shut up, DJ. The bartender and I chatted a little when I bought our first round, and he gave me his number. He's gay, and you know it. Your gaydar's much stronger than mine. Would you show him your dimples if you sensed he wouldn't notice them?"

"Well yeah. I know he's gay, but I had no plans of hooking up with him. I just couldn't resist smiling at him, he's got a cute butt."

Lee rolled his eyes. "As I was saying, you might have a little dalliance with the bartender, while with Jenni, Enzo is just—"

"Enzo's fucked that girl before, Lee. And he might fuck her again tonight just to prove his virility."

"You think so?" Lee said. "Oh gosh. This is why I hate relationships. You get hurt when your partner fucks someone else."

DJ stood up and pulled Lee's hand. "Come," DJ said.

"You're not going to pull Jenni's hair, are you?"

"Of course not. We'll just dance."

"Alright."

DJ took Lee near Enzo and Jenni. Enzo was almost lying down—his hands were on the floor, supporting his upper body—and Jenni was sitting on his crotch, humping up and down. Their college friends cheered them on.

DJ danced with Lee, acting as though Enzo didn't exist. He gyrated and bumped his hip on Lee.

"Hey," Lee said.

Enzo and his friends started to notice DJ and his obviously gay moves. DJ dropped to his knees and bobbed his head up and down in front of Lee's crotch, as though he was sucking him.

Lee chuckled and slowly pulled DJ up. He led him back to the table.

"What did you think you were doing, DJ?" Lee said when they were seated.

"Dancing," DJ said.

"Don't give me that shit," Lee said. "That was gross. We're fourth cousins. If you want to make Enzo jealous, don't use me."

DJ took a deep breath. "I'm sorry. Let's get out of this place, Lee."

"Alright," Lee said. "I'll tell Enzo to take you back to your apartment."

"No," DJ said. "Let's leave him here. Let's let him enjoy the night with his ex."

"Why do you two like hurting each other? Instead of fixing the problem while it's still small, you avoid dealing with it and do things that make it worse. You and Enzo should go home together and talk."

"No. There's nothing to talk about. It's over between us." DJ's voice started to shake. "I'm tired of helping him hide in the closet. I'm tired of understanding why he is ashamed of me."

"He's not ashamed of you. You said yourself he's just not ready to come out yet."

DJ sniffled.

"Hey, don't cry here," Lee said, standing up. "Okay, let's go." He put his arm around DJ and led him out of the bar.

It was almost midnight, but the night had just started in Mango Square. A group of rowdy teenagers passed by. The girls checked out Lee and DJ, and Lee checked out the boys. DJ barely noticed them. "Lee," DJ said. "You're staying in a hotel, right? Can I stay with you there for a while?"

"Sure," Lee said. "No problem. But don't you think you should patch things up with Enzo? Let's wait for him here. I think he saw us leave. He must have followed us right away."

"I'm sure he didn't," DJ said. "He's—"

"I'm sorry," Lee cut DJ off. He took his phone from his pocket. "Someone texted me." Lee fumbled with his phone and smiled. "Gosh, it's the bartender," he said. His smile disappeared, though, when he looked at DJ.

DJ understood right away what was going on. "It's alright," he said. "I'll just go back to our apartment."

"Well, the bartender said in the text that his shift had just ended, and... I'm really sorry, friend."

DJ forced himself to smile. "No, no. Don't worry about me. I want you to enjoy your last night here in Cebu."

"Maybe you should really wait for Enzo to come out of the bar."

"No, I'll just leave ahead now," DJ said, hailing a taxi. "Take care."

As the taxi was leaving Mango Square, DJ saw Lee and the bartender greet each other. He smiled sadly. He had never felt so alone since he came to Cebu to work in a call centre, two years ago.

When DJ reached the room he was sharing with Enzo, he headed straight to the closet and started putting his clothes in a large bag. He had stuffed half of the bag when he realised he had nowhere to go. It was the middle of the night, and he could not just barge in at the place of any of his friends at such an hour. He also couldn't afford to get a room in a hotel. The money in his wallet and ATM card was just enough for his food until the next payday.

Depressed, he slumped on the bed. He thought maybe Lee was right. Enzo would come right after him. He would be opening the door with his own key any moment now. DJ decided that if that happened, if Enzo said he was sorry, he would forget everything that had happened tonight and forgive him.

The clock ticked by, and whenever DJ heard a sound, he stared at the door, expecting the knob to turn and Enzo to walk in. The door remained closed, however. DJ did nothing in particular; he would sit on the bed, walk around the room, and sit on the bed again. He couldn't and didn't want to think; he didn't want to imagine where Enzo was or what he was doing.

By the time the door opened, DJ had been waiting for an hour and had resolved not to forgive Enzo no matter what he would say, in case he cared to explain.

Neither of them said a word for what seemed like a very long moment. DJ remained sitting on the bed, not looking straight at Enzo but observing him at the corner of his eye.

Enzo pulled up the hem of his shirt and walked to the closet, intending to change clothes. He stopped in his tracks when he saw the half-packed bag. He straightened down his shirt again and said, "So what now, Lee has decided not to go back to Mindanao and to stay here in Cebu so you can move in with him?"

DJ was surprised with what Enzo said. But instead of setting straight the wrong assumption, he said, "No. I've decided to leave Cebu so that I can move in with Lee in Mindanao."

"Alright," Enzo said. "Why don't you hurry and finish packing up?"

"I'm still tired from fucking Lee. I just got in here."

Enzo chuckled bitterly. "I knew it. You and Lee are not relatives. Or are you really that itchy that you fuck even your cousins?"

"Yes, I'm that itchy. I admit I'm itchy. Unlike you, Enzo. You would fuck a girl just to hide from other people what you truly itch for."

"You made me do it!"

"So you did do it!" DJ said, standing up and pushing Enzo on the shoulder. "You did fuck that Jenni." He pushed Enzo on the chest.

Enzo held DJ by the wrist. "We're even now, aren't we?"

DJ pulled his hand out of Enzo's grip. He continued packing his clothes. "You cheated on me, and I cheated on you. But that doesn't make us even, Enzo. I invested more in this relationship. I tried to understand your fears. I cut off my connection to the world to keep our relationship a secret. I did—"

"Don't yap about what you've done for me," Enzo said. "You really wanted to help me keep our relationship a secret? What do you think you did in the bar? Minutes after I told my friends that you're my roommate, you danced on the floor with Lee and showed everyone how gay you are."

"So you were afraid your friends would think that your gay roommate isn't just your roommate. You were pressured to fuck Jenni to dispel any possible notion that you're gay. Is that it, Enzo? You're saying now that it's my fault? Well, tell you what, I wouldn't dance with Lee that way if you weren't humping with Jenni on the dance floor."

"I wouldn't dance with Jenni that way if you didn't flirt with the bartender."

"Oh yeah. That's another thing I admit. I was flirting with the bartender. I showed him my dimples. Now let's talk about what you did. You wrapped your arms around a girl and licked the salt on her shoulders. Now, are smiling and doing body shots the same?"

"You started it all!"

"You always blame me and never yourself. Yes, I started it. It's all my fault. I'm the bad guy, you're the innocent victim. I hope you're happy now." Fumbling with the large bag, DJ walked out of the room. The wind outside blew softly on him.

He walked toward the highway, and he remembered that he had nowhere to go. He dropped the bag on the ground. He thought right away, though, of Lee. He hoped Lee and the bartender just had a quickie and the bartender had left Lee's room. He had to call Lee. He groped in his pocket and realised he had left his phone on the bed. He lifted the bag again and went back to the apartment.

Enzo was sitting slumped on the floor, crying.

DJ felt the impulse to rush to Enzo and hug him. But he controlled himself. He reminded himself that Enzo had slept with Jenni. He said, "So you're sorry now for cheating on me?"

Enzo wiped his tears with the back of his hand. "I feel sorry for myself for wasting several months on you."

"So am I," DJ said, taking his phone from the bed. "But I'm not shedding a single drop of tear for you. I'm not the bad guy in this relationship, Enzo. You are. Whenever I commit a little mistake, you use it as an excuse to do something worse, to do something you've been wanting to do."

"I didn't want to fuck Jenni."

"Let's put an end to this conversation," DJ said. "It's not going anywhere. You would just keep on insisting that I am to blame. Before I leave for the last time, though, before I disappear completely from your life, Enzo, let me tell you that I didn't fuck Lee. You have no justification whatsoever for cheating on me."

Enzo's jaw dropped.

DJ walked away, unable to hold back his tears. When he reached the door, Enzo said, "I didn't fuck Jenni, either!"

DJ stopped in his tracks. Sobbing, but not turning to Enzo, he said, "Stop lying, Enzo."

"I'm not lying," Enzo said, standing up. He came to DJ and said behind him, "I only told you I went with Jenni because you told me something happened between you and Lee. Jenni actually left the bar with someone else, with one of my old teammates."

"No," DJ said, calming himself. "You're only saying that because you don't want to admit your mistake, that I didn't cheat and you did."

"DJ, please. Believe me."

DJ turned to Enzo. "If you didn't hook up with Jenni, what did you do? Why did it take you an hour to come here?"

"I just stayed there in the bar, drinking with my old schoolmates."

"You continued having fun with your friends while I was waiting for you?"

"I didn't know you were here. I thought you went with Lee to his hotel."

"Why did you think I'd do that? You long knew I don't sleep with just anyone. Though I've had several relationships, not one of them was just a fling."

Something seemed lodged in Enzo's throat. "I... I'm sorry," he said.

DJ felt that all his defences had crumbled down. He knew it was difficult for Enzo to own up to his mistake. Whenever they had a misunderstanding, it was usually DJ who would ask for forgiveness first.

"I'm so sorry," Enzo repeated. "I just got jealous. I shouldn't have accused you of flirting with the bartender. I shouldn't have used Jenni to get even with you. And I shouldn't have assumed that you were having an affair with Lee."

DJ took a deep breath. He no longer had any reason to cling on to his pride. "I'm sorry too," he said. "I was really flirting with the bartender. I shouldn't have done it. And I shouldn't have made you believe that something's going on between Lee and me."

"No, you shouldn't apologise. It's my fault."

"Alright," DJ said, chuckling. "It's both our fault. Let's not have another fight because no one wants the other to admit it's his fault. In this relationship, no one's the good guy and the bad guy."

"No one's the good gay and the bad gay," Enzo said.

They both laughed, and then they kissed, as sweet and passionate as the first time they tasted each other's lips. When they moved apart, Enzo took DJ's bag and put it inside the closet. DJ locked the door of the room and told Enzo, "If you didn't go with Jenni to her place, your friends might be thinking now that we're more than just roommates."

Enzo shrugged. "Let them think whatever they want to. The more important thing for me is you. What I care about is what you think of me."

"Enz, I don't want you to come out because of me."

"Why not? It's as good as any reason. Hiding our relationship has been such a burden to you."

"I'm just being whiny sometimes, but really, it's a burden I'm willing to carry. It's the least I can do for you. If you want to come out, do it for yourself. Do it because you want to."

"Thank you," Enzo said. "One of these days, I'll have enough courage to do that."

"I'll just be here."

They kissed again, their hands exploring each other's chest and waist. Enzo lightly pushed DJ to the bed, and DJ pulled Enzo down to him.

After some time, they lay spent in each other's arms. They listened to each other's heartbeat and to the waking city outside the room.

"I have to text Lee," DJ said. Still lying in bed, he picked up his jeans from the floor and took his phone from the pocket. After texting, he put the phone down. "Lee was a little worried about us," he told Enzo. "I told him we're okay now and wished him a safe trip home. And oh, I also asked him if he had fun with the bartender."

"He hooked up with the bartender?"

"Yeah. He enjoyed the night. He enjoyed Cebu."

The phone vibrated. DJ checked it. "Lee has replied. 'I shagged the bartender blind. Do me a favour please. Bump your head and your boyfriend's head against each other. Drama queens. You two are so gay.'" DJ and Enzo laughed.

"Why do we get so affected by each other's actions?" Enzo asked DJ. "Is it because we're gay?"

"It's because we love each other so much."

Once more they kissed and made love.

ABOUT JUDE ORTEGA

Jude Ortega's work has appeared in *Expanded Horizons, Philippines Graphic, New Asian Writing, Likhaan: The Journal of Contemporary Philippine Literature,* and other publications. He lives in Mindanao.

NO MAGICAL VANILLA

Jo Wu

On the day she moved in right next door to my studio apartment, I noticed her down the hall. She stood hardly any taller than five feet, with skin like milk, lacking the bronzed glow most Asian girls had. Her straight black hair fell to her hips, along with blunt bangs chopped just above her eyes. She wore army boots and a red plaid dress with heart-shaped buttons trailing up her neck. Judging from her attire, and the fact that her parents were helping her carry in boxes, I surmised that she must be an undergraduate at the university where I'm earning my PhD.

As I watched them, her father's head shot up with a glare at me, making me jump. He looked like a stone-jawed samurai who would impale me with the coat hanger he carried into his daughter's room.

Retreating into my apartment, I gazed in the mirror that hung on my closet door, stroking back my gelled black hair and straightening my back as I watched how my crimson shirt flaunted my muscled torso and biceps. I wasn't particularly tall, about five-seven, something I wasn't proud of. I tried to compensate for it by working out and weight-lifting. Scrutinising my tanned face, I was pleased by my wide eyes, complete with double eyelids and a square jaw. But I've had crow's feet since my twenties, and I didn't like how my cheeks crinkled when I grinned.

Dammit, I'm thirty, I thought, *and I'm still a broke graduate student. I would have never had the guts to do this ten, no, five years ago. How would she react if she knew my age? She can't be too young. She's gotta be at least twenty-one.*

I waited until the evening, when her parents were gone.

"Hi. I'm your neighbour, Trent."

She held out a slim, smooth hand. Her nails were clean, unmanicured, and about a centimetre past each fingertip. "I'm Kira. Pleased to meet you! Are you a student as well?"

"Yes, getting a PhD in chemistry. You're an undergrad, right? Senior?"

She shook her head as she smiled. "Yes, but I'm not a senior."

"Junior?"

"Yep!"

"Twenty-one years old?"

"No, I'm twenty."

Darn it. Ten years younger than me. She wasn't even drinking age.

"Um... err..." How do I say this without sounding like a creeper? "May I come in? I've never been inside one of the smaller apartments before, and I'm curious about how it looks."

She pressed her lips as she considered for a moment. It didn't take long for her to open her door wider. "Sure."

What did I expect to see upon entering her room? I felt confused entering it, taken aback by the dichotomy of girlish decor and darker, forbidding tastes. Her room was tinier than mine, with a single window that did not face out into the streets, but into a furnace. To cover up the homely view, she had black curtains printed with skulls hanging over the window. Her bed was piled with stuffed tigers and dogs. A poster of the Disneyland castle, glowing lavender against a sapphire sky studded with sprays of coloured fireworks, made a stark contrast with an Iron Maiden poster, a vase of plastic black roses on her desk, and skulls upon her bookshelf.

"Wow... erm... I guess you're the creative type? A child at heart?"

"Yes." She grinned. "You as well?"

"Me?" I laughed at the absurdity of the thought. I had always been a small, skinny kid who got beaten up and was stuck in remedial English classes all the way through high school. "No, no. Not a bit, thank God no!"

She put her hands on her hips. "Now that you've seen my room, can I see yours? I'm curious about the bigger rooms. My room is the most I can afford."

My studio was significantly bigger than hers, complete with a window that looked out into the city streets. I admired the smile on her face as she gazed out through the window, the soft twilight glow illuminating her pale skin. She had an innocent quality to her, with dark eyes glimmering with wonder. We could hear hums of the busses and cars driving by on the streets, and buskers singing and strumming on their guitars.

"I love city streets," Kira remarked. "I used to paint all the time in high school."

"Oh, really? Were you a good artist?"

She shrugged. "I'm okay."

I couldn't help but chuckle. "That must mean you're really good."

"No, I'm not!"

"I think you are. Listen, I play basketball with a lot of guys, and the good ones are the ones who always go, 'Eh, I'm okay,' but the mediocre ones are the ones who say, 'Yeah, I'm good!' because they don't want to be embarrassed and play with people beyond their league."

As she sat with the thought of what I told her, I asked, "If you don't mind, can I see your artwork?"

She pulled out her iPhone from the pocket of her dress and held it out to me so I could watch her flip through her photos. I saw coloured pencil drawings of candle-lit skulls, ravens bursting out from rivers of ink and crimson apples, acrylic paintings of distorted castles, wide-eyed little girls amidst storybook landscapes complete with smiling moons and dogs dressed in suits, and samurai warriors wielding swords within cyberpunk cityscapes.

"Damn, you can really draw!" I flopped back onto my bed with a grin. "Now that you've shared your artwork with me, let me show you one of my own."

I pulled up my left shirt sleeve. On my bicep was a roaring black oxen surrounded by clouds and stalks of bamboo, standing above a great waterfall that poured all the way down to my wrist.

"That's a beautiful tattoo!" She sat in the chair by my bed, and rested her chin in her hands. "It looks like a Chinese painting."

"After my father passed away, I wanted to do something to honour him. He was born in the year of the ox, and my friend designed this tattoo for me."

"He has a good eye for colour and composition." Kira then softened her voice. "I'm sorry about your father."

I shrugged. "It's been over a year. His time had come, but I loved him so much. He was a good father."

She prodded my left ankle with her toes, shooting me a playful grin as she met my eyes. "What about this tattoo?"

There, in an amateurish scrawl with thin black ink, was the name *Jade*.

"Oh, that!" I crossed my right ankle over it. "That was my first girl-friend. I used to tell myself that I would wait until marriage, but I lost my virginity to her when I was sixteen."

Jade, that bitch. She had threatened me to get her name tattooed, otherwise she would leave me for the thirty-three-year-old bastard she had her eye on. She still left for the fucker anyway. Even though my next two girlfriends weren't half as crazy, the memory of them made me burst with the question I had in mind for Kira. "So, um... have you ever had a boyfriend?"

"Well... um... er..." She giggled. "Yeah."

I laughed. "What is that supposed to mean?"

"Well, I had a boyfriend back when I was fourteen."

"Six years? That's a long time!"

"I had a girlfriend too, when I was seventeen. We broke up shortly before graduating high school, and I'm in a poly relationship now."

"Wait... you're bisexual? And polyamorous?"

She nodded.

"Oh wow... I've never met a bi or poly person before."

"Really?"

"I was raised Catholic."

"Oh."

Seeing her furrowed brows, I blurted, "But it's not a big deal! It's just a cultural thing, but everyone I know doesn't really practice it! I mean, I've had sex, c'mon! I know this sounds so crass of me, but why poly? How does that work?"

She twirled the ends of her hair around one hand. "I'm waiting for marriage. No one wants to be in a relationship with a virgin. Or at least, not a monogamous relationship. This way, the guy can at least have sex with other partners."

"Oh... that's noble of you." I coughed into my fist. "And... so you're... with a guy seeing other girls?"

"He's married, and has two girlfriends. One of them is me."

"Doesn't that get awkward?"

"No. We're all very communicative, and it was his wife's idea for him to see other women in the first place."

What? None of my exes would put up with that. "Um... why was it her idea?"

"She couldn't fulfil things that he wanted."

"Well, you're not having sex with him. So what do you do with him?"

She narrowed her eyes and tapped her chin over her smooth lips. "You know so much about me already. I should wait before I tell you more."

My eyes widened. "What is it?"

She shook her head, still smiling. "Another day."

"C'mon, tell me!"

"I need to get to know you better."

"If you're not going to tell me, then leave." I pointed to my door, adopting a mock-angry expression.

"Fine." She stood up from her chair and turned.

"No!" I reached out a hand. "Come back! Please, just tell me!"

She turned her face, her hair half-hiding her smirk. "Well, well... you really want to know?"

"Yes!"

"My, you're very hungry for information, are you?" Her fingers fluttered for my doorknob.

"No, Kira, stay here! Why won't you tell me?"

She threw her head back in a laugh. A laugh that was girlish but cold and mocking. "You might not like me so much when I tell you."

"At least let me guess! You do drugs with the guy? Don't worry about that, I used to do molly whenever I went clubbing!"

She wrinkled her nose. "I don't do drugs."

"You go on killing sprees? I've got a friend who has a stabbing fetish!" Oh shit, I was just spewing random stuff out my mouth, wasn't I?

Her jaw dropped as she slapped a hand to her chest. "What the heck? That's a thing?"

"Well, I don't associate with him very much, but yeah, he's a weirdo. C'mon, why wouldn't I like you? You're cute! You must have guys drooling all over you!"

That cold laugh again. It was like being pricked with pins, augmenting my humiliation over my spewing admittance that she was cute. My younger and shyer self would've dropped dead with shame.

"C'mon, Kira, I'm not gonna tell anyone. Promise!"

Walking towards me, slowly, like a wary cat, she narrowed her eyes, and bent, staring straight into my eyes without a single blink. Shadows cloaked her face, making her grin all the more menacing.

"I do bondage."

"Wait... What? B-B-Bondage?"

Still smiling, she nodded.

"Well... Well... Well, hey! That's cool! You mean, get tied up while you have sex?" I tried imagining this girl, who looked barely legal, naked and spread-eagled on a bed, with the shadow of a man looming over her. Would she be grinning at him, or look terrified?

"Oh, wait a minute, you can't have sex... you're waiting until marriage."

"No. I'm a domme. I like to tie up and torture my boyfriend. His wife is a sub, and so she has no interest in topping him."

Tie up? Torture? My head was spinning. "Do you ever get tied up?"

"Yes. I've been suspended for photoshoots."

What? Was it like in the pornos, where she was hogtied and let some guy do whatever he wanted with her? Or even gangbanged? How was she a virgin?

"Well, Kira, when the time comes to finally do it, my advice for you is to find someone experienced. This way, you'll ensure that you'll have a good first time."

She giggled. "Gee, thanks for the advice, Trent. Now, I gotta have dinner with a friend. Night!"

She skipped out of my room. I lay in bed, staring at the ceiling, wondering what it would be like to have Kira curled next to me. How smooth was her skin? She was completely covered head-to-toe. Hopefully it was for the cute and innocent facade, and not because she has an acne-riddled back... like Lanh.

Lanh. I checked my phone:

LANH: U ok baby? Gonna come see you soon, k? What days work?

Dammit, I have yet to respond. She wanted to work things out between us, but to Hell with that for now. Thinking of her stressed me out.

How do kinky virgins exist? What a giant contradiction. And how in the world does a wife let her husband see other girls? If I ever did that, my testicles would be sliced off. Nothing she said made sense to me.

Maybe Kira was a virgin who wasn't shy about what she wanted? Maybe I could be the first one for her. Maybe.

Fall semester started. I returned to the routine of autoclaving beakers, pipetting acids, and instructing lab courses for apathetic freshmen who would fall asleep if I didn't administer pop quizzes. I wondered why they decided to pursue chemistry. I felt empowered when I lit a bunsen burner for the first time and received a perfect score on the periodic table test in middle school. After becoming a PhD candidate, my interest waned—failed experiment after failed experiment were only aggravated by grant money droughts. What was the point of all this? For a fancy title, to show how superior in society I was?

Kira majored in art history, so I never saw her strolling through the chemistry territory of campus. Yet, I'd see her traipsing through the halls of our apartment building. Sometimes she wore heavy eyeliner and black or red lips, and dresses emblazoned with skulls, which was kind of cool but extreme. Sometimes she would go barefaced and just throw on a blue hoodie emblazoned with our school's name.

"Hi, Trent!" She grinned and waved, like she always did when she saw me.

"Hey there." I unlocked the door to my apartment, still wearing my glasses and button-up with long sleeves that hid my tattoo. "Whatcha up to?"

"Homework." Kira wrinkled her nose and stuck out her tongue. What a cute tongue it was, with a pointed tip.

"Hey, um, wanna work in my room? You can use my desk. I always sit on my bed anyway."

"That sounds great! Let me grab my stuff."

In five minutes, she came clutching a spiral notebook to her chest, while fisting a pen and a highlighter. As she highlighted and scribbled notes, I glanced up from my laptop. I liked that she didn't wear make-up today. By daylight, I could see how pale she was, though there were a few acne scars on her cheeks, like almost-inconspicuous chocolate stains. I thought of photos of make-up-free porn stars that I've seen online. Some of them were nice-looking, while others were hideous. If Kira did bondage, would that mean she did porn?

Without looking up at me, she adopted a sing-song voice. "What are you staring at?"

"Nothing!"

She threw back her head and laughed. Her black hair snaked down her bum. "I so believe you."

"If you really want to know, I was curious about what it'd be like to kiss you."

"Really?" She grinned, like a kid. "You know, I noticed you down the hall when I moved in, and thought, 'Hey! That's a really handsome guy!'"

Wow. This cute girl who was maybe a total porn star underneath the student persona thought I was handsome?

"Um... I remember you saying you do photo shoots. Do you have photos I can see?"

"Sure! I model part-time." She crossed her legs next to me on my bed, and pulled out her iPhone. I saw photos of her in Victorian gowns, fairy wings, vampire fangs dripping with blood, and curly mint-green, blue, purple, and red wigs.

"Where's the bondage stuff you told me about?"

"Here." She pressed a tab titled *Fetish*.

I was surprised by how classy she looked compared to what I had seen in porn. She looked older in her photos, maybe twenty-five. She wore black latex dresses moulded to her body, shiny with lubricant, while balancing on knife-sharp ballet boots. In some photos, ropes criss-crossed over her torso and squeezed her breasts as she parted her gleaming ruby lips, shooting me come-hither gazes from beneath heavy lashes. Other photos were of her suspended in midair, some of them of her upside down, and many of them with her hands behind her back.

"These... These are... wow..." Here, before me, in flesh and blood, she looked so... normal. No spidery lashes, no tight shiny clothes, no Photoshop, and she looked like she could be seventeen.

"I'm not as glamorous as my photos. I'm really just a normal girl!"

I laughed as she snatched away her phone. "They're really cool!"

"You're the first guy from school to tell me that."

"You don't even have guy friends?"

She stared down at her fists in her lap, still clutching her phone. "Not here. They all think I'm weird. Whenever I talk to them, they just ignore me."

"I'm not ignoring you."

"No." She raised her head, meeting my eyes. "I appreciate that."

We stared at each other. The sunlight from the window illuminated her porcelain complexion. Was my face really coming closer to hers?

I tasted mango on her soft lips. I wrapped my arms around her, and pulled her on top of me, running my hands down her back. The apex of her rear was prominently round and firm.

I flipped her onto her back. "What would you like me to do?"

Her voice was eager, matching her wide eyes and parted lips. "I want your tongue in my mouth."

Careful not to crush her with my weight, I pressed my open lips over her soft ones. She reciprocated by flickering her sweet, pointed tongue over mine and digging her nails into my shoulders.

I stroked her hair. As I did so, she tore her lips from mine, and then gnawed on my neck.

"That feels really good." I closed my eyes, relishing the playful sharpness against my jugular.

"Really?" With a little growl, she flipped me onto my back, pinning my shoulders. Whoa. Usually, Lanh just lies there and makes me do all the work.

"What's one of your biggest fantasies?" I asked.

Her grin mirrored the gleam in her dilated pupils. "Having a male submissive."

I pictured Kira standing over me, in a black leather corset and tall boots glimmering by moonlight, brandishing a whip pulled taut between her gloved fists.

"Could I be a sub for you?"

Her eyes widened. "You want to?"

"I've never met a girl as forward as you. So dominant. To be honest, I find it such a contradiction that you're waiting for marriage, but you're also... kinky. And poly."

She stuck a tongue out at me. "I'm one-of-a-kind."

I saw how erect her nipples were, plump and bursting from beneath her dress. I kissed one. "Do you like that?"

"Yes."

"How about this?" I clenched my teeth over her nipple, biting harder and harder.

"That feels good." She smiled. "I'm thinking of nipple clamps in a fetish photo that I like."

I curled my long fingers over her slim hand. As I kept biting down on her, I pressed atop of her and pinned her down. When I moved my lips from her nipple to her lips, she threw her arms around my neck, rolling both of us around until she pinned me once again.

I laughed. "You're an aggressive little lady, aren't you?"

I slipped my hands under her dress, but she slapped them away.

"No, Trent. Not without permission."

"What? Why?"

"Haven't you ever heard of consent?"

"Consent?"

Before she could elaborate, my phone rang.

Dammit, Lanh.

"Sorry, gotta take this." I turned my back on Kira. "Hey babe. Sup?"

"*Trent!*"

Oh gosh, I had to hold the phone inches away from my ear as Lanh screeched, "*Why haven't you responded to me?*"

I shrugged. "Busy."

"The Hell you are! Don't forget I'm coming over this Saturday, you hear me?"

"Yeah, I know."

"Can you come get me at the airport?"

"I won't be able to. You know how to get here. You've come by yourself before."

"Such a meanie." Lanh's voice was pouty over the phone. "Well, I'll see you! Bye bye, honey!"

I hung up. Kira glared at me.

"That was your girlfriend?"

"Ex. She's my ex."

She crossed her arms and narrowed her eyes. "She's coming here."

"We broke up three months ago. She wants to get back together." I kept staring at the floor. "It's not happening."

"But you're letting her come."

My shoulders hunched up to my ears. "She's twenty-six. She's a big girl. She knows what she's doing."

"How long were you together?"

"Four years."

"Has she had other boyfriends before?"

"I'm her first real boyfriend."

"No wonder she wants to get back with you. And you're just betraying her like that? How could you do that?" Kira's voice kept rising, like nails on a chalkboard. "Just letting her come with these expectations?"

"W-W-Well, you've never been in a relationship with someone you've had sex with. So you know nothing, and you know it!"

Kira's jaw dropped. Her eyes darted between the floor and me before she finally growled, "I may have never had sex, b-b-but... but at least I have an idea of how to treat others!"

She stormed out of my room. Her door slammed down the hallway.

✐

Saturday came. The cheers and chants of the soccer video I was watching when I should have been grading papers were interrupted by the knocks on my door.

I groaned.

"Trent!"

The second I opened my door, I was assaulted by giddy shrieks and squeals, the gagging scent of floral perfume, and showers of glitter shedding from Lanh's eyeshadow as she threw her arms around me.

"Trent! You bad boy!" She playfully shoved my chest. "You couldn't even bother to come pick me up at the airport."

I shrugged. "I had stuff to do."

She dumped her luggage by my bed. Pink, plastered with stickers from Bueno Aires, England, Vietnam, South Korea, and Mexico. She zipped across the room to open my mini-fridge.

"Gee, nothing?"

"I had Chinese takeout last night."

She yanked my hand. "C'mon! Let's go grocery shopping!"

By the time we returned to my apartment, potato chips and chocolate chip cookies sprouted into a mountain by my bed.

"Omigod! This is *so* going on Instagram!" She hooked her elbow around my neck and grinned as she yanked me against her, nearly choking me. I smiled half-heartedly as her iPhone flashed us.

"Help me think of a clever caption, Sweetie!"

I hunched my shoulders as I stared at my laptop on my lap, pretending to be engrossed with emails. "Mmmm... sure..."

"How about... 'Junk food with the bf! We are SO adults.'"

"Okay."

"Oooooh, hashtag love, hashtag boyfriend, hashtag loveforever..."

Um, let me just type out this response to one of my student's questions about 1,4-benzoquinone—

"Trent? Trent?"

My head snapped up, meeting Lanh's large brown eyes. They were one of the first things that drew me to her. Her large eyes, as black as night, and wide as a doe's, complementing her mocha skin. "Yeah?"

"You know I love you, and I don't ever want to let you go."

"Um…" I ran my fingers through my gelled hair, trying to think of something that she would like to get her to shut up about the mushy stuff. "You wanna go shower? Together?"

She shot up to her feet, clapping her hands. "Yes! You know I *love* showering with you!"

Without waiting for a response for me, she began stripping, crossing her arms to inch her t-shirt up from her waist, unhook her nude-coloured bra, and bunch down her jeans. As she bent over to gather her Hello Kitty bathrobe, I smacked her butt.

She whirled in surprise. "Trent?"

I grin. "You like that, don't you?"

"Of course! Omigosh, it's been so long since you've done that!" She grabbed my hand, her bony fingers pressing against my palm like wooden chopsticks.

Flexing my fingers as I followed Lanh out through the halls, I thought of how Lanh's butt lacked the plump and muscular roundness of Kira's—

Shit. There's Kira.

Just as we turned a corner in the hall, Kira also turned the corner, past us. What the Hell was she wearing? Red heels and a tight leather skirt with a leather jacket? Eyeliner and black lipstick? The Hell was she up to?

Lanh was four-ten, so Kira wasn't that much taller, but in those heels, she was about my height. Kira glanced at Lanh, who just brushed past her, oblivious, her eyes glued to her phone as she squealed, "Ooooh, we got fourteen likes on the photo of us already!"

As Kira looked up from Lanh, I turned my head to the floor. *Pretend not to know her, pretend not to know—*

"Hi, Trent!"

Fuck.

With that smirk of hers, Kira brushed past me, her hair fluttering against my triceps like a ghost's caress. Her heels click-clacked against the floor as she sauntered back to her room.

In the bathroom, after I locked the door behind us, Lanh whirled around, gnashing her teeth. Strands of hair from her bun fell over her eyes and knitted brows, giving her a deranged look. "Who was that?"

"Oh, I dunno! She's a weirdo!"

"You're turning red."

"I don't know her! I swear I don't! I... I just see her around the building!"

"She knows your name."

"I've only spoken to her, like, once! I guess I told her my name, but I totally forgot hers! I swear, Lanh!"

"Well..." Lanh unfastened the sash of her robe, and flung it open, exposing herself to me, crossing one leg in front of the other as she put her hands on her hips. She pursed her lips. "Am I hotter than her?"

Lanh's form was twig-like. Despite being twenty-six, her breasts looked barely more than buds, and she had no ass to speak of. Her stomach was as flat as a board.

I gulped. "By a million, baby."

Nodding with satisfaction, she turned on the water. As we lathered up, I ran my hands over her body and kissed her as if she was a bland slice of white bread. She lacked the muscles of Kira's thighs, the softness of Kira's stomach, the generous roundedness of Kira's bum, and the perkiness of Kira's breasts. It was almost like trying to copulate with a hybrid of a prepubescent girl and a bag of bones.

By the time I was done rinsing myself off, Lanh was still combing conditioner through her hair.

"I'm going back to the room, babe." I wrapped my towel around my waist and left the bathroom.

✎

For the next two weeks, even after Lanh left, I never ran into Kira. Lanh and I were still exes. I guess you could say that. She still thought we were a couple with on-going disagreements. So stubborn.

I kept thinking of Kira. Whenever Lanh and I fooled around in bed, especially if it was dark, I imagined that Lanh was paler, and pretended that her moans belonged to Kira. Waking up one morning after Lanh was gone, the first thing I did was pull out my phone.

ME: Haha what did u think when u saw us?

No response. I didn't think much on it until my phone vibrated while I supervised my students in their lab course.

KIRA: I tried very hard not to laugh

My fingers flew over my phone's keypad.

ME: Hahaha laugh why?

KIRA: Lol u couldnt look at me when we passed by each other in the hall

ME: Well I was surprised, as I'm sure u were

KIRA: I wasnt. I expected to run into both of u at some point. Is she still with you?

ME: Nah, she left. We're not together.

Yo, I'm still interested about being a sub.

KIRA: Hmm...never had a Vanilla approach me with this desire before.

ME: Vanilla? Wuzzat supposed to mean?

KIRA: You know how in Harry Potter, the wizards call non-magical people Muggles?

We kinksters call non-kinky people Vanillas.

ME: Haha, very funny.

KIRA: You also need to learn about consent.

ME: You just say no, and I stop if you don't like something, right?

I heard an explosion of shattered glass: a student had dropped an acetone-filled beaker. Twenty minutes later, after cleaning up after him, my phone vibrated against my thigh.

KIRA: That's how it should work. Are u open to being tied up? ;)

Being tied up? My mind raced at the possibility.

ME: Wanna try on me?

"Trent?"

My head snapped up to look at one of my students, a tall girl with ponytailed blonde hair.

"Sorry to interrupt. You looked cranky, and I didn't know if—"

"Don't worry, it's my job to answer questions." I stuffed my phone into my pocket, even though it vibrated against my thigh like an electric erection. "What's up?"

"I lost two points from the quiz you handed back." She handed me her red-marked sheet. "I know answer two is right, so I was wondering why you marked it wrong."

After confirming that I had made a grading error, I watched my student bounce away. She wasn't much younger than Kira—two years? Blondes weren't my type.

I whipped my phone back out.

KIRA: How does 9 tonight sound?

ME: Sure. Later.

She came to me in a getup none of my exes, not even Lanh, would have dared to wear: a crimson under-bust corset tightly laced with black ribbons in the back, and lace panties with a pattern of black roses. Her scarlet lace bra made her B-cups look large and supple. It was a wonder to watch her saunter into my room in sky-high black stilettos. A heart-shaped red purse dangled from her elbow.

"What's in there?"

Her voice adopted an authoritative tone. "If we're going to be dominant and submissive, we need to negotiate."

"Negotiate?"

"Yes. Tell me what's off-limits, and I'll be sure to stay away from that."

"But… if you're dominating me, doesn't that mean you get to do whatever you want with me?"

She rolled her eyes. "No. If I did that, that's a crime. If I'm dominating you, it means your wellbeing is my responsibility."

"Um… what are examples? I was expecting you to just tie me up."

"Yes, I have rope." She placed her purse on my couch, and began to take implements out, laying them side by side. Bundles of hemp rope came out first. "I also have floggers, crops, whips, gags, a violet wand—"

"Violet wand? What's that?" I imagined a violet flower in bloom.

She held up a little plastic wand attached to an electrical plug. "It's meant for shocking."

"Oh, Hell no! Nothing electric, please!"

She smiled, stifling a laugh. "Very well." She laid it next to the gags. "So, take your pick. Anything you'd like?"

"Can we start with rope?"

"Anything else?"

"Um…" I never had options before. This was my chance. "We could *try* the flogger."

"Do you have a safeword?"

"A *what*?"

"Safeword. An out-of-context word that signals to me that you want me to stop everything I'm doing and tend to your needs."

"Couldn't I just say stop? Isn't that obvious?"

"No. Some people like playing victim to create authenticity when they're in subspace."

"Huh?"

"Some people like to use the word 'Red' for instance. It's quite a common one for beginners to use."

I didn't quite understand what she meant by *authenticity* or *subspace*, but I wanted to get going. "Fine. Red, then."

"Are you ready?"

"Yes."

"Get on your back."

I laid on my bed.

"Put your arms above your head." Her hands were very gentle even though the rope scratched my wrists.

She was careful not to cut into my joints, and bound them to the bedposts. I watched her weave a pattern of diamonds over my chest and down my stomach. Then she wove columns down to my ankles before securing both of them to the other bedposts. I was surprised by the sensuality of the tightness of the rope cocooning my skin. They even smelled faintly of tangerines.

"Try struggling."

I writhed against the bonds. They bit into my muscles.

Kira nodded. Then, she pulled out a black blindfold from her purse.

"Hey! Don't blindfold me!" I thrashed against the ropes. "I actually want to see you!

She frowned, looking quite displeased.

I stammered. "Y-Y-You're so pretty, it's a waste to have you here but not be able to see you!"

The blindfold fluttered to the floor. "Very well."

I sighed. Who said flattery didn't work on girls?

"You are doing good so far, Trent. You're communicating your needs to me."

"Damn. You and this S and M shit aren't as crazy as I thought."

"Excuse me?" Her voice sharpened. "What is that supposed to mean?"

"Normal people don't do this."

Kira held her hands behind her back and thrust her nose into the air, appropriating authority despite her scandalous getup. She even paced back and forth from one wall to the other. "When did I ever claim to be normal? Since you're a PhD student, I'll let you know that studies have been done in which conclusions state that BDSM practitioners are mentally healthier than Vanillas. For your shameful ignorance, I believe it's time for a flogging."

She picked up the flogger from the couch. I'm suddenly thinking of party streamers, but these long, black leather strips look deadly.

My erection throbs, hard and hot with blood pulsing at the pointed bulb. She caressed my thighs with the flogger. The leather ribbons felt so soft, so buttery.

The flogger slapped my thighs with a moderate *thud*, making me yelp more out of shock than pain. With fluid twists of her wrists, the leather ribbons painted figure eights in the air, hissing as they flung about in looped blurs. I flinched, but at the same time, I relished the blows. At the right intensity, it felt like a massage.

"How's that on a scale of one to ten, with ten being the most painful?"

"Five."

"Would you like it harder?"

"Yes."

She slapped me harder, provoking me to jump within my bonds. I writhed as she adopted a sing-song tone, all while smacking me harder with the flogger. "'Yes, *Mistress*.' That's the proper response."

Goddammit, this was not feeling like a massage any more. I swear welts were sprouting on my thighs. "Red!"

The blows of the flogger were replaced by Kira's soft, smooth hand gently stroking my thigh, cool and assuaging against my burning skin. "Are you okay?"

"Yeah. I think I've had enough for tonight."

Placing the flogger back on the couch, she zipped to my side to free my wrists from their binds. "Do you need me to get you anything? Water? I'm supposed to administer aftercare now."

"Aftercare? What's that?"

"It's standard practice after a scene. The top gives special attention to the bottom, such as cuddling, talking, fetching food or water, or anything else the bottom needs to be brought back to reality."

What? This exists? This was so unlike anything I've ever experienced. The complete opposite of picking up a chick, banging her, and then zipping out the door without saying so much of a farewell or even knowing her name. I've just been tied up and flogged by this girl, and she asks me if I *want* anything?

"Cuddling would be nice."

After the ropes tumbled to the floor, Kira curled herself against me and entwined her soft arms around my neck, pulling me into a kiss. Our tongues met, hot and wet. With her long nails, she traced the ridges of my clavicles, drew circles over my cheeks, scraped down my belly, and zipped down my legs, straight past my dick, as if my erection was an iceberg for her hands to sail past. Her nails were like little knives, sparking shivers through me.

"Will I be your sub?" I asked, gasping when she pulled away.

"Yes." She placed a hand on my cheek. "I want to take you to a place and have you meet members of the community."

The BDSM community? Meet them? "Um... sure. When would you like to go?"

"Sometime next month. I need to check online for the date, but if you're available, we can go together."

"Sure!" It's gotta be better than boring Lanh. Something more exciting than labwork.

*

"Thorny?" I stared up at the neon red sign of the black building she brought me to. "What a terrible pun for horny."

Kira laughed. "Of course it's a bad pun. But thorns are also sharp, and sharp things are some people's kinks!"

I came dressed in a black t-shirt and black jeans, as those were the only remotely BDSM-y things in my pile of laundry. I tugged at the black leather collar around my neck, which Kira had given me. Kira wore a leather corset, fishnets, and knee-high boots. Her hair was in a high ponytail, and she carried her heart-shaped purse.

"Glenn!" Once inside, like an excited little girl, Kira, in her heels no less, ran up to an Asian guy who had two hot women by his side. All three of them hugged her. One of the women was a tall redhead, the other a more stocky brunette.

There were many pretty girls roaming with male dominants, many collared and leashed to the man. Sure, there were some guys like me, who had a woman as a dominant, but I felt envious of the male dominants. Especially Glenn. I learned that the redhead was his wife, Giselle, and the brunette was Annie, his nineteen-year-old girlfriend. He wasn't bad looking, but how did a guy like him get all these girls? Kira too?

Kira sauntered towards a giant wooden structure shaped like an X. I pointed at the structure, racking my brains for what she had taught me through the aid of Google and Wikipedia. "That's a... a St Andrew's Cross, right?"

"Yep!"

"I could go for a blindfold tonight."

She slipped a blindfold over my eyes. Seeing nothing but darkness, I could hear the pounding industrial music, overlaid with the sharp whistles and cracks, whipping out delighted shrieks from women interspersed with giggles that bounced throughout the air.

Leather cuffs embraced my wrists and ankles. Ropes snaked along my limbs as she bound me to the cross.

"What would you like me to do?" Her breath seared my cheek.

My heart leapt to my throat. "Surprise me."

"But what if I do something you don't like?"

"I'll say 'Red.'"

Kira's breath blasted in my ear as she dug her nails at the bottom of my scalp, yanking back my head. "I *love* your willingness to try."

I moaned as her soft lips and sharp teeth fluttered over my throat, and gasped when she spanked me. Who ever heard of a girl spanking a guy?

I gasped again when I felt the lash of her flogger. As the leather ribbons struck along my thighs, the stings flirted along the lines of pain and pleasure, making me alternate between crying out in laughs, screams, and sounds that I couldn't distinguish as either one.

When she stopped flogging me, she cupped my throat. Her hand felt so hot against my neck, pressing down on my Adam's apple. As I gasped for breath, she kissed me. I kissed her back, wanting to drink her in, wanting her small, slim fingers to caress away the red, burning marks she imprinted on me.

"I... I think I'm done," I gasped when she tore her lips away.

As she unfastened my bounds and slipped off my blindfold, I realised that heavy, dark music pounded throughout the room, and now beat into my ears. Some guy's creepy chants and screams set to heavy guitars and drums, clashing with high screams from female subs throughout the room. My head spun.

Kira's soft voice contrasted with the discordant noise. "Did you enjoy it?"

If I had to be honest, I wasn't sure. I felt weird, like I wasn't as masculine as the guys dominating the women. I hadn't felt weird when

Kira did things to me in my room. But here, surrounded by people, I felt strangely insecure. "Yeah."

"You're gonna need aftercare." She took my hand. "C'mon. Let's go to the couch."

"Actually, I'm kinda hungry..."

"Oh, there's food at the refreshment table."

"No, I mean... like, a burger or something." I broke off her hold and started walking to the entrance, showing the bodyguard the red smiley-face stamp on my hand to let him know I'll be back. "Gonna go out to grab a bite. Want me to get anything?"

She shook her head. "Nah. I told Annie I'd tie her up."

There was a bar a block away. There, I savoured the cold bitterness of a beer, gulping it so it dowsed my insides like medicine. Gosh, I just felt so nervous, to be that vulnerable in public. Was this what I was in for? Did I think it would be like this? Would I have preferred to top Kira instead? I tugged on the collar around my neck, half-wishing it would choke me to death.

I didn't care that my hands shook as I stumbled back to Thorny. That my head spun a bit. Well, I'm a sub. I get punished for things like this, right?

Back inside Thorny, Kira was cuddling with Giselle inside some sort of glass case in one of the black walls of the room. Weird. Like one of those glass aquariums you'd see in a restaurant, but with women inside.

There was a tall, slender Asian girl wearing nothing but panties and walking around alone like a lone doe. A long braid snaked down to her knobby knees, and a diamond sparkled in her navel. She was walking past me when I snatched her hand.

"You're really hot." I pressed up against her against a wall and kissed her cheek.

"Wait—what are you—" Her hands were flimsy against me.

"C'mon, you're asking for it, dressed like this, aren't you?"

As I fondled her breasts, she began to shriek, her voice an alarm piercing my ears.

Before I knew it, a fist struck my cheek. Hands locked my arms behind my back, and large, burly bodies piled atop of me in a torrent of yells of "Bastard!" and "Get off her!"

I coughed and nearly suffocated if it hadn't been for that one voice: "*Trent!*"

The men atop me looked up. Promptly, they scattered apart, revealing Kira glaring down at me.

"K-K-Kir—" My hand shook as I reached out for her. She snarled, digging her nails into my palm, making me yelp.

"We're going home, Trent."

"Kira, don't go home alone with him!" Glenn put his hand on her shoulder.

"He's my responsibility."

"We'll go with you."

Glenn, Giselle, Annie, Kira, and I boarded the train. Kira had hooked her leash to my collar, yanking my neck in hard jerks, not caring that eyes were on us. Some pretended not to look, but they stole glances at us.

I would have taken the collar off myself, but Kira had tied my hands behind my back. "Kira, this is humiliating."

"Stupid Trent."

"C'mon, red." She doesn't meet my pleading eyes. "Please?"

"Shut up."

Glenn placed a hand on Kira's fist. "Kira, that's enough."

"He needs punishment, Glenn!"

"But not like this. You're violating codes, you know. This isn't an act of consent. Do you really need me to lecture you on this?"

Side-eyeing me, it took a good few seconds before Kira sighed. She unfastened the collar and rope.

After walking me back to my apartment, Kira didn't look back at me as Glenn and his women escorted her back to hers down the hall.

❧

Kira didn't look at me. Instead, she stared out the window, into the streets of students hustling by as she slurped up at least ten tapioca pearls through the pink straw of her iced jasmine green tea in one gulp.

"Kira, I'm so sorr—"

She snapped her head towards me. "Sorry for *what*, Trent?"

"For... for..."

She glared.

"For being drunk."

She tapped her foot. "And?"

"Hurting that girl."

She rolled her eyes. "What an understatement."

"Kira—"

"Do you have any *idea* how embarrassing that was? How you humiliated me in front of everyone like that? You know how damaging that is?"

"Please, I—"

"So you sneak out, telling me you just wanted to eat, and you come back *drunk*? You idiot!"

"I promise I won't do it again. Please, kick me, beat me, hurt me all you want! Just don't leave me!"

"No, Trent."

"Kira!"

Ignoring the gasps from people around us, she shot up from her seat, raising her hand. Cringing in anticipation for her blow, I also felt a surge of joy for her impending touch.

Her hand froze in the air, though her face softened. "You want me to punish you, don't you?"

"Yes, please! Just don't leave me!"

She lowered her hand. Grabbing her drink, she stormed out of the boba shop, like a cold siren who trampled upon a pathway of lovers' broken hearts.

"Kira!"

"Go away, Trent. Go away, before I call a restraining order on you."

December arrived. After the semester ended, I went to knock on her door after she didn't respond to my text.

"Kira? Are you home?"

Silence.

"Kira, if you're listening, I'm so sorry. I really miss you. Miss talking to you. Miss playing with you." I knocked again. "If you—"

The door creaked open. But there was no hand on the doorknob. The door swung inwards, revealing an empty room. Even the curtains were stripped from the window, through which the hazy winter light rained through, flooding the vacuumed murky-brownish carpeted floor.

She didn't even tell me goodbye.

When I returned home for Christmas. I accompanied my family to church. The children choir sang in high notes of purity and humility, coating the hypocrisy of the Lord's Words. It couldn't paint over my hypocrisy and stupidity. I, an idiotic Vanilla who couldn't understand or fit into her world. Her magical world. Of course I was unfit to be by her side.

Lanh and her family was there too, sitting at the front pews. Afterwards, we all went over to my house with other families in our church community for *banh mi* and shrimp rolls. Lanh sat in the backyard, sitting on the stone bench watching the children run around, kicking a soccer ball at each other. Well, more like taking photos of the kids playing and posting to Instagram.

"Hey, Lanh."

"Hey, Trent." Although her eyes remained glued to the phone, she scooted over.

Sitting down, I placed an arm around her shoulder and kissed her on the cheek. "Merry Christmas."

Her eyes widened as she turned her head to look at me.

When the children ran inside with the announcement of mango pudding, I gently cupped Lanh's face. She gazed into my eyes with those large doe eyes, as black as onyx, her caramel skin warm beneath my palms. She was just as pretty as when we first met, and her lips were still as soft as always. Softer than Kira's lips.

After breaking off the kiss and resting my chin atop her head the way I used to, she gasped, "Trent... this is the most romantic I've seen you in a long time."

"I've just missed you, Lanh."

Running my fingers through her shoulder-length hair, I tried to ignore the fact that it was nowhere near as long as Kira's hip-length tresses.

ABOUT JO WU

Jo Wu is a student at UC Berkeley, where she studies Integrative Biology and Creative Writing. She has been published in a few anthologies, and her short story, "Devoured by Envy," from the anthology *Darker Edge of Desire*, was praised by Publishers Weekly. Born and raised in the San Francisco Bay Area, she can be found scribbling in notebooks or typing away in her Google Docs, accompanied by a giant Jack Skellington mug that's constantly refilled with green tea and hot water, and earbuds blasting a mix of metal, alternative rock, industrial, film scores, and classical crossovers. You can visit her at JoWu.co, or Tweet her @Jo_Wu_Author.

CPSIA information can be obtained at www.ICGtesting.com
Printed in the USA
BVOW08s1821111016

464752BV00001B/41/P

9 780980 508451